CALL ME
SONNY

CALL ME SONNY

STEVE LAZARUS

Boyle
&
Dalton

Book Design & Production:
Boyle & Dalton
www.BoyleandDalton.com

Hardback ISBN: 978-1-63337-754-7
Paperback ISBN: 978-1-63337-755-4
E-book ISBN: 978-1-63337-756-1
LCCN: 2023917634

Printed in the United States of America
1 3 5 7 9 10 8 6 4 2

TO MY FATHER,
WHO TAUGHT ME EVERYTHING.

ALLAN R. LAZARUS
1936-2020

PART I

CHAPTER 1

IT WAS the last day of Travis Conway's life.

If he got his final wish, it was also the beginning of the end for the people who put him in the maximum security prison he had called home for the past four years, a place its former warden described as a cleaner version of hell. He waited alone for his visitor.

A few hundred feet away, the attorney made his way through the crucible of the prison security system, suffering the indignity of a full-body search in stocking feet while the contents of his pockets and briefcase were picked over as if each were a potential deadly weapon. When they finished, he put on his belt, shoes, and jacket, and reached for the rest of his belongings.

"Everything stays here," the morbidly obese guard barked. "You can take a notepad and a pen or pencil, nothing more. This way." He motioned his charge to follow him, and led the way down a dank, dimly lit corridor.

It was the attorney's first time in ADMAX, the nation's only federal supermax prison, and he hoped it would be his last. He knew the stories of prisoners going insane here, confined to their cells 23 hours a day, devoid of human contact for years, even decades on end. He had seen the inside of dozens of prisons—most were raucous, dirty places that provided the stereotypes on which the average Hollywood jailhouse movie was based. This place was cold, antiseptic, and deadly silent. It made his skin crawl, and the farther he was guided through the maze of unmarked hallways, the more he wanted to leave.

They stopped at a solid steel door marked B-11, where they were joined by a second guard, as lean and muscular as his colleague was soft and round. Fat Guard produced a key from a lanyard on his belt and opened the steel door, revealing another door with a small window to the room where he would meet his client. Skinny Guard carried the key that opened the second door.

"One hour," said Fat Guard as he gestured toward the folding chair, the only piece of furniture in the room. The sound of the two doors closing and bolting behind him did little to assuage the visiting attorney's growing anxiety.

Travis was waiting for him, seated in his own chair in an identical room, a thick plexiglass window separating them. Small holes formed a circle in the window that would allow them to speak to one another, and a slit at the bottom was just large enough for a piece of paper to pass through. The room itself was as cold and sterile as the rest of the prison—a windowless box of gray-painted cinder block and polished concrete floors.

Travis was 62 years old and looked 80. The entirety of his four years at ADMAX had been spent in solitary confinement, and time had taken its toll. His jaundiced eyes were sunken deep in their sockets, a pair of dim headlights in a skeletal face framed by a cascade of matted, thinning gray hair that hadn't seen a barber since his arrival at the Colorado prison. His khaki uniform was at least two sizes too large. To those who didn't know any better, Travis Conway appeared to be a helpless, frail old man who couldn't hurt a fly. The attorney knew better. Much better.

Travis waited silently for the coded greeting.

"Good morning, Mr. Conway. I'm James Todd, your attorney. Call me Jim. How can I be of assistance?"

Travis pulled a folded piece of paper from his pocket and passed it through the slit in the plexiglass. "It's all there," he said in a quiet, thick Southern drawl.

The attorney read the note carefully, then re-read it while Travis waited, his face devoid of expression.

"This seems harsh, Mr. Conway."

Travis scowled. "Not as harsh as living the rest of my life in this place, Mr. Todd. Do you know what happens to inmates here?"

"I'm sure it's not pleasant."

"You could say that. Men lose their minds, Mr. Todd. You're the first human being I've talked to in over a month. I don't even know what month it is, and I'm not near as bad off as some around here. A lifer down the block from me tied a tourniquet around his wrist and amputated all five of his fingers with a razor blade. Then he cooked one of them and ate it in a cup of ramen soup. They had to cover another fellow's bars with plexiglass on account of him throwing his shit at the guards every time they walked by. Like a monkey in a goddamned zoo. You're right, Mr. Todd. This is not a pleasant place."

"I apologize, Mr. Conway, I didn't mean to trivialize your situation." He held up the note and pointed to it. "It's just that this seems over the top. The partners may take issue with it."

"And why would the partners all of a sudden have a case of conscience?"

"Conscience has nothing to do with it. They may see it as provocative and bad for business. You know we have always avoided drawing attention to ourselves."

Travis was indignant. "You say 'we' like you were one of the founding members, Mr. Todd. Well, since you weren't and I was, let me remind you of a few things. First, the Network is in the business of making money, and I'm paying in full for the jobs you're holding in your hand. Second, the Network has never, EVER refused a request from a member, and make no mistake, I am still a member in good standing."

James felt his stomach begin to tighten, and he began to backtrack. "I'm not saying it can't be done, Mr. Conway, I was just saying—"

Travis cut him off. "Don't interrupt me. And don't think just because you're walking out of here you somehow become untouchable. Same goes for the partners. I don't leave things to chance, Mr. Todd. An old friend used to say, 'Wear a belt and suspenders.' I can always hire another attorney."

(Translation: *There's already a Plan B, in case you and the partners don't want to do your job. And if my backup guy has to take care of it, you'll all be looking over your shoulders for the rest of your short lives.*)

James composed himself, took a deep breath, and replied, "No need to worry, Mr. Conway. I assure you this will be taken care of. You have my word."

Travis stared at his attorney through the plexiglass. "Trust me, I'm not worried. Are we good?"

"We are. Just. . . well, I'm a little concerned about the guards finding this on me when I leave." He held up the note again. "They were pretty thorough on the way in."

"Which one walked you back here, the fat one or the thin one?"

"The fat one."

Travis allowed himself a chuckle. "That's Ernie. He's a friend of ours. You'll be fine."

Ernie was indeed a friend, and he reappeared on the one-hour mark to escort the attorney past the security checkpoint and out of the prison. Travis's handwritten instructions remained unchecked and untouched in James's jacket pocket as he walked through the outermost gates of ADMAX and made his way to his rental car. He guarded the piece of paper all the way back to Atlanta as if his life hung in the balance.

––––––––––––––

Travis made his decision weeks before. He had already suffered a half dozen panic attacks and was having more frequent hallucinations, the last of which involved his long-dead mother visiting him in his cell. He knew there would come a time when his lapses in lucidity became more enduring, even permanent, and by then he would no longer control his fate. It was a nightmare he had no intention of living.

The night before his meeting with the attorney, he tore several strips from a bedsheet and braided them together into an improvised rope, hiding it under his mattress and hoping the next 24 hours would not bring a shakedown inspection of his cell. It did not. After the meeting, he came back to his cell and retrieved the rope and a toothbrush to which he'd attached an inch-long piece of blade he had extracted from a prison-issued disposable razor. He tied the rope to the upper bars of his cell's door and fashioned a slipknot on the other end, placing it around his neck so that it was just slack while he was standing upright.

Without allowing himself to ponder the moment, he began to kneel, taking out the slack, feeling the noose tighten and the pressure begin to build around his neck. As his consciousness waned, Travis placed the razor against his wrist and plunged it into the flesh, pulling it lengthwise toward the palm of his hand until he saw bright red blood start to flow, then to gush. *Belt and suspenders*, he thought as he used the last of his strength to kick his legs out in front of him, transferring all his body weight to the bedsheet noose. His peripheral vision narrowed, pinpointing as his carotid artery closed and the flow of blood to his brain slowed to a trickle. There was a moment of fear, then a moment of peace. And then there was nothing.

CHAPTER 2

THREE MONTHS LATER

Vincent began his day like most of his fellow Americans, pouring a cup of black coffee and checking his phone. There was a text message from his dentist reminding him of an upcoming appointment, and three more from his daughter: She had arrived safely with her girlfriends at the resort in Cabo, she loved him, and she would send pictures. His online streaming service sent two notifications, each recommending a show they thought was right up his alley. The first was for a romantic comedy, and the second was for an animated series that appeared to be geared toward adolescent boys. He made a mental note to cancel the service. There were four emails, two spam and one from his bank, reminding him of the pre-approved credit card with the $20,000 limit they were waiting to send him. Three quick deletes.

The fourth email caught his eye.

All Inclusive Getaway in the Breathtaking Maldives! Luxury Beachfront Accommodation With Airfare from $1995.00/Week! Click Here for Details!

The link took him to a page with color photos of a paradisiacal stretch of sand surrounded by crystal blue waters and dotted with thatched-roof villas. The details of the offer were spelled out below the pictures:

Seven days, six nights at the Maldives #1 adults-only resort. 15 luxuriously appointed individual suites, each with their own private beach and 24/7 butler service. $1995 offer is per person, and includes airfare from New York, Charlotte, or Miami with transfers in Dubai. 50% deposit required with booking; may be cancelled up to 7 days before travel for a full refund. Click below to book now!!!

There was no need to click below. He went to his safe and retrieved a laptop, powered it on, and used an Ethernet cord to plug it directly into a router. This would have seemed archaic to the casual observer, but for the task at hand, even secured and encrypted Wi-Fi was a risk he was unwilling to take. Moments later he accessed the Tor browser that would take him to the dark web, and navigated to the online chess club site Checkmate. A quick login brought him to the main menu, where he selected *New Game*, then *New Opponent*. Another menu appeared, this one listing international destinations where opponents were also logged on and waiting for a game. He selected Dubai. When prompted for his player identification number, he pulled up the original email on his phone and began copying numbers directly into the laptop. From *7 days. 6 nights. #1 resort. 15 villas. 24/7 butler service*, he typed in: *76115247*. He continued plucking the numbers from the text until he had entered the required fifteen-digit verification code: *761152471995507*.

When he clicked *Enter*, the chess site disappeared, replaced by a nondescript, monochrome spreadsheet with headings labeled: *Job Number*, *Category*, *Description*, and *Bid*. There were four new listings, each offering the same fee in cryptocurrency upon completion and verification, and they all appeared to have been posted by the same person, someone who apparently had a large axe to grind.

The description page for each job listed only the target's name, a few biographical details, and their last known location; the individual contractor was responsible for conducting their own advance work and making certain the task was completed as specified. Vincent studied the listings carefully, plotting a strategy and risk assessment for each. Big cities were big headaches, with their well-staffed police departments and video cameras on every street corner and storefront. Plus, the target was a female, and even hit men had their standards. He struck number one. Number two was fifty miles from the city in which he grew up, and the risk of being seen by someone he knew was too high. Another strike. He alternated back and forth between the two remaining listings, sorting the pros and cons of each, before clicking *Accept* next to number four.

He considered bidding on both, but balked at the idea of doubling his exposure. If he was correct, it wasn't going to take the authorities long to figure out the links between these four murders, and they would be looking for anyone they could connect to multiple crime scenes. Better to stick to one, do it quickly and anonymously, and disappear. "No need to get greedy," Vincent muttered to nobody in particular as he logged off and stowed his laptop.

One hour later, all four jobs had been taken.

CHAPTER 3

"**THE PLAINTIFF CALLS** Bryce Chandler."

He rose from his chair in the gallery and walked toward the witness stand, still not believing this day had actually come. Who in God's name takes a divorce to trial? And for that matter, who in their right mind allows their dirty laundry to be aired in open court in a tiny community like Marathon, where everyone knows everyone, and gossip is a commodity unto itself?

April and Stanley Murtaugh, that's who. He was the owner of Monroe County's largest and most successful marina, and she was a former Miss Miami-Dade County, twenty years his junior. After ten years of marriage, they found themselves locked in a battle that would surely be the biggest and nastiest of its kind since . . . well, since EVER in this sleepy town, best known as the midway point along the island chain of the Florida Keys. At stake was half the couple's community assets, or at least that's how April Murtaugh saw it. Stanley had dangled two million dollars for her to go away quietly, final offer, not subject to negotiation. In response, April hired an attorney and Bryce.

Under Florida law, divorce proceedings were heard by a judge, not a jury. Still, unless the parties could present a compelling reason, the trials were held in open court, and on this day the courtroom saw more than its share of casual observers and a reporter or two from local news outlets. The Murtaughs were well-known in this part of Florida, and there was a sense among the onlookers that they would get to hear some lurid details about the doomed marriage.

Bryce was sworn in and took his seat in the witness chair. Morgan Landover picked up his yellow legal pad, walked from the plaintiff's table to the podium, and began his questioning.

"Please state your name and occupation for the record."

"Bryce Chandler. I'm a private investigator."

"And how long have you been so employed, Mr. Chandler?"

"Four years."

"Mr. Chandler, were you hired by my client, Mrs. Murtaugh, and if so, for what purpose?"

"Yes, about a year ago. Mrs. Murtaugh wanted me to investigate her husband's professional and personal life. She was concerned about his business dealings and how they might affect her financial interests. She was also concerned that he might have been having an affair."

Ashley Oliver stood at the defense table, and every red-blooded man in the courtroom took notice, Bryce included. She was about 40 years old, tall and athletic, with auburn hair and green eyes highlighting a face worthy of a professional model. She had actually done a bit of modeling to pay the bills during law school, but any courtroom adversaries who wrote her off as just another pretty face did so at their own peril. She was the number two graduate in her class at the University of Houston, had a voracious appetite for the law, and she was fearless.

"Objection, Your Honor. Relevance. Mr. Chandler is testifying to issues not in evidence."

Morgan Landover countered. "Judge, my witness is merely giving the background for the substantive portion of his testimony. But if it pleases the court and Ms. Oliver, we can strike and move on."

Judge Myron Troxley, in his thirtieth year on the bench, was a man of few words, but they were always well chosen and served notice to counsel that he was in charge of his courtroom. "It pleases me greatly, Mr. Landover, and thank you for the offer. The objection is sustained. Move on."

Landover continued. "Mr. Chandler, tell us about your investigation."

Bryce repositioned himself in the chair, reorganized his thoughts, and stuck to the rehearsed script. "I began following Mr. Murtaugh about a year ago, tracking his activities as far north as Tavernier, and as far south as Key West. I kept notes on his destinations, arrival and departure times, his contacts—"

Landover interrupted, "Contacts?"

Bryce explained, "Who he met with, if I was able to tell."

"And how would you be able to tell who he was meeting with?"

"Usually by running their license plate. If they weren't in a car, I might take a picture and ask around. Folks in the Keys are pretty helpful."

"And Mr. Chandler, were you able to establish any regular patterns of behavior or contacts for Mr. Murtaugh during your investigation?"

"A few, yes. Most of what he did, I would describe as unremarkable. He looked at and test drove a lot of boats, which made sense for someone who owns a marina and is a licensed yacht broker. He played golf in Key West about once a week with friends.

Belonged to a gym and worked out there three times a week. Church on Sundays."

"Well that all seems pretty tame, Mr. Chandler. Were there any activities you felt Mr. Murtaugh would have wanted to keep secret from Mrs. Murtaugh?"

Ashley Oliver rose again. "Objection, Your Honor. Speculation and relevance."

Judge Troxley shot her an incredulous glance; surely she knew the flimsiness of such an argument. "It's a divorce proceeding, Ms. Oliver. Overruled."

Landover refocused his witness. "Any secrets Mr. Murtaugh was keeping?"

Bryce answered, "He had a standing appointment at the Sandpiper Inn on Sugarloaf Key, every Thursday between noon and two p.m. Always the same room, number 142. He always used the same alias, Donald Romine. Always paid cash, and always had company."

"Tell us about his company, please."

"They were young females, no older than thirty. I never saw the same one twice. Once, there were two of them. They would pull up in front of the room about ten minutes after him, then go inside. And they always left after he did. I figured they were either working girls or online hookups."

So much for church on Sundays.

Landover asked, "And how long did this go on?"

Bryce replied, "For as long as I was following him, about four months. He never missed a Thursday."

Ashley Oliver sat quietly through the brutal line of questioning. There was no sense alienating the judge with endless objections;

she knew there were pictures and records of all the comings and goings Bryce was describing, and she didn't want to shine a bright light on all that evidence just for the sake of attacking the witness's credibility. That would come later. Her client's extramarital sex life was the least of her worries, so she held her tongue and waited for the other shoe to drop, and it did in short order.

Landover continued.

"Besides the activities at the Sandpiper Inn, what else about Mr. Murtaugh did you think would be relevant to this proceeding?"

"Over the course of a month, Mr. Murtaugh had several business lunches at Panama Jim's in Islamorada, always with the same individual. It wasn't part of his routine, and I wanted to know more. I started by identifying his lunch partner."

Landover asked, "And who did you determine that to be?"

"His name is Roger Mackenzie. He's Chase Worthing's personal attorney."

Landover clarified, "And would that be Chase Worthing, as in Worthing Motors?" The exotic foreign car dealership specialized in high-end vehicles—Lamborghini, Maserati, Ferrari, and Aston Martin, to name a few—and was the largest of its kind in Miami. Worthing, a 1980s NASCAR sensation, had gone on to own and operate his own race team, and in the early '90s he opened the business that bore his name.

Bryce answered, "One and the same."

"And Mr. Chandler, were you able to ascertain the nature of those business lunches?"

Ashley Oliver knew what was coming, and she knew it would be devastating to her client. She also knew she couldn't stop it, but still she rose again. "Objection, Your Honor. This witness is not an expert in business matters, and he is not qualified to state conclusively what my client may or may not have been discussing with Mr. Mackenzie."

Landover and Chandler were both surprised at the slip—she had just conceded the lunch meetings as fact. Not that it mattered, as there were photographs, credit card receipts, and eyewitnesses at the ready if the defense wanted to make an issue of it all.

Judge Troxley was unmoved by the latest objection. "Ms. Oliver, it seems to me Mr. Landover is inquiring as to the generic nature of a lunch conversation. If I find the answer wandering into expert witness territory, I'll address it. And of course you can always dispute the witness's findings during cross examination. But I'm going to allow him to answer the question."

Landover asked again, "What were they talking about, Mr. Chandler?"

Bryce replied, "At their final meeting, they were discussing the sale of Mr. Murtaugh's marina."

"And how do you know that?"

"Because I was sitting at the table next to them, about three feet away."

Landover asked, "Now when you say they were discussing the sale of the marina, what exactly do you mean?"

"It was clear from their conversation that Mr. Murtaugh was going to sell the marina to Mr. Worthing."

Landover continued, "And did they discuss a price?"

"Yes."

The moment Morgan Landover had waited for was here.

"And what was that price?" he asked.

"Twenty-six million dollars."

———————————

Ashley Oliver had urged her client to settle with his estranged wife months ago; he refused to discuss the matter. She knew the plaintiff had a private investigator, a good one, and that they had uncovered Stanley's plan to sell the marina and conceal the proceeds from April. She had hoped against hope the judge would exclude Bryce Chandler's testimony regarding the meetings between her client and Roger Mackenzie, but even that was a long shot; there were other ways for opposing counsel to get the evidence into the record. By the time the witness was tendered, the damage was done. Stanley Murtaugh was a greedy serial philanderer who would be forfeiting half of everything he owned to his wronged, soon to be ex-wife. Ashley's last hope was to destroy the credibility of the witness. She attacked.

"Good morning, Mr. Chandler. Please tell the court again how long you've been a private investigator?"

He knew exactly where it was all going and was powerless to stop it.

"Four years."

She continued, "And during that time, Mr. Chandler, has your private investigator's license ever been suspended or revoked by the State of Florida?"

"You know it has."

"Perhaps I know, Mr. Chandler, but would you please share with the court the circumstances behind your suspension?"

"I was arrested for driving under the influence three years ago. I pled guilty to a reduced charge of reckless driving, attended a defensive driving course, and performed 100 hours of community service. And yes, my PI's license was suspended for six months."

Ashley smiled. "I see. And was this the first time your professional life was affected by your alcohol use?"

It was Morgan Landover's turn to object.

"Your Honor, I'm not sure where defense counsel is going with this, but Mr. Chandler isn't on trial here. Just how far back are we going to allow Ms. Oliver to pry into Mr. Chandler's life?"

He knew how far she was going to pry, because Bryce had told him everything when he was hired on. Still, he wanted to stop the bleeding if he could.

Ashley responded, "Judge, I'm not asking about his personal life, I'm questioning his use of alcohol in a professional capacity. Surely that's relevant here. I mean, we're talking about the reliability of an alleged eyewitness who claims to have overheard a damaging conversation involving my client."

Judge Troxley pondered the issue for a moment and issued his ruling.

"I'll give you a bit of leeway, Ms. Oliver. Keep it short, and keep it relevant. The objection is overruled. Please answer the question, Mr. Chandler."

Bryce wouldn't give her the satisfaction of seeing his expression change or hearing his voice waver. He nodded toward the judge, faced the microphone, and answered the question.

"There was another incident."

"And when was that, Mr. Chandler?"

"Five years ago."

"So, before you were a private investigator, and before you moved to the Keys?"

"That's correct."

"And where were you, and what line of work were you in at the time?"

"I was an FBI agent in Atlanta, Georgia."

"Why did you leave the FBI, Mr. Chandler?"

Bryce smiled. "I retired. They let you do that after twenty-two years."

Her voice turned syrupy sweet and was brimming with sarcasm. "I'm sure they do, and thank you for your service. But isn't it true, Mr. Chandler, that you retired while under investigation for another alcohol-related incident? Isn't it true you chose retirement over losing your job because you came to work drunk and assaulted a supervisor?"

She had it mostly right. "Drunk" wasn't an accurate assessment. To be fair, he was still feeling some effects of the previous night's bourbon, and witnesses claimed they could smell it on his breath. But it was anger, not alcohol, controlling him when he grabbed his supervisor by the tie and threatened to throw him out the window of his seventh-floor corner office. The target of his anger was Greg Peoples, a skinny, bespectacled, thirty-three-year-old accountant with fewer than five years' of experience as a street agent, and he had just informed Bryce he would be spending the next sixty days conducting background investigations for new FBI agent applicants. Peoples was intimidated by the older veteran agents on the violent street gang squad, especially the men, and had already succeeded in getting two of them to seek transfers and a third to retire. He hoped sending Bryce to the "land of misfit toys" (the office nickname for the applicant squad) would force him into a similar decision. It probably would have if Bryce had been in a better mood on the morning in question. But it had been a rough twenty-four hours.

He gave the defense attorney his rehearsed answer. "I had a disagreement with a supervisor, and unfortunately, I did have alcohol in my system at the time. It was poor judgment on my part, and in retrospect I wish I had shown more restraint. I could have stayed on with the FBI, but I felt it was time to begin the next chapter of my life, and so I retired." In fact, he was given the option to either retire or face an inquiry that could have led to his dismissal sans benefits. He took the pension and ran.

Ashley Oliver smiled and continued as if he hadn't said anything. Her next question was going to infuriate the judge and maybe even get her held in contempt, but she was running out of options.

"And isn't it true, Mr. Chandler, that you were still drunk that morning because the previous day your wife served you with divorce papers, and the grounds for that divorce included the disruption to the marriage caused by your habitual use of alcohol?"

She had barely completed her sentence before Morgan Landover jumped to his feet.

"Objection, Your Honor! Ms. Oliver is way out of line here. Mr. Chandler's marital record has no bearing on this court's business. The defense was instructed mere minutes ago to stay out of his personal life."

"The witness will not answer the last question." Judge Troxley glared at the defense counsel. "Ms. Oliver, you disappoint me. One more stunt like that, and you'll not be happy with what happens next, I promise you."

She was on thin ice and needed to proceed carefully.

"Apologies, Your Honor, and to you as well, Mr. Chandler. Just a couple more questions. First, I'm going to ask you to recall the day you claimed to overhear a conversation between my client and Roger Mackenzie at Panama Jim's Bar and Grill in Islamorada. May I assume you were performing your professional duties as a private investigator at the time?"

"I was."

"And do you recall what you had for lunch that day?"

"Sorry, that was nearly six months ago."

"Fair enough, but can you tell me what you had to drink that day, either before or during lunch?"

"You mean, as in alcoholic beverages, Ms. Oliver?" Bryce asked.

Her tone turned from inquisitive to accusatory.

"That's precisely what I mean, Mr. Chandler."

"Well, I can tell you I didn't have a drink all day, if that's what you're after."

"Good for you, Mr. Chandler. So if, perchance, I was able to obtain a copy of your bill from the restaurant, are you positive there wouldn't be a record of you ordering any alcohol with your lunch?"

It was a rookie tactic. He had used it countless times himself during interrogations of street-level thugs. *What if I told you there was a security camera on the street corner where the shooting occurred, and what if I told you I've got video of you firing the pistol?* Only an idiot would fall for it. Fortunately, many of Bryce's subjects in those days were, in fact, idiots. Bryce was not.

"Ms. Oliver, I am certain of two things: I did not consume any alcohol that day, and you don't have a copy of my restaurant bill that shows otherwise."

She glared at him as she picked up her legal pad from the podium. "Nothing further, Your Honor."

Judge Troxley asked, "Redirect, Mr. Landover?"

Morgan Landover stood at the plaintiff's table and addressed his witness. "Just one question, Your Honor. Mr. Chandler, you testified that you couldn't remember what you had for lunch on the day in question, but you were positive you didn't have anything to drink. Can you explain for the court how you can be so sure you didn't consume alcohol that day?"

"Yes, sir. I am an alcoholic. The day after I was arrested for DUI, I went to my first Alcoholics Anonymous meeting. I've been a regular ever since, and I've been sober for three years." He glanced into the gallery and saw a half dozen approving smiles and nods.

"Thank you, Mr. Chandler. Nothing further, Judge."

Judge Troxley said, "The witness is excused, and we'll be in recess for lunch."

As the courtroom emptied, Bryce stopped at the plaintiff's table, chatted with Morgan Landover and April Murtaugh, and wished them well. He walked without comment past the defendant and his frustrated attorney, and out of the Monroe County courthouse into the stifling heat and humidity of a mid-July afternoon. Beads of sweat gathered on his forehead and ran down his back before he made it as far as his truck, where he sat for a few minutes, allowing the air conditioning to cool the interior before starting for home. As he waited, Bryce reflected on the indignity of having the two great failures in his life aired to a live audience. He had come to the Keys to start over after his divorce and forced retirement from the Bureau, but his past seemed determined not to let go. *Progress, not perfection,* he reminded himself as he pulled out of the parking lot and turned southbound onto US-1, the iconic Overseas Highway that linked Miami to Key West.

Five minutes later he was driving across the Seven Mile Bridge, the vast expanse of the Atlantic Ocean to his left and the Gulf of Mexico on his right. It was his favorite stretch of road anywhere, his happy place, and the ten-minute drive in either direction never failed to brighten his mood.

Still, he could have really used a drink.

CHAPTER 4

ANDY PITTMAN was always an early riser, but especially so over the past year. Once a dedicated bachelor, he now found himself enjoying the very antithesis of the single life, married with a new baby and a mortgage on a three-bedroom fixer-upper in the tiny Terre Haute suburb of Fairview Park, Indiana. His shift at the prison started at 7:00 a.m., which meant he had to be on the road by 6:30, earlier if he wanted to stop for breakfast. He preferred to let his wife and infant son sleep rather than wake them with the sounds of clattering about the kitchen, and so most mornings his commute included a stop at the local fast food drive-through for a sausage biscuit and coffee.

On this day he woke at 5:00 a.m., showered, dressed in his uniform, kissed his sleeping wife on the cheek, and pulled the door closed on their darkened bedroom. He padded down the hallway in stocking feet and stopped at the next room, cracking the door just enough to gaze in on his sleeping son, then closing it again. He continued into the living room, where he retrieved his shoes from the mat at the front door, donned them, stepped outside, and locked the door behind him.

The sun was beginning to lighten the horizon, and Andy could see the faint outline of the garbage bin he had wheeled to the curb the night before. He made a mental note to avoid it when he backed down the driveway. He climbed into his SUV and started the engine; the radio was already tuned to a classic country station, and he hummed along with the lyrics of "I'd Love to Lay You Down" as he buckled his seatbelt, shifted into reverse, checked the rearview mirror, and reminded himself: *Don't hit the damned trash can.*

He wouldn't make it that far. The blast occurred halfway down the driveway, throwing the back end of the SUV upward in a shock wave of explosive energy as the entire vehicle flipped upside down. The gas tank was full, and when it ruptured, flaming gasoline sent a fireball twenty feet into the dark morning sky. By the time his wife and neighbors ran outside to see the horror, the SUV was an unrecognizable shell, a mass of twisted metal engulfed in flames. Mercifully, Andy was dead microseconds after the initial explosion, spared the agony of burning alive.

The Terre Haute fire department extinguished the blaze, and police cordoned off what was left of the vehicle and covered it with a tarp to conceal Andy's charred remains. A police bomb squad and no fewer than two dozen FBI and ATF agents descended on the scene, squabbling over who was in charge. The argument was settled when the victim was identified as a federal correctional officer, thus granting the FBI jurisdiction. They would pick over the scene for the next twelve hours, photographing the carnage from every angle, swabbing for explosive residue, and gathering a thousand or more bits and pieces of scorched metal and plastic in an attempt to reconstruct the explosive device and identify its maker.

As night fell, Andy's body was removed to the state crime laboratory for an autopsy, which seemed perfunctory, but was required by state law and would be necessary for a murder trial in federal court. The vehicle carcass was **flipped** upright, forklifted onto a flatbed, and driven to the FBI office in Indianapolis, where it would be preserved as evidence. Andy's wife and son had been ushered away from the scene by neighbors following the explosion, and by day's end were with family a hundred miles away from the shattered home to which they would never return.

CHAPTER 5

THE USED, twenty-two-foot center console fishing boat was Bryce's second purchase in the Keys, after his nine-hundred-square-foot, two-bedroom home (the "box on stilts," he liked to call it), which sat on one of the myriad canals linking Big Pine Key to the open waters of the Atlantic Ocean and the Gulf of Mexico. By Florida Keys standards, both the house and the boat could be at best described as "modest," although in the Keys even a modest lifestyle was expensive. His ex-wife got half his FBI pension, and what was left barely covered his mortgage and utilities, thus the private investigator work. Besides giving him a reason to get out of bed in the morning, it was the safety net that kept him from dipping into his guarded retirement savings.

Boaters in the Keys could choose between the rougher, deeper waters of the Atlantic Ocean with its treasure of big game fish, or the more serene shallows of the Gulf of Mexico, where the Keys themselves served as a sort of protective barrier to a lush ecosystem of sandbars, mangroves, and marine life. Bryce preferred the relaxed vibe of the Gulf and its abundant supply of smaller but easy-to-catch mangrove snapper, yellowtail, and stone crab. At least three days a week, he headed out early enough to watch the sun rise from one of his preferred fishing spots along Big Pine's western shore. He found his time on the water more beneficial to his mental health than any two-hundred-dollar-an-hour shrink, and between his failed marriage and drinking issues, he had seen his share of those.

He had just dropped his chum in the water when his phone rang. It was Morgan Landover.

"Good morning, Morgan. You're up early."

"Morning, Bryce. No rest for divorce attorneys here in paradise. Anyway, I wanted to call and update you on the Murtaughs. The judge ruled as we thought he would and partitioned the estate. He granted our petition to force the sale of the marina, the house, and most of the marital assets. Stanley is not a happy man."

Baiting a hook with a live shrimp, his phone tucked between his shoulder and his ear, Bryce replied, "Stanley's a piece of shit."

Morgan laughed. "That seems to be the consensus. Anyway, April said he's furious with you, and he even went so far as to make some threatening remarks. I got a courtesy call from Ashley Oliver, and she said the same thing. Stanley's going on about how you have no idea what you've stepped in, he's not afraid of you just because you used to be a Fed, blah, blah, blah."

Bryce dropped his line and began playing it out into the chum stream. "Well, hopefully he'll feel a little better when he gets his half of the sale proceeds from Chase Worthing. I mean, thirteen million bucks is still more money than you and I will ever see in our lifetimes."

"True," Morgan replied, "except that's not happening anymore. The day after you testified, Worthing's lawyer called Stanley and told him the deal was off. We think the publicity of the divorce trial spooked them. After you told us about the meetings at Panama Jim's, April did some snooping of her own. She found an unsigned draft copy of a sales contract in Stanley's desk, and Chase Worthing's name was nowhere on it. The deal was between Murtaugh Marine and a company called Atlantis Global Trading."

Bryce was finding renewed interest in what had been a routine divorce investigation.

He asked, "So why do you think Worthing wanted to keep everything hush-hush?"

Morgan answered, "Your guess is as good as mine, buddy. All I know is I've got a client worth about twenty million on paper, but paper is all she's worth right now. With Worthing out of the picture there aren't any serious buyers for the marina. The house will sell, but it's a multi-million-dollar mansion so the process is going to take a while. And to top it all off, the judge didn't issue an order of occupancy, so they're holed up on opposite sides of the place, fighting like two cornered cats."

Bryce laughed. "And let me guess, you and Ashley Oliver get to play referee?"

"You got it. I shouldn't complain; with all the notices and motions I'm filing, April Murtaugh accounts for twenty percent of my billable hours right now. And let me tell you, those two deserve each other. She's as mean as he is, maybe meaner. Anyway, watch your back where Stanley is concerned. He's in a bad way."

"I'll do that, Morgan. Thanks for calling."

Bryce put his phone back in his pocket and turned his attention to the water, where over the next half hour he caught and released a dozen or so gray snapper, none of which met the minimum size to be a keeper. Ordinarily, he would have moved to another spot, but by now his mind was swirling with thoughts of

Stanley Murtaugh, the entitled little pervert with the big mouth and the sudden shot of courage.

Bryce weighed anchor and headed for home.

CHAPTER 6

IN ATLANTA, the name "Buckhead" was synonymous with luxury and affluence. The stylish suburb due north of the city had long been known for its upscale shopping, fine dining, art galleries, and trendy nightlife. Its residents laid claim to the highest median income in the metropolitan area, and nothing said "I've arrived" quite like a Buckhead mailing address.

At 4:30 a.m. the gunman pulled onto a side street in a residential neighborhood off West Paces Ferry Road, shut off the engine, and smoked a cigarette while he waited, watched, and listened. It was his fourth visit to the area, and he was confident in his choice of time and location. Buckhead didn't come to life much before sunrise, with the exception of the occasional jogger or dog walker. There were few streetlights off the beaten path, and an abundance of places to lay in wait.

He crushed out his cigarette and put the butt in his pocket, left his car, and walked northwest toward the governor's mansion, donning gloves along the way. When he reached Habersham Road, he turned right and ducked into a stand of trees alongside the street, fading into the darkness and vegetation. He pulled the Glock nine-millimeter pistol from his waistband, checked the suppressor, and waited for his prey.

At 4:45, a short, fat man in an Atlanta Braves T-shirt passed, half-walking, half-running, wheezing as he went. The gunman watched him until he disappeared from sight. Five minutes later, a young Asian woman with a runner's gait passed in the other direction, oblivious to his presence. As the minutes ticked by, he began to have second thoughts; the target had always reached this point between 4:45 and 5:00. At 5:01, he would leave and reevaluate his options for another day.

There. About two hundred feet up the road, running along the sidewalk in his direction. The right height and build, the familiar stride, the Adidas warmup pants he had seen twice before, their reflective stripes catching the light from a nearby porch. He was 95 percent sure, but needed to be positive.

As the target passed, he stepped out of the trees and onto the sidewalk, calling out a name just loud enough for the two of them to hear.

"Julia."

She turned, still running in place, and barely had time to register the presence of the stranger before the first bullet struck the center of her chest. As she fell backward, another round tore through her neck, paralyzing her as she collapsed in a heap on the sidewalk. He walked toward her, pausing over her body just long enough to deliver a third and decisive shot to her temple, then returned the Glock to his waistband and retraced his steps back to the car.

He made two stops on his way to the airport, disposing of the pistol in one dumpster and the suppressor and gloves in another. By the time the Atlanta Police Department arrived at their latest homicide scene, he was twenty miles away, and before they left he would be 30,000 feet in the air and halfway home.

CHAPTER 7

TWO DAYS AFTER his conversation with Morgan Landover, Bryce opened his own investigation into Chase Worthing and Atlantis Global Trading. Maybe Stanley was just blowing off steam, maybe not. But according to April Murtaugh, the sale of the marina had been scuttled over the publicity of the divorce trial, and that piqued his interest. Why was Chase Worthing so determined to keep his name out of the deal?

He began with a search of the public business records for Atlantis Global Trading. It had been founded just over a year ago, incorporated in Delaware but with a Miami address. There were no tax liens or records of bankruptcy, no court judgments or UCC filings. The principal and CEO was Roger Mackenzie, and the type of business was listed as "General Trading, Import/ Export." There was no listed phone number. Other than the filing with the Delaware Secretary of State, Atlantis Global Trading had no online presence, not even its own website. All the signs of a shell company.

Chase Worthing wasn't nearly as bashful about his public persona. His dealership's splashy website had an entire section devoted to his life's story, replete with pictures and tales of his glory days on the NASCAR circuit. A tab marked *Our Customers* took browsers to a photo gallery of well-known entertainers, professional athletes, and prominent business and society figures, all posing with Chase in front of their new luxury cars. The dealership's inventory included both used and new models, ranging in price from a $55,000 pre-owned Aston Martin Vantage to a brand-new Ferrari LaFerrari with a sticker of $1.7 million. The website advertised in-house financing, but Bryce doubted many of Worthing's customers were into car payments.

Land records showed Chase and his wife owned a house and land in Miami's North Beach, with an assessed value of $4.2 million. The Florida Department of Motor Vehicles listed a seventy-three-foot, 2004 Donzi Convertible motor yacht under Worthing's name, and Bryce estimated its value to be around $1.25 million. The DMV had no records of ownership for passenger cars, but that made sense for someone like Worthing who had an endless supply of luxury vehicles at his disposal.

Chase Worthing had never been arrested, filed bankruptcy, or been named as a defendant in a lawsuit. He had been divorced twice and was five years along with wife number three. He held a Florida driver's license and was certified as both a boat captain and a private pilot. He was a registered Republican, voted in Florida's last four general elections, and contributed the legal maximum to the campaigns of the state's GOP gubernatorial candidates during that period.

Bryce hadn't expected to find much in the public domain, and his expectations were met. Still, this was only entry-level snooping. The real dirt came from old fashioned detective work—surveillance, informants, and an occasional payoff for sensitive information. He pulled out a pad and began jotting a to-do list, barely getting started before his phone rang. It was his former partner in Atlanta, Donnie Morris, no doubt calling to catch up.

He answered on the second ring. "Donnie, my brother! How are things in the ATL?"

Donnie's voice was somber, and he got right to the point. "Hello, Bryce. Have you been watching the news?"

"As little as possible. What's up?"

"Julie Martinez is dead."

Julia Martinez, "Julie" to her friends, was far and away Bryce's favorite Assistant United States Attorney, the official title for federal prosecutors. Unlike many of her contemporaries, she saw FBI agents as partners rather than servants, and that went a long way with veteran investigators like Bryce and Donnie. She respected the concept of staying in one's lane, taking a back seat during the investigation process, and expecting agents to do the same when the matter came before the court. Most of all, she was tough as nails, and was known for charging every possible statute and seeking maximum sentences for her defendants. If there was such a thing as a hanging AUSA, it was Julie Martinez.

Bryce found himself searching for words. "Oh my God. . . what happened?"

"She went out for a run early yesterday morning, and somebody shot her three times. Another jogger found her. It looks like an execution."

There was a pause as Bryce processed what he hoped he wasn't hearing correctly. "Do we have any idea who did it? Any leads at all?"

Donnie replied, "It's not our case. Julie quit the US Attorney's Office six months ago and went to work for a local firm. Since she was no longer an AUSA, there's no federal jurisdiction. APD homicide has the lead."

Bryce's mind was reeling. He had dozens of questions and doubted his friend could answer any of them. He asked anyway.

"Are they looking at Sean? Had there been any threats? What was she working on at the new job?"

"Julie and Sean divorced a year ago. He was out of town on business and flew back last night. From what I've heard he's shook up, but he's cooperating with the detectives and they don't think he has anything to do with it. That's all I have. My source says APD is keeping a tight lid on everything. I'm lucky to know what I know."

One last question. "What do you think happened?"

Donnie sighed. "I don't know, buddy. I really don't. This doesn't make sense. I mean, Julie put away her share of bad dudes, but so did everyone else in the criminal division. I think our best bet now is to hope whoever did this messed up somehow, maybe left behind some forensic evidence. But it sounds like a professional job."

Bryce was suddenly tired of talking, even with an old friend. "All right. I appreciate you calling. And please let me know the minute you hear anything."

"You know I will."

Bryce hung up and reached for his laptop.

He entered *Atlanta prosecutor murdered* in the search engine and clicked on the link to the first result:

Police Seek Clues in Murder of Local Attorney

By Kevin Forrester
Atlanta Tribune

Atlanta -- Authorities are investigating the murder of a former federal prosecutor found slain in her Buckhead neighborhood yesterday, a spokesman for the Atlanta Police Department said.

Julia Martinez, a former Assistant United States Attorney for the Northern District of Georgia, was found dead along a jogging path near West Paces Ferry Road at about 5:30 a.m. Thursday. Witnesses say she had been shot by an unknown assailant, but the Atlanta Police Department homicide unit, which is leading the investigation, refused to confirm or deny those claims.

Ms. Martinez, 44, was a graduate of the Emory University School of Law, and served 12 years at the United States Attorney's Office before leaving earlier this year to take a position with the Atlanta law firm of Callaway and Moriarty. The Atlanta Police Department is asking anyone with information to call their tip line, or to contact them online using the Crimestoppers tab on the APD website.

The story left Bryce with more questions than answers. He went back to the results of his search and scrolled a little further to see if another outlet was offering a different perspective. There were none, but at the end of the list there were multiple links under the heading *More Stories Like This*. He scanned the offerings:

Ohio Prosecutor Charged With DUI in Wild Police Chase

*Texas Attorney General: No Charges in "Pay for Play"
Scandal at State House*

*FBI Investigating Bombing, Murder of Federal
Correctional Officer*

*Federal Prosecutors Indict 6 in Massive Government
Fraud Case*

To most retired agents, an FBI story was always worth a read.
He clicked on the third link, which was dated two weeks earlier:

*FBI Investigating Bombing, Murder of Federal
Correctional Officer*

*By Deborah Spate
Indianapolis Journal*

*Terre Haute -- The FBI, ATF, and Indianapolis Police
Department Bomb Squad descended on the chaotic
scene of a car bombing that took the life of a Federal
Correctional Officer in Fairview Park outside of Terre
Haute on Tuesday.*

*The blast occurred around 6:00 a.m., shaking neigh-
bors from their beds and shattering windows as far as 100
yards away. Witnesses described seeing a large fireball immediately after hearing an extremely loud explosion. Bomb
technicians and evidence recovery experts worked until
nightfall trying to determine the cause of the explosion.*

*Agents at the scene declined to comment, other than
to say they did not believe the explosion was accidental.*

> *Killed in the blast was Andrew Pittman, 33, who*
> *had worked as a prison guard at USP Terre Haute for the*
> *past 10 years. Mr. Pittman's body has been taken to the*
> *state crime laboratory for an autopsy. His wife Tanya and*
> *their infant son were shaken but unhurt in the blast.*
>
> *Anyone with information is asked to contact the*
> *FBI's Indianapolis office.*

As a rule, Bryce didn't buy into conspiracy theories. If a career as a criminal investigator had taught him anything, it was that the simplest and most logical answer was usually the correct one. And at first glance, logic told him the deaths of Julie Martinez and Andrew Pittman were likely unrelated. Still, two murdered federal officers in the space of two weeks? And not just murders, but what looked like a pair of professional hits.

Chase Worthing and Stanley Murtaugh could wait. Bryce walked outside and down the stairs to his garage, where he retrieved a large, worn footlocker weighing close to a hundred pounds. He cursed every step on the way back up, nearly dropping the locker twice before setting it on the floor next to the kitchen table he used as an office.

He hadn't seen the inside of the box since he retired, and it took him three tries to remember the combination on the lock. But it was all still there: every note, every report, every photograph from every case he had been assigned over a twenty-two-year career. Bryce pulled the oldest file from the box and started reading.

CHAPTER 8

MOVIES AND TV almost never got it right. For whatever reason, they insisted on depicting FBI agents as superbeings who could solve a crime or locate a criminal anywhere on the planet with a few strokes on a computer keyboard, before jetting off on a waiting Gulfstream to catch the bad guy. In reality, the bedrock work of the Bureau was tedious and boring, and it was conducted by a corps of case agents for whom long hours, drudgery, and anonymity were badges of honor. Among the rank and file, there was almost no regard for the speed with which a fellow agent secured promotions. To the contrary, those who moved up too quickly were dubbed "Blue Flamers" and seen as lacking in the ability to conduct case work (as it was with Bryce's nemesis, Supervisory Special Agent Gregory Peoples). Street agents, or "brick agents" as they were sometimes known, respected investigative achievement above all else, and among them you were known for your work ethic and the quality and magnitude of your cases. There was no greater insult among street agents than "he never worked a case."

Bryce Chandler was a career street agent. It wasn't that he disliked the Bureau's management or would have minded the extra pay, but sitting behind a desk and conducting case file reviews wasn't why he signed on with the FBI. He was a cop before joining the Bureau, and like most cops, he saw himself as a guardian of the masses, a sheepdog whose reason for being was to keep the wolves at bay. When he landed on the Atlanta division's gang task force early in his career, he knew he had found his home.

A major case against a violent street gang could take years, and it would occupy the entirety of the case agent's time and attention from its inception until the final defendant was sentenced. Charting the structure and leadership of a violent street gang could take months. Informants had to be identified and developed. Phones were tapped. Crimes committed on behalf of the enterprise were catalogued—from drug deals to assaults and murder—every overt act in furtherance of the organization's agenda could be charged against every member of the organization, whether they participated in the actual crime or not. Such was the beauty of the Racketeering Influenced and Corrupt Organizations (RICO) Act: If you were part of the organization, you were held responsible for every criminal offense committed on its behalf.

During his nineteen years on the gang squad, Bryce was the primary agent on twelve cases, five of which were prosecuted by Julie Martinez. If the murders of Julie and Andrew Pittman were connected, the most likely explanation was that one of her defendants ended up in his prison. The *Indianapolis Journal* reported that Pittman was thirty-three years old and had worked at USP Terre Haute for ten years, making it likely that Terre Haute was his only assignment within the Bureau of Prisons. It also meant that if there were a common defendant responsible for both their deaths, they must have gone through the system during the past ten years, which included the final five years of Bryce's FBI career. That eliminated all but two of the cases he shared with Julie

Martinez: the Rollin West End Crips, and an Atlanta offshoot of the deadly and notorious MS-13.

The Crips were a well-known gang with origins in South Central Los Angeles. They branched out nationally and internationally since their founding in the early 1970s, and there were several Crip nation gangs, known as "sets," in Atlanta during the 1990s and 2000s, when Bryce began his work with the gang task force. Most of the sets were loosely organized groups with membership numbers in the single digits, whose criminal activities rarely rose above the level of spray-painting gang signs on street corners to mark their territory. When they did step out of line, the Atlanta Police Department dealt with them swiftly and effectively.

The Rollin West End Crips were a different story and a criminal enterprise in the truest sense of the term. They took their name from the West End neighborhood of Atlanta where they were founded, and when Bryce began investigating them, there were upward of fifty identified members. Not content to engage in petty turf wars, they ran a cocaine and heroin business with revenues in the millions, and they protected their operation and territory with sheer brutality. The organization was structured, with veteran leaders calling the shots and street soldiers doing their bidding. Four murders had been attributed to the gang before the case was opened, and two more would occur before the massive takedown that ended their control over South Fulton County's hard drug trade. When all was said and done, two dozen of the gang's members either pled guilty or were convicted at trial of a spate of felony charges, including the dreaded RICO and the crushing sentences it carried with it. A few of the soldiers escaped with five to ten years, but the top three leaders of the gang were each sentenced to multiple life terms in prison.

MS-13's ruthlessness made the Crips look tame by comparison. In 2012, the Salvadoran street gang was the first to be designated a trans-national criminal organization by the Department of Justice, and its motto "kill, rape, control" fit their business model well. Like the Crips, the gang originated in Los Angeles but soon spread nationwide, taking with it a reputation for brutality on par with the most violent of the Mexican drug cartels. In Georgia, MS-13 occupied a sizeable territory northwest of Atlanta, where they engaged in human trafficking, child prostitution, methamphetamine production and distribution, extortion, and murder. When it came to violence, nobody was off limits for MS-13—not women, not children, and not law enforcement. On the day Bryce and his team arrested twenty of the gang's members in a coordinated roundup, every one of them was armed, some with high-powered, military-grade rifles. The weapons charges were added to the list of felonies that made up the indictment, and by the time the plea deals and trials were finished, over five hundred years' worth of prison time had been handed down, including life sentences for the gang's leaders.

Bryce combed through the sentencing reports, building a list of names and dates of birth that he would pass to Donnie Morris in Atlanta. From there, Donnie could meet with his contacts at the Bureau of Prisons and run the names through their system, checking to see which, if any, of the defendants might have spent time at USP Terre Haute. It was a long shot, but it was all he had for the moment, and the least he could do for his friend Julie.

CHAPTER 9

THE NEWS CAME three days later. Of the forty-four defendants from the Crips and MS-13 cases, none were sent to Terre Haute. Bryce was disappointed but not surprised that his efforts had failed to advance the investigation into Julie's death. It had been a long shot at best.

Donnie updated him on what he knew of the Atlanta Police Department's case. Two shots were fired from about six feet away, the third from point-blank range. Three shell casings from a Glock nine-millimeter pistol were found within twenty feet of Julie's body, but evidence technicians were unable to develop any usable fingerprints or DNA on them. The only witness was the jogger who found her body; there were no reports of gunshots or suspicious activity in the neighborhood; and they had cleared her ex-husband Sean of involvement. Computer forensic examiners had Julie's laptop and phone, and they were poring over the details of her phone calls, texts, emails, and online activity. Although they had not announced it publicly, homicide detectives had grown convinced it was a professional hit. As none of the neighbors on the quiet street reported hearing gunshots, it was likely the assailant had used a silencer. An expensive gold necklace and Apple Watch were left on Julie's body, and other than the gunshots, she hadn't been assaulted, sexually or otherwise.

Everything about her death seemed sterile and planned, with all the markings of an emotionless murder for hire, and the detectives surmised the most logical scenario was a former defendant bent on revenge. Beyond that, they had nothing. A reward for information had been offered by her law firm and, with contributions from the United States Attorney's Office, it had grown to a hundred thousand dollars. The tip line was mostly silent.

Donnie was as frustrated as Bryce. "She prosecuted almost two hundred people in twelve years," he told Bryce. "And I hate to tell you this, buddy, but you're the only one who thinks there might be some connection with that guard in Indiana. When I brought it up with APD, they didn't want to hear it. They're convinced this was a standalone crime."

Bryce replied, "Maybe. Still, all we looked at was the possible common denominators between my cases and Julie's. What about yours? What about everyone else on the squad? What about DEA and ATF?"

"I suppose anything is possible, but to be honest, it seems like a stretch. And at the risk of repeating myself, APD isn't going down that road, and nobody around here wants to look like we're poking our nose in their case."

Bryce knew he was fighting an unwinnable battle. "I guess so. Keep me in the loop, will you? I need to get back to my day job."

"Yeah, how's the whole PI thing going?"

"Not bad, it keeps gas in the boat. I'm actually doing some pro bono work right now."

"Who's the client?"

"Me, I suppose. I had a divorce case a few weeks back that took an interesting turn. I caught the husband screwing around and trying to hide eight figures worth of assets from the wife, and now he's running his mouth, threatening me. I think he's also into some shady business with a car dealer up in Miami."

Donnie chuckled. "You sound like you're still on the job. What are you gonna do, throw the guy in jail?"

"Nah," Bryce replied. "I'm just going to play some defense."

CHAPTER 10

CHASE WORTHING MOTORS sat on a corner two blocks from the water, one block west of the A1A, the main artery that ran the length of the Florida coast from Key West to Georgia's Amelia Island. The garish collection of six- and seven-figure luxury cars might have attracted gawkers elsewhere, but in South Beach there was no such thing as over the top, and the dealership was right at home in the neighborhood it shared with upscale shopping outlets, art deco hotels, and celebrity chef-owned eateries. The area was the embodiment of all that was glamorous and desirable about the South Florida lifestyle.

If anything stood out, it was Bryce Chandler, the middle-aged man in cargo shorts and a faded Jimmy Buffett T-shirt driving a dirty, rusty, seven-year-old pickup truck. He chose his perch carefully in a nearby parking lot shared by a vegan sandwich shop and a Cuban cigar store, able to see the comings and goings at Worthing Motors without making himself too obvious. It was his third trip to the area in as many days, and if nothing of interest happened this day, it was going to be his last. There had been no sightings of Chase Worthing, his attorney Roger Mackenzie, or Stanley Murtaugh, all of whom Bryce had planned to follow if they made an appearance.

On day one, a transport truck delivered eight vehicles, and Bryce watched and snapped photos as six of the new arrivals were positioned on the sales lot and the remaining two were driven through a roll-up garage door into the on-site body shop. Day two's highlight was the delivery of a brand-new, fire-engine-red Porsche Cayenne to an overjoyed blonde twenty-something who could have passed for a Miami Dolphins cheerleader. She arrived on the lot in a Mercedes AMG roadster driven by a tanned, heavyset man at least twice her age and, judging by her reaction when the Porsche was wheeled around from out of sight, it was a surprise gift. Bryce looked on as she alternated between fawning over the new vehicle and showering her benefactor with hugs and kisses, and he couldn't help wondering if he was watching a father and daughter or an ambitious millennial with her doting sugar daddy. He assumed the latter, and smiled to himself as he thought of the words of warning Stanley Murtaugh might offer.

Day three had thus far been a bust. Bryce finished his quinoa and avocado flatbread and re-lit the half-smoked Cohiba lying in his ashtray. If you camped out in someone's parking lot, it was always a good idea to buy something from them to keep the questions to a minimum and the cops from being called. As three o'clock approached, he thought about the traffic southbound toward home, and made his plan to call it a day after another hour, two at the most.

At four o'clock, a large truck with an enclosed trailer pulled alongside the dealership on an adjacent street. Shortly afterward, the garage door to the body shop opened, and two cars, a yellow Lamborghini and a white Ferrari, were driven out. Bryce recognized them as the vehicles that had arrived on the transport truck on day one but weren't placed on the sales lot. The cars were loaded into the transport trailer while the truck's driver went inside the dealership, and Bryce pondered the investigative value of following the truck and its cargo. For all he knew, it could be a delivery to a customer on the other side of the country, and he had neither the time nor the resources to get involved in a surveillance of thousands of miles, or even hundreds for that matter.

He decided to follow the truck for fifty miles in whatever direction it went, after which he would re-evaluate his options and either stay with the target or break off. The truck pulled away from Worthing Motors ten minutes later, turned south on the A1A, and stayed on the main thoroughfare as it wound its way through South Beach, across the south end of the Biscayne Bay, and into downtown Miami, where the road remained the same but the signage changed from A1A to US-1. In half an hour, they were through Miami proper and enroute to Homestead, and Bryce was beginning to think he had made the right call. The truck held steady at the speed limit as they passed through Homestead and Florida City, entering the vast expanse of swampland that made up the Southern Everglades. US-1 only went one place from there, and Bryce congratulated himself on his decision as they drove toward the Keys.

CHAPTER 11

THE TRICKY PART of surveillance wasn't following your subject—anyone could do that. The difficulty was in following a subject without them knowing about it. As an FBI agent, Bryce had the luxury of running surveillance with a half dozen or more fellow agents in separate cars. Their numbers allowed them to divide responsibilities between a lead car, or the "eye" as it was called, and a cadre of follow vehicles that stayed well out of sight of the target. Periodically, a follow vehicle would move up and assume the eye, allowing the lead vehicle to back off and creating a different look in the target's rearview mirror. If a Bureau aircraft was available, the eye was in the sky, invisible to the target, and the pilot or copilot called the play-by-play from above while the ground surveillance team followed from an undetectable distance. A well-equipped, well-staffed FBI surveillance team could follow a target across multiple state lines without being detected.

As he drove toward the Keys on US-1, Bryce was a surveillance team of one. He had been careful to stay well back of the truck and trailer since leaving South Beach, always keeping at least two or three vehicles between himself and his target. As they approached Key Largo, he knew the truck would have to turn off the highway at some point, and when that happened, he would need to make a decision. If the driver had even the slightest inkling he was being followed, taking the same turn would confirm it. If he allowed the truck to make a turn without following, he could lose his target.

He decided when the truck turned, he would continue straight, then make a U-turn, double back, and try to spot the truck again, perhaps as it pulled into its destination. It wasn't a perfect plan, but it was all he had.

As they approached Tavernier, the truck slowed and signaled a right turn. Bryce knew the area well, so well, in fact, that he couldn't believe his eyes and his luck. The truck made the right turn, and Bryce continued on. There was no need to double back. The road the driver took led to precisely two destinations: Tres Gatos taqueria, and the Upper Keys Yacht Club and Marina.

Stanley Murtaugh's marina.

CHAPTER 12

THE SOCIAL HIERARCHY in the lower Florida Keys wasn't based as much on your net worth as it was your residency status. At the top of the pecking order were locals, and as the name implied, that meant you lived and worked in the Keys full time.

One rung down the ladder were seasonal residents, or snowbirds, who earned the scorn of more than a few locals by driving up real estate prices and making affordable housing hard to find for the working class. Many of them also annoyed the natives by complaining about everything in the Keys that wasn't the same as "back home." (Nobody cares how they make pizza crust in New York City, and if it's that big of a deal to you, drive your ass back there and take your snooty friends with you.) Still, for the most part, they were tolerated.

At the bottom of the food chain were vacationers and tourists, and they were responsible for every series of unfortunate events that happened in the Keys. If there was a pileup on US-1, some tourist must have been driving too fast. Boating accident? Obviously an unqualified idiot vacationer on a rental. Scurvy outbreak? Check for out-of-state plates.

Harley Christian was a local. His entire forty-five years had been spent in the Keys, save for an abbreviated stint in the Navy, which did not end well, and which, according to Harley, was the result of a misunderstanding. Misunderstandings seemed to follow Harley. Neither of his two ex-wives understood his frequent dalliances; a former employer failed to understand why Harley sold ten thousand dollars' worth of company tools on Craigslist; and the Monroe County Sheriff's Office never reached a full understanding with Harley as to why they found a pound of marijuana in his car, along with rolls of twenty-dollar bills, a scale, and six boxes of Ziploc baggies. Yes, Harley Christian was a poor, misunderstood soul.

He was also the most street savvy, connected person Bryce knew. Back in the day, he would have been a dream snitch. There wasn't a small-time drug dealer between Marathon and Key West Harley didn't know. There wasn't a card game at which he was unwelcome, or a prostitute who wouldn't give him the friends and family discount. His wiry body was festooned with tattoos, including a giant colorful parrot covering his right upper arm and a marijuana plant on the left. A ponytail reached halfway down his back, and Bryce couldn't recall ever seeing him dressed in anything other than cargo shorts, a T-shirt, and flip-flops. He was the quintessential Keys native who fit in everywhere and knew everyone. When Bryce showed Harley the pictures he'd taken of the girls coming and going from Stanley Murtaugh's room at the Sandpiper Inn, he identified every one of them.

Ironically, one of the reasons Harley stayed so well-connected was that he didn't snitch. Not to the police, anyway. Monroe County was a small community, and the locals were a close-knit bunch. It didn't take long for informants to be found out and shunned by everyone they knew. After the marijuana arrest, he was offered the opportunity to cut a deal for himself and turn over his supplier. He told the prosecutor to go to hell and took his year in jail like a man. Like a local.

Harley had no such moral quandaries when it came to working for Bryce Chandler. Bryce wasn't a cop, and nobody was going to jail. He would never have to testify or have his name mentioned in court or on an official document. Bryce paid him well; not as much money as he made repairing boat motors and slinging weed, but enough to make it worth his time. Above all, the work Bryce had for him was easy and often fun. Where else could you pocket a quick hundred for chatting up a hooker or making a few discreet inquiries in circles where a retired FBI agent dare not show his face?

Over the two years they had known each other, a friendship of sorts had developed, or as much of a friendship as could exist between a retired federal agent and a drug dealer. Normally Harley wouldn't have answered his phone at 10:00 p.m., but when he saw it was Bryce, he picked up.

"What's going on, boss?"

Bryce got right to it. "I need to use your car."

"And good evening to you too, sir. Did your truck break down?"

"No, it's fine. I just need to run an errand, and I can't take the truck. Can you help me out?"

"Well, now you've got me intrigued. What sort of errand are we talking about here? Is there a woman involved?" Absent evidence to the contrary, Harley assumed every unexplained situation revolved around sex.

Bryce was growing impatient. "No, this is just me and some business I need to finish up from earlier today, but I can't take the truck. Can you help me out or not?"

"I can, and I will, but it's gonna cost you."

"I'll bring it back full of gas."

"Nothing like that. I want to come along. Whatever you're doing sounds sexy. Who knows, maybe I can even help you out."

"That's the worst idea I've heard all day. I don't need company. I need a car."

"Well, good luck getting one this time of night. I'm sure you have other options."

The line went silent while Bryce pondered those options. There were no rental car companies nearby, and a cab or Uber was out of the question. He had a few friends who might loan him their car, but Harley was the only one awake at this hour, and the only one who would understand why he needed to run off on some mysterious "errand" in the middle of the night. His truck was too hot to be seen near the marina, and by morning the truck, trailer, and cargo he followed might all be gone. *Hell, it might all be gone right now,* he thought.

He had no choice. "I'm driving. You're riding shotgun and keeping your mouth shut. Non-negotiable."

Harley sounded giddy. "I'll be over in ten minutes."

The drive to Tavernier took forty-five minutes, and when they arrived, there was no sign of the truck or the trailer. Along the way, Harley broke the first rule of their agreement and peppered Bryce with questions. Bryce responded with equal parts truth and lies: His client owned a luxury car leasing business but lived out of state and trusted his brother-in-law to run the day-to-day operations for him. Lately, he had grown suspicious that the brother-in-law was leasing cars off the books and pocketing the money for himself. Bryce was hired to look into it, and earlier in the day he watched as two cars left the business in a trailer and ended up here in Tavernier. He told Harley to keep his eyes open for a yellow Lamborghini and a white Ferrari.

Tres Gatos was still open, and most of the action looked to be on the front porch, where a half dozen or so customers were whooping it up with pitchers of margaritas and longnecked beers. Bryce found a spot in a dark vacant lot behind the restaurant that gave him a clear line of sight to the marina.

Harley was itching for action. "What's the plan, boss?"

"Right now, the plan is for you to be quiet while I think. And while you're being quiet, keep your head on a swivel for anything that looks out of place."

"Uh-huh, got it. Head on a swivel. Stuff that looks out of place. That's the plan. I just have one more question: Are you sure you used to be an FBI agent?"

Bryce stared straight ahead, his patience dwindling. "Don't make me sorry I brought you along. I've told you before, this is boring work. It's not like in the movies. We may find what we're looking for, we may sit on our asses for a few hours and get nothing. We may even—" He caught a familiar whiff and turned toward Harley. "Holy shit, are you smoking a joint?"

He was.

"Wow, you sounded just like my dad there for a second. I cracked the window, relax. You know this stuff is legal in Florida now, right?"

Actually, it was legal in Florida for medicinal purposes only. "I don't need a cop wandering by, smelling that, and pulling us out of the car while he checks your doctor's note. Finish it up and put it out. Please."

Harley changed the subject. "What do you think *that* baby costs?" he asked, gesturing toward the marina.

There was no need to specify which "baby" he meant. In the crowd of dozens of boats Bryce could never afford, the 110-foot yacht stood out like the crown jewels in a pawn shop. It looked brand-new, and its name and home port were emblazoned in gold leaf across the transom: *Pablo's Revenge, Nassau.* It was easily twice the size of the next largest vessel at the marina.

Bryce replied, "I'll take a wild guess and say between ten and fifteen million. Why? You in the market?"

Harley laughed. "Nope, too rich for my blood. I've never understood where folks get that kind of money."

"You and me both. Where are you going?"

Harley had opened the door and was stepping out. "Gotta take a leak. I'll be back in a few."

Bryce was grateful for the peace and quiet, and as he surveyed the marina and the surrounding area, he weighed his options. He knew the area well from the time he spent tailing Stanley Murtaugh, and he figured if the cars were nearby, they were locked up in the marina's massive boathouse. Even if they were parked in the open, getting close to them would mean either breaking through a locked gate or scaling a ten-foot fence topped with barbed wire, neither of which appealed to him.

He began to doubt himself, questioning his judgment and decision-making. *What if the whole thing is one hundred percent legitimate? What if somebody bought a couple cars from Chase Worthing and had them delivered here? What if that's all there is to it?*

And even if that's not it, what did you expect to find when you came back here tonight? A Ferrari and a Lamborghini doing donuts in the parking lot, dropping leaflets that spelled out the details of a shadowy criminal conspiracy?

An inventory of his situation proved depressing. Here he was, parked behind a low-rent taqueria at midnight in a borrowed car, waiting for his stoner informant to finish peeing. This after three days lurking in South Beach, eating vegan food that tasted like wood pulp and smoking Cuban cigars at fifteen dollars a pop. All for not so much as a single billable hour. And all because he let Stanley Murtaugh get under his skin. *No more*, he decided. When Harley came back, they were calling it a night, and he was done with Stanley, Chase, and whatever drama they had going on between them.

Harley had been gone for at least twenty minutes before Bryce took notice. He punched his number into his cell phone and shot out a text.

Where you at?

The reply was immediate. *Ten min.*

Nope now.

Ten minutes passed as Bryce fumed. He tried again.

Get your ass out here NOW.

Five more minutes went by, and Bryce considered walking around to the front of the restaurant to find Harley, but thought better of it. Whatever he was doing, and whoever he was doing it with, there was no upside to introducing himself as Harley's six-foot, four-inch friend with a demeanor that screamed COP! to everyone in the room.

Ten minutes later, Bryce's phone buzzed. *Coming out.*

Harley appeared from the corner of the taqueria, his cell

phone in his hand, his steps quicker than when he left nearly an hour ago. As he opened the door, he was already talking, and he reeked of cheap marijuana and cheaper tequila.

"Sorry, boss, I know you're pissed. But trust me, you're gonna love me in a minute. Wait 'til you see what I've got."

Bryce had a rant at the ready, but before he had the chance to unleash it, something caught his eye. Three men had emerged from the bar following the same path Harley had, and when they crossed momentarily through the patio light, Bryce saw one lugging a baseball bat. Behind him came another, also armed with a bat. A third followed, and Bryce made his decision as soon as he saw the glint of the pistol in his right hand.

As it turned out, there were four of them. No sooner did Bryce place the car in drive than the back window exploded, and he glanced in the rearview mirror just long enough to see yet another bat-wielding attacker scream, "Get out of the car!" at the top of his lungs as he drew the bat back for another strike.

Bryce floored the accelerator and aimed for the one with the gun. Harley had already shrunk down beneath the passenger side dashboard, and Bryce made himself as small as he could while still maintaining control of the car's speed and direction. There were loud thumps on each side of the vehicle as Bryce drove past the remaining batsmen and they took their swings. As he accelerated, the gunman raised his pistol and began firing.

The first shot skipped off the hood, went through the windshield, and exited the vehicle through the newly created opening where there once was a rear window. The second shattered the driver's side headlight. The third pierced yet another hole in the windshield, passing inches from Bryce's head.

As Bryce bore down on him, the shooter dodged to his right to avoid being hit head-on. By this point, Bryce was on automatic pilot, using the vehicle as his own weapon, focused on eliminating the threat rather than fleeing from it. He steered toward the gunman, whose evasive move had put him near the corner of the building, and when he hit him at nearly twenty-five miles per hour, he pinned his assailant between the side of the vehicle and the taqueria's wall. The car roared ahead without slowing, grinding and spinning the shooter like a ragdoll between cinderblock and sheet metal. Bryce watched him collapse in a crumpled heap in the rearview as he sped away. From start to finish, it was over in less than ten seconds.

Bryce turned southbound on US-1, accelerated to eighty miles per hour, and watched for followers in his rearview. When he saw none, he slowed to the speed limit and began worrying about the next most likely threat: a sheriff's deputy with nothing more important to do than pull over a car with a missing headlight. At which point, of course, the discussion would shift from headlights to bullet holes in windshields, and Bryce's day would go from bad to worse.

He turned to Harley. "You all right?"

Harley merely nodded his head, too frozen with fear to speak.

"Okay, listen carefully to me. I think the car will make it home, we just can't get pulled over. If we do get stopped, and Harley, I mean this most sincerely, shut the hell up and let me do the talking. We're going to park it in my garage, and I'll take you home. Anything past that we'll figure out in the morning."

Harley managed his first words since re-entering the car. "What about the cops? They're probably on their way to the Mexican place now. If anyone got my plate number—"

"Harley, they just tried to kill us. They're not calling the cops, and they're not going to let anyone else call them either. Were they in the restaurant at the same time you were?"

"Yeah, it was just them, me, and two dudes I was talking to. We were all out on the patio. The manager let me use the bathroom, but I think the inside of the restaurant was closed. It was empty, anyway."

Bryce felt better already. "All right then. We just have to make it home. Sit tight."

He drove and prayed.

CHAPTER 13

THE CABIN was a labor of love, and Wendell Branch knew every log and every stone. It had taken ten years to complete the weekend getaway turned retirement home in the north Georgia mountains, and he boasted to visitors that the only professional contractors who ever set foot on the lot were those who poured the concrete basement floor. A wooden sign next to the front door paid homage to the other great love of his life, Beatrice, who he married between finishing his tour in the Marines and starting law school in 1970. She fought him tooth and nail over naming the cabin "Bea's Nest," though she would eventually concede it added a certain charm to their little slice of heaven, sixty miles north of Atlanta and three miles from the nearest neighbor.

A stream bisected the property, running about a hundred yards behind the cabin along a thick line of Georgia pines. It was where Wendell and Bea would take their coffee every morning, sipping it while sitting on a flat rock and chatting, mostly about their children and grandchildren. It was where they mutually decided he would retire from the bench and begin enjoying more time with those kids and grandkids. It was where Wendell had spread Bea's ashes three years earlier. He hadn't missed a coffee date since.

The intruder knew Wendell's routine and was waiting for him to return.

Wendell unlocked the back door and stepped into the kitchen. He filled his dirty coffee cup with water and left it to soak in the sink. He hung the keys on a rack by the refrigerator and walked toward the living room at the front of the house. As he was about to cross the threshold between the two rooms, the stream of light caught his eye, changing everything in a fraction of a second.

When you live thirty years in a house you built with your own hands, you know every square inch, every leaky faucet, every flickering light fixture. You know every drafty corner and loose doorknob. And you know there shouldn't be light streaming through the gap between the front door and the jamb, because you replaced the weather stripping two months ago. Unless, of course, someone didn't fully close the door.

Unless someone was in the house.

Wendell hadn't been down to the stream without his Springfield Hellcat nine-millimeter pistol since the day Bea had nearly been bitten by a copperhead hiding under their favorite rock. He kept the compact gun in a holster that fit snugly inside the waistband of his khakis, and Bea had always teased him that the snake he was most likely to shoot was the one already in his pants. He was amused, but undeterred by her chiding.

He reached for the pistol as he stepped into the living room, and at the same instant felt the rope snap against his neck and begin to tighten. The intruder pushed him forward with his knee while pulling his head back with the rope, and he knew he had only seconds before he would black out. His hand was firmly on the pistol, but he couldn't see his target, so he drew it from the holster, pointed it behind him at waist level, and blindly fired three quick shots. The rope eased as the intruder screamed in pain and fell to the floor.

Judge Branch turned and saw his attacker slumped against the wall, blood spilling from wounds in his belly and groin.

Still standing with the gun in his hand, he pointed it at his assailant and began with the most obvious question. "Who the hell are you?"

Silence.

He tried again. "Is there anyone else in my house?"

More silence, then a moment of clarity.

"Who sent you?"

The would-be assassin stared back at him and began to vomit. Wendell pulled a chair from the dining table, placed it a few feet from his attacker, and sat down facing him.

"Call an ambulance," he muttered through the bloody foam seeping from his mouth.

Wendell pulled out his cellphone and dialed 911. He placed his thumb over the green button and paused as he stared at his attacker. A silent rage swept over him as he contemplated his brush with death, and he moved his thumb instead to the red button, pressed it, and replaced the phone in his pocket.

"An ambulance isn't going to do you any good, friend. Now I'm going to ask you again: Who sent you?"

His voice was lower and weaker. "Call an ambulance," he pleaded before lapsing into unconsciousness. Over the next half hour, his labored breathing turned to wheezing, then to what sounded like heavy snoring as his respiratory system filled with blood. Wendell watched his chest rise, fall, and finally go still. He watched and waited for five more minutes, then made his call.

CHAPTER 14

THE MORNING after the showdown at Tres Gatos, Donnie texted Bryce a link to a story in the *Atlanta Tribune*. Bryce read it while sipping coffee on the porch overlooking the canal behind his house.

> *Retired Judge Shoots, Kills Attacker in Dawson County Cabin*
>
> *By Rhonda Majette*
> *Atlanta Tribune*
>
> *Dawsonville -- The Dawson County Sheriff's Office is investigating an apparent attempt on the life of a retired federal judge in his north Georgia home Saturday, according to sources.*
>
> *Wendell Branch shot and killed the unnamed attacker with a handgun early Saturday morning after a brief struggle inside the house, according to sources. Mr. Branch was treated at the scene for minor injuries, but did not require further medical attention.*
>
> *Officials from the sheriff's office declined to comment, citing departmental policy. A law enforcement official familiar with the investigation said the motive in the attack appeared to be robbery.*

Mr. Branch retired from the bench in 2016, after serving 21 years as a District Court judge in Atlanta. Prior to that, he served as a prosecutor for both the Fulton County District Attorney's Office and the United States Attorney's Office for the Northern District of Georgia. Phone calls to Mr. Branch requesting an interview have not been returned.

Donnie picked up on the first ring, and Bryce skipped the pleasantries.

"Can I assume my wild-eyed conspiracy theory is being taken seriously now?" he asked his friend.

Donnie paused, then sighed deeply enough for Bryce to hear. "I wish I had better news. We're not touching it."

Bryce was incredulous. "What? That's a former AUSA, a federal corrections officer, and a retired federal judge, all within the span of a month! How could we possibly be turning our heads on this?"

"Politics and pride, I think. Atlanta PD isn't letting go of Julie's case, and Dawson County says everything at the judge's cabin looks like a robbery gone wrong. They don't get many homicides up there, and one this open and shut is a gift they're not going to share with anyone, least of all the FBI."

"That's bullshit and you know it. He's a retired judge and we could take the case if we wanted it. Same with Julie's murder. Who's the gutless wonder calling the shots?"

"I'll give you two guesses, and the first one doesn't count."

"Oh, sweet Jesus. Not him."

"Yep, although it's ASAC Peoples now, and if you forget and call him Greg, he'll remind you."

Assistant Special Agent in Charge was the title bestowed on upwardly mobile agents who occupied the management space between squad supervisors and the overall office boss, known as the Special Agent in Charge or SAC. ASACs oversaw entire programs within a field office, and Bryce guessed (correctly) that his old nemesis would have been in charge of the Atlanta division's vast criminal investigations operation, encompassing everything from drugs and gangs to fugitives, white collar crime, and public corruption.

He was amused and angry all at once. "I wish I could say I'm surprised. He always did have a six-foot blue flame shooting out his ass. Does he even have ten years on the job yet?"

Donnie laughed. "He just hit twelve. He's really insecure about it, too. We weave it into the conversation whenever we can. It's fun to watch the smoke come out his ears."

"I still don't get it. Peoples was always a prick, but one thing he wasn't was lazy. And this just seems lazy to me. I mean, how much effort would it be to try and connect the dots here?"

"I think this is more politics than laziness. We've been on thin ice with APD since we arrested three of their officers for civil rights violations last year, and nobody here or in the US Attorney's Office wants to piss them off right now. Their chief is in tight with the governor, who's on the GOP's short list to run for president next year. The US Attorney is a political appointee, and he doesn't want to be out of a job next November, so he's playing go along to get along."

"What about the prison guard in Indiana? The Bureau is running that case, aren't they?"

"They are, and they uncovered a smuggling ring that was using guards to run cell phones and dope to the inmates. So far they've arrested a half dozen guards, and every one of them has implicated Andrew Pittman as the ring leader. So as far as they're concerned, he got on someone's bad side, probably shorted a dealer or broke a promise to a prisoner. They don't think his murder has anything to do with the cases here in Georgia, and they're not interested in looking into it."

Bryce was undeterred. "You feel like doing some side work, partner?"

"As long as it doesn't get me fired. You're already collecting your pension. I've got three years before I'm eligible to retire."

"No heavy lifting, I promise. Just some more checking with your contacts at the US Attorney's office and Bureau of Prisons."

"We already checked to see if any of Julie's defendants went to Terre Haute, and we struck out. We can do the same thing for Judge Branch's cases, but if none of them were prosecuted by Julie, there's no nexus between the three."

Bryce had already considered that very problem. He was about to concede the point to Donnie when the idea struck him, and it was so obvious he could have kicked himself for not thinking of it earlier.

"When your BOP contact ran the prison records on Julie's defendants, what exactly did they check?"

Donnie answered, "I would assume either the prison they were sent to after sentencing, or where they were currently locked up. To be honest, I didn't specify. I just told them we needed to know if any of her convicts were sent to Terre Haute."

"Okay, this time we need the entire prison record. Where they were sent initially, where they are now, and any stops they made in between. Remember, sometimes inmates get transferred from one prison to another for disciplinary issues, medical treatment, overcrowding, or whatever. We may be looking for someone who spent time at Terre Haute but isn't there anymore."

"Fair enough, I can do that. Give me a few days. I need to keep it quiet. If Peoples finds out I'm poking around, he'll have my ass."

Bryce replied, "That's what I would call a badge of honor, amigo. I'd be more worried if someone like Greg Peoples thought highly of me. That guy snuck into the gene pool while the lifeguard was on break."

Donnie laughed. "I'll call you."

Bryce hung up, energized by the prospect of what information the new leads might uncover. His optimism was still guarded, but he was more convinced than ever that this was no string of random, unconnected crimes. His mind spun endless possibilities as he prepared his breakfast and caught bits and pieces of SportsCenter on the living room television, and in his preoccupation he never noticed the late model black sedan that drove up his street, stopped for several minutes near his house, and then slowly drove away.

CHAPTER 15

THE TEXT FROM HARLEY was short and to the point:
Meet me at the DS?

The Dive Shack was, as its name implied, a dive. Half bar and half short-order grill, it was a local hangout near Harley's house on nearby Cudjoe Key, and it was the sort of place where "What happens here, stays here" was more than just a catchy slogan. The owner, Slyde Richards, was the sheriff's half-brother and, in recognition of their familial bond, his place was given a wide berth by the department. In return, Slyde kept the noise down, the fights short and mostly bloodless, and the petty drug dealing under the table. His one strike policy kept the clientele honest and obedient, and it had been years since a uniformed officer had entered the establishment during operating hours.

Bryce typed back: *Come to the house.*

No wheels, remember?

Bryce had almost forgotten the bullet-riddled car hiding in his garage. He also knew that he and Harley had yet to discuss the details of their chaotic night, including what precipitated the violent encounter outside the restaurant.

He texted: *What time?*

I'm here now.

Give me thirty minutes.

Bryce had been to the Dive Shack only a few times over the years, and it was just as grimy, dimly lit, and smoke-filled as he remembered it. The walls were covered with thirty years' worth of pen-and-ink graffiti, the floor was strewn with discarded peanut shells, and a pair of 70s-era pinball machines blinked incessantly in a corner. There were a half dozen patrons in the bar when Bryce arrived around 10:00 a.m., all nursing drinks at the bar. Harley was seated in a booth in the rear of the dining area, and Bryce slid in across from him.

As was his custom, Harley began talking immediately. "How's my car doing?"

"It's ready to go, buddy. I spent all night filling the bullet holes, repainting the hood, and pulling out the dents where your friends played whack-a-mole on it. I also found a junkyard that delivers at three in the morning, so I replaced the windshield and back window. Good as new."

Harley rolled his eyes. "No need to be an asshole. I'm still freaked out over the whole thing. Are you sure they're not going to try and find us?"

"I never said they weren't going to try and find us. I said they weren't going to call the cops. And I stand by that. Whatever mess we made there last night, it's already been cleaned up. And if there were any witnesses, rest assured they've been paid off or threatened to keep their mouths shut. These people weren't playing games."

"If they got my license plate number, will they be able to find me?"

"Probably. DMV records are pretty much public these days. Let's worry about that later. Why don't you tell me what exactly happened after you got out of the car?"

"I walked around the front of the restaurant and, like I told you, there were four guys sitting at one table out on the patio, two at another table, and the manager. I asked the manager if I could use the bathroom and he pointed me toward the back of the place. It was empty inside, and when I finished, I came back out and was about to head back to the car when I realized I knew one of the guys drinking on the patio."

"One of the guys in the twosome or the foursome?"

"The twosome. He's a former customer of mine, Zeke, and he used to hang out in the Lower Keys. Anyway, he saw me, called out my name, and told me to come have a drink with them."

Bryce interrupted. "What's Zeke's last name?"

"We don't do last names in my world, man. Just Zeke."

"Okay, what happened next?"

"They had a half empty pitcher of margaritas and a full one on the table, so Zeke asked the manager for another glass and he poured me one. We shot the shit for a while. He said he'd been there about four hours, watching boats come and go at the marina, drinking, hitting on girls. I was getting ready to leave when he asked if I wanted to see a cool video. When I saw it, I knew you were gonna want to see it too."

"Tell me about the video."

"How about I show you? I had him WhatsApp it to me."

Harley cued the video on his phone and handed it to Bryce. The point of view was from the patio of Tres Gatos, and the background was of the marina, and specifically the parking slip occupied by *Pablo's Revenge*, the 110-foot luxury yacht Bryce and Harley were ogling the night before.

The yellow Lamborghini and white Ferrari were parked alongside the yacht. Workers were manipulating a pair of ramps into position between the yacht and the dock, and when they finished, the cars were driven up the ramps, onto the yacht's rear deck, and into a garage on board the massive boat. The garage door rolled shut, and the video stopped. It lasted about four minutes, start to finish.

Bryce had a newfound appreciation for Harley's information-gathering prowess. "Nice work, but I sure wish you could have done it without almost getting us killed. Did you notice the guys at the other table eyeing you and your friends? Did they say anything to you?"

"Nope. They were cool, up until the part where they shot up my car."

"Play it again."

The second time through, Bryce took his time, pausing and zooming in, paying more attention to mundane details than to the glitz of the megayacht and supercars. There was a pickup truck parked on the dock near the spot where the ramps were deployed, and he was able to copy down a license plate number. A food truck drove by but did not stop. A man dressed in what appeared to be a white Navy uniform walked briefly into the frame from the front of the boat while the cars were being driven aboard, watched for a few seconds, then left in the direction from which he had appeared. Bryce figured him to be the ship's captain.

As the second of the vehicles was being driven into the ship's garage, two men appeared in the frame for just a few seconds, walking from the shadows of the garage and onto the ship's rear deck. Their faces were visible for a mere second before they turned away from the camera, and Bryce tried and failed more than a few times to freeze the video at the exact moment he needed. He finally managed to capture the image of their faces, and he recognized one of them as Stanley Murtaugh. He Googled a recent photo of Chase Worthing, and confirmed him as the second man on the screen.

Bryce turned to Harley. "This is important. Try and remember exactly what you and your friend Zeke were saying when he showed you the video."

"Uhh, it was something like, 'Hey man, you missed a pretty cool show earlier.' And I asked him what he was talking about, and he showed me the video. So I said I had a friend who would love to see something like that, and could he WhatsApp it to me? And that's pretty much it."

"All right. Finish up and let's get out of here."

"Can you drop me at my house?"

"Nope, we're driving to Miami. I found a salvage yard that has a mostly intact 1983 Cutlass, and it's got all the parts we need. If we're lucky we can be back early this evening and get your car out of my garage in a day or two."

"Then what?"

"Well, then we wait and see if this massive pile of shit we stepped in goes away by itself."

"And if it doesn't?"

"If it doesn't, we are in a world of hurt."

CHAPTER 16

THE REPAIR WORK took two days. Harley protested that the hood from the salvage yard was a different color than his car, but Bryce convinced him the two-tone look gave the car character, and if he didn't like it, he could find another 1983 Cutlass in the right color with a hood for sale.

There was no mention of the incident at Tres Gatos in the news. Bryce made a few discreet inquiries among his law enforcement contacts, and there had been no police or ambulance response to the area that night. It was as if it never happened, except Bryce knew the people who attacked them would be out for blood. He had stumbled onto something bigger than he expected, big enough to elicit a violent and potentially deadly response. And in trying to avoid a confrontation, he may have maimed or even killed one of his attackers. No, this was not over.

Between rebuilding Harley's car and watching for fallout from their adventure, Bryce had forgotten about his last conversation with Donnie. When his phone rang, he hoped for some good news.

"Talk to me, partner."

"Well, it's been an interesting couple of days, most of which I've spent bouncing back and forth between the US Attorney's Office and the prison. All, of course, while trying to keep our buddy ASAC Peoples out of the loop."

"And what did you find?"

"I started with the cases Julie had in Judge Branch's court. There were about a dozen in total. Two of them were found not guilty, so I assume they're of no interest. Another was dismissed based on an error in the discovery process and was never re-tried. So I threw that one out as well."

"Okay, so that leaves, what, about nine convicted defendants?"

"Yep, so next I took the list over to my contact at the prison, and we spent half a day checking every name, where they were originally sentenced, if they were transferred within the system, who was still in, who got out, you name it."

Bryce hung on Donnie's every word. "And?"

"And while nobody on the list was originally sent to Terre Haute, two of them were eventually transferred there. They both started at lower security institutions, got in trouble, and ended up at Terre Haute because it's a higher security prison that handles problem inmates."

"You're killing me. Cut to the chase. Did we find our guy or not?"

"I'm getting there. One of the two is an inmate named Felix San Diego, and he's still in. He copped a plea in front of Judge Branch on a thirty million Ponzi scheme, got fifteen years, and was sent off to the Federal Correctional Institute at Texarkana. About a year into his sentence, they caught him with a cell phone, found out he was running yet another Ponzi scheme, sentenced him to five more years, and shipped him off to Terre Haute for good measure. He's been a model prisoner since his arrival. Found Jesus, works in the prison ministry, and with time for good behavior he's up for release in another two years. He does not strike me as the sort of prisoner who wants to risk everything by ordering a hit on his enemies."

"Okay, what about the other one?"

"Three time loser, took a jury trial on a weapons trafficking charge and was found guilty. Julie proposed a twenty-year sentence, and Judge Branch gave him even more than she asked for. He started off at FCI Edgefield, assaulted multiple inmates and a guard, and got sent to Terre Haute in 2012. He killed an inmate during a riot there in 2016, was convicted and sentenced to life in prison, and they relocated him to ADMAX in Colorado."

"And you think maybe this is our guy?"

"You tell me. Does the name Travis Conway ring a bell?"

CHAPTER 17

"Hold all your questions until the end of the briefing."

Bryce surveyed the team assembled around the conference table, and felt confident he had what he needed to pull off the night's operation without a major malfunction. His trusted partner, Donnie Morris, sat to his right, and four more seasoned agents from the violent gang squad lined the left side of the table. Seated past Donnie was a medic on loan from the SWAT team, and beyond him a pair of FNGs, or Fucking New Guys, freshly minted agents less than two years out of Quantico who needed arrest and search experience in order to fulfill the requirements of their probationary agent program.

"So, as you all know, we're starting to wrap up the MS-13 case, and one of the defendants, Arturo Salamanca, has had a change of heart. It may have had something to do with the twenty-year recommendation in his pre-sentence report. Anyway, Mr. Salamanca's lawyer called Julie Martinez last week and said his client wants to cooperate."

Bryce continued. "You all remember the military-grade weaponry we found when we arrested the subjects last November. We never could find out where they came from, but Mr. Salamanca says he can set us up with the dealer, who he claims works through some shady internet-based organization. It's all anonymous, so we don't know the dealer's name, description, or where he's coming from. What we do know is that he has agreed to deliver a dozen fully automatic M4 rifles with night optics for fifteen thousand apiece, cash. We're meeting him tonight behind the Home Depot on Sidney Marcus at eleven o'clock."

Bryce filled in the details of the operation, including the role of the undercover agent who would play the part of the weapons buyer, and the $180,000 in "show" money that was on loan from a local bank branch and could not, under any circumstances, be lost. He assigned Donnie and the squad's two most senior agents the responsibility of the arrest itself, as it was the most critical and dangerous aspect of the plan. He would direct the overall operation and be responsible for the safety of the undercover agent and the recovery of the show money. The remaining agents from the gang squad and the FNGs would monitor the parking lot for the approach of the subject, and when the arrest signal was given they would move their cars to the front and rear of the subject's vehicle to prevent an escape.

"Questions?" Bryce pointed a finger to the agent directly to his left, moving it slowly down the table until he reached the last occupied chair. Not a word was uttered. He repeated the gesture to his right, starting with Donnie, the medic, and finally the two FNGs, one of whom spoke up.

"Yeah, what else do you want us to do?"

Bryce stared for a moment. "What do you mean, what else? Was the briefing not clear enough for you?"

"No, I got what you said in the briefing, but my supervisor told me to come help your squad with an arrest. It doesn't sound like I'm arresting anyone. It sounds like I'm a glorified security guard."

Bryce and Donnie gave each other the "you have to be kidding me" look. The veteran agents across the table were trying their best to hide their amusement, but a few light chuckles were heard.

Bryce broke the silence. "What's your name, kid?"

"Greg Peoples. And I'm not a kid."

"Okay, fair enough. Well, Greg, I don't know what squad you're on—"

Peoples interrupted. "I'm on the cybercrimes squad."

"That's great, Greg, and I'm sure you've been doing a wonderful job for the past . . . how long have you been out of Quantico?"

"Six months."

Bryce stared incredulously at the young agent. "Six months. That's awesome. Anyway, Greg, here on the gang squad we give the most dangerous and difficult assignments to our most experienced agents, and that ain't you. This isn't some computer hacker in his mom's basement, it's an arms dealer delivering a couple hundred thousand dollars' worth of high-powered weapons to the most violent street gang in the country. So do me a huge favor and just complete your assignment as you've been instructed. Any more questions?"

Peoples stared at Bryce in silence, then lowered his head without further comment.

"Great. Let's roll in fifteen minutes and be on site at the Home Depot no later than ten-thirty. Come up on channel A8 and give Donnie a comms check as soon as you're in place. Everyone be safe."

———————

Bryce gave a final briefing to the undercover agent who on this evening was playing the part of Oso, or "Bear." His real name was Victor, and he was a ten-year veteran from the Bureau's San Diego office. This job was a "cameo," meaning the UC wouldn't be engaging with the criminal organization on a long-term basis, but rather was in town for one night to play a part and then go home. He fit his stage name well, tall and burly with a thick beard and full-sleeve tattoos on both arms. Bryce turned on one audio/video recorder concealed in Victor's eyeglasses, and another secreted in the cargo area of the ten-foot box truck Victor would use to pick up the load. He sent the UC to the meeting location, positioned his arrest and support teams around the area, conducted a final radio check with his team, and waited.

At a couple of minutes past eleven, one of the support teams checked in. "Okay, everyone, gray Suburban, Georgia tags, just pulled into the parking lot, sitting in the shadows across from the riding mowers. Tinted windows, can't make out whoever's inside."

Two minutes later, the same team was back on the radio. "Suburban is moving slowly, coming around the building counterclockwise, and he just turned his lights off. Bryce, you should see him driving your way in a few seconds."

Bryce did see the Suburban, and when it stopped behind the store's loading dock, the UC flashed his parking lights. The Suburban pulled alongside the box truck and both men got out of their vehicles.

Bryce narrated to the team as the scene unfolded over the next few minutes:

"Okay, subject and our guy are out of their vehicles, looks like they're just talking."

"Our guy is reaching into the truck, pulling out the backpack with the show money."

"Subject looks satisfied with the show money. They're walking around to the back of the subject's Suburban."

"Doors on the rear of the Suburban are open. I don't have an angle to see inside, but I think our guy is inspecting the rifles."

The undercover appeared from the rear of the Suburban and removed his baseball cap.

"Okay, the UC just gave the signal. Donnie, move your team in and take him. Support teams, cut off the escape routes. Let's go."

The night exploded in blue strobes and siren blasts as the squad announced its presence. Donnie and his team moved toward the subject, weapons drawn, shouting, "FBI! Show me your hands!" He did as he was told and obeyed Donnie's commands to turn away from him, go to his knees, and place his hands behind his head with his fingers intertwined.

Donnie approached the subject with his handcuffs at the ready. Without warning, Greg Peoples rushed past him, leaped in the air, and executed a flying tackle that caught everyone, including the subject, off guard. Compliant up until that moment, he was now fighting back, landing a solid right fist to Peoples's jaw before being pummeled in return by the rogue youngster. As Donnie and Bryce rushed toward the scrum, the subject knocked Greg's pistol from his hand, then gained control of it as Peoples continued flailing away with his fists.

But rather than turning the gun on his adversaries, the subject pointed the muzzle toward his own head and wrapped his finger around the trigger. It all happened in a few seconds, and in that time Donnie had gotten to within striking distance of his target. Much as Peoples had done moments earlier, he went airborne, bulldozing Peoples out of his way and plowing into the subject with a force that knocked the gun from his hands and sent it clattering to the asphalt. A dogpile ensued as the other arresting agents joined the fray, each of them pinning down a separate limb as the subject fought, then submitted to the overwhelming force.

Bryce grabbed Peoples by the collar and pulled upward, yanking him almost off the ground, and continued pulling him backward until they reached the Suburban, thirty feet away. He spun Peoples around, slung him against the driver's door, and moved his grip from the back of his shirt to his neck. He drew his face to within inches of Peoples's, his eyes bloodshot with rage.

"What the fuck was that?" Bryce screamed, relaxing his grip just enough to allow Peoples to form an answer.

"I told you, I need credit for an arrest, not for watching a parking lot," he hissed. "Get your goddamned hands off me."

"Bryce, everything okay?" Donnie called out. Bryce turned and saw that Donnie had the subject handcuffed and on his feet. Bryce loosened his grip further but kept one hand on Peoples's throat while placing the index finger of his other hand an inch from his nose.

"You ever do something that stupid again, I swear to God I will beat you to within an inch of your life," Bryce warned. He let go of Peoples and began walking toward Donnie and the subject.

"Are you going to charge him with assaulting me?" Peoples asked.

Bryce stopped, turned around, and stared. "You can't be serious. You're lucky I don't charge you with assaulting him. Don't ever volunteer for one of my details again." He broke eye contact, walked away, and left Peoples alone with his wounded ego.

The cargo was exactly as advertised: twelve brand-new, fully automatic, M4 rifles fitted with sophisticated night vision sights. The subject was identified as Travis Conway, fifty years old, a life-long Georgia resident with a lengthy arrest and prison record. He was taken to the FBI booking room, fingerprinted, photographed, and advised of his Miranda warnings. When Bryce tried to question him, he opted to remain silent, other than demanding to be provided with an attorney. He was transported to a holding cell to await an appearance in federal court the following morning.

By the time it all wrapped up, it was 3:00 a.m., and Travis Conway was Julie Martinez's problem. Bryce gathered his team, thanked them all for their hard work, and invited them to join him at the Waffle House for an early breakfast, his treat. It was a squad tradition, an opportunity to decompress, share a laugh or two, and strengthen the bonds of their brotherhood over some seriously good hashbrowns. Everyone took Bryce up on his generous offer, with one exception.

Over breakfast, the team members decided the incident between Peoples and Travis Conway would stay in the Home Depot parking lot.

CHAPTER 18

"JESUS, DONNIE. I completely forgot about him."

"I figured as much. His name wasn't on the list of MS-13 defendants you sent me."

"Partner, that case lasted almost three years. Travis Conway's involvement was one night. We didn't even know his name until after we arrested him," Bryce said.

Donnie replied, "Well, if this isn't our guy, I don't know who would be. I dug a little deeper into his time at Terre Haute and the details behind his murder conviction. BOP called it a riot, but it was more of a gang fight. Remember the smuggling ring I told you about?"

"The cell phones and dope?"

"That's the one. According to the case agent in Indianapolis, Travis Conway was a major player, and there was friction between his operation and a similar one being run by some black inmates. So about five minutes before this alleged riot breaks out, a video camera catches a guard passing by Travis's cell, where he stops and unlocks the door. Doesn't go in, just keeps walking. Five minutes later all hell breaks loose on the block, two black males walk up to Travis's cell, open the unlocked door, and one stumbles out thirty seconds later, bleeding from a half dozen stab wounds. The other one was already dead inside the cell. Travis had a shiv hidden in his mattress and used it to defend himself."

Bryce asked, "So you think the so-called riot was a cover for a hit on Conway?"

"Looks that way. It happens all the time in the rougher prisons, and Terre Haute is as rough as they get. You know the deal, a guard gets paid to look the other way, leave a door unlocked, or maybe just not be in a certain place at a certain time."

"And dare I ask if we know the identity of the guard in the video?"

"No surprises there, Bryce. It was Andrew Pittman."

A wave of vindication swept over Bryce. "So when are we going to visit Mr. Conway? I assume he's still at ADMAX?"

Donnie laughed. "What's this 'we' thing? You think there's any way a retired agent is going to be allowed to interview an inmate in a supermax prison? Anyway, nobody's talking to Travis Conway anymore. He killed himself in his cell almost six months ago."

"Wait a minute. If we think he's behind all this, and he's been dead for six months, then who's calling the shots?"

"That's the mystery. He was at ADMAX for three years, never made or received a phone call, never had a single piece of incoming or outgoing mail. He had one visitor, an attorney who came to see him on the day he died. Hours before he died, as a matter of fact."

"And what do we know about the attorney?"

"His name is James Todd, and he's a small-time criminal defense attorney here in Atlanta. DUIs, petty thefts, a little dope work here and there. He hangs out in the county courts and picks up low-hanging fruit. Oh, and he wasn't Conway's attorney during the trial or for any of the appeals."

"Then why was he visiting him at ADMAX?"

"Like I said, there's your mystery. If our buddy Peoples wasn't being such a hardass, I'd go find this Todd fellow and at least interview him to see what he had to say. But nothing has changed. I don't even dare mention this to management or I'll be processing new agent applications until I'm eligible to retire."

"What does the SAC have to say about it?"

"He hits mandatory retirement age in six months, and he's checked out. Spends most of his time sucking up to the CEOs at the big companies trying to line up his next job. Greg Peoples is practically running the office."

"Why am I not surprised? Well, I guess that means we're going to have to keep this under wraps. I can be in town by this time tomorrow. When do you want to go find James Todd?"

"You got a mouse in your pocket, or are you just trying to get me fired?"

Bryce laughed. "If there's one thing we know, partner, it's discretion. If you want, I can go talk to him by myself. Just let me know where I can find him."

"Stop it. You know I'm not going to let you go solo on this. But seriously, we have to be quiet. Promise me you can do that."

"You know I can. You got room for me at Casa Morris?"

"Yep, I'll make up the guest bed. See you tomorrow."

CHAPTER 19

THE ADVANCE WORK was done. Vincent had already made two trips to the Lower Keys, scouting the house and neighborhood and making meticulous notes of the target's comings and goings. Vincent checked out of his Homestead hotel room at 2:00 a.m., loaded his rental car, and used his phone to book a one-way flight home out of Miami at 1:00 p.m. He drove south on US-1, planning to be in Big Pine Key by 4:00 a.m. and driving north again less than an hour later if all went according to plan.

The plan was simple. Bryce Chandler woke every morning at 4:30 a.m., went to his kitchen and brewed a cup of coffee to drink while he watched SportsCenter. The dimly lit rear porch overlooking the canal was difficult for neighbors to see, and it would be all but impossible for someone in the bright lights of the kitchen to spot anything or anyone in the darkness outside the house. He had test fired the suppressed Kimber 1911 through glass windows enough times to know that a fully jacketed round would provide the most accurate performance. Sacrificing the lethality of a hollow point for a solid bullet meant he might have to expend a few more rounds of ammunition for a guaranteed kill, but that's what the suppressor was for. In any event, he did not want to chance leaving forensic evidence inside the house or on the target, and that meant doing the job from a distance. He would park well up the street in a dead zone between the streetlights, approaching and departing the house on foot. Total time in the neighborhood would be less than twenty minutes.

He immersed himself in his planning during the drive, so much so that he lost track of his speed in the strictly enforced forty-five miles per hour stretch of road through Key Largo. The blue lights in his rearview mirror snapped him back to the here and now, and he cursed his lack of attention as he pulled the rental to a stop on the shoulder. He rolled the window down, placed both hands on the wheel, and waited for the officer to approach.

The trooper shined a flashlight first into his side view mirror, then directly into his eyes as he approached the driver's window. "Good morning, sir. May I see your driver's license and registration?"

He smiled through the blinding light, replying, "It's a rental."

"The rental agreement, then."

He found the documents and handed them over.

"Wait here. I'll be back in a few minutes."

And now it was decision time. He had only been stopped once before, and that one did not end well. Fortunately, it was on a deserted stretch of road in East Nowhere, North Dakota, in the middle of the night, and the poor soul who pulled him over was some sort of local constable who had no concept of the danger that awaited him. Not satisfied with Vincent's explanation of where he was going and what he was doing on the road at 2:00 a.m., the constable made the fateful decision to order him out of the vehicle. In response, Vincent put two rounds in his chest and another in his forehead without so much as unbuckling his seatbelt, then drove off, leaving the body and crime scene for the highway patrol to find just after dawn. They never developed a lead.

But this was no local constable, and he wasn't in the middle of nowhere. It was the Florida Highway Patrol, and that meant the stop (and thus the license plate on the rental) had been called in. There was probably a dashboard camera behind him recording everything. And the trooper who now held his fake driver's license was no inexperienced local yokel, but more likely a well-trained and deadly adversary who'd had a gun pulled on him at least once during his career. Vincent eyed the Kimber stuffed between the driver's seat and the center console, and ran the permutations in his head. There were no good outcomes, but the worst of them was the one in which he went to jail. If the trooper wanted a fight he would give him one, but he silently prayed it wouldn't come to that.

The trooper was back. "Mr. Petty, where are you headed this morning?"

He smiled again. "Key West, sir. Going to grab a charter and see if the tarpon are biting, then hit Duval Street. The usual tourist stuff, you know?"

It was the trooper's turn to smile. "I do, sir. The reason I stopped you is because you were doing sixty-two miles per hour in a forty-five zone. This is a dangerous stretch of road, and it's also the only road in and out of the Keys, so if it gets blocked by a wreck it can shut down the whole economy for a half day or more. We take our speed limits very seriously."

"Absolutely, officer. My apologies. Won't happen again."

"I hope not, sir. I do have to cite you, though. The department put a stop to warnings for speeding more than ten miles an hour over the limit." He produced his ticket book and began writing. "Is this your current address in Kansas City?"

Vincent smiled. "Sorry to say, but yes. It was a nice place when I moved there ten years ago, but it's really gone to hell, if you know what I mean."

The trooper continued writing. "Tell me about it. I grew up in Miami, and you can't even walk the streets at night where I went to school. It's happening all over the country. Some people have no respect for the law."

"Damn shame, isn't it? Well, I hope you know there are still those of us who appreciate what you're doing, even if it's going to cost me a few bucks. Small price to pay if you ask me."

He finished writing, handed the ticket book to Vincent, and said, "Thank you, sir, and I'm sorry to have to do this. Sign right there on the bottom line, and of course that's just a promise to appear or pay the ticket, not an admission of guilt. Please press hard, there are three carbon copies."

He signed the ticket, wished the trooper well, and drove away. The entire process had taken fifteen minutes of his time, but Vincent Kamara (or Robert Charles Petty, as he was now known by the state of Florida) was confident he could still make Big Pine Key on schedule, and he could think of no reason to abandon or change his plan.

———————

The drive from Big Pine Key to Atlanta was every bit of twelve hours, and Bryce was not looking forward to it. He had planned to be on the road by 6:00 a.m. and get to Donnie's place in time for dinner, but he'd spent most of the night tossing and turning, the details of the day's conversation with his former partner spinning in his brain and denying him the rest he needed for the long, solo road trip. At 1:00 a.m. he woke from a final period of fitful sleep and knew there would be no more. He showered, brewed enough coffee to fill a travel mug, and grabbed three energy shots from a cupboard. He threw a suitcase in the rear seat of his truck, chugged the first of the energy shots, and began his long journey north along the mostly deserted Overseas Highway.

Deserted or not, the sheriff's office and highway patrol were out in force, trying their best to keep the speed and mayhem in check on what had become one of the most dangerous stretches of roadway in the state, if not in the country. A Monroe County deputy was running radar on the north end of the Seven Mile Bridge, and another had a pair of Harley Davidsons stopped north of Marathon in Duck Key. A trio of Florida Highway Patrol troopers had a U-Haul truck pulled to the shoulder in Islamorada with the back door opened. *Waiting on the drug dog*, Bryce thought to himself. Another trooper was standing alongside a small black sedan stopped on the southbound side of the road in Key Largo, and it looked like he was writing a ticket.

Bryce watched his own speed as he drove toward Homestead. He could open it up a little more once he hit dry land, but everyone knew US-1 in the Keys had turned into one long speed trap. Well, apparently not everyone.

CHAPTER 20

THE WEATHER WAS PERFECT, and Bryce made the early decision to avoid Miami, the turnpike, and the tolls, opting instead to follow US-41 through the Everglades and pick up Interstate 75 outside of Naples. It would add perhaps an hour to the drive, but the scenery and solitude would be just what he needed to clear his head of all the noise generated by the events of the last two weeks. He tuned the radio to a classic rock station, rolled his window down, and rid his mind of all things related to luxury cars, megayachts, bat-wielding restaurant patrons, and Travis Conway.

By ten o'clock he was passing through Lake City, and the state line loomed ahead, an invisible partition between his current and former lives. He had returned to Georgia only once since his humiliating departure five years earlier, on the occasion of his daughter's high school graduation. At the time, he was still living in the bottle, the scars still fresh from his divorce and near-firing from the FBI. The graduation was, of course, a gathering of the friends and family from whom he had become alienated, and he could see it in every one of their faces. *Poor guy. He had a beautiful family, a great career, and blew it all on booze and God only knows what else.* It didn't help that Janet dragged her new boyfriend to both the graduation ceremony and the celebration dinner afterward, and the humiliation of the weekend was enough to keep Bryce away for another three years. Until today.

Three years of sobriety and some serious alone time had cleared the lens through which he viewed his life. Bryce had long since accepted responsibility for the damage he had done to himself and those around him, both personally and professionally, with his drinking. Alcoholics Anonymous taught him the power of self-forgiveness and, as he drew closer to Atlanta, this time the familiarity of his surroundings gave rise to feelings of nostalgia, rather than of failure and shame. There had been happy times, to be sure. Georgia was where he and Janet met and were married, where they bought their first home, where their daughter was born and raised, and where he had carved out a more than respectable career in the profession he had dreamed about since he was a teenager. He stopped for gas outside Macon and briefly considered running into town for a Pig and fries from Fincher's, the barbecue landmark where he had taken Janet on their first date nearly thirty years earlier.

He dismissed the idea in favor of trying to beat Atlanta's afternoon rush hour and make it to Donnie's house at a reasonable time. He pressed northward, enthusiastic about the reunion with his oldest and best friend, and eager to delve into the mystery of Travis Conway. He was happy and optimistic, two feelings he hadn't associated with Georgia in years, but his good mood would not last.

The sign was waiting for him twenty-five miles ahead, in the same spot where it had been since long before he had even heard of the place. It sat on the offramp to State Route 18, green with white lettering and a left-pointing arrow, and Bryce first caught sight of it a couple hundred yards in the distance: *BARNESVILLE 13.*

STEVE LAZARUS

afterward, and the humiliation of the weekend was enough to keep Bryce away for another three years. Until today.

Three years of sobriety and some serious alone time had cleared the lens through which he viewed his life. Bryce had long since accepted responsibility for the damage he had done to himself and those around him, both personally and professionally, with his drinking. Alcoholics Anonymous taught him the power of self-forgiveness and, as he drew closer to Atlanta, this time the familiarity of his surroundings gave rise to feelings of nostalgia, rather than of failure and shame. There had been happy times, to be sure. Georgia was where he and Janet met and were married, where they bought their first home, where their daughter was born and raised, and where he had carved out a more than respectable career in the profession he had dreamed about since he was a teenager. He stopped for gas outside Macon and briefly considered running into town for a Pig and fries from Fincher's, the barbecue landmark where he had taken Janet on their first date nearly thirty years earlier.

He dismissed the idea in favor of trying to beat Atlanta's afternoon rush hour and make it to Donnie's house at a reasonable time. He pressed northward, enthusiastic about the reunion with his oldest and best friend, and eager to delve into the mystery of Travis Conway. He was happy and optimistic, two feelings he hadn't associated with Georgia in years, but his good mood would not last.

The sign was waiting for him twenty-five miles ahead, in the same spot where it had been since long before he had even heard of the place. It sat on the offramp to State Route 18, green with white lettering and a left-pointing arrow, and Bryce first caught sight of it a couple hundred yards in the distance: *BARNESVILLE 13.*

Countless thousands of travelers passed it every day, nearly all of them on their way to somewhere else and none needing its guidance, even if they were heading to the self-described "Buggy Capital of the South," population 6,500. It seemed as if the only reason for the sign's existence was to taunt Bryce, to drag him back to the darkest day of his life, to the beginning of the end for most of what mattered to him at the time. He slowed as he passed, his gaze fixed on the road ahead but his mind fully aware of the sign in the periphery, like a jogger trying to run past road kill without processing the unpleasantness of the blood and gore.

CHAPTER 21

MAY 3, 2011

The target location wasn't actually in Barnesville, but rather in an unincorporated part of Lamar County due west of the quaint little town. The single-wide trailer sat on a twenty-acre tract of heavily wooded land, a narrow dirt road marking the only way on and off the property from the nearby county two-lane. Menacing signs near the entrance proclaimed: *Posted, Keep Out, No Trespassing,* and *We Don't Call 911,* complete with a cartoonish drawing of a revolver pointed at the sign's reader.

Over the past two months, the informant had made three purchases of methamphetamine from the house in increasing quantities, the last buy being a sizable two pounds of good quality crystal. He reported that the meth was being cooked on the premises in a converted bedroom on the southwest side of the trailer. There were no neighbors for miles in any direction, making it plausible that the noxious odors one normally associated with a meth cook could go unnoticed and unreported in the rural area.

The cook, according to the CI, went by the name "Ice," and he lived in the trailer with his wife, Shayla. Bryce's investigation revealed the property owners were Douglas and Shayla Parkerson, forty and thirty-eight years old respectively, married nearly ten years, with no apparent means of support. Georgia Department of Labor checks showed Douglas Parkerson's last reported job was in 2008, as a high school custodian, prior to which he held an assortment of menial positions in the food service industry. Shayla had no record of employment. Both had petty criminal records: his for a series of minor drug possession charges and hers for a half dozen shoplifting offenses. Their most recent mug shots could have been standalone public service announcements warning others considering a similar life's journey.

Bryce secured a no-knock warrant based on the CI's reports of seeing Ice armed with a handgun, but the judge refused to waive the daylight hours provision in the warrant's conditions, meaning the team could not execute their plan before 6:00 a.m. He didn't see that as much of an issue, seeing as how most dopers went to bed around 4:00 a.m. and slept until well past noon.

Donnie and Bryce stood behind their cars, parked alongside one another with trunks open in the darkness on the county road about a quarter mile from the entrance to the Parkerson's land. As usual, they were the first to arrive. While they waited for the rest of the team to join them, they went through the pre-arrest ritual of donning protective gear, checking weapons and equipment, and getting their minds right for the sixty seconds of mayhem they knew lay ahead. It was usually a time for silence or idle chit-chat, but this was no ordinary day. The news stream from Pakistan and the White House had been unending.

"I still can't believe we got the son of a bitch," Donnie marveled, pulling his body armor from the trunk and sliding it over his head. "I mean, think about the logistics. Think about the technology. Think about the intelligence. Halfway around the world, we land two helicopters in some dude's backyard, stroll into the house, and shoot him in the face. It's like something out of a Tom Clancy novel. It's badass."

Bryce fiddled with his own protective vest, securing the radio earpiece and microphone in place with Velcro straps. "Well, according to the news reports it was Seal Team Six. And they're about as badass as it gets."

Donnie asked, "Do you really think it was him?"

"Come on, man, lose the tinfoil hat. The president said it was him. Said he saw the pictures. I know he's a politician and all, but that would be a pretty big lie. And if it wasn't him, you can bet he'll show his face somewhere pretty soon, just to prove he's still alive."

Donnie pulled a H&K MP-5 from the rack on his trunk lid, drew the bolt to the rear, and inserted a thirty-round magazine filled with ten-millimeter hollow point rounds. With a swipe of his right hand, he released the bolt with a loud thwack, launching a round into the chamber and, but for the safety lever, making the weapon ready for action. He hung the submachine gun over his neck and adjusted the sling to allow for a quick transition to his pistol on the chance the H&K malfunctioned.

"I guess that makes sense. Still, it would have been nice to see the corpse. I think it would have been therapeutic for a lot of Americans, especially anyone who lost family on 9/11. But I get it. And I get the whole burying him at sea thing too, so his gravesite doesn't become some kind of holy site for his followers. It just would have been nice to see the body."

"Yep, he's crab food for sure by now."

Donnie looked at his partner. "What do you mean, crab food?"

Bryce kept his attention focused on his handgun, as he ran

through a press check, pulling the slide just far enough to the rear to confirm there was a round in the chamber, then pressing it back forward to ensure the weapon was in battery and the first pull on the trigger would send a round through the barrel. Satisfied, he returned the pistol to its holster on his right leg and secured the retention strap.

"Crabs are bottom feeders. You ever watch that show in Alaska about the guys who fish for them in thirty-foot seas and twenty-degree weather? They sink those cages all the way down to the bottom of the ocean, then come back after a couple days and haul up all the crabs that wandered into the traps. That's where crabs hang out, eating and screwing and shitting and doing all the rest of their crab stuff on the ocean floor all day long. And they eat whatever falls down there. Like your buddy bin Laden. That's why I don't eat crab."

"Dude, that's nasty. I had a crab salad sandwich from the Sub Station for lunch yesterday."

"Not to worry. I doubt you consumed any actual crabmeat," Bryce said while he inserted a red lens into his tactical flashlight, checked the beam against the inside of his raised trunk lid, and returned the flashlight to its holster on the front of his vest.

"Well if it wasn't crabmeat, what the hell was it?"

"My guess would be flounder, pollock, and cod scraps, pressed and formed with some red dye thrown in to give it a crabby appearance. The stuff that doesn't make the cut at the fish stick factory."

Donnie smiled. "You know, you're not making me feel any better."

"I'm not trying to. If you want to feel better, throw away

your punch card to the Sub Station. That place is nothing but a processed food factory."

"Yeah, whatever. How did we get talking about my diet, anyway?"

"Beats me. I thought we were discussing international terrorism. Who's bringing the ram?"

Donnie replied, "Dave Kinney."

"Good, he's a beast. Probably knock the whole trailer over. Put this in your pocket." Bryce handed Donnie a signed copy of the warrant, which they were required to leave on the premises, along with an inventory of everything they took during the search.

Four sets of headlights appeared in Bryce's rearview mirror, and he checked his watch. It was 5:45 a.m.

"They're here. Let's do one final brief and get this thing done. I would really like to be home at a decent hour for once."

———————

At precisely 6:00 a.m., the battering ram separated the trailer's front door from its frame, and six FBI agents swarmed into the Parkerson's home, announcing their presence as required with multiple alternating shouts of "FBI! Search warrant!" As they cleared the threshold, Bryce and his team were met with the faint aromas of anhydrous ammonia and toluene, and he knew in an instant the CI's reporting on the in-home meth lab was solid.

The Parkersons were sleeping in their bed, and neither of them moved or made a sound when their front door crashed in and two men in body armor appeared in their bedroom. They were, as Bryce's father used to say, "stoned to bejesus," and had to be roused by the agents who handcuffed them and moved them to a seated position at the foot of their bed.

Bryce and Donnie moved as a team through the second bedroom and into the rear of the trailer, where one quick look through another bedroom door confirmed the presence of the lab equipment and several plastic bins stuffed with baggies full of freshly made product. Score.

With the house cleared and the Parkersons under control, Bryce gathered his team and gave them assignments for the search, then sent them off while he and Donnie questioned Douglas and Shayla in the bedroom. Their old mug shots, as unflattering as they were, didn't do justice to the drug-ravaged faces Bryce saw sitting before him on the edge of the queen-sized mattress. Neither looked like they had slept or bathed in a week, and their yellowed eyes, scabbed skin, and gaunt features gave them a zombie-like appearance as they gazed up at the unknown intruders looming over them.

Donnie broke the silence. "Mr. Parkerson, do you know why we're here?"

Douglas cocked his head, squinted, and answered in a low, almost whispering tone. "No . . . we're sleeping. Let us sleep."

Donnie tried again. "Mr. Parkerson, my partner and I are with the FBI, and we have a warrant to search your house because we believe you are manufacturing and selling methamphetamine. Do you understand?"

"I need to go to sleep."

Donnie shook him by the shoulder. "Mr. Parkerson, do you know where you are or what day it is?"

There was no response. Douglas appeared to be sleeping in a

seated position, and Shayla wasn't in much better shape, though she at least appeared to be conscious. Bryce made the decision.

"These two are way too far gone to give us anything useful, and even if they did it would never be admissible in court. We can't even Mirandize them like this. We've got enough to arrest them both, so let's get them out of here, finish our search, and let the DEA boys handle the lab cleanup. We have what we need."

Donnie nodded. "All right, you two, you're both under arrest for possession and sale of methamphetamine. You're going to be transported to the nearest federal courthouse for an initial appearance in front of a magistrate, but first we need to search you before we put you into our cars. You first, Douglas."

Donnie pulled him to his feet, patted him down, checked the security of his handcuffs, and put him back on the bed. Bryce turned his attention to Shayla.

"Stand up right where your husband was, Mrs. Parkerson. Sorry, but we don't have a female agent with us today, so I'm going to have to search you. This is for your protection and mine, and I'm not going to do anything inappropriate. Do you have anything on you that could hurt me, like a weapon or a needle?"

By now Shayla was spread-eagled against the wall. She turned her head partway toward Bryce, who was standing behind her, and gurgled out what sounded like "turn it off."

Bryce shot Donnie a look, then re-addressed his subject. "What did you say? Turn what off?"

She repeated herself. "Turn it off."

Bryce moved to Shayla's side and looked her in the eye and repeated his question. "Turn what off?"

"Turn it off. It's gonna burn."

"What's going to burn? Donnie, did we miss something in the lab? A hotplate, a Bunsen burner, anything like that maybe left on?"

Donnie replied, "We gave it a good look, but I can run back in there. I don't think anything was burning."

"Yeah, run and check, will you? I can handle these two." He finished searching Shayla and put her back on the bed next to her husband.

Donnie disappeared down the hallway. Douglas fell back on the bed, his hands cuffed behind him, and began snoring. Shayla looked up at Bryce and started again.

"Turn it off, it's gonna burn."

Bryce was annoyed. "We're checking it, okay? Trust me, we're not any more interested in getting blown up than you are."

"The oven. Turn it off. It's gonna burn."

"The oven? Are you saying you left the oven on? What, did you leave your dinner in there?"

There was no response other than a nod.

"That's great, lady. A smoking hot oven twenty feet from a meth lab. It's a wonder you two were still alive when we got here."

Donnie reappeared, shot Bryce a thumbs up, and said, "Lab's good to go. Nothing was on, and I unplugged a couple of things just to make sure."

"Thanks. The issue appears to be in the kitchen. Watch these two and I'll take care of it."

The kitchen was in a separate space, with a door closing it off to the rest of the trailer. The oven was at least as old as the trailer itself, rusted around the edges and coated down the front and sides with years of spilled grease and crusted food residue. For the first time since entering the house, Bryce smelled the faint aroma of burning meat over the chemicals from the meth lab, and a quick glance at the oven's dials showed it was indeed on, set to 400 degrees. He turned the dial to *Off*, cracked the door just enough to let some of the heat escape, and immediately regretted his decision.

The thick, black smoke billowed from the open door and made its way straight up, catching Bryce in mid-breath and coating the insides of his nose and throat. He stopped inhaling and turned his head away, but it was too late. He lost his grip on the oven door and it fell open, releasing more smoke as he stumbled backward into the wall and began to retch. On his hands and knees, Bryce crawled back through the smoke toward the open oven, his eyes watering and bile building in his throat as he felt along the floor for the door handle. The smoke cleared just enough for him to see inside the oven before he flung the door shut, fell backward again, and emptied the contents of his stomach onto the floor.

Donnie heard the commotion and called out from the bedroom. "You okay in there, Bryce? What's going on?"

His throat burning from smoke and stomach acid, Bryce could barely manage a response. He stepped to the kitchen door and tried to speak, but his voice failed him. He slammed the door shut behind him and stumbled back to the bedroom where Donnie greeted him with a look that was equal parts horror and curiosity.

"Jesus Christ, what happened to you?"

His voice barely above a whisper, Bryce replied, "Stay out of the kitchen. Nobody goes in there, understand?"

"Yeah, no problem. What happened, did you—"

Donnie stopped in mid-sentence as Bryce lunged across the room at Douglas Parkerson and caught him flush on the side of his face with a closed fist. He landed on top of the handcuffed meth dealer and was about to deliver another blow when Donnie grabbed him from behind and pulled him off.

Donnie screamed at his partner as he knelt over Douglas Parkerson's unconscious body. "What the hell are you doing?!"

Bryce stood up slowly on unsteady legs, his breathing labored, his heart beating triple its normal rate. He felt his chest tighten and his vision began to tunnel as the room became smaller and darker. He looked at Douglas, then at Shayla, then back to Douglas.

He could manage no more than a raspy whisper. "You piece of shit. You piece of shit." His eyes rolled back in his head, and his world went black as he fell to the floor.

"Don't touch that." The paramedic moved Bryce's hand away from the oxygen mask covering his nose and mouth. As he regained consciousness, he realized he was lying on a gurney outside the trailer, and a crowd had gathered that far outnumbered the half dozen agents he had brought with him before dawn. He scanned the area and made out a Georgia Bureau of Investigation crime scene van, a DEA clandestine lab cleanup crew, and at least ten marked units from the county sheriff's office and the state patrol. Down the dirt road that led to the trailer, he could see a couple of news crews, no doubt being held back by even more state and local cops.

Donnie was standing outside the trailer's front door, and he walked toward Bryce, who was becoming annoyed with the paramedic taking his blood pressure.

"How you feeling, partner?" Donnie asked.

Bryce pulled the oxygen mask away, ignoring the paramedic's repeated orders. "Okay, I guess. What's going on inside?"

"DEA and GBI are doing their thing. We recovered about thirty pounds of meth, and Shayla and Douglas are on their way to the marshal's office for booking. We'll get them in front of a magistrate for an initial appearance later today. And you, my friend, are going to the hospital to get checked out."

"Like hell I am," Bryce replied as he reached for the straps and buckles securing him to the gurney.

The paramedic grabbed his hand again. "Agent Chandler, you are in terrible shape. Your blood pressure is 180 over 120, your breathing sounds asthmatic, and your oxygen levels are borderline. God only knows what you inhaled into your lungs inside that trailer. Everyone in there right now is wearing full body suits and respirators. You need to see a doctor."

Bryce was unimpressed, and he brushed away the paramedic's arm a second time. The frustrated young man raised his hands in the air in a symbol of surrender, walking away without further comment toward the open rear doors of a nearby ambulance. Bryce released the strap around his waist and swung his legs over the side of the gurney as he sat up. "Donnie, where are the rest of our people?"

"They're all gone, either transporting the Parkersons or taking the drug evidence back to Atlanta. I stayed to make sure you were taken care of. We're done here." He approached Bryce on the gurney, his voice lowered to a whisper. "Nobody knows what happened to Douglas in the bedroom except you and me, so don't mention it to anyone. He's so wasted he's not going to remember it anyway."

Bryce nodded his understanding. "I need to get out of here. Help me make these guys understand I'm not going to the hospital."

Donnie walked over to the paramedic, had a brief discussion, and came back with a clipboard in his hand.

"Sign this. It says you are refusing medical attention, and if you die, they're not to blame. At the very least, you need to let me take you home. We can have someone come get your car. You're in no shape to drive."

Bryce scribbled a signature, stood up on wobbly legs, and slowly made his way toward his vehicle. "Tell the bosses I'm going to take a few days of sick leave. I'll see you back in the office next week."

He drove back to the interstate and turned north toward Atlanta. When he reached the southern suburbs, he pulled off the highway and found a liquor store where he paid cash for four liter-sized bottles of Jack Daniel's. About a mile away, he checked into a Super 8 motel, turned off his phone, and cracked open the first bottle.

Bryce would never remember the next three days of his life.

CHAPTER 22

THE TIGHTNESS IN BRYCE'S CHEST decreased as Barnesville faded in the distance. Seeing the road sign had stirred feelings he had not known in years, ones he had never discussed with anyone but his AA sponsor. The psychiatrist the FBI forced him to see never got a full accounting of what happened that day. He even refused to talk about it with Janet, despite the continuous questioning as to why her husband had become a distant, binge-drinking stranger. In the end, his stoicism cost him his marriage.

In the years since his DUI arrest, he had worked through the twelve steps of the AA program, from accepting that he was powerless over alcohol to working with other alcoholics and trying to set an example with his behavior. The most difficult steps of the process were those that required him to compile a list of the people in his life he had wronged and humbly ask their forgiveness. He took the task to heart, even calling Greg Peoples and apologizing for the overblown "assault" incident that spelled the beginning of the end of his time in the FBI. Still, as he pondered the amends he had made since his fall from grace, he knew there were instances when he could have done better, and one in particular.

The Atlanta skyline loomed ahead, and Bryce figured it would take another hour to reach Donnie's house in the northeast suburbs. There was time for a stop in between. He exited Interstate

285, the Atlanta perimeter loop, at Peachtree Industrial Boulevard and drove the familiar route to Norcross. Several turns later, he pulled into a subdivision and drove past the well-manicured lawns and brick and wood facades of the traditional Georgian style homes. At the end of a cul-de-sac, he parked his truck, walked up the driveway, and rang the bell.

Through the leaded glass, he could see her unmistakable silhouette as she approached. The door cracked slightly, then opened fully as she stood before him, the look on her face a mix of surprise, irritation, and resignation.

She spoke first. "Hello, Bryce."

"Hello, Janet. Can I come in?"

———

The kitchen was as he remembered it, save for the absence of any family photos that included him. They sat at the table where they had planned countless family vacations, where he served his traditional Sunday waffles, and where she served him with divorce papers five years earlier. She offered coffee, but he opted for a bottle of water. After the perfunctory greetings and a minute of uncomfortable silence, Janet got to the point.

"Why are you here?"

"I'm going to see Donnie. We have some leftover business on an old case, and there wasn't much going on in the Keys, so I decided to take a poor man's vacation."

"I didn't mean here in Atlanta. I mean why are you here in my house?"

The word choice stung him. *My house. It used to be my house too,* he said to himself, and decided the thought was better left inside his head.

He replied, "I need to talk to you. There are some things you don't know, things I should have told you years ago."

She looked down at the table, her head in her hands. "Bryce, nothing is going to change things between us. Please don't try. I accepted your apology when you were doing your AA program. I've moved on. Let it go."

Bryce was unfazed by the rejection. "Give me ten minutes. This isn't about trying to change anything between you and me. But of all the people I hurt, you were the one who deserved an explanation for why I became what I did. You don't owe me anything. I'm asking this as a favor. Please, Janet."

She folded her hands on the table, refocused on Bryce, and remained silent.

"You remember the three days I didn't come home?"

Her response was acerbic. "You mean the three days the entire office, the police, and the sheriff's department were looking for you? The three days when we didn't know if you were dead or alive? The three days when your daughter cried herself to sleep because she didn't know if she still had a father? Yes, Bryce, I remember all that."

He continued. "We had a search warrant down in Lamar County. It was a couple of meth heads cooking and selling out of a trailer. It was Donnie, me, and four other guys from the squad. We hit the door, cleared the house, just like we'd done a hundred times before. It was a husband and wife, both stoned out of their minds. While we were searching them, the wife told me to . . ." He took a deep breath. "She told me to turn off the oven."

Janet looked at her former husband and saw something she had never seen before. He was struggling with his words, and his eyes were moist with tears. He stared down at the table as he spoke.

"I went into the kitchen and turned the oven off. When I opened the door I almost choked to death on the smoke. I actually fell down and puked on the floor. DEA said it was ammonia gas, and that the oven had probably been used during a cook." He took in another deep, steadying breath.

"It smelled so bad, all I could think about was closing that oven door. And when I got closer to the oven, I saw it."

Janet remained expressionless, silent and still, her hands folded in front of her on the table and her gaze fixed on Bryce.

"It was a baby," he sobbed.

Tears were streaming down his face, and he took a moment to regain his composure. "They cooked a baby. Because it wouldn't stop crying. Because they wanted to sleep. They cooked a little baby girl, Janet."

He finally looked up. Her eyes were steely and dry, and they bore no sign of surprise.

"I know, Bryce."

Bryce stared at his former wife in disbelief. "You knew? How did you know? When did you find out?"

"Donnie told me. About a week before my attorney drew up the divorce papers. I called him and asked to meet for coffee, and I had to beg him to tell me what was going on with you. He was actually surprised you hadn't shared it with me."

"You could have told me you knew."

"Seriously? You want to go down that road? You want to make the lack of communication in our marriage my fault?"

He instantly knew he had said the wrong thing. "No, of course not. I'm sorry I said that. I guess by that point, the damage was done anyway."

"You could say that. Look, let's not pretend everything was perfect in our marriage before all this happened. But after you came home, you were a completely different person. We barely spoke. You lost interest in our relationship, our friends, our social life, our sex life. You reeked of alcohol nearly every time you walked through that door. It was like living with a stranger. And as bad as I felt for you after talking with Donnie, I knew it was something I couldn't fix, and at the same time something I couldn't live with. I hope you can get over the pain one day, I really do. We made a beautiful girl together, and I'll always love a part of you. But you're broken."

There was no sympathy in her eyes, and her voice was businesslike and emotionless. This was not the joyful, kind, and loving Janet he had courted twenty-five years earlier. She had become a hardened, battle-scarred version of her former self, and Bryce would never forgive himself for the role he played in the metamorphosis. She backed her chair away from the table and stood as his cue that it was time to go.

They said their goodbyes, and as he stepped through the door and onto the front porch, he turned to offer a final apology, but she had already closed the door.

CHAPTER 23

STANLEY WAS BACK, and as usual, he was in a foul mood and reeking of gin. His weekly drop-ins had increased in frequency to every other day, always under the pretense of wanting to know what progress was being made in his case. Ashley suspected he had at least one additional motive, and the thought of it sickened her. He was a squat, portly, balding little man, clothed in garish '80s disco attire, dripping gold chains and pinky rings, sporting a cheesy toupee and patchy goatee that screamed, "I'm still young and virile . . . right?" When she looked at him, she felt pity for his shrewish, gold-digging wife who was a colossal pain in the ass in her own right.

Ashley glared at him from behind her desk, her patience worn well past thin. "Stanley," she said, "we've been over this a hundred times. You lost. We're appealing Judge Troxley's decision, but our chances of having his order amended, much less over-turned, are about zero. I begged you to settle this with April, and your exact words, if I recall correctly, were, 'That bitch will get nothing.' Well, here we are, and that bitch got half of what you own. You have nobody to blame but yourself."

"How do you figure that?" he asked, bewildered.

"You're kidding, right?" Ashley replied. "For starters, there was your little Thursday afternoon whore parade at the Sandpiper Inn. That didn't exactly set you up for Man of the Year honors, did it? Then the falsified affidavit in which you listed your assets at less than half their actual value. Oh, and then the cherry on top, your pathetic attempt to sell the marina without April's knowledge, like you didn't know it was community property. Like I didn't specifically advise you not to try and hide it from your wife or the court." She jabbed the air, her index finger pointed toward him to accentuate her words.

"She doesn't deserve it," he slurred through bloodshot eyes. "I built it all from nothing. It was my blood, sweat, and tears. She sat on her ass hosting dinner parties and playing bridge with her friends."

"Well, Stanley, the state of Florida saw it differently, and I'm surprised Judge Troxley didn't give her more. I can still petition the court to allow the sale of the marina if you think you can get Chase Worthing back to the table. But everything will have to be completely above board, and make no mistake, April will get half of the proceeds."

"You don't get it, do you?" he asked. "That deal was dead the moment it became public record during the divorce trial. Chase Worthing didn't want his name associated with the marina. That's why he put together that bullshit shell company and had Roger Mackenzie's name on all the paperwork. Come on, sweetie, you knew what was going on. You had to."

She bristled at the inappropriate term of address. "My name is Ashley. And no, Stanley, I don't know why Chase Worthing wanted your marina, and I'm sure I don't want to know. Frankly, I don't think you should be talking about it in this office. It has nothing to do with your divorce case, and that is the only legal matter for which I represent you."

Stanley was undeterred. "Seriously? You're a smart girl. Do

the math. A businessman from the country's cocaine capital needs a quiet place in the Keys where his boats can come and go discretely, so he can do what? Fish for grouper out of season? Please. Don't act like you don't know what's going on."

She had suspected it, but the boldness with which Stanley spoke out of school still surprised her. And if what he was saying was true, running his mouth about it would put them both in danger.

"Stanley, shut the fuck up!" she yelled, loud enough to startle him. "I don't want to know any of this. It's outside the scope of the divorce, so we don't have attorney/client privilege. Do you understand that? I can be forced to testify about all the stupid shit coming out of your mouth right now, and I don't need that aggravation in my life. Whatever's going on between you and Chase Worthing, leave me out of it."

Stanley didn't stop. "I've seen it, you know. Not the actual drugs, but I've seen them unloading the boats after midnight, putting boxes into trucks . . . there's more. Much more."

"Get out. Stanley, I'm telling you, get out of my office and don't come back unless I invite you." She stood and motioned toward the door. He didn't move, but kept talking, staring straight ahead with dead eyes and an expression of hopelessness that frightened Ashley. There was no stopping him. She couldn't physically throw him out, there was nobody she could call, and involving the police was out of the question, at least for now. She thought about just walking out and leaving him alone in her office, but that too seemed like a bad idea.

Stanley's alcohol-fueled confession went on for another thirty minutes, and by the time he voluntarily stumbled out of her office, Ashley Oliver knew she was in real trouble.

CHAPTER 24

DONNIE'S PENCHANT for unhealthy food hadn't changed, but Bryce could hardly complain. They dined on thick New York strips and baked potatoes the size of footballs covered in butter, sour cream, and bacon. The salad was a formality and went mostly untouched. Donnie's wife Crystal baked her self-described "world famous" death-by-chocolate cake, and the three of them devoured most of it, laughing and teasing one another as they proclaimed each successive slice to be their last.

"It's so good to see you again, Bryce," Crystal said. "Donnie tells me you're doing private investigator work down there in Florida. What's that like?"

Bryce pushed away from the table, stifled a belch, and answered, "Well, I'm never going to get rich, but let's just say there's enough work to keep a roof over my head. Lots of divorces, some shady business partners screwing each other over, and the occasional family member trying to track down a missing sibling or child."

Crystal asked, "Missing persons . . . wouldn't that be a police matter?"

"Not necessarily. If they're over eighteen and haven't committed a crime, there's nothing for the police to investigate. The Keys is one of those places that isn't on the way to anywhere else, so people don't just pass through. It's kind of a lost and found. Some folks go there to get lost and others go to find themselves. It attracts dreamers, poets, and artists, but it also has its share of drifters, deadbeats, and people who've just checked out on life in the mainstream."

"So which one are you?" she asked.

The question caught him unprepared. He'd had more than one conversation with his therapist and AA sponsor, exploring the reasons he chose a remote island chain as his post-divorce, forced retirement landing spot. He could have gone anywhere, but he opted, in his own words, for the lost and found.

"I guess I'm a little of both," he replied. "I don't know. The Keys just seem to fit me."

Crystal asked, "So is it safe to live there?"

"Oh, absolutely. The Keys are no more dangerous than your average American city, and knowing where and where not to go will keep most people out of trouble. Truth be told, spring breakers and partyers from out of town account for most of the crime. There's an old saying that I've learned is funny but true. The Florida Keys: Come on vacation, leave on probation."

Crystal and Donnie both laughed. She said, "Okay, I'll leave you boys to your business, whatever that is. Help me clear the table and I'll take it from there."

Bryce and Donnie carried the dishes into the kitchen and retired to the deck, where Donnie produced a pair of Cohibas and a torch.

"What's the plan for tomorrow?" Bryce asked as he lit his cigar and passed the torch back to Donnie.

"Well, I'm going to assume Mr. James Todd, Esquire, isn't going to book an appointment with an FBI agent without knowing what it's about in advance," Donnie answered. "Also, there's the issue of him calling the office to raise a stink, and if he talks to ASAC Peoples, we're finished before we get started."

"Yeah, good point. You have a ruse in mind?"

"I got a little something planned. Just play along. If all goes well, by the end of the day we'll have him singing like a bird. Or he might call my bluff, report me to Peoples, and then I can start working on that truck driving career. But I'm not letting him off the hook easy. I'm going to make him sweat."

"Damn. Sounds like your balls finally dropped."

Donnie laughed. "I guess you could say that. You were one hell of a training agent, and the most important thing you showed me was to stick to my guns when I knew I was right. And we are right on this one. Screw Greg Peoples, screw Atlanta PD, and screw the US Attorney's Office. Julie's murder is somehow connected to Travis Conway, and James Todd was one of the last people to see him alive. I want answers."

Bryce silently admired his former protégé's newfound determination and courage. They had spent enough time on business, and so he changed the subject to a shared favorite, that of their love for the Atlanta Braves and the team's potential for making the playoffs. Sports talk turned to discussion of children and college, then to war stories and reminiscences of two decades' worth of FBI casework. Crystal said goodnight at 10:00 p.m., and the two friends continued on until well past midnight. Bryce made no mention of his visit with Janet.

CHAPTER 25

JAMES TODD'S OFFICE occupied a two-room suite in a South Fulton County strip mall, wedged between a nail salon and a frozen yogurt store. The glass entry doors gave way to a small reception area that contained seating for clients and a desk for his secretary. Lashelle Washington was a sizeable, middle-aged black woman with a sharp tongue and a no-nonsense attitude, both of which served her well in her dealings with the stream of riffraff who called James their lawyer.

Donnie told Bryce to dress street casual, and they entered the waiting room wearing jeans, T-shirts, and sneakers. Lashelle greeted them as coldly as she did all of James's clients, told them to take a seat, and picked up the phone.

"Mr. Webster here to see you. Plus one."

"Who's the plus one?"

"He says it's his brother. DeKalb PD took his license and he needed a ride."

"Okay, send them in."

James didn't bother to stand from behind his desk, motioning his visitors to a pair of chairs across from him. James began as soon as they sat down, barely looking up from the laptop in front of him.

"Okay, Mr. Webster, it says on your intake sheet you were arrested for DUI in Stone Mountain a few nights ago. Obviously you've bonded out, so our next issue is a preliminary appearance at which you will plead not guilty. I haven't had a chance to pull your police report, but Lashelle will get that for me after today's meeting. Today I need a $2,500 retainer, and I will bill you at $150 per hour against that. I will take cash or a personal check, and if the check bounces I will terminate my services as your attorney immediately. Do you understand?"

Donnie nodded his head in agreement. "I do."

James continued. "William, you indicated to Ms. Washington on the phone that you've never been in trouble with the law before, and that's good. The marijuana complicates things a bit, but nothing we can't get past. Why don't you tell me exactly what happened from the moment you saw the flashing lights in your rearview mirror?"

Donnie leaned forward in his chair. "Mr. Todd, I was never arrested by the DeKalb County Police, or anyone else for that matter." He retrieved his badge and credentials from his back pocket and showed them to James. "I'm Special Agent Donald Morris of the FBI."

A puzzled look came over James's face as he leaned forward and closed the laptop, his attention focused on the two men in front of him for the first time since they walked in. He folded his hands underneath his chin and fixed his gaze on Donnie.

"I suppose you're going to tell me why you're in my office and why you lied to get in here?" he asked.

"I am," Donnie replied. "We want to talk to you about one of your clients."

James smiled. "Surely they taught you at your academy the nature of attorney/client privilege. Do you think I'm going to violate it just because you waved an FBI badge in my face? I've got a better idea. How about I call your boss, and tell him a couple of his agents are in my office right now, pretending to be clients, and trying to get me to break the law? How's that sound?"

Donnie stood his ground. "It sounds like a rash, premature move on your part, Mr. Todd. If I were you, I'd want to know more about those agents and what they're after. You can always call my boss later."

James's smile broadened as the realization set in. "They don't know you're here, do they? What is this, some sort of shake-down? I'll tell you what . . . get the hell out of my office in the next thirty seconds, never come back, and we'll forget this ever happened."

Donnie glanced at Bryce and realized the time had come to play his cards. "Mr. Todd, we're here to talk about Travis Conway."

His involuntary reflexes betrayed him as the blood left his face and his breathing quickened. The smile was gone, and he looked down toward his desk as he mumbled a feeble reply. "Never heard of him."

"Sure you have, James," Donnie replied, switching to the more familiar form of address as he gained the upper hand. "You visited him at ADMAX earlier this year. It was an attorney visit, which we found puzzling seeing as how you were never his attorney of record. Equally puzzling was the fact that he hung himself in his cell an hour after you left."

James stared straight ahead and offered no response.

Donnie continued. "And most perplexing of all is the fact that a few months after your meeting with Mr. Conway, people connected to him started dying. His prosecutor was shot to death execution style, a former jailer was blown up in his driveway with his wife and baby nearby, and the judge who sentenced him was almost murdered in his house, but got the drop on his attacker and shot him to death."

It was the first chink in his armor. James was rattled, but had no intention of giving in, at least not so quickly. "And what does that series of unfortunate events have to do with me?" he asked.

It was Donnie's turn to smile. "Is that how you want to play it? Fair enough. I'm sure this meeting has left you with more questions than answers, and it's a lot to take in, isn't it? You need some time to process all this and get your head right, so let me explain what's going to happen next. Tomorrow we are going to have another meeting, only this time it will be at a location I will choose. At that meeting, you are going to tell me everything I want to know about your dealings with Travis Conway. You will also agree to tell your story to a grand jury, and in return, we will arrange for you to plead guilty to a minor offense, avoid spending the rest of your natural life in prison, and enter the witness security program. You're dealing with some very bad people, James, and this is your only option."

James maintained his stoic façade. "And if I decide on another option?" he asked.

"Like I said, this is all you've got. Here's my number." Donnie handed him a business card. "Call me before ten o'clock tomorrow morning."

James took the card, placed it on his desk, and glared at Donnie and Bryce. "Get out of my office."

"Ten o'clock. Don't make me come back."

As soon as they got back into Donnie's car, Bryce started in.

"Jesus Christ, Donnie, a grand jury? A plea deal? WITSEC?

Have you even spoken to an AUSA or the Marshals Service about any of the promises you just made this guy?"

"Of course not. This is all a calculated risk, but I think it went well. He was white as a bedsheet when I brought up Travis Conway's name. If we can nail down a statement from him tomorrow, then we can make it all official. But we both know nobody's going to give us the time of day unless we can bring them a smoking gun, and James is holding that gun. I think he's going to play ball."

"Partner, I sure hope you're right. I don't even want to think what Peoples will do to you if this all blows up in our face. Oh, and by the way . . . William Webster? That's your alias? A former FBI director?"

Donnie laughed. "You always said I needed to lighten up and get a sense of humor. I think it had a certain degree of whimsy, don't you?"

Bryce shook his head. "Three years 'til retirement, you say? At this rate you'll be lucky to make it three months. I guess we'll see what he decides. What do you want to do in the meantime?"

"The North Georgia mountains are beautiful this time of year. Let's go see Judge Branch."

Lashelle knew something was off. She didn't like those two from the minute she saw them. Something just wasn't as it seemed. They didn't carry themselves like Mr. Todd's usual low-rent clientele. She heard parts of their conversation through the closed door, and now she could hear him in there alone, cursing a blue streak and slamming his fists on his desk. She knocked softly and pushed the door open just far enough to see him, red-faced and flustered, stuffing his briefcase with files.

"You okay, Mr. Todd?" she asked.

He never shifted his gaze from the desk. "I'm fine, Lashelle. I'll be taking the rest of the day off, and maybe tomorrow as well. I need you to clear my calendar."

"You've got a bond motion at one, Mr. Todd. That Whitman boy. The aggravated assault."

"Call Brad Levy and ask him to handle it. He owes me one."

"I'll take care of it, Mr. Todd. Is there anything else?" she asked.

"No." He picked up his briefcase, threw his jacket over his shoulder, and left without another word.

Lashelle called Brad Levy, then half a dozen of James Todd's clients. She let them know their attorney had been unexpectedly summoned to court on a most urgent matter, and they would need to reschedule their appointments. She then turned her keyboard over to reveal a small sticky note taped to its underside. Written on the note in pencil was a telephone number she had been given two years before, and it was one she thought she would never need to dial. A female voice answered on the other end.

"McNair Industries, how may I direct your call?"

"I need to speak to Mr. Jackson."

"Hold, please." The line was silent for what seemed like an eternity while Lashelle waited. Finally, whoever was claiming to be Mr. Jackson answered, his voice low and steady, marked with a slight Texas accent.

"How may I help you, Mrs. Washington?"

Lashelle was taken aback. "How did you know my name?"

The voice was sterner this time, almost scolding. "How may I help you, Mrs. Washington?"

She realized she was in no position to be asking questions. "Sorry. I was told to call this number and ask for Mr. Jackson if, umm . . . if certain things happened."

"And what has happened, Mrs. Washington?"

"Well, I work for James Todd, an attorney in Atlanta—"

The voice interrupted her. "I know where you work and who you work for. Please tell me what happened and why you called this number."

"Sorry. I'm just nervous is all. Anyway, Mr. Todd had a visitor today, two of them actually. They said they were with the FBI. And they were accusing him of something."

"What exactly were they accusing him of doing?"

"It was hard to tell. One of the FBI men did all the talking, the younger one. He said they wanted to talk about one of Mr. Todd's clients, somebody named Mr. Conway. He said Mr. Todd went to visit Mr. Conway at some place called Mad Max or something like that, and afterward some people started dying."

"And what did Mr. Todd say to them?"

"He told them to get the hell out of his office, pardon my language. Just like that. Twice. But they kept on. And then they told him he had until tomorrow to make up his mind. They left, and then Mr. Todd left about fifteen minutes later. Had me cancel all his appointments for the rest of today and tomorrow."

"Did Mr. Todd discuss the meeting with you at all?"

"No, sir. He just told me to clear his calendar for the rest of the day."

"Okay, Mrs. Washington. All of this is very helpful. Have

you told anyone else about the meeting in Mr. Todd's office?"

"Oh, no sir. The man who gave me this number was very clear about when I should call it, and that I wasn't to talk about it to anyone, not even Mr. Todd."

"Very well done, Mrs. Washington. We will be in touch, and we will keep our end of the agreement. Until then—"

Lashelle cut him off. "Mum's the word." She had already begun spending the money in her mind.

"Indeed. Good day, Mrs. Washington."

CHAPTER 26

HARLEY CHRISTIAN LEFT the Dive Shack around midnight, half a dozen drinks under his belt but certain he was below the legal limit in the event he was pulled over. For good measure, he lit a joint and smoked it as he navigated the two-minute journey from the bar to his house in his patchwork Chevy Cutlass.

Work, both legitimate and otherwise, had been sparse, and he was happy to have a small job waiting for him the next morning. It was just a lower unit service on a friend's outboard motor, but he would pocket a couple hundred bucks after paying for the parts. He pulled into his carport, shut off the engine, and double-checked to make sure the doors were locked. There had been a rash of break-ins on Cudjoe Key over the past few weeks, and he could ill afford to lose the tools he stored in the trunk of his car.

His senses were more dulled than he estimated, and he never saw the two men until it was too late. As he turned the key in the front door lock, the larger of the pair pushed him through the door and into his living room, where Harley landed on his face. He turned over and dismissed the idea of charging his assailants when he saw the guns in their hands.

They each grabbed an arm and manhandled him onto a kitchen chair, then took up positions in front of and behind him. The one standing in front of him began the questioning.

"Do you know who I am, Harley?" he asked. A long, perfectly straight white line ran from the corner of his right eye to the middle of his jaw, made all the more noticeable by the assailant's deep tan. Harley had seen enough knife fights to know the scar's likely genesis.

Harley stared, squinted, and replied, "I give up. Who the fuck are you?"

The pain was immediate and intense as he was struck across the right side of his face from behind with an open palm. The force of the impact ruptured his eardrum, loosened one of his molars, and made his eyes water.

"Watch your mouth, Harley. I'm not here to hurt you, but I will hurt you and a whole lot worse if you don't tell me what I want to know. You and your friend almost killed one of my men a couple of weeks ago. You were sticking your nose where it didn't belong, and I need to know who your friend is. The one who was driving your car."

Harley touched the side of his face and it felt hot. With his tongue, he felt the spot where the tooth had loosened and tasted the blood pooling at the back of his mouth. The buzz was gone, replaced by fear and confusion. He knew there was no way of talking his way out of it, but he tried anyway.

"I don't know what you're talking about. Where did all this supposedly happen?"

The second blow came again from behind, this time from his left and delivered with a closed fist. It caught him in the temple just behind his left eye, shattering bone, collapsing his eye socket, and leaving him nearly unconscious on the floor.

They picked him up and put him back in the chair, and his interrogator continued. "Harley, don't make me kill you. This isn't about revenge. The people I work for need to know why you and your friend were making their business your business, and they are some very serious people. I'm just doing a job here. So I'm going to ask you again: What's your friend's name, and what were the two of you doing at Tres Gatos the week before last?"

Harley was fading in and out, his left eye already starting to swell shut, a shattered jaw and mouthful of blood making it difficult to speak. He stared up at his attacker and managed a final reply.

"His name is Big Dick. We had just finished tag teaming your mother and decided to celebrate the occasion with tacos and margaritas. Now go fuck yourself."

The final series of blows came from straight ahead, as the interrogator smiled, balled his fist, and drove it forward repeatedly with all the strength he could muster, sending Harley sprawling backward onto the floor and into the darkness.

CHAPTER 27

THE RIDE TO DAWSONVILLE took two hours, and the judge was waiting for them on the front porch of the cabin when they arrived. He wore jeans, Western boots, and a flannel shirt, and sported hair well below his ears and a full gray beard. Both Bryce and Donnie were taken aback by the radical transformation of the clean-cut jurist they had only known to wear dark suits and black robes. The Springfield Hellcat, no longer concealed, now rode prominently in a holster on the judge's right hip as he stepped off the porch to greet his visitors.

"Agents Morris and Chandler, I presume? Pardon me if I don't remember our time together in the courtroom, gentlemen. It has been a few years."

"Not at all, Judge," Donnie replied as the three exchanged handshakes. "We appreciate you taking the time to meet with us. Can we go inside and talk?"

They settled into leather chairs in the same room where Judge Branch's attacker died just weeks earlier. As he took his seat, Bryce noticed a dark stain on the heart pine flooring, about the size of a dinner plate. Somebody had tried to scrub it away, and they were unsuccessful.

As with James Todd, Donnie led the conversation while Bryce listened.

"Sir, what has the Dawson County Sheriff come up with so far?" he asked.

A puzzled look appeared on the judge's face. "Any reason you're asking me that and not them?"

"Politics, Judge. You know the whole state-versus-feds pissing contest thing. Sheriff Freeman has never been a big fan of ours, and word has it they've written it off as a home invasion gone wrong."

The judge smiled. "Yep, that's what they told me."

"And you don't believe it?"

"Hell, no. I don't know who that son of a bitch was that broke in here, and I certainly don't remember seeing him from across the bench, but whoever he was, he wasn't some junior varsity burglar. He was waiting for me. The Rolex they gave me when I retired was sitting on my nightstand next to my wallet, which had three hundred dollars cash in it. That's an original Remington print hanging on the wall behind you. And he was standing right next to it with a rope in his hands to strangle me. Burglar, my ass. And one more thing: The sheriff sent his DNA and fingerprints to the GBI crime lab, and you know what came back? Nothing. Not one goddamned hit. His plane tickets, the name he used to rent the car, the name and address on his driver's license . . . all fake. He's a ghost. Or was."

Wendell removed his glasses, wiped them with a handkerchief, and stared directly at Donnie. "I assume you boys have a theory yourselves or you wouldn't be here. Am I right?"

Bryce spoke up. "You are, Judge. We think your attacker was somehow linked to whoever killed AUSA Martinez and a prison guard in Indiana."

"I heard about Julie. She was a fine prosecutor. A terrible loss. So what do you think the connection might be?"

Donnie stepped back in. "Sir, do you recall a defendant named Travis Conway?"

"Refresh my memory."

"He was a gun runner, and we caught him selling a dozen military-grade rifles to MS-13. Twice convicted prior felon, the presentence report recommended twenty years, and you upward departed to twenty-five."

The judge stroked his beard and gazed at his feet as he tried to remember the case. "Was he a local guy? Priors for arson and armed robbery?"

Donnie replied, "That's him, Judge. He continued his bad behavior in prison, and eventually got sent to ADMAX. After a few years there he killed himself, but not before he met with an attorney from Atlanta named James Todd."

"That name doesn't ring a bell."

"Nor should it, sir," Donnie said. "Todd is a local hack who represents low-level felons and DUIs, mostly in Fulton County. He's never set foot in federal court."

"Then why was he meeting with a federal convict at AD-MAX?" the judge asked.

Donnie continued. "Yes sir, there's the mystery. We spoke with him earlier today and gave him until tomorrow to fill us in on the details."

"So I take it Julie was the prosecutor on his case, and I sentenced him. I get the connection there. But you mentioned something about a prison guard in Indiana?"

Bryce took over. "After you sentenced Conway, he was sent

to FCI Edgefield. He messed up there and was transferred to Terre Haute where the guard worked. The guard was running cell phones and drugs to the inmates, and Travis Conway got on his bad side. During a riot, which we think was planned, Pittman left the door to Conway's cell open so two inmates could kill him. Only Conway killed one of the inmates and nearly killed the other one. He got himself a life sentence and a final transfer to ADMAX."

Judge Branch couldn't hide his amazed expression. "So do we think this Conway fellow put out hits on the three of us?"

Donnie replied, "That's exactly what we think, and we also think he issued the orders through James Todd right before he killed himself in his cell. Sort of a final screw you to the system. What we don't know, and are trying to figure out, is how Todd arranged for the hit man or hit men to perform the jobs."

"So do you believe it was more than one hit man? Because if it was just one, then I may have killed a double murderer in my home."

Bryce answered, "Almost certainly multiple hit men, Judge. Julie was shot execution style, Andrew Pittman was blown up in his driveway, and your guy tried to garrote you. These fellows usually have one method they're comfortable with and they stick to it."

"Well, I think you're onto something. Who's the prosecutor?"

Bryce and Donnie looked at each other uneasily.

"You do have a prosecutor, don't you? I can't imagine the Bureau working something this complex without buy-in from the US Attorney's Office."

Donnie answered, "Judge, this one is a little . . . sticky. There are competing jurisdictions, and political friction has kept everyone in my chain of command from signing on to the case. Truth be told, there isn't a case, at least not officially. Agent Chandler is retired, and he and I are working this one off the books."

The judge howled a deep belly laugh that caught Bryce and Donnie off guard. "Well, it's a good thing I'm retired, or I'd have both your asses in a sling. I can't begin to imagine how many procedural violations you've racked up. What's your long-term plan?"

"It's all hinging on what we find out from James Todd. If he tells us to go to hell, there's not much more we can do, but hopefully he doesn't know that. We've got him in a tough spot. If he cracks, I will take what he gives me to my ASAC, and at that point he won't have a choice but to open a full investigation. This is murder for hire, and the three victims are all federal officials. I'll probably spend the rest of my career picking up brass at the firing range, but I really don't care."

The judge smiled warmly. "Well, what you're doing certainly takes courage, and I appreciate that. For my part, nobody will know you were here, least of all Sheriff Freeman. But I sure would like to see whoever sent an assassin to my home get what he has coming to him." He rose from his chair, walked toward the door, and held it open. "Keep me informed, will you?"

Donnie shook his hand once more on the way out. "Count on it, Judge."

CHAPTER 28

JAMES TODD rolled over and looked at the alarm clock on the bedside table. It read 1:45 a.m., or ten minutes since he had last checked. His wife was asleep next to him, unaware that her husband hadn't closed his eyes since they retired four hours ago.

He hadn't mentioned a word to her about his meeting with the two FBI agents in his office earlier that day, and how could he? She knew nothing about the Network, and would leave him if she knew the details of his involvement with the quasi-anonymous circle of for-hire criminal entrepreneurs. Not that a divorce would be the worst thing that could happen to him. He had funneled a small fortune in ill-gotten earnings to an offshore account in Belize, and she was none the wiser. She could take him for everything he legitimately owned and he would still live comfortably for the rest of his days. The problem, for the moment, was the number of those days, and he predicted it to be a small number indeed if the Network's partners decided he was a security risk.

He laid awake for another few hours, running the scenarios through his head, judging the risks and rewards of each, calculating the odds of emerging from his situation alive and not spending the rest of his life in a federal prison cell. In the end analysis, there was only one logical path, and so, at 5:00 a.m., he rose from his bed, walked into the kitchen, poured himself a cup of coffee, and made his decision.

———————

Lashelle Washington arrived at the office promptly at 8:00 a.m., as was her routine. She liked her alone time in the mornings before her boss and his endless parade of derelict clients robbed her of the peace and quiet that was in short supply in the law offices of James Todd. She fixed herself a cup of coffee, skimmed the office copy of the *Atlanta Tribune*, and set about organizing James's calendar for the day, assuming he showed up. He had left in such a hurry the day before, she wasn't sure if she needed to start calling clients to reschedule their appointments. The first one was set for 10:00 a.m., and if he wasn't in by nine, she would do just that.

At 8:20, there was a knock at the office's exterior glass door, which she kept locked until just before Mr. Todd showed up for work. She looked up from her desk and saw a towering young man dressed in khakis, a button-down shirt, and a sport jacket, a briefcase in his hand. He was athletically built, good-looking, and . . . Nordic? His close-cropped blond hair and steel-blue eyes reminded her of one of her favorite movie villains, Russian boxer Ivan Drago from the *Rocky* series. *Too clean-cut and respectable-looking to be a client in this place,* she thought. *Probably lost.*

"Can I help you?" she asked without getting up from her seat.

The visitor replied through the glass. "Is this James Todd's office?"

"Yes, but we're closed. Mr. Todd doesn't come in until at least nine, and you need an appointment to see him. You can come back during business hours and I'll set you up with one."

"I have a delivery."

She barely looked up this time. "Honey, we take deliveries during normal business hours. You'll have to come back."

"From McNair Industries."

Lashelle sprang from her chair, nearly knocking it over, and rushed to unlock the door. Once her visitor was inside, she threw the bolt behind them as her standoffishness evaporated. "You have something for me?" she gushed.

"I do," he replied with a smile. "Could we maybe do this somewhere out of the view of the general public?"

"Let's go in Mr. Todd's office," she said, leading the way. Once inside, she closed the door behind them, and he placed the briefcase on the desk.

"Do you want to count it?" he asked, as he opened the briefcase and retrieved a brown envelope.

"I really don't know. I mean, I don't see why I can't trust you, but maybe just let me take a peek."

"Sure thing. Take your time." He put the envelope on the desk and she sat in Todd's chair, her hands trembling as she opened the flap. She pulled a small stack of hundred-dollar bills from inside, still wrapped in the orange-and-white paper band that identified the amount as ten thousand dollars.

"And Mr. Todd will never know I called you, right?" she asked, staring down, mesmerized at the sight of more cash than she had ever held in her hands.

He had moved behind her, retrieving the silenced pistol from the shoulder holster concealed under his sport coat and releasing the safety. "Guaranteed, sweetheart," he answered, as he placed the muzzle to the bottom of her skull and squeezed the trigger.

He left her body in the chair, her head lolled back and eyes wide open, as he retrieved the money, stuffed it back into the envelope, and replaced it in the briefcase. With his business complete, he turned to the personal task at hand, retrieving a pair of dental extraction forceps from his jacket pocket and positioning himself once again behind Lashelle Washington's motionless corpse. He pulled her head toward him with his left hand and pried her mouth open with his thumb and forefinger. With his right hand, he inserted the forceps past her front teeth and felt for the first molar behind the bicuspids, the tooth dentists would call number twenty-seven. If asked, he would never be able to explain why he extracted that particular tooth from all his victims, other than it was the first trophy he had ever taken and he was a creature of habit. He grasped it tightly with the forceps and began wiggling back and forth until he felt it loosen, then pulled it up and out of her mouth. It was a perfect, clean extraction, and he wrapped the bloody tooth in a tissue, placed the tissue in a ziplock bag, and put the bag in the briefcase alongside the cash-stuffed envelope.

Then he turned one of the client chairs toward the door and took a seat, his pistol at the ready, and waited for James Todd to come to work.

———

The clarity and focus from four hours ago had been replaced by fear, doubt, and a nagging voice in his head, taunting him with "what if?" scenarios. What if the partners didn't care that he did the right thing and told them about the visit from the FBI? What if they decided the only way to truly ensure his silence was to silence him themselves? On the other hand, what if the FBI wasn't bluffing, and they had what they needed to indict him and take him into custody? If the Network was concerned now, the news that he was facing federal charges would only reinforce their decision to eliminate him as a potential government witness.

Rock, meet hard place.

In the end analysis, it had come down to either running from the FBI or running from the Network. One meant legal trouble, another certain death. He was an experienced defense attorney and would take his chances with the legal system.

Still, he continued second-guessing himself as he parked his car next to Lashelle's in the strip mall lot. He took his briefcase from the passenger seat, locked the car, dropped the keys into his pocket, and walked toward his office.

The voice chided him as he approached the door. *What if?*

The lights were on, but Lashelle wasn't in her usual spot at her desk.

The voice was a little stronger now. *Where is she?*

He paused at the door, scanning the waiting area for his secretary. The *Atlanta Tribune* lay open on her desk, despite her longstanding practice of placing it next to his daily calendar on the desk in his office.

Louder. *What's going on?*

His heart raced and his mouth went dry. He stood frozen at the door, almost reached for the pull, and then he saw it, in the space between the door itself and the jamb. The deadbolt was thrown in the locked position. In four years, Lashelle had never failed to have the office door open and the newspaper on his desk when he arrived for work. Until today. Of all days.

The voice in his head was screaming at him now, just a single word, over and over.

RUN.

Donnie checked his watch as they finished their breakfast at the kitchen table.

"He's got one hour."

Bryce chugged the last of his coffee. "And what's the plan if he stiffs us?"

"I haven't thought that far ahead. We don't have enough to charge him, and he probably knows that. We shot our wad in his office when we told him we knew about his visit to Travis Conway. What we need is a wiretap, surveillance, and a forensic examination of his computer. We need James Todd working for us. And we're not going to get any of that until I have enough to convince Greg Peoples this is a real case."

Bryce nodded. "It was a long shot at best, partner. And it's not like we're giving up. We know what we have, we just need to find another way in. We will."

"So when are you heading back?"

"Today, I suppose. You need to show your face around the office and I need to get back to work, or what little of it there is right now."

Donnie's phone buzzed. He looked at it and showed the screen to Bryce. "Unknown number."

"You think it's him?" Bryce asked.

"One way to find out." Donnie put the phone on speaker

and barely got "hello" out of his mouth before James Todd started talking.

"Listen very carefully, you're only getting one chance at this. When I hang up this phone, I'm throwing it out the window. Tell me where to meet, and it had better not be anywhere near the FBI office."

"Fair enough. How familiar are you with Atlanta?"

James answered, "I've lived here my whole life."

"Okay, do you know Little Five Points?"

"I do."

"Meet us in the Vortex parking lot. I'm driving a black Ford Expedition. We'll be there in thirty minutes."

"You'd better be."

PART II

CHAPTER 29

TRAVIS CONWAY wasn't always a cautious man. To the contrary, his hardheaded, reckless personality was the reason he spent nearly half of the first thirty-seven years of his life in prison. And while he was destined to die behind bars, it probably would have happened decades sooner had he not had the good fortune to share a cell with Devonte Carter.

As an unwritten rule, black and white inmates were separated at Reidsville, at least on the cellblock. But overcrowding in the late 1980s supplanted the loose system of segregation designed to keep the peace, and Travis returned from the exercise yard late one afternoon to find his new cellmate settling into their shared ten-foot by ten-foot home. He was surprised, but not offended or upset. His personal shortcomings were plentiful, but racism was not among them. They introduced themselves and then quietly went about their lives without becoming too familiar too fast, as etiquette dictated in their situation.

Over time, they began to trust one another and share the parts of their life stories that led them to being guests of the government. Devonte was several years older than Travis, tall and lean, with a shaved head and deeply set eyes that contrasted sharply against his skin, projecting a sense of sorrow and wisdom at the same time. He was soft spoken, and when he did speak, he did so with a quiet confidence that made Travis stop and listen intently, something he had rarely done before. One of Devonte's favorite sayings was, "The loudest one in the room is the weakest one in the room."

Devonte was in the later stages of a fifteen-year sentence for aggravated assault, stemming from a drive-by shooting of a rival gang member's house. As it turned out, his target wasn't home, but the target's daughter was. She took a bullet to the leg as she lay sleeping in her bed, and the prosecutor, fueled by community outrage, wasn't taking deals. Devonte wasn't the shooter or even the driver, but being along for the ride was enough. He pled guilty and received the same statutory maximum sentence as everyone else in the car. Shortly after being incarcerated, he renounced his gang affiliations and refused to associate with the prison-based sets of his former brotherhood. It was a choice that cost him dearly. In his first few years behind bars, he was assaulted no less than six times, including a pair of stabbings that landed him in the prison infirmary, and a beating that left his right arm withered and useless. When they realized there was nothing they could do to bring him back into the fold, his tormentors gave up, leaving Devonte to survive on his own, and he did by abiding the prisoner's code: Mind your own business, don't ask questions, and don't ever, EVER snitch.

If Devonte was older, wiser, and reformed, Travis was still young, dumb, and looking for trouble. As their bonds grew, Travis began sharing details of the exploits that had landed him behind bars, including the one that started it all. Devonte's reaction was a mixture of surprise and amusement.

"Let me get this straight," he said. "You robbed a cop hangout . . . during lunch?"

Travis shrugged. "I didn't know it was a cop hangout. There were about five of them eating at a table around the corner from the register, and when the clerk screamed they all came running. What can I say? It wasn't my lucky day."

"You weren't unlucky. You were careless and unprepared."

"What do you mean? How was I supposed to know who eats lunch at the Varsity? I thought it was just a college joint."

"By doing your homework," Devonte scolded. "You don't just run into a business, stick a gun in the cashier's face, and take off with the money. You should have been in there half a dozen times before you robbed them. Eating. Watching. Listening. At different times of the day. Seeing who came and went. Stuff like that."

"I didn't have time for that," Travis replied. "It was just a hot dog stand, for Christ's sake. I wasn't planning some fancy train robbery."

"And how did that work out for you?"

"About the same as your drive-by. If you're so smart, why are you in here?" Travis sneered.

"Because for one moment in time, I didn't have the sense to listen to my father's advice," Devonte answered. "He was an electrician, and he had this saying . . . belt and suspenders. He got it from working around high voltage electricity, and knowing the importance of checking and double-checking a line was dead before grabbing hold of it. Leave nothing to chance. Trust nothing but your own instincts, and double-check those, too."

Devonte continued. "I knew who I was getting in the car with that day, and I knew they had a beef with another gang member. I could feel something was wrong, but I made myself believe them when they told me we were just going to the liquor store. The next-door neighbor caught our license tag as we drove off, and the cops were on us in five minutes." He turned his palms toward the ceiling. "And here I am."

Travis laughed. "I guess we're not so different after all, are we?"

"We're very different, Travis. I know what I did wrong, and I've owned it. You're still making excuses. And all that poor unlucky me shit is going to keep landing you in the same place until you're really unlucky and it gets you killed. Start thinking things through. Have a backup plan for the backup plan, and for crying out loud, learn to trust your instincts. Belt and suspenders, Travis. Belt and suspenders."

A year and a half after he landed in Travis's cell, the state of Georgia deemed Devonte's debt to society paid, and he was paroled. His replacement was Sal Pinti, and Sal and Travis got along famously. Sal was a leg breaker for a small-time gangster in Atlanta, and he looked every bit the part—a swarthy behemoth of a man with fists like volleyballs and a giant head that seemed directly affixed to his shoulders. He was loosely affiliated with the Genovese crime family, and was serving seven years on an aggravated assault charge after roughing up a strip club owner who was late on his payments.

Once the two trusted each other, they shared their stories, as Travis had with Devonte. It turned out Sal was much more than just a leg breaker, and he had an impressive number of mob-ordered hits under his belt. He was also everything Devonte had warned Travis not to be: impulsive, reckless, and a slave to his temper. When Sal came to him late one night with the plan, it was Travis's turn to be the voice of reason.

"Say that again . . . a helicopter?" he asked.

"Yep. It's so simple I can't believe nobody ever thought of it before," Sal replied. "Everyone thinks about tunneling out, or trying to climb the fence, or cutting through it, or sneaking out in the laundry, stupid shit like that. These guards have seen all that before. It won't work."

"But a helicopter will?"

"Think about it. Who in their right mind would even expect it? A fight breaks out in a corner of the yard, and the guards are distracted for a minute or two. We move to the opposite corner where the chopper swoops in, drops a rope, we grab ahold, and he flies away with us. Start to finish, the whole thing takes thirty seconds."

For a moment, it sounded like a good idea. It was dangerous, but it was a prison break, after all. If they were successful, the reward was freedom, which was more than worth the potential risk.

"And who's flying this chopper?" Travis asked.

"You know Kiki?"

"The Rasta-looking white dude?"

"That's him. His brother was an Army medevac pilot until he got discharged for failing a drug test. Since then he's been flying loads for Kiki's former supplier between Jamaica and Key West. Kiki says he can rent a chopper that will do the job. There's room for six of us, Kiki plus five."

"And what is Kiki getting out of all this?" Travis inquired.

"Better odds. He's pretty sure a sniper will try and pick off the prisoners hanging onto the end of the rope. It's a tough shot, hitting a moving target like that, but if there's six of us dangling from the helicopter, the chances of him getting hit are lower."

"What do you know about this brother? Does he have the skills to pull this off?"

"How would I know that?"

"By asking. How long did he fly for the Army? Did he do any combat tours? If he's running dope, does he get high? I want to get out of here as much as you do, Sal, but a stoner chopper pilot might not be the best plan."

"Yeah, well, I'm not gonna look a gift horse in the mouth. You want to ask Kiki for a résumé, go ahead."

Travis wasn't done. "What about the chopper itself? Where's he getting it? Is it capable of lifting six full-grown men off the ground? How long do we have to hang onto the rope? Where is it dropping us, and where do we go from there?"

Sal saw he wasn't convincing his cellmate, and he raised his hands in surrender. "I get it, Travis. You're out. We'll find a sixth guy. There's plenty of guys who want out of here and are willing to take the risk."

"Good luck. And if you have a brain in that cannonball you call a head, you'll take a pass too. You've got six years left, less than that if you don't do anything stupid. And Sal, this escape plan is one of the stupidest things I've heard in a long time. Somebody's going to get killed."

The escape unfolded mostly as Kiki had planned. Moments after four inmates staged a fight in the southeast corner of the prison's largest exercise yard, a Robinson R44 appeared from behind a tree line a half mile away, piloted by Kiki's brother Dennis and trailing a fifty-foot rope. The distraction gave the escapees the time they needed to assemble under the hovering chopper at the facility's northwest corner, grab the loop handles tied into the rope, and signal the pilot they were ready to be lifted away.

The sniper was almost too late. He brought his Winchester .308 to bear on the scuffle, where he remained focused until the noise of the rotor blades broke his attention and he turned to see the last of the prisoners taking hold of the tether. The rules of engagement were clear: Deadly force was authorized to prevent the escape of a fleeing prisoner. They were about two hundred yards away, and as the helicopter started pulling the slack out of the rope, he placed his crosshairs in the center of the group and began firing.

The first round struck the dirt at the prisoners' feet. The second tore through an inmate's thigh as they were being hoisted upward, and he fell twenty feet to the ground, right back where he had started, but with a bleeding femoral artery that would spell his end. Kiki's plan was holding, as he had surrounded himself with his fellow escapees and was, for the moment, unscathed.

The Robinson R44 was designed to carry a pilot and four passengers comfortably, and it strained under the load of the five remaining prisoners tied to its belly, but made enough altitude to get the job done. When the end of the rope was clear of the fence, Dennis pushed the cyclic control forward and began putting distance between himself and the prison. His load lightened when another prisoner was struck by a sniper round, this time falling some sixty feet to an immediate death on the asphalt surface of the visitor's parking lot.

The sniper's final round missed the prisoners altogether. Instead, it pierced the plexiglass on the pilot's side of the windscreen, where it entered Dennis's left temple and exited the right, taking with it the upper half of his skull and most of his brain. The chopper stopped in midair, where it seemed to hover perfectly for a second or two, its forward momentum ceased as the pilot's hands fell away from the collective and cyclic sticks.

But with nobody at the controls, the tail rotor caught the prevailing wind and spun the rear of the craft violently around, beginning a final, corkscrewing death dance toward the ground two hundred feet below. The remaining four prisoners, Kiki included, hit the ground a split second before the doomed aircraft, where two of them were sliced in half at the waist by the still-spinning main rotor. Kiki and the other less fortunate member of the escape party were crushed by the falling aircraft carcass, but did not die immediately. Their demise came as the fuel tank gave way and ruptured into a ball of flame, cooking them alive. Sal was right. From start to finish, it was all over in less than a minute.

And since Travis had stayed in his ear since their conversation one week prior, Sal ended up being right about one more thing. He decided, in his own words, the "juice wasn't worth the squeeze," and opted out of the plan the day before it unfolded. Kiki found another inmate more than willing to take his spot.

It was the bloodiest day ever in the Georgia State Prison system, and Travis congratulated himself for not being a footnote in its historical accounting. For the first time in his life, he had considered the consequences of acting on his impulses, and it saved him. He was pleased with his personal transformation, and while he knew he wouldn't leave prison a better man, he would at least be a better criminal.

And he would never go back.

CHAPTER 30

STONE MOUNTAIN, GEORGIA, OCTOBER 1995

Lloyd Daniel stared at the ticket in his hand, then back at the "Life" section of the *Atlanta Tribune* laying on the desk in front of him. He compared the numbers for what must have been the dozenth time, reading them aloud and in his head, pointing to each with his finger, then with a pencil. He placed the ticket directly underneath the numbers in the newspaper and compared them another two or three times. They didn't change. He had won the lottery. Five million, two hundred thousand dollars.

He knew most lotteries paid out their advertised jackpot as a twenty-year annuity, and winners who chose the "lump sum" option could expect about two-thirds of the jackpot sum, which he calculated in his head at around three-and-a-half million. Uncle Sam and the state of Georgia would take 40 percent of that in taxes between them, leaving him just over two million dollars, free and clear.

But he would have to share it. Not that a million dollars was anything to sneeze at, but the idea of giving his wife a seven-fig-ure payday was more than he could stand. And she would get her half, probably more. It wouldn't matter that she had been sleeping with her therapist for the better part of the last year. Lloyd had his own skeletons and indiscretions, ones she knew about, and she

150

would use them mercilessly against him if he dared serve her with divorce papers. He would be publicly embarrassed. He would be thrown out of his own house. His five-minute-old dream of being a single multimillionaire would end before it started.

She had to go.

He thought about killing her after he discovered the affair, but dismissed the idea. It was too cliché, too obvious. The enraged, cuckolded husband confronting his cheating wife and her lover in the act and shooting them both in the marital bed they had defiled. He would spend the rest of his life in prison, and for what? Their twenty-year marriage had long since gone cold, and Lloyd was more meal ticket than husband to her. Her death, like their relationship, would be devoid of passion. This was a business decision, not an affair of the heart.

And that was why he knew he couldn't do it himself. He mulled the idea of hiring a hit man, but how exactly did one go about finding a mercenary killer who wasn't actually an undercover cop? Lloyd Daniel had done some bad things in his forty-five years, but orchestrating a cold-blooded murder was out of his league.

He secured the lottery ticket in his safe and walked into the garage where his three mechanics were all at work on separate vehicles. Walking past the first two, he stopped at the far service bay where his latest hire was installing new front discs and pads on a Ford F-150. He stopped what he was doing just long enough to acknowledge Lloyd's presence.

"Morning, boss," he said over his shoulder.

"Good morning, Travis. Have you got a minute? I need to see you in my office."

Lloyd beat around the bush, making small talk for a few minutes. *How are you liking the new job? Making the transition from prison okay? Your parole officer stopped by last week; he seems like a nice guy.* Eventually he got to the point of the conversation, though he made no mention of the winning lottery ticket, allowing Travis Conway to believe his only reason for wanting his wife dead was her serial philandering.

Travis leaned back in his chair and folded his hands across his chest. "Why are you telling me this?"

"Well, Travis, you spent . . . what? The last ten years of your life in prison?"

"Fourteen, between Jackson and Reidsville. So you think because I'm an ex-con, I'm also a murderer?"

Lloyd shook his head. "No, not at all. What I do think is that you know people who could help me. I also think I can trust you when it comes to whether you might call the cops. And finally, I think—I know—you could use some extra money. I'm paying you ten bucks an hour, right?"

There was a long silence while Travis pondered the offer. If Lloyd was working with the cops himself, this would be the most obvious case of entrapment in legal history. He dismissed the idea of a setup.

"Let's say I knew someone. Let's say we could get this done. There are conditions."

"Such as?"

"Such as it would cost you. Ten thousand each, twenty thousand total. And once you commit, you don't call the shots anymore. It gets done the way I say it gets done. And the biggest condition: When your wife ends up dead, the cops will be looking at you for it. If you point your finger at me or anyone else, you join her. Understand?"

Lloyd nodded. "I understand."

"Good. Now tell me everything about your wife. And I mean everything."

CHAPTER 31

TRAVIS HAD HIS PARTNER IN MIND before leaving Lloyd's office.

Sal Pinti had been released six months before Travis, and he'd settled in Augusta, about two hours east of Atlanta. He was surprised to get a phone call from his former cellie, and was intrigued by the offer of a visit to catch up. After all, two old friends can always reminisce over the phone, unless there's something to discuss that can't be subjected to prying ears. They agreed to meet at a barbecue joint just off I-20, midway between Atlanta and Augusta, and within ten minutes of sitting down, Sal was in.

"Sounds easy," Sal said as he shoved a trio of greasy fries into his mouth. "Wait 'til she's alone in the house, break in the back, and get it done. Couple of minutes tops."

"No," Travis countered. "We're doing this my way. No offense, but the last time you said something was going to be easy, it involved a helicopter and ended badly."

Sal winced. "I guess I deserved that. What's your plan?"

Travis replied, "The therapist has a cabin on Lake Oconee. She makes an excuse to get away about once a month. I followed them up there last month and they stayed put for three days straight. So if we do it as close as possible to their arrival, we buy at least a couple days when nobody will be looking for them. The cabin is way off the beaten path, and there are no neighbors for at least a half mile in any direction. It gives us time to get there, set up, and clean up properly after the job is done."

"Why involve the shrink? Are we doing them both?"

"That's how it has to be," Travis answered. "Murder/suicide. Make it look like the husband had nothing to do with it. I told him to get out of town and give himself an alibi the cops can check out. Go to New Orleans or Vegas for a few days, use his credit cards at the hotel, you know—leave a trail."

"Okay, well, if I'm doing two jobs, I'm getting paid for two jobs. Twenty large."

Travis smiled. "I figured you'd say that, and I thought about upping the ante as soon as I decided to make this a two-fer. I'll talk to Lloyd and tell him the price of his freedom just went up. He does a good business and a lot of it is in cash, so I don't think he'll bat an eye."

"Good. So tell me about the therapist. Is he a big tough guy? Bodybuilder type? Are we gonna have trouble with him? I don't want to have to beat on him or tie him up and leave rope marks on his wrists. Cops know how to look for that stuff, and it doesn't jibe with suicide."

"Way ahead of you, Sal. He's an average-sized guy, but that won't matter. He's the murder victim. She's the suicide."

"Really? That sounds a little backward from the normal storyline. Usually it's the guy who loses his shit, kills the girlfriend, then realizes what he's done and eats his own gun."

"I know," Travis answered. "But then I thought . . . she's the one seeing the shrink, right? Maybe he decided to call it off. Maybe we knock her around a little bit and make it look like he

155

beat her. There are lots of ways to play it, but in the end it looks like a loony bitch went off the deep end and took her boyfriend with her. They're both married and he's screwing his patient, so there won't be much sympathy for either of them. The cops aren't going to bend over backward to solve this one."

"If you say so. When do you want to get this done?"

"Well, first I need to go back to Lloyd and tell him about the new fee structure. I'll get half for each of us up front. Then we have to wait until our two lovebirds plan their next getaway. I'll give you a call."

"Sounds good."

CHAPTER 32

AS TRAVIS PREDICTED, Lloyd didn't flinch when he explained the plan and demanded the additional twenty thousand dollars for the job. What Travis did not know beforehand was that Lloyd would hand him the down payment right there in the office, and that he had the money stored in the safe beside his desk. Travis watched silently and without expression as his boss dialed the combination, opened the steel door, and retrieved two bundles of cash, which he handed over as casually as if he were tipping a valet.

"She said she's going to visit her mother weekend after next. Maybe the only person on this earth she hates more than me is her mother, so there's your opportunity."

Travis pocketed the bundles and replied, "All right, then. You're getting out of town?"

"Yep. I liked your idea about Vegas. Everywhere you go there's a dozen cameras on you. And I'll use my credit card for the flight and hotel. I'll stay gone for three or four days, then when I get back I can play the part of the concerned husband and call the police to report her missing."

"Whatever makes you happy. One last question: Is your wife right- or left-handed?"

"Right-handed. What the hell does that have to do with anything?"

Travis ignored the inquiry. "Okay, Lloyd. We've now entered the binding part of the agreement. It's a green light from here on out, and you remember all my conditions, right?"

"I do. Good luck."

———

Trisha Daniels was not, in fact, visiting her mother, and the job went according to plan. Travis and Sal were waiting in the cabin when they arrived, and the boyfriend was dispatched immediately with a pair of shots to his chest. For good measure, Travis grabbed a knife from the kitchen and inflicted a series of a dozen stab wounds on his face, neck, and torso, believing it supported the narrative of an enraged lover.

Trisha made it easy on them, collapsing into a near catatonic state and curling into a fetal position in a corner of the cabin's living room. As she lay dazed and sobbing, Travis dragged her across the floor to where her lover's body lay, and where Sal was waiting with the gun he had used to end the man's life. She barely resisted as Sal transferred the gun from his gloved hand into hers, raised it to her temple, and fired a single shot. He placed the gun on the floor next to her body, then retrieved the knife and curled her right hand around the bloodied handle before leaving it next to her therapist.

Sal and Travis spent the next half hour double-checking their work and waiting for nightfall. As the sun set below the horizon, they walked back down the long dirt road to the car they had parked a mile away.

"So when's your boss back in town?" Sal asked as they pulled out of the marina parking lot. "I need to get paid."

"He's going to stay gone for about three more days. Don't worry, we'll get our money. Maybe a little more."

"What's that supposed to mean?"

"I'm not sure yet. Do you know a good safecracker?"

CHAPTER 33

MYLES MCCLURE was an expert safecracker, and Sal had used him on several occasions when breaking the legs of an overdue debtor was uncalled for or too risky. A former locksmith from Camden, New Jersey, Myles lost his state license and bond after pleading guilty to an aiding and abetting charge for copying post office box keys at a hundred dollars apiece on behalf of the leader of a petty theft ring. He went underground, and had since offered his services to clients on a strict "no questions asked" basis. His fee for a safe job was five thousand dollars plus expenses, and Travis and Sal decided to split a portion of their earnings to finance the job, provided Myles could get to Georgia before Lloyd Daniels returned from Las Vegas.

At 2:00 a.m. the following day, Travis and Sal crouched in the darkness of Lloyd's office while Myles went to work. Neither the single cylinder deadbolt nor the antiquated magnetic reed alarm sensor on the garage's rear door had proved a challenge, and the vintage Mosler floor safe wasn't putting up much of a fight either. On his fourth try, Myles found the correct combination on the spin dial and opened the door.

Travis motioned him away from the safe and took his place on the floor, where he began removing the contents under Sal's watchful eye. There was more cash, but nowhere near the amount

Lloyd had plucked from the safe a week ago, or the amount Travis was hoping to find. There were two guns, a Smith and Wesson .38 revolver and a Glock nine-millimeter pistol, both loaded. A half empty bottle of Johnny Walker Blue Label and roughly two ounces of marijuana in a plastic baggie rounded out the inventory, along with a nondescript brown accordion folder containing miscellaneous business and legal documents.

Sal was visibly disappointed. "I thought he kept all his cash in there?" he asked.

"I never said that. What I said was that he pulled twenty thousand out like it was no big deal, and so I thought maybe there was more. He probably got it from the bank and had it in there to pay us afterward, so when I came in for the advance it was already in the safe."

Neither Travis nor Sal wanted to discuss their dealings with Lloyd in front of Myles, so they paid him and sent him on his way. After he left, they discussed their options.

Sal said, "There's about thirty-six hundred dollars there. Not worth the hassle of taking it and getting the cops involved. The guns are worth a couple hundred each on the street, so it's the same thing . . . the juice ain't worth the squeeze. I don't smoke weed, so that's no good to me. I think we just blew a few grand apiece on an empty hole. Your boy had damned sure better pay us when he gets back."

"Oh, he's good for it. I explained to him in detail what happens if he goes back on his word or talks to the cops."

Sal sighed. "Alrighty then, let's put all this shit back and get out of here."

"In a minute. Go grab two cups off the coffee bar. This is a hundred-dollar bottle of scotch. I made almost a year's salary off this job, and the least I can do is toast it with Lloyd's booze."

Sal retrieved two paper cups and set them on the desk. As Travis lifted the bottle to pour, something caught his eye.

"What's that?" he asked.

"What's what?" Travis replied.

"On the bottom of the bottle. Looks like there's something on it."

Travis re-corked the bottle and turned it over. A small baggie was taped to the underside, containing a piece of white paper that had been folded into the same size as the square bottle bottom. He carefully removed the tape, then the paper from the bag, unfolding it to reveal the printed side. When he realized what he was holding, his curiosity morphed into anticipation.

"It's a lottery ticket."

"I can see that," Sal replied. "Is it a winner?"

"I can't tell from this. It's not an instant win ticket, so you have to see if the numbers match the drawing for that date. And this ticket is six weeks old. We would have to find a newspaper from the day after the drawing or call the Georgia lottery and ask them."

"Well, do you think it's a winner?"

Travis thought for a moment, then answered. "Why else does someone keep a lottery ticket, and why do they keep it hidden under a bottle of booze in a safe?"

"So what do we do now?"

Travis's eyes gleamed, and his smile stretched from ear to ear. "Who do you know in Las Vegas?"

CHAPTER 34

THE STORIES APPEARED two weeks later in the *Atlanta Tribune.* The first—*GBI Seeks Clues in Disappearance of Dead Woman's Husband*—was just below the fold on page three. Buried twelve pages back in the Metro section was the second, barely three column inches long, sans byline: *Richmond County Woman Agnes Shepard Claims Lottery Jackpot.*

A small photo of Agnes accepting the oversized check accompanied the story, with her looking every bit the demure Southern matron—the kindly grandmother personified and just the sort of kindhearted soul who made the losers say, "Well, if it couldn't be me . . ."

Which was ironic, because in truth, Agnes Shepherd was one of the meanest, nastiest excuses for a human being that Sal Pinti had ever met, including his mob associates and fellow inmates. On more than one occasion he heard her threaten her overdue tenants with castration and all other forms of mutilation if they were late on another rent payment, and he was sure she meant it. She was a virulent racist who would not allow Blacks, Hispanics, Asians, or Jews in her boarding house, either as tenants or guests. Her cursing made even Sal blush on occasion, and he never saw her without a cigarette dangling from her lips. When she drank, which was every day from noon until bedtime, she was even more difficult to tolerate.

But Sal paid his rent on time, in cash, every month, and kept his room quiet and neat, which somehow endeared him to the old coot. When he approached her with the offer to pocket ten thousand dollars for playing the role of jackpot winner, she accepted without question. Twenty-four hours after her performance at the Georgia lottery headquarters, the money was in her bank account, and the day after that it had been equally divided between Sal and Travis Conway.

Lloyd Daniels's body was never found.

CHAPTER 35

AT TRAVIS'S INSISTENCE, the two of them put their winnings in safety deposit boxes, and other than normal living expenses, spent none of it for six months. When they were sure there were no eyes on them and Agnes Shepherd's fifteen minutes of local fame had expired, Sal delved yet again into his seemingly endless Rolodex of criminal associates and found somebody to clean their money.

Red Acheson owned a string of "Buy Here, Pay Here" used car dealerships between Destin and Panama City, catering to a high-risk, low-credit-score clientele who wanted to drive something newer and more stylish than the stereotypical bargain lot clunker. Long before the advent of anti-predatory lending laws, dealers like Red were free to charge upward of 30 percent interest to buyers who were either too desperate or too ill-informed to make wise financial decisions. His average customer ended up spending two to three times the book value on their purchases, with Red, of course, carrying the note. It was lucrative, cash-based, and tailor-made for laundering money.

Red was sixty-five years old, tall and thin, with a dark tan and a thinning head of gray hair pulled into a ponytail that draped halfway down his back. He wore a loud Tommy Bahama flower print shirt, khaki shorts, and flip-flops for their meeting at a café near one of his lots, and Travis would have mistaken him for a tourist if Sal hadn't called across the room to his old acquaintance, who was already seated at a booth near the kitchen. They slid in across from him, shook hands, and ordered a round. Once the beers arrived, the car dealer got right to business.

"Sal tells me I can be of service. How much are we talking about?"

Travis was still uneasy about the idea of discussing his new-found wealth with a stranger, but Sal shot him a reassuring nod. "A little over a million."

Red didn't blink. "Cash?"

"It is. I have it in a safety deposit box for now."

"Very good. And how do you want to do this? All at once or a little at a time?"

Travis hadn't thought that far ahead. He looked at Sal, then back at Red. "What are the pros and cons of each?"

Red took a long draw from his beer. "Well, it depends on your objective. If you want to cash out and spend it all at once, say to buy a new house for instance, we can set something up through my contacts at one of the Indian casinos. You'll walk in, play dollar slots for about an hour on the machine they set up for you, and hit a million-dollar jackpot. All said and done, you'll keep about seventy-five percent of your million after they get their points and I get mine. But don't forget they're going to have to generate a W-2G to the IRS, so count on another thirty percent of that going to Uncle Sam. In the end, you'll keep about half a million, but you will have access to every dime of it right away, and it will be pure as the driven snow."

Travis winced at the idea of sacrificing half his money just to keep things legal. "And the long-term plan?"

"The short answer is, it's cheaper. First off, you deal with me and only me. I can't move a million through my business all at once, but if you want something that looks like a monthly salary, I can do that. My rate is twelve percent, so let's say you give me a hundred grand and you want it back over the course of a year. My cut is twelve thousand, so the remaining eighty-eight thousand we split into twelve monthly payments that we disguise as salary. You keep more of your money to start with, and by taking it over time you probably save half what you owe the IRS by staying in a lower tax bracket. And, at the risk of stating the obvious, it's just going to generate less attention than a sudden influx of cash. But it's your choice."

Travis mulled his options. "I like the low-key option, but how do we explain that I'm your employee when I live in Georgia?"

Red replied, "That's the beauty of this business. I have a network of independent haulers who pick up and deliver cars for me from all over the country. I moved over four thousand units last year alone, so it's nothing for you to invoice me as just another contractor who delivered a hundred cars at nine hundred bucks a pop."

"Would I need to buy a trailer to make myself look legit?" Travis asked.

Red laughed. "My friend, you are WAY over-thinking this."

Travis replied, "No one's ever gotten pinched for overthinking. Prisons, on the other hand, are full of under-thinkers."

"You're right, but trust me, the IRS doesn't audit returns for honest, working-class Americans making less than a hundred thousand dollars a year, unless you do something stupid like try and claim eighty percent of your income in deductions. I've been doing this for twenty years, and I've never had a client get hurt."

Travis looked at Sal, who once again indicated his approval with a silent nod. "All right, let's get moving. How do we start?"

Red replied, "We start with your money. Decide how much you want to give me, how fast you want it back, and how you want me to send it back to you. I can mail you a check or direct deposit it into a bank account. At the end of the year, I'll generate a 1099 form with the amount I've disbursed to you, so you can use that to file a tax return. And like I said, at that point it's completely clean, for you to use as you wish."

Travis nodded. "Sounds good. I'll make another drive down next week, and we can get this thing rolling. How do I get in touch with you? I'm not a fan of talking on the phone, too many prying ears."

"Do you have an email address?"

A puzzled look came over Travis's face. "What the hell is email?"

Red answered, "It's a new way of communicating over the internet. Every provider has their own email system, but you can send messages to anyone, no matter who their provider is. My tech-geek friends tell me it's not completely secure, but much more so than running your yap on an open phone line."

Travis winced. "I guess I'm going to need to buy a computer and some internet, however that works."

Red laughed. "Just go to one of those big box stores that sells computers and tell them you want their tech team to come out to your house and set everything up for you. It costs about fifty bucks. They'll have you up and running in no time."

CHAPTER 36

FOR ALL ITS HYPE, Travis was unimpressed with the World Wide Web. A week after the bespectacled, pimple-faced kid from Best Deal delivered and installed his new computer, he had yet to appreciate the allure of what everyone else was calling "the future of information sharing." He logged on once a day to see if he had any email, and he spent ten minutes browsing the latest news stories, any of which he could just as easily read in the newspaper or watch on television. There was a surprising amount of pornography, but like the news, it wasn't anything he couldn't find elsewhere. He predicted that the internet, like pet rocks and Rubik's cubes, was a passing fad.

On a Monday morning nearly two weeks into his experiment with technology, he received his first email. It was from RedAuto@asn.com and read:

Hi, and thanks for your interest in the 1992 Jeep Wrangler. It is still here on the lot, but I've had quite a bit of interest in it, so I would suggest you don't delay if you are planning to take it for a test drive. How about Wednesday morning at ten? Does that work for you?

Travis clicked on the *Reply* button and typed, *See you then.* The following morning, he withdrew $100,000 in cash from his safe deposit box and headed south.

Red met him in his office at one of his three Panama City locations, and they went over the details of the arrangement again. Travis could expect to receive his first paycheck the following week, and with Red's urging he agreed to have it electronically deposited into a bank account in Georgia. "The less paper, the better," Red advised, and Travis knew he was right, even though the idea of money he couldn't see was still well outside his comfort zone.

Red placed the cash in his safe, and a thought momentarily crossed Travis's mind, which he quickly dismissed. *Let's not go to the well one too many times*, he told himself. He stood from his chair and offered his hand to Red, who shook it firmly. "Pleasure doing business with you," Travis said.

Red smiled. "There's more business if you're interested," he said. "I'm always looking for someone I can trust."

Travis asked, "What did you have in mind?"

"Well, that depends on your appetite for money and your tolerance for risk. I've developed a few side jobs here and there I could offer someone like you to increase your income. Sal speaks highly of you, and I trust his judgment. Do you mind if I ask, what did you do time for?"

Travis was silent for a moment. He didn't share the details of his prison record with most people, but then, most people weren't laundering his money, either. He felt a show of faith was in order. "The first stretch was for armed robbery. A buddy and I held up a hot dog stand called The Varsity in Atlanta, and I didn't know it was a cop hangout. I never made it out of the parking lot. The second time was for arson. The company I was working for fired me for getting into a fight with my boss, so I torched one of their trucks. I mean, who else were they going to look at but the ex-con they'd shit-canned the day before? Looking back, I was one dumb son of a bitch in my younger days. But I did my time, never snitched on anyone, and I think I've learned from it all."

Red replied, "What do you think you've learned? How to be a better person?"

Travis laughed. "I wouldn't go that far. Let's just say I'm not going to do something stupid enough to land me back in the joint."

Red smiled. "That's good, Travis, and I won't ask you to do anything stupid. I'm also a careful man. Can you open a few more email accounts and get me the addresses?"

CHAPTER 37

WITHIN TWO WEEKS, Travis received another cryptically worded email. It was from a different address than the first, but seeing as how Red Acheson was the only person with whom he corresponded via the internet, the sender's identity was obvious.

Hello, and thanks for inquiring about the Mercedes. I've got it priced at $10,000. If you're interested, please give me a call.

After their previous meeting, Travis had learned of another piece of technology that had debuted while he was in prison: single-use, pre-paid "burner" cell phones that could be purchased at discount stores, used for a short period of time, and then thrown away. Travis suggested using them as a supplement to email communications, and Red reluctantly agreed.

Travis pulled a fresh one from its box, inserted the SIM card, powered it up, and dialed the first number on the list of a half dozen phone numbers he had been given.

Red answered on the second ring. "How are things in Georgia?"

"Good enough, I suppose. What do you have for me?"

"Pickup and delivery. You'll need to rent a twenty-four-foot truck in Macon and drop it off in Miami."

"Anyone getting hurt?" Not that he minded from an ethical standpoint, but if the job involved violence, he would expect to be paid a premium.

Red replied, "Absolutely not."

"Any candy on board?" Travis had made it clear to Red that he would not, under any circumstances, dabble in the drug trade or with drug dealers. If he had learned anything during his lengthy prison stretches, it was that dopers were more likely than the average criminal to get caught, and once caught, far more likely than their colleagues to cut a deal with the police and rat out their associates. Too many of them violated the dealer's cardinal rule: "Don't get high on your own supply," making them unreliable, unpredictable, and prone to cave under the slightest pressure once they were in handcuffs.

"No candy. If you're up for it, I'll have the contact in Macon email you. That's about all we need to talk about over the phone."

"Good. Let's do it."

The load consisted of three dozen Yamaha 225 horsepower outboard boat motors, worth a half million dollars on the retail market. A week earlier, they were on a shipment bound for a marine dealer on Long Island before the truck was hijacked and the driver beaten into a coma. The details were of no interest to Travis, who was smart enough to figure out he was driving a truck full of illegal or stolen goods from Point A to Point B, and that was all he needed to know.

He parked the rental at a nondescript warehouse on Macon's west side, walked three blocks to a local coffee shop where he ate breakfast for one hour, and returned to find a beefy padlock and fresh railroad seal on the rear door's hasp. The keys, as promised, were on the front seat, and he began his journey toward south Florida without speaking to or meeting his contact in person. He obeyed the speed limit religiously, signaled all his turns, and stopped for a full three-second count at every stop sign.

Twelve hours later, he pulled into the parking lot of yet another warehouse, parked the truck, and left the keys in the glovebox. He made the final call on his burner phone to hail a cab to Miami International Airport, where he rented a car for the one-way trip back to Atlanta, with a stop in Panama City to collect his pay.

CHAPTER 38

TRAVIS WAS neither greedy nor reckless, and the next year saw him declining more job offers than he accepted. Still, Red valued and trusted him, and the offers kept coming via coded emails and thirty-dollar disposable flip phones. Usually, the work involved transporting stolen goods up and down the East Coast. On one occasion, Red enticed Travis to venture outside his comfort zone and earn what he jokingly called "danger pay."

The client in Salina, Kansas, owned a failing restaurant and needed it burned to the ground for the insurance money. Red remembered Travis's conviction for arson and assumed, correctly, that he would have no moral objections to the assignment. Two weeks after Travis agreed to take the job, the 220-volt line powering a deep fryer at the Spicy Chick shorted out, overheating and starting a fire. The blaze spread through the kitchen and engulfed the dining area before the town's volunteer firemen could be roused from bed and respond. Investigators ruled it an accident, the insurance company paid out, and Travis redeemed himself as a professional arsonist after his miserable failed attempt some fifteen years prior.

All in all, Travis liked his new life. Almost a year to the day after his first payment, he delivered another $100,000 to Red, leaving him a comfortable, debt-free existence for at least the next eight years. A man of modest means, he lived quietly in a small two-bedroom house and drove a five-year-old pickup that was neither showy nor dilapidated. He carved out an existence that kept him off the radar of the police and the IRS, but he still kept his eyes open for something more—the next big score that would bankroll him for the rest of his life.

He never could have dreamed that opportunity would present itself when Sal Pinti was arrested.

Sal had a higher tolerance for risk than his friend, and thus fewer qualms about dipping his toe in the drug trade. Unbeknownst to Travis, Sal had been running dope for Red Acheson and his associates since well before the three of them met together for the first time.

The phone call was from a number Travis didn't recognize, so he let it go straight to voicemail. The message was short and to the point:

"Mr. Conway, my name is Louis Nardozza, calling from Columbia, South Carolina. I represent Mr. Salvatore Pinti, with whom I believe you are acquainted. He is currently indisposed and asked that I get ahold of you. Please call me at your earliest convenience."

Travis plucked a new burner phone from its box, powered it up, and dialed the return number.

"Louis Nardozza speaking. Mr. Conway, I presume?"

"Uh-huh. How did you get my number?"

"Well, as I said, I am the attorney of record for Salvatore Pinti, and he is currently incarcerated in Myrtle Beach, South

Carolina. He asked me to get ahold of you and advise of his situation, which is, to put it bluntly, not good. Before we get into that, perhaps we should discuss your representation, which I am happy to provide. As a matter of fact, I recommend it."

"And why is that?"

"Because it gives us latitude to discuss matters pertaining to your legal interests. I'm sure you're familiar with attorney/client privilege."

Because the cops can't listen to this call if I'm your lawyer.

"Okay, do I need to sign a contract or something like that?" Travis asked.

"A verbal agreement will do for now. Do you agree to retain my services as your attorney?"

Travis thought for a moment. Law enforcement officers could play some dirty tricks, but calling and pretending to be a lawyer was so beyond the pale, he could take credit for the Kennedy assassination during this call and walk away. Plus, this Nardozza fellow had his personal number, which only Sal and a few other close friends knew. He decided to take the chance.

"Yes. You can be my lawyer."

"Great, let the record reflect that I, Louis Nardozza, am now attorney of record for Travis Conway. Gentlemen, if you are listening, it is now time to hang up."

"Is that some kind of a joke?" Travis asked, clearly not amused.

"Mostly, but you never know. If a tape of this conversation ever makes its way into a courtroom, it'll be thrown out faster than a can of rotten tuna. I'm just dotting all my i's and crossing my t's."

"Okay, so what's the deal with Sal then?"

"The police stopped him two days ago with fifty kilos of cocaine hidden in the tires of the pickup truck he was driving. With his record, he's looking at some significant time behind bars, even if he cooperates and takes a plea deal. Which I'm sure you know is not going to happen."

"Uh-huh. Well, even if he did, how would that concern me? I don't have anything to do with dope or dopers, and Sal knows that."

"Understood. What you should know is Mr. Pinti is certain he was set up. The arresting officer told him he failed to signal a lane change when he pulled him over, which is nonsense because Mr. Pinti was traveling in the right lane, at the speed limit, and hadn't changed lanes in several miles. Further, the officer asked Mr. Pinti if he could search the vehicle, and when Mr. Pinti agreed, another officer with a drug dog was on scene in less than two minutes. The dog went straight to the tires, the vehicle was impounded, and Mr. Pinti was detained while they got a search warrant and pulled off the first tire. After that, he was arrested. It was all just too perfect, too scripted to have been a random vehicle stop on a deserted stretch of road in the middle of nowhere."

"Okay, I'm sorry this happened to my friend, but again, what does it have to do with me?"

"Mr. Pinti's concern is due to the fact that you and him have worked for the same person. The person who gave him this particular job. The one with the colorful name. If there's a leak in the organization, you could be at risk as well."

"All right. I get it, and I appreciate the advice. Does Sal need anything from me? Money?"

"No. Mr. Pinti is well prepared to deal with his situation. He and I have done business for many years, and he will accept the consequences of his situation without turning on his friends and associates. It's regrettable, but it comes with the territory in his line of work. He just wanted me to reach out to you so you could protect your own interests."

"I will. Thanks for calling, and please give my regards to Sal."

"Done. And keep my number, Mr. Conway. I'm not your average attorney. People like you need people like me. Good day, sir."

Travis closed the flip phone, thought for a moment, and packed an overnight bag. This was not an email conversation, and certainly not a phone conversation, not even on a throwaway. This would have to be dealt with in person. He went to bed early in preparation for the next day's drive to Panama City.

CHAPTER 39

RED WAS visibly unhappy to see him, but he closed the door to his office and offered Travis a seat.

"What brings you to town?" he asked, his eyes betraying the fact that he knew full well the reason for the visit.

Travis spoke in a near whisper as he stared across the desk. "What happened to Sal?"

Red sighed. "That was unfortunate. Like you, he accepted a job, and like you, he knew the potential consequences. My understanding is that he was unlucky. Some backwater cop pulled him over and found the cargo. End of story. It doesn't happen often, but it does happen."

Travis was having none of it. "Great story, Red. The only problem is he was pulled over for some bullshit violation like not using his turn signal. By an interdiction unit from a specialized drug task force. And they had a dog waiting around the corner when Sal gave them permission to search the car, because he knew they wouldn't find the load in the tires. And all of this on a back road fifty miles west of Myrtle Beach, not on an interstate where those interdiction cops normally work. Somebody knew what he was driving, what he was carrying, where he was going, and how he was getting there. Sal was set up, and I need to know by who."

Red held his hands up in protest. "Travis, if you're trying to insinuate for even a second that I—"

Travis cut him off. "I'm not saying it was you. If it was you, I'd be in jail too. But whoever it was, you know them. You brokered the deal. So I need their name. And that's not a request."

Red folded his hands in front of him on the desk and cleared his throat. "Travis, try to understand. I can't let that sort of information go. In my business, all I have is the trust of people like you, who know that no matter what, I won't give up their identities. Not to you, not to the police, not to anyone."

Travis leaned back in his chair, reached upward in an exaggerated stretching motion, and brought his hands to rest with his fingers interlaced behind his head. In so doing, he intentionally exposed the Colt Python he was wearing in a shoulder holster so that Red could see it and understand the gravity of the moment. He posed that way for a few seconds, then leaned forward in his chair and drew his face to within inches of Red's.

"You know what?" he hissed. "I'm thinking maybe it was you."

It wasn't the first time Red had been threatened with a gun. But there was something about Travis's voice and demeanor that told him this was no idle threat. He kept his voice calm and measured, but the fear in his eyes was unmistakable.

"Travis, don't."

"Don't make me."

Ten minutes later, Travis left Red's office with the identity of the cocaine supplier who sent Sal on his fated mission.

———————

"Nice to meet you in person," Louis Nardozza said as he shook Travis's hand. The leather and mahogany appointed office sat on the fifteenth floor of Columbia's newest and shiniest high-rise, boasting views of the Congaree River and the University of South Carolina. A receptionist brought coffee service on a silver-plated tray, and Travis felt uneasy in the luxurious setting.

"You're still my attorney? What I say here stays here?" Travis asked.

"Most certainly. As long as you don't tell me about your plans to commit a crime, and particularly a violent one, I am prohibited by law from discussing our conversations with anyone else."

"Okay then. And the same thing applies when you talk to Sal? They can't tape you talking to him in the jail?"

Louis laughed. "They wouldn't dare. But even so, I'm careful when I talk with clients, whether it's here in my office or at the county lockup. I take it you need me to tell Sal something?"

"Actually, I need you to get some information from Sal. He has a friend in Las Vegas I need to talk to. I don't know anything about him, except he helped us out a couple years ago. Sal will know who I mean. I just need to know how to get ahold of him. Can you make that happen?"

"Sure, that shouldn't be a problem. Sal has pretrial motions set for next week, so I need to go see him anyway. We may have caught a break."

"How so?" Travis asked.

"The state police bungled the chain of custody on the cocaine. There's a 24-hour period during which it cannot be accounted for. I'm going to petition the court to exclude the drug evidence."

"So if you get the dope thrown out, Sal's in the clear?" Travis asked.

"It's certainly better for him. But if he was set up as I suspect, then there's probably an informant on the other end who's going to testify. At a minimum, they could still pin a conspiracy charge on Sal."

"What if there's not a snitch?"

"We've been over this. There are too many coincidences for an informant not to have been involved."

Travis shook his head. "That's not what I mean. I mean, what if there's *no* snitch? As in, what if the snitch goes away?"

Louis didn't blink. "Then I would say Mr. Pinti's prospects of walking away from all this are dramatically improved. And beyond that, I strongly recommend we not discuss this any further. I need to maintain plausible deniability."

"Yeah, sure. Just get me that name."

CHAPTER 40

THEY MET at the Four Queens on Fremont Street in the heart of old Las Vegas. Travis arrived early and got a table in a dark corner in the bar's seating area near a row of noisy nickel slot machines he hoped would keep their conversation private. The room smelled of stale smoke and musty carpet, and it was crowded with locals and tourists looking for the low-stakes table games and cheap buffet food that had all but disappeared from the glitzier, new Vegas strip.

He was nothing as Travis imagined—short and wiry, with a shaved head, thick glasses, and salt-and-pepper goatee, dressed in blue jeans, an untucked button-down shirt, and an oversized navy blazer with leather elbow patches. He looked more like a disheveled college professor than a mob hit man, and Travis dismissed him as he strode by the table and stood at the bar for a minute, his eyes surveying the room. After a minute he walked directly toward Travis and stopped three feet away.

"How's our friend?" he asked, without looking Travis directly in the eye.

Surprised, Travis answered, "As good as can be expected. He sends his regards."

He pulled out the second chair and sat down. "Nice trip?" he asked.

"Not bad," Travis replied. "Ever since they made air travel cheaper than taking the Greyhound, it's all gone downhill, but what are you gonna do, right?"

"Try business class once. You'll never sit in the back of the plane again. And speaking of business, are you looking for same as last time? The guy at the MGM?"

"Pretty much. This one's in Florida. I had him checked out, and he's not a cop or anything like that. He got jammed up on a possession charge, so he set Sal up to make a deal for himself with the prosecutors. Needless to say, he has to go. I can give you all the details if you want the job."

"Why not do it yourself? From what Sal told me, it wouldn't be the first time."

Travis winced. "Sal shouldn't have been talking about that. But anyway, I'm not willing to risk the exposure. The guy I'm putting you on is tied to some of the same people as me and Sal, and I need to stay clear of it all."

"Hey, no problem. Snitches are my specialty. You want me to send a message? Leave a rat in his mouth or something cinematic like that?"

Travis stifled a laugh. "No, nothing like that. Just get it done."

"Okay, and Sal told you it was twenty? Half now, half after."

"Yep, no problem. Are we in business?"

"We are. Let me see what you've got."

Travis slid the envelope across the table and waited patiently while his new acquaintance made his way through the identity and address information he had been able to cobble together.

"This looks straightforward enough. You have a timetable in mind?"

"As soon as you can get it done. Even if he's made a deal with the cops, he's probably going to jail at some point, and then it becomes a more difficult situation."

"Actually, if you ever need a job done on the inside, I can handle that too. But I'll get this one done next week. You brought the down payment?"

Travis reached inside his jacket pocket for another envelope, this one much thicker than the first. "I did," he said as he handed over the cash.

"Then we are all set." The man extended his hand and shook Travis's as he stood to leave.

Travis said, "Wait. Sit back down with me for a minute."

"Sure. What's on your mind?"

"If there was another job, it would be forty?"

"You're smarter than you look. Yes, twenty times two is forty. What's this second job about?"

Travis replied, "I can get you the details tomorrow with the rest of the money. I've been tossing this one back and forth in my mind, and I think it's a loose end that needs tying up."

Charred Remains ID'd as Local Businessman

By Felipe Ortiz
Panama City Journal

Panama City – The state crime lab in Tallahassee has identified the charred remains found after a fire at a local car dealership as the owner of the business.

*Red Acheson, 65, of Destin, is **believed** to have been murdered by a single gunshot to **the head** before the fire was intentionally set at the dealership on Pennel Street last week. Police have not released **a motive** or any suspect information, and inside sources tell **the** Journal there are no leads.*

*Acheson was a fixture in the **local** business community, and well known for the slew **of** "No Money Down" and "No Credit, No Problem" **television** ads in which he personally appeared. Consumer **advocates** routinely decried his business practices as "**predatory**" and accused him of luring financially **vulnerable** clients into paying interest rates sometimes in excess of 25%.*

*Additionally, sources close to **the investigation** tell the Journal that Acheson was "on the **police radar**" for a number of suspicious dealings with **criminal** elements including narcotics dealers and interstate **theft** rings. Those same sources say the investigation has **been** hamstrung by the fire at Acheson's dealership, which **may** have contained a treasure trove of business records **but** was entirely gutted during the blaze.*

CHAPTER 41

THEY MET back at the same table, in the same corner of the bar at the Four Queens. He was more relaxed this time and ordered beers for both of them to celebrate the completion of their business.

"Thanks for the drink," Travis said as he raised his longneck in a toast and slid the third and final envelope across the table. "I take it everything went according to plan?"

"Zero drama," he replied, pocketing the envelope without looking inside. "Neither one of them saw it coming. I still wish you had let me have some fun with the rat, but that was your call. The other guy . . . what was he, like your boss or something?"

"More like an associate. I did some side work for him, and he's the one who put Sal on the job that got him locked up. Problem is, he was also a nice steady source of income, and he was cleaning my money to boot. So now I have to fill those two voids."

"Smurfs are a dime a dozen. The trick is finding one you can trust with your cash. As for income, there are more opportunities than you could imagine in my line of work."

Travis shook his head. "I'm sure there are, but I don't think it's for me. Don't get me wrong, I have no problem getting my hands dirty, and yes, I have been down that road. But when you're a convict, everything you do puts you under a microscope. You can't leave town without telling your PO. Your prints and DNA are on file with the FBI. And whenever something goes wrong, you're the first person the cops come talk to. I think this whole deal with Sal has put some things in focus for me, and I need to start being a little more careful."

"I hear you. But keep in mind, you don't necessarily need to get dirty yourself to make money in this business. The brokers take in more than the shooters."

"Brokers?"

"Yep. Some guys like me are independents. I've got a set list of clients and friends I've developed over the years, and lucky for you, Sal was on that list. Others work for brokers, who set up their deals, get them paid, and take a cut. And then there's guys who do a little of both. If you know how to get a hold of the right people, you can stay in the shadows and you've got a license to print money."

Travis smiled. "Well, that's a problem. I don't exactly have a list of clients and contractors for that sort of thing. And after Sal, I'm not sure I trust email and the internet anymore."

"What are you talking about?" he asked.

Travis laid out the details of the communication plan he used to transact business with Red. The more he spoke, the more incredulous the look on his drinking partner's face became.

"You gotta be kidding me. Emails? Were they end-to-end encrypted with PGP or something like that?" he asked.

Travis shrugged. "I have no idea what that is. Red said it was a safer way to talk than using the phone."

"Well, Red sounds like he didn't know shit about computer security, and it's a wonder you weren't snapped up before Sal, if that's really how you were doing business. Entire industries are making billions of dollars a year creating new ways to protect your privacy on the internet. There are secure places called chat rooms now, where you can have an online conversation with whoever you invite in, and only them. My tech-geek friends tell me that within the next couple of years, there will be a whole new part of the internet that will be completely secret, and they're calling it the black web or the dark web. It's going to be like a shopping mall for everything you can't find on the legit internet."

Travis was wide-eyed, taking it all in. "That's good to know, but like I said, I don't have the contacts to get into your line of work."

"What if I could help you?"

"And why would you do that?"

"This is not a business with a long shelf life. Sooner or later you get ratted out, or someone decides you've become a liability, or maybe even a target gets the drop and you end up dead instead of him. In any case, the operations side of it has become a young man's game, and I've been thinking about a different business model as part of my long-term plan."

Travis asked, "Okay, but why partner up with someone? Why not go it alone? I'm not trying to talk you out of it, but what's that saying? Two people can keep a secret if one of them is dead?"

He laughed. "Based on our history, and especially the last two weeks, I know I can trust you. You have no idea how valuable that is. Guys like you and Sal who keep your mouths shut are a dying breed. Old school, you know? Kids these days get rolled up by the cops and start singing before they get to the jailhouse. And I like how you don't take chances. You could have handled the Florida jobs yourself, but you knew better than to risk the exposure. That was smart."

"Thanks."

"How's Sal doing? He was always a good guy, and I hated to hear he got pinched again."

"His lawyer thinks he can get the case dropped. Getting rid of the snitch might have been the last obstacle."

"Good. We could use him. Anyway, my idea is a system that makes money for the brokers and the shooters, keeps everyone safe and secure, and keeps the cops away. It would be members only, no independent contractors, with a vetting process for everyone, background checks, the whole thing. Bring on a tech guy or two to manage security. And we would need oversight to make sure we don't go off the rails and do stupid shit, like green-lighting a hit on the president. Some kind of system for the most trusted members to review and approve jobs before they're assigned. Almost like a board of directors, or partners in a law firm, you know what I mean? Contract killing meets risk management."

Travis took a long draw from his beer while he pondered the offer. "I might be interested in something like that. I'm supposed to leave for Atlanta in the morning. Let me push it back a day and we can talk details tomorrow."

"Fair enough. But let's find another joint, somewhere on the new strip. This place reminds me of my grandmother's house."

Travis laughed as he stood and offered his hand. "You know what? It just occurred to me, all the shit we've done together and we haven't even exchanged names. I'm Travis."

He took Travis's hand, shook it firmly, and smiled. "Call me Sonny."

PART III

CHAPTER 42

"SO IS IT JUST MURDER for hire, or does the Network dabble in other criminal activities?" Bryce asked, a pen in one hand and a Diet Coke in the other.

They had been at it all day and into the night, in the hotel suite Donnie rented near the Mall of Georgia in northeast Gwinnett County. Pizza boxes and fast-food bags littered the couch and a nearby counter. The table they were seated around was empty, except for a tape recorder, Bryce and Donnie's notebooks, and their cell phones. James, true to his word, had thrown his phone out the window after calling Donnie. His abandoned Audi sedan sat in the Vortex parking lot, keys on the driver's side floor mat, and it would remain there for several more days until it was towed and impounded by the FBI.

James replied, "As I understand it, Sonny and Travis started out with just the murder angle. Later, they dipped their toes in gun running, and that's what got Travis locked up. After Travis went away, Sonny recruited some more partners and returned the network to its roots. Hit men only, because he felt they were more reliable and less likely to run their mouths to the police when they got caught. Also, the demand is higher than you could imagine, and the fees they charge give them a nice healthy profit margin. There are over a dozen partners now, and every one of them made over a million dollars last year."

"Explain the lawyer part to me again," Bryce said.

James answered, "Even with all the precautions, the founders knew it was only a matter of time before somebody ended up in jail, where all the encryption and dark web secrecy in the world won't do you any good. And they wanted a way to communicate with them, to make sure they weren't going to turn on the Network and start making deals. Sometimes that meant taking care of their family and keeping them happy. Sometimes it meant reminding them we can get to them, even on the inside. In any event, lawyers were the messengers, seeing as how we enjoy attorney/client privilege and they can't listen to or tape our conversations."

Donnie cut in. "So I'm sitting there in jail, and some lawyer I've never met shows up and says they work for me. Why am I supposed to believe them?"

James replied, "When you're brought into the Network, all the rules are explained. You know how to bid on jobs. You know how you're getting paid. You know what's expected of you if you get locked up. And you know if a lawyer shows up at the jailhouse, tells you their full name, and then tells you to call them by their nickname, that's a representative of the Network. Like if I walk into the room and say, 'My name is James Todd, but call me Jim,' then I'm the guy. You can trust me and you can talk to me."

"Pretty simple," Bryce said. "So, do you have a whole cadre of lawyers around the country on retainer for whenever one of your hit men screws up?"

James replied, "It doesn't happen all that often. I'm the only full-timer, the only one who knows how the Network operates. So when Travis Conway got word out of ADMAX that he needed to speak to us, I got the call. Other than him, I've handled maybe half a dozen clients over the past couple of years."

Donnie asked, "And what happens if you're not available?"

"We have a bench. Local lawyers who can use the occasional quick fix of cash and know how to keep their mouths shut. No high-profile guys; nobody who runs commercials, and none of them know where the bodies are buried, no pun intended. I mean, they know what they're doing isn't exactly kosher, but at the end of the day, they're paid messengers, nothing more."

Donnie continued. "Changing subjects for a minute. Let's talk about the guy who tried to whack Judge Branch and got himself killed instead. He laid on ice at the county morgue for a month while they tried to identify him. Fingerprints, hair, DNA, everything came back negative. Zero record of him ever existing. Which in this day and age is almost impossible."

James smiled. "Well for that one, you can thank your own people."

"Meaning?"

"Meaning the FBI, and in particular your guys in West Virginia who keep all the criminal databases. As you know, that's where all those inquiries go, straight to the records complex in Clarksburg. We've had one of your folks on the payroll for the last ten years, and whenever a new operator is brought on board, the first thing we do is send his DNA and fingerprints to our contact and make sure he's not in the system. If he is, twenty-five grand and about three minutes of keyboard time makes the record go away. Then we outfit the operator with a new identity that he uses only when he's working, so if he gets rolled up by the cops or shot dead like what happened in the judge's case, there's nothing to find. The only ones who know his real name are him and the Network."

Bryce said, "So tell me again about your meeting with Conway. He gave you the list, and you told him it was a bad idea?"

"I told him the partners would see it as provocative. And at the risk of patting myself on the back, it would appear I was correct."

"So why did you release the list to the Network? Why not just say screw you and let him rot in prison?"

"You have no idea the connections Travis Conway had. He all but told me that if we didn't take care of it, he would find someone else, and that 'someone else' would take care of us. He knew the names of the partners and where they lived. He had at least one of the guards at ADMAX on his payroll. They decided it was less risky to make him happy than to make him angry, so they put the contracts out. It was a split decision, by the way."

Bryce continued. "So he gives you a list with four names. Julie Martinez is dead. Andrew Pittman is dead. Judge Branch is lucky to be alive. And the fourth name?"

James stared at Bryce in amused wonderment. "You're kidding, right? I thought for sure you had that one figured out. Frankly, I was surprised when you told me your name. I mean, you're supposed to be dead by now."

They went on until midnight, then Bryce and Donnie slept in shifts, one sprawled on the king-sized bed while the other watched James, who collapsed on the sofa and didn't stir until

8:00 a.m. While he slept, the two former partners discussed the way forward.

"When are you going to tell Peoples?" Bryce asked.

Donnie shrugged. "I can't keep this guy locked up in a hotel room forever. If we're going to use him, we need to get the US Attorney's office and Marshals on board, probably today, tomorrow at the latest. He needs to get into Witness Security or he's dead as fried chicken."

"You want me to stick around for moral support while you brief Peoples?"

"I'd love to have you there, but it's not a good idea. Greg dislikes me, but he hates the air you breathe. Knowing you were with me for this whole ordeal would only make things worse. As it is, I'm already contemplating my future career in the pizza delivery industry."

Bryce smiled. "I don't think he can hurt you that bad. At the end of the day, you were right. His ego's going to take a hit, that's all. With what you're giving him, he's got no choice but to open a case."

"We'll see," Donnie said. "And what about you? It looks like there's a bounty on your head. Are you going to lay low until we sort all this out?"

"Nope. I'm heading home, getting back to work. I can take care of myself," he said, patting the bulge in his waistband where the Glock forty-caliber pistol was concealed in its holster. "Besides, if the Network's all in a panic knowing their lawyer just got scooped up, maybe I stayed alive just long enough for them to call everything off. That's what I'd do if I thought the FBI was going to be knocking on my door."

"Bryce, I really wish you'd rethink that," Donnie said. "These guys, whoever they are, they're for real. And it's obvious they don't care who you are or what you used to do for a living. When I talk to Peoples, I'm going to recommend putting a protective detail on you, at least for the time being. This is no time to be a hero."

"Do what you think is right, Donnie. You know where I'll be."

They bade one another goodbye, and Bryce took a taxi back to Donnie's house to pick up his truck. During the cab ride, he checked his voicemails and found two new messages. The first was from a woman whose voice he did not recognize.

"Hello, I'm looking for someone named Bryce. This is Robin Diego, and I'm a nurse in the intensive care unit at Miami Methodist. I'm treating a Mr. Harley Christian, who was admitted three days ago in a coma. It looks like he suffered a rather severe beating. He's in bad shape, but this morning he was able to give us your name and number when we asked if there was anyone we could call. If you know Mr. Christian, please call the nurse's station in ICU and ask for me. I'll be at work from seven in the evening until seven in the morning. Thank you."

Bryce's mind was spinning. There were any number of reasons why Harley might end up in the hospital, but a "severe beating"? It could only be one thing. They found him. He thought back to his casual dismissal of Harley's concerns for his safety, and a wave of guilt swept over him. He could make Miami by late evening, and decided a personal visit was in order rather than a phone call.

He recognized the second caller's voice immediately as that of his former courtroom nemesis.

"Agent Chandler, I hope you are well. Ashley Oliver here. When you get a chance, could you give me a call? I want to discuss a matter with you and possibly retain your services. Hope to speak to you soon."

Ashley Oliver? The woman who humiliated him before a packed courtroom? The attorney for the man who might very well have Harley Christian's blood on his hands? *What could she possibly want?* He would return her call when he was home in the Keys, after he had time to speak with Harley and sort out that particular mess. One crisis at a time.

The cab dropped him off at the foot of Donnie's driveway. He threw his bag into the back seat of his truck and headed for the interstate. It was at least ten hours to Miami, and he drove in silence for much of it, the radio off and the events of the past two weeks whirling in his head as he tried to make sense of it all. Two murdered federal officials. An anonymous hit man dead at the hands of a retired judge. A rogue lawyer running for his life from the deadly Network behind it all. On the home front, a mystery soup of supercars, luxury yachts, philandering millionaires, and violent taqueria patrons. Oh, and the other thing.

Somebody wants me dead.

He repeated his earlier prediction, this time in his head. The Network was on defense now. Surely they would hunker down, call off their dogs, and see if they could weather the storm. The last thing they wanted was for one of their operators to be compromised. Whoever had the ticket on him was probably back home, thinking of another way to pay his bills.

CHAPTER 43

HARLEY WAS UNRECOGNIZABLE. His head appeared swollen to twice its normal size, and a large swath of his hair had been shaved away on the left side to allow a path for the surgeon who had cracked open Harley's skull, relieved the pressure caused by the beating, and saved his life. His eyes were blackened, and the left one was swollen completely shut. Multiple lacerations, some stitched and some not, littered both sides of his battered face. At least three teeth were missing from the front of his mouth, and his lips had the appearance of mangled raw hamburger. Tubes ran from both arms, his nose, and underneath his hospital gown.

"We took him off the ventilator yesterday," Nurse Diego said, "but he's still not out of the woods. The ambulance took him to Mariners Hospital in Marathon at first, then they life-flighted him up here to let the neurosurgeons take over. He's a very lucky man. The initial attending gave him a twenty percent chance of making it out of surgery."

Bryce stared at the body laying before him, finding it hard to believe this was the same Harley Christian with whom he had dodged death just a few weeks earlier. "Can he hear us? Does he know I'm here?"

"He's been awake a couple times. Still woozy from all the pain meds, but he's been able to communicate by squeezing our hands and blinking his eyes. There have been a few one-word responses to questions, but he's not easy to hear. It took twenty minutes to get your phone number out of him. The MRI showed extensive damage around the area where the swelling was, and right now he's touch and go. At the very least he's going to have chronic headaches, confusion, and memory loss over the long term. Worst case scenario, he needs professional assistance to live a normal life. But it's too early to tell right now."

"What's his short-term prognosis? How long will he be in the hospital?"

"He'll be in ICU another few days, maybe a week after that on the neurology floor. They're going to watch him very closely to make sure his brain doesn't keep swelling. Even when he is released, they will recommend he go to a rehab facility to evaluate his ability to live on his own. People who suffer these kinds of traumatic brain injuries have to learn to do everything for themselves all over again, from walking and feeding themselves to bathing and using the toilet."

The same wave of guilt Bryce felt when he got the phone message washed over him again. This was his fault, not only for allowing his ego to goad him into pursuing Stanley Murtaugh down the rabbit hole, but for allowing Harley to come along with him to the marina that night. Still, as bad as he felt, he knew Harley wouldn't blame him. It wasn't in his nature. For all his poor life decisions, he had always accepted personal responsibility for his actions. It was a trait Bryce admired from his first dealings with Harley, and one that set him apart from the dozens of snitches and informants Bryce had employed over his years as an FBI agent.

He took Harley's hand, squeezed it gently, and whispered, "You're going to be okay, buddy. You're going to be okay." He didn't know if he believed his own words, or if Harley could hear him, but when he spoke them, the term "buddy" somehow seemed right. Harley Christian was his friend, and it was time he started treating him accordingly.

"Can I stay?" he asked.

Nurse Diego replied, "Sure, I don't see why not. Normally it's family only in the ICU, but from what I can tell, he doesn't have any, at least none who care. Nobody's been here or asked about him since he came in. It looks like you're all he's got."

———————————

Harley woke up the next morning and managed a gruesome smile at the sight of Bryce standing at his bedside.

"How you feeling?" Bryce asked.

"Ike a tuck an me oh-uh." *Like a truck ran me over.*

"The doc says you're going to be okay, but it's going to take a while. Do you know who did this to you?"

Harley breathed deeply through the pain. "Air wah two uh dem." *Two of them.*

"Okay. What did they want?"

"Dey . . . dey wan know who you wuh. I tol dem go huck demsell." The mere effort of forming sentences was exhausting, and Harley appeared to be about to drift back into unconsciousness.

"You did good, Harley, but to be honest I wish you would have just given them my name and avoided all this."

"No way." Harley's eyes closed.

"All right, buddy, rest up. I may need to head down to the house and take care of a few things, but I'll be back. I want you to know how much I appreciate everything you've done for me."

"Ryce."

"Go to sleep, Harley. I'll be back to check on you."

"Ryce," he mumbled. "Dey got eye hone."

"You're not making sense. Go to sleep and we can talk later."

His voice raised to a near panic. "Ryce! Dey got eye hone." As he spoke, he lifted his trembling right hand to his face, mimicking a phone call by extending his thumb and pinkie. When he finished speaking, his hand fell back to his side and he slipped back into his morphine-induced slumber. All at once, Bryce understood what his friend was saying.

They got my phone.

He pressed the call button, and Nurse Diego appeared. "How can I help you?" she asked.

"Where are his personal belongings?" he asked.

"Right there in that nightstand in a plastic bag. There wasn't much. They threw away all his clothing because it was soaked with blood. There was a set of car keys, his wallet, a shark's tooth necklace, and some loose change in his pocket. That's about it."

"Did he have a cell phone when he came in?"

"No, and he was pretty worked up about it the first time he woke up. Wanted to know if we had it, and I told him we did not. It was causing him some obvious distress. Can't say I blame him. If I lost my cell phone I don't know what I would do. All the contact information for everyone I know is in there."

Bryce rubbed his temples and breathed a deep sigh. "Yeah, that's the problem with those things, isn't it?"

There were no less than a dozen roadside liquor stores along the drive back to the Keys, and as he passed each one, his resolve waned. The demons they warned him about in AA spoke to him in loud, clear voices. *One drink. Just one drink. It'll take the edge off. Being an alcoholic doesn't mean I can't drink, it means I can't get drunk. It means I have to drink responsibly. I can handle this. I handled it before Barnesville, I can handle it now.*

None of which, of course, was true. One drink would lead to another. And another. If he was fortunate enough to make it home, he would continue drinking himself into a stupor, black out, and throw away three years of hard-earned sobriety. If he wasn't lucky, he would either get arrested for another DUI and lose his investigator's license permanently this time, or worse. He couldn't recall wanting a drink this badly in years, but he knew the story all too well, and he didn't like the ending.

"Let's change the channel," he said to himself as he drove through Key Largo. He thumbed through his phone to his voice-mail messages, found the one he was looking for, selected "redial," and waited.

She answered on the third ring. "Ashley Oliver."

"Hello, Ms. Oliver. Bryce Chandler here, returning your call."

"Hi, Bryce, and it's Ashley, please. Thanks so much for getting back to me." She sounded nothing like the attack dog he had faced off against in court. "Are you free to meet for dinner this week? My treat. I have something I need to discuss with you."

Bryce proceeded cautiously. "What's it about?"

"I really don't want to get into it over the phone," she said.

"You're going to have to do better than that."

"Look, Bryce, I hope you're not holding a grudge over our encounter during the divorce trial. I'm sure you know I was just vigorously defending my client. It was business, not personal. And the reason I called you is important. It has to do with Stanley Murtaugh, and some of the things I learned about him while I was his attorney. Simply put, I think I might be in danger."

"Call the cops."

"It's not that simple. I'm not sure who to trust."

"But you trust me?"

"I do. I know I said a lot of terrible things while you were on the stand, but like I said, that was business. I also know you're one hell of an investigator, and you're not wrapped up in any of what Stanley was doing. I can explain much more when we meet, and I'll be happy to pay your hourly rate for the work."

As she spoke, Bryce weighed his choices. Telling her off would have been the most satisfying option, but now more than ever, he wanted to know details about the relationship between Stanley Murtaugh and Chase Worthing, and Ashley Oliver might hold the missing pieces to the puzzle.

"I can meet you tomorrow night. Pick a place in the Marathon area."

"Thank you. Are you familiar with Sundown Grille? Great spot on the water if you've never been."

"I've been. Nice place. See you there at seven?"

"Sounds great. And thank you again."

He hung up and kept driving, taking in the endless expanse of blue ocean on either side as he passed from key to key on his way home. He was back in his happy place, but between Harley being beaten nearly to death and the unaddressed threats to his own safety still hanging in the balance, he was anything but content. He drove on, the natural beauty of the Keys welcoming him home, but every passing liquor store calling to him like an old friend.

CHAPTER 44

"TWO-MINUTE WARNING!" the pretty young administrative assistant chirped above the low noise of the crowd. Reporters moved toward their seats, and camera crews took up positions behind their tripods in anticipation of the impromptu press conference. There were at least a dozen print and broadcast media outlets on hand, all lured to the fourth floor of the ultra-modern steel and glass building by the brief press release sent out only hours before. *FBI to announce break in cases of murdered federal officials. Press conference at 2:00 p.m.*

Right on time, Greg Peoples strode into the room and up to the podium, barely able to contain his exuberance during what would surely be the finest moment of his FBI career. He chose his most expensive suit, pairing it with a crisp white shirt with French cuffs adorned by tiny Bureau seal cuff links. His shoes were shined to a high gloss, and he had fussed over his hair for ten minutes in his office before taking the elevator to the presser.

Normally, the principal at such an event surrounded himself with colleagues who played a part in the success of the operation. It was common courtesy to invite subordinate agents or members of sister law enforcement agencies to share the podium and the spotlight, perhaps to even make a short statement of their own. But Greg Peoples didn't want any of that. This was his moment, his day, his case. This was the stuff that made Special Agents in Charge and Assistant Directors, and it was no time for "aww shucks" credit-sharing with the street agents or the local yokels.

"Good morning. I am Assistant Special Agent in Charge Gregory Peoples, and I've called you all here today to announce a major break in the murder of two federal officials, including Atlanta's own Assistant United States Attorney Julia Martinez. As you no doubt remember, Mrs. Martinez was brutally gunned down as she went for an early morning run a few months ago. Shortly before that murder, a federal corrections officer was killed in a car bombing at his home near Terre Haute, Indiana. We now have solid evidence to believe the two killings were linked to one another."

He continued. "Additionally, around the same time there was an attempt on the life of a retired federal district court judge in North Georgia, during which the judge was able to defend himself and kill his assailant. We believe this was to have been the third of a round of four murders which were contracted by a prisoner in the federal penal system and carried out by a secret network of hired assassins who ply their trade on the dark web."

The astonishment in the room was palpable. Reporters alternated between their notebooks and laptops, scribbling questions on the former while drafting their stories on the latter.

"The FBI has worked diligently to solve these crimes since the day they were committed, and our hard work has paid off in the discovery of this murderous network and the arrest of one of its key members. We will continue to investigate the entire organization until we hold every single member responsible for their heinous crimes. I will be happy to answer your questions now."

Nearly every hand shot up at once as the entire press corps clamored for the first question. Greg Peoples pointed to a comely young woman in the front row.

"Good afternoon. Cynthia Alvarez, WST-TV. Agent Peoples, are you saying the person you have in custody is the one who shot Julia Martinez and killed the prison guard in Indiana? And if so, who was the individual killed by the judge?"

"It's ASAC Peoples, and no. We believe those were three different people."

The TV reporter stole a follow-up question. "So who did the FBI arrest?"

"As I said, it's an associate of the criminal enterprise we believe is behind the murders. He is in protective custody at the moment, but we anticipate he will be trading information on the enterprise in exchange for a reduction in the charges he could be facing." He pointed toward the rear of the room. "In the back."

A tall, middle-aged man rose from his seat. "Charles Mizell, Associated Press. What can you tell us about the man who tried to kill the judge, and do you have the identities of the people who murdered the prosecutor and the prison guard?"

"We have not been able to positively identify the judge's assailant, due to what we believe is a sophisticated fake identity scheme the network uses to protect its hit men. As for the other two, we are working diligently on identifying them. I expect to develop more information during continued debriefings of our cooperating witness."

The AP reporter shot back his follow-up. "So in reality, you haven't arrested anyone for the actual murders, is that correct?"

Peoples appeared wounded by the retort. "I never said we had arrested the murderers. We have in custody a significant cooperating witness who knows how the Network operates and can help us navigate the complex system of encrypted communications they used to solicit and pay for murders for hire, not only in the United States, but around the world. The principals in this organization can run, but they can't hide." He congratulated himself on the ability to weave the wisdom of Joe Louis into his performance.

Another television reporter stood. "Amy Black, American News Network. With regard to the cooperating witness: You've already referred to him as 'he,' so I'll assume he's a man and is somehow highly placed in the organization. What else can you tell us?"

"Nothing, other than the fact that he is in a unique position to help us peel back the layers of the organization, and is willing to do that in order to avoid going to prison for the rest of his life. Trust me, he is very well protected. Only the United States Marshals Service and a few select senior law enforcement officials even know his whereabouts."

"And are you one of those senior officials?"

It was a fateful moment, one a less ambitious man would have recognized and navigated more cautiously. Greg Peoples was not merely ambitious, but blindly so, and his ego simply would not allow him to concede the image of complete authority in which he had cloaked himself.

"Of course."

The questioning continued for another half hour, peppering the aspiring FBI Director with everything from the legitimate ("Did you uncover any other murder-for-hire schemes?") to the irrelevant ("What software program did the network use to communicate on the dark web?") to the downright inane ("Is the FBI considering consulting with psychics to find out more about these murders?"). He answered some directly, some less so, and offered the standard "no comment" on others.

The final question came from Kevin Forrester of the *Atlanta Tribune*, who asked, "You said there were four murders contracted by this federal prisoner . . . who was the fourth intended victim? Are they in harm's way, and if so, what is the FBI doing to protect him or her?"

Peoples answered quickly. "The fourth intended victim is well aware of the situation and can take care of himself. And considering the fact that we have effectively dismantled the criminal organization behind these murders, there's really nothing to worry about. Thank you all for your time."

He moved briskly toward the door, ignoring the chorus of follow-up questions, and took the stairs back to his office. He spent the next few hours combing through paperwork, answering emails, and awaiting his starring role on the evening news. Through it all, he remained blissfully ignorant of the hell he had just unleashed.

At 5:00 p.m., the story led the news on all three local networks. American News Network and their conservative competitor, Guardian News, aired excerpts from the press conference on their evening reports, and Guardian News invited a former mob hit man, one who had been thrown out of the witness security program, to provide commentary. The story was front page, above the fold in the *Atlanta Tribune* and three major national newspapers. By 8:00 p.m., the catchphrase "Murder.com" was trending on a half dozen social media platforms, and a small cadre of news vans set up an encampment outside the FBI Atlanta field office. Greg Peoples had finally garnered the attention he aspired to.

———————————

Fifteen hundred miles away, in a modest, nondescript three-bedroom ranch on the outskirts of Fort Collins, Colorado, the stooped, aging man went about his evening ritual. He donned his pajamas, took his daily dose of fiber along with the small pharmacy of pills that kept his blood pressure in check and his prostate from exploding, and let the Boston Terrier out for its final break of the day. As he locked the door and drew the shades, his phone rang. He didn't bother to look at the number; he knew who would be calling and why.

"Hello."

"You saw the news?" the caller asked.

"I did."

"Sounds like they got the lawyer."

"Umm-hmm. I thought we were taking care of him."

"We tried. Our guy got his secretary, but somehow he must have gotten spooked and ran."

"I see."

"You don't sound too upset about it."

"Why, because I'm not cursing a blue streak and slamming the phone down? Of course I'm upset. I have just as much exposure as you and the rest of the partners. Goddamn Travis Conway, that stupid son of a bitch. Gets himself arrested running guns to a street gang, then orders up a hit on the people who put him away? Talk about exposure . . . we should have told him to go fuck himself and let him rot."

"We went over that, boss. He had other ways of reaching out and touching us."

"Yeah, we're still screwed, only now it's the FBI who'll be knocking on the door. How much can the lawyer give them?"

The caller paused. "Well, definitely the details on Travis's job. And the operators he visited in jail, so if memory serves me that's the jobs on the Albuquerque hedge fund CEO and the guy who was screwing his daughter in Baton Rouge. And that's just over the last couple of years. He's been with us, what . . . five, six years? Plus he's seen our faces and knows where we live. Let's just say he can ruin us and leave it at that."

"What about this fourth victim they talked about in the press conference? Can we at least call that off?"

"I can try, but the operator isn't checking his messages; he's on autopilot and we can't recall him."

"And dare I ask who the fourth victim is supposed to be?"

"The FBI Agent who arrested Travis. I think he's retired now."

"Oh, Jesus Christ almighty. This just keeps getting better and better. Call it off. And we need the lawyer gone."

"He's in protective custody, isn't he? That's going to be a tough job."

"Then pay double. Or triple. I don't care. Just take care of it."

"I'll get on it. Any thoughts on where to start looking for him?" the caller asked.

"That cocky little bastard in the press conference said he knows where they're keeping him. Start there."

"Will do," the caller said.

"Let's suspend all operations until we get this sorted out. Once the lawyer is taken care of, we can all meet and figure out the way forward. Let me know when it's done."

"You got it, Sonny."

CHAPTER 45

BRYCE DIDN'T WATCH the news, and he missed the story altogether. The phone call from Wendell Branch the next morning brought him up to speed.

"Good morning, Judge. This is unexpected."

"Good morning, Bryce. Wondering if you had a chance to catch the news last night. Your ASAC put on quite the show. . . Peoples, is it?"

Bryce flipped open his laptop as he replied. "No idea what you're talking about. Did something happen in Atlanta?"

"Well, it looks like the case you and Agent Morris came to me about has blown wide open. The FBI, or at least this Peoples fellow, was on TV last night bragging about how they've solved it and have one of the co-conspirators locked up."

"Dear God. He didn't."

"Oh, but he did. That idiot told the whole world he's got somebody in custody who's going to spill the beans on the rest of the organization. I've seen some poorly advised press conferences in my time, but this one takes the prize. I spoke with a couple of friends who are still on the bench, and the word at the federal building is the US Attorney is livid. He sent a cease and desist order to Peoples's boss, demanding there be no more public statements on the matter from the FBI."

"I don't even know what to say. I knew Greg Peoples was never the sharpest knife in the drawer, but honestly I didn't think he was this stupid."

"So was it you and Agent Morris who rounded up this conspirator-turned-government-witness?"

"It was, Judge. You may remember we told you we had met with a local lawyer earlier in the day and gave him an ultimatum. Well, for one reason or another, he decided to accept our offer, and we spent the next day and a half debriefing him. After that, Donnie was going to let Greg Peoples know everything, and I assume that's when he decided to hold a press conference."

"I think I know why he took your offer," Judge Branch said. "There's another story running on the local news, and I don't think anyone in the media has put the two together yet. A legal secretary was found murdered in her office, and her attorney employer is missing. What did you say your guy's name was?"

"James Todd."

"That's him. Anyway, it's only a matter of time before some junior detective wannabe reporter connects the dots and breaks the story that the dead secretary's boss is the same guy the FBI has under lock and key."

"Well, Judge, I'm sure Assistant Special Agent in Charge Peoples will work that one out. It's not my problem anymore."

"All right, Agent Chandler, I'll let you go. One more thing: You think they'll try and re-order the hit on me? Or are they running scared now that they've been exposed?"

"That's a good question. My instinct is that they're battening down the hatches and don't want to risk drawing any further attention to themselves. But I wouldn't put that sweet little

Hellcat pistol up in the closet just yet. You never know."

"Oh, she's not going anywhere. You have a good day, Agent Chandler, and stay safe."

"You too, Judge. Thanks for the call."

Bryce hung up and spent the next half hour reading online news accounts of the press conference. The arrogance and naivete of Greg Peoples was astounding. The FBI had a long-standing practice of refraining from commentary in ongoing cases, unless it was to ask for the public's help in identifying a suspect. In his quest for his fifteen minutes of fame, Peoples aired sensitive details about the murders and the attack on Judge Branch that would serve no purpose other than to provide fodder to a defense attorney and taint a potential jury pool. Worst of all, he disclosed the existence of a cooperative witness, and then all but dared the membership of the Network to try and find him. Was he trying to get James Todd killed?

He dialed Donnie's number, but it rolled immediately into voicemail. He texted him twice but got no response. After an hour of waiting with no reply, he called Crystal.

"Hello, Bryce."

"Good morning, Crystal. Is Donnie okay? He's not answering his phone."

"He's right here. And I'll let him fill you in on the details."

Crystal handed the phone to Donnie, who sounded like a beaten man. "Morning, Bryce. Sorry I didn't call you earlier."

"What's going on? Did something happen to your phone?"

"They took it. They also took my gun, my badge, my credentials, and the keys to my car. Right before they walked me out of the office and told me not to come back for at least thirty days."

"Holy shit, Donnie. They put you on the bricks?"

"Come on, Bryce. We both know the rules, and I probably broke a dozen of them, the worst of which was trying to strong-arm a lawyer into betraying his attorney/client privilege under false pretenses. Oh, and doing it all without an open case. No Bureau approval, no oversight . . . I'm screwed. Peoples says they're going to seek termination. The thirty-day suspension is just to give them time to put the case together. And then he goes and holds a press conference to take credit for the work we did. You have to admit, it is in keeping with what we've always known about him."

"Donnie, I am so sorry. I never wanted it to go this way. What can I do to help?"

"None of this is your fault. I'm a big boy. I made my own decisions, and I'll live with the consequences. The Agent's Association attorney thinks we have a chance for me to at least keep my job, but even if I do it won't be anything as glamorous as picking up brass at the firing range. Maybe I'll be that guy's assistant."

Bryce stifled a laugh at his friend's gallows humor. "Don't give up. We can't let assholes like Peoples win. He'll get what's coming to him eventually."

"At this point, I don't even care what happens to him. I just want to keep my job. I'm three years from retirement, and if I have to start over again at this point, I'm financially screwed for the rest of my life. Still, I'd do it all again. We did the right thing, didn't we?"

"You bet your ass we did. And I know it sounds awfully convenient coming from a guy who's already collecting his pension, but I'm proud of you. What you did took guts."

"Thanks, brother. I take it you made it back to the Keys okay?"

"I did. Made a stop in Miami to visit a friend who got roughed up by some guys on account of a case he was helping me with down here. They almost killed him, and now I think they might be looking for me."

"Really? What kind of case?"

"That's just it, I'm not sure. Maybe drugs. Maybe money laundering. Maybe both, or something else altogether. It all started as an hourly gig to catch some guy screwing hookers and hiding assets from his wife, and sort of snowballed from there. As a matter of fact, I've got dinner tonight with the target's former attorney. Apparently she's realized what a scumbag her client was and for some reason she wants to discuss it with me."

"Was that the one you told me about? The one who roughed you up on the stand?"

"Yep. Easy on the eyes, but mean as a snake, at least in the courtroom."

"So, dinner?" Donnie asked.

"Yes, dinner."

"Not lunch, not coffee, but dinner?"

"What are you getting at?"

"Nothing. It's just that dinner is the most intimate of all the dining options. Usually when I want to meet someone to talk, at least in our business, it's a cup of coffee, maybe a sandwich at the most. Dinner is dimly lit restaurants, shared appetizers, and if she orders the lobster, it's game on, if you know what I mean. Expectations and all."

This time, Bryce laughed out loud. "You're hopeless. And for the record, she's picking up the tab."

"Well then, you should order the lobster."

He laughed again. "I'll keep that in mind. But this is business, and I'm sure I'm not her type anyway, unless she has a thing for older men who spend their days taking pictures of cheating husbands and medical insurance fraudsters."

"If you say so. But keep your options open. And when you get to the table, pull out her chair. Women love it when men do that."

"You're killing me. I gotta go. Give my best to Crystal and keep me up to date on your situation."

"Will do. And tonight . . . wear something nice. Trust me."

Bryce shook his head as he ended the call. If there was one thing about which Bryce was certain, it was that Ashley Oliver was not interested in him, at least not physically.

Still, he thought, *It never hurts to iron a shirt and maybe throw on some aftershave, right?*

CHAPTER 46

BRYCE ARRIVED five minutes early at the Sundown Grille and waited for Ashley at the hostess stand. She was right on time, and for the second time, he was struck by her raw beauty. The business suit had been replaced by a flowery sundress that showed off her tanned, athletic body. Her hair, pulled back in court, now flowed halfway down her back, and swayed from side to side as she walked toward him. Even in his prime, he told himself, this woman would have been out of his league.

"Hi, Bryce," she said as she extended her hand. "It's nice to see you again."

"Is it?" he asked. "After last time, we could have done just as well never seeing each other again." She responded with a smile and a slight eye roll, and he almost retracted the statement. But the sting of her courtroom assault was still fresh and he wasn't ready to forgive it, especially after the events of the last few weeks.

The hostess led them to their table by the water, where Bryce did in fact pull out Ashley's chair, not because Donnie told him to, but because it was how he was raised. The sun was hovering just over the horizon, glinting off the calm waters dotted by commercial fishing boats on their way into and out of the nearby marina.

Their waitress took their drink orders, and Bryce was impressed that Ashley asked if he would mind her having a glass of wine. Being around social drinkers was never a problem for him, and he assured her of as much before ordering a glass of iced tea for himself. They made small talk about the weather and Keys traffic until the waitress arrived with their drinks.

"Anything to get you started with?" she asked the pair.

"The calamari here is delicious," Ashley said. "Want to share an order?"

Bryce couldn't help himself and laughed out loud.

"Am I missing the joke?" Ashley asked with a smile.

"No, sorry. Just thinking of something a friend told me recently." He ordered the calamari and the waitress left them alone.

Ashley got the real conversation started. "I want to start off by clearing the air about what happened during our unfortunate encounter in the courtroom. I know I took a cheap shot, but you had us over a barrel and it was all I had. My duty is to defend my client's interests, even if they're a scumbag. I'm sure you've been subjected to worse over your career. Do you think we can move past it?"

Bryce appreciated her bluntness. "I guess that's as close to an apology as I'm going to get, so I'll take it."

"Good," she replied. "So how have you been?"

"In a word, busy. There's been some continued fallout from the whole Stanley Murtaugh thing, and a good friend of mine was nearly beaten to death over it. He's recovering in the ICU up in Miami as we speak."

"Oh, no. What happened?"

"I'm not sure how much of it I want to share right now. To be honest, I wish I had never heard of Stanley Murtaugh, or Chase Worthing, or Roger Mackenzie."

She took a long sip from her wine glass. "They're horrible people, all of them. I only represented Stanley, but I met Chase and Roger through him."

"In what capacity?" he asked.

"Well, the whole reason for the contested divorce was that Stanley didn't want April to find out about the sale of the marina and take her half of the proceeds. He figured if he could get her out of his life before he closed with Chase, he would keep the whole twenty-six million in his pocket. Chase had Roger Mackenzie representing his interests, but Stanley never hired an attorney to represent him with regard to the marina. He was a cheap SOB and figured if he was paying me to handle his divorce, I could review the sale documents as a sort of side job. I explained that wasn't the way it worked, but he didn't care. I explained I wasn't a real estate attorney, but he didn't care. All he cared about was selling that marina and getting April off his payroll. So against my better judgment, Stanley, Chase, Roger, and I sat down in my office and hammered out a draft sales agreement. Remember the meeting at Panama Jim's where you heard Roger and Stanley discussing the twenty-six million sale price? This was the formalization of that verbal agreement."

The waitress arrived with the calamari and took their dinner orders. April chose the blackened mahi-mahi, while Bryce ignored Donnie's advice and opted for the Gulf shrimp linguine.

"So that agreement . . . I assume it's the one April found in Stanley's desk?" he asked.

"I never saw a copy of what she found, but that sounds right. Anyway, it's all moot now. The sale is off, and even if it was still on, the judge partitioned the estate, so April won."

"You said Chase and Roger were 'horrible people.' You got all that from a business meeting?"

She shook her head as she swallowed a piece of calamari. "No, that came later. After the trial. When Stanley started going off the rails and getting chatty."

"Chatty?" he asked. "What do you mean by that?"

"Stanley has a drinking problem. A pretty bad one. He kept it in check while he thought things were going his way, but after the judge ruled against us and Chase backed out of the marina deal, he lost control. He was in my office nearly every day, drunk and ranting about Chase, Roger, April, you name it. He even made some not-so-veiled threats against Morgan Landover and you, and I of course called Morgan to let him know. He said he would contact you."

"He did."

"Good. So for whatever reason, during these daily rant sessions, he started telling me about his business dealings with Chase. That's when I found out what sort of people I had become involved with. Chase Worthing is the biggest cocaine dealer in Miami. He's been using his car dealership as a front to hide drug and cash shipments between the United States and Mexico for the past ten years, and he's been laundering the proceeds through his business and Stanley's marina."

Bryce finished off the last of the calamari just as their dinner arrived. April ordered another glass of Cotes du Rhone.

He ate a few bites of linguine, then restarted the conversation. "Why was Stanley telling you all this? I mean, I get the whole attorney/client privilege thing, but why? What did he have to gain?"

She shrugged. "Like I said, by this point he was living in the bottle. Not stumbling and falling down, but drunk enough that

all his filters were turned off. The things he said. . . well, if Chase
Worthing is what Stanley says he is, his big mouth is going to get
someone killed, and I don't want that someone to be me."

"So how much detail did Stanley share about Chase's drug
dealing activities?"

"Chase never brought Stanley fully into the fold, so to speak.
Stanley only saw an actual shipment of drugs one time, when it
was being offloaded from a boat at his marina and put onto a
truck that was taking it to Miami. From the way he described it,
Chase's people weren't happy that he was around, and when word
got back to Chase, he told Stanley to stay away from the marina
after hours, which is when they usually did their business."

"So the drugs came in through the marina and were driven
up to Miami. How did the cash flow back to Mexico?"

"Like I said, Stanley wasn't in on the details of the drug side
of the business. He never saw any money going out, only cars.
There was this one huge megayacht that came into the marina
once every month or so, and it always left with a couple of cars
on board."

"What kind of cars?"

"Exotic sports cars like Ferraris. Stanley said all the big dealers
in the Mexican cartels love their sports cars, but they can't buy them
on the legitimate market because most of them are wanted men,
and they can't show their faces in public down there. So he figured
Chase was providing them as partial payment for the drugs."

He was half right, Bryce said to himself. There was only one
plausible explanation for a pair of supercars spending two days in
a body shop before being shipped to a drug cartel in Mexico. The
money was hidden in the cars, and not just in the glovebox and

under the seats. Chase's men had more than likely removed entire body panels, hidden the cash in the innards of the vehicles, and then put everything back together to look legitimate to the eye of the casual observer, or even a cop or customs inspector performing a routine inspection.

"You said Chase was laundering money through his car dealership and the marina. Any idea how he was doing it?" he asked.

"I don't know anything about the dealership. Stanley told me he generated fake invoices for non-existent fuel sales, boat repairs, and storage fees. He said that kind of stuff is almost impossible to trace."

Bryce shook his head in disbelief. "I still can't believe he told you everything he did. What was he thinking?"

"Probably that he was protected by attorney/client privilege. Which in this case isn't true, because none of the information he gave me had anything to do with our attorney/client relationship. He wasn't telling me this stuff in order to get legal advice, but just to blow off steam and, I imagine, to brag."

"So why didn't you go to the police with the information you had?"

"Because according to Stanley, Chase has at least two local cops on his payroll. And he made it very clear what happened to people who cross Chase Worthing. They disappear. There's this guy named Manuel, a former cartel enforcer from Mexico, and he's Chase's personal goon. Chase offered to let Manuel take care of the April problem before the divorce trial, but he just wanted her out of his life, not dead. After the trial, Stanley wouldn't shut up about how he should have taken Chase up on the offer. I don't want to meet Manuel."

"So why are you telling me all this?" Bryce asked.

"Because Stanley's gone missing, I don't want to be next, and I'm not sure who to trust."

"Define 'missing.'"

She shrugged. "Like I said, he was becoming a regular at my office. If he didn't come by, he called. He was always asking about our next legal steps, even when I assured him we had none. It's not like you have any real hope of winning an appeal when a judge rules against you in a divorce trial, especially when the evidence paints you as the world's worst husband who was trying to deny your poor wife her share of legitimate community property."

"And he stopped coming by?"

"Stopped coming by. Stopped calling. Stopped replying to my gentle email reminders about the $15,000 or so in unpaid invoices he still owes me. I do okay for myself, but that's still a large chunk of change to have floating in my 'receivables' column."

"I imagine so." Bryce didn't have that much in his checking and savings accounts combined. "How long since you last heard from him?"

She drained the last of her wine. "About two weeks. Do you think I have anything to be worried about?"

"Hard to say. On the one hand, if something has happened to Stanley and you're still here, that's obviously a good sign. But if Chase Worthing is running the amount of dope Stanley said he was, then you need to understand those types of people stop at nothing to protect their drugs, their money, and their freedom. And if he's dealing with the Mexican cartels, we're talking about a whole other level of ruthlessness. Those guys don't just kill thieves and snitches. They kill family members to set an example."

Bryce saw the horrified look on Ashley's face and knew he had overshared. The poor woman looked as if she was about to cry.

"Sorry, I didn't mean to scare you, but you need to know these are serious people. Let me ask around with some friends who are still in the business. If Chase Worthing is as big a dealer as you say, he's got to be on somebody's radar."

The waitress showed up to clear their plates, and asked if they wanted coffee and dessert. Ashley ordered a cappuccino.

Bryce asked, "How's the key lime pie here?"

"Best in town," the waitress answered.

He laughed. "Yeah, everyone says that. Let me have a slice, and a cup of decaf." He smiled at Ashley. "You sure you're going to pass on the best key lime pie in all of Marathon?"

She glanced up at the waitress. "Bring two spoons," she said. *What was it that Donnie said about dinner and intimacy?*

There was no more talk of Stanley, or Chase, or nefarious cartel thugs for the rest of the evening. The pie was good, but nowhere near the best in town, and they ordered a second round of coffee and cappuccino as the conversation turned to each other's personal story and how they ended up living and working in paradise. Time passed quickly, and when Bryce heard a vacuum cleaner whir to life nearby, he knew they had outstayed their welcome and the restaurant staff was politely telling them it was time to go.

The waitress brought their bill, and as Bryce reached for it, Ashley snapped it up. When he protested, she reminded him a deal was a deal, and she said she was taking him to dinner. He relented, his masculine pride wounded, but not enough to spoil what had turned into a surprisingly pleasant evening with his former adversary.

As they stood to leave, Bryce said, "I'll start making some discreet inquiries tomorrow. When I know something, you'll know something."

Again, Ashley surprised him. "Good. Walk me to my car?" She reached for his arm and he instinctively bent it at the elbow, giving her a proper spot to rest her hand as he led her through the empty restaurant and out into the warm South Florida night air.

CHAPTER 47

BRYCE WASN'T SURE if the goons at Tres Gatos got a good look at him, but he knew enough not to show his face there or at the marina, at least not during daylight hours. Still, if Chase and Stanley were partners in a drug trafficking operation using the marina as a transshipment point, there was a potential treasure trove of information to be gained, if he could penetrate their inner sanctum.

Developing a source inside the business would be risky, time consuming, and a waste of effort if the source didn't have access to the information Bryce was after. Between Harley's beating and what Ashley relayed to him at dinner, it was obvious he had stumbled onto more than he bargained for when he started looking into Chase Worthing's business. But he still needed to know if Stanley's claims were real, or drunken fabrications, or somewhere in between. He needed a place to start. And he knew one of the most underappreciated yet highly effective means of identifying a potential drug dealer was to steal his garbage.

In the Bureau they called it a "trash pull," and it wasn't always a tool FBI agents had in their bag. The Fourth Amendment to the Constitution prohibited searches and seizures without a warrant, but in 1988 the Supreme Court, in *California v. Greenwood*, ruled in favor of law enforcement. The justices found that trash put out to the curb, or anywhere outside the so-called "curtilage of the home," was considered to have been abandoned by the owner, and thus fair game for the police.

The effectiveness of the technique laid in the simple premise that most people don't pay attention to what they throw away. And not just ordinary citizens, but experienced criminals who should damned well know better. During Bryce's career, he routinely pulled "kilo wrappers," cellophane used to bundle cocaine into uniformly weighted packages, from the trash cans of dopers who had purchased the large bricks of powder and then broken them down into street-level amounts in their homes. A colleague who worked white collar crime and fraud matters found a complete set of printed tax returns in the garbage bin of a subject who was laundering millions of dollars in ill-gotten gains. It stretched the human imagination to believe someone could be so stupid, but as Donnie was fond of saying, "If they were rocket scientists we'd never catch them."

Not that absconding with the contents of a trash can, or multiple trash cans, or an entire dumpster, was an easy task. You had to have a plan, including knowing when the trash would be set out and how you were going to carry it away without being noticed. With a simple pretext call to the trash company, Bryce learned pickup along the marina's route was scheduled for Tuesdays. He planned his approach for the hour between 3:00 and 4:00 a.m. He knew from experience this was a dead zone during which most criminals, even night owls, had gone to bed, and all but the hardest of the hardcore morning people had an hour or two before their alarms went off.

Even under the cover of darkness and with the rest of civilization nestled in their beds, Bryce needed to work quickly. He cleared the bed of his pickup truck, drove to Tavernier along a deserted Overseas Highway, and parked in an overlook position a few hundred yards away from the marina to assess the situation.

Tres Gatos was dark. There were no cars in the parking lot or along the side of the building between the restaurant and marina where Bryce and Harley escaped a violent attack just a couple of weeks earlier. The marina also appeared unoccupied, although lights shone brightly along its backside, illuminating the boats entrusted to its care in the various slips and dry racks. Bryce retrieved a pair of binoculars and scanned the front of the building for security cameras. He found none, which made sense given that everything worth watching was around back, on the water.

He found the targets of his pre-dawn mission: three large, rolling trash cans that had been wheeled to the curb, waiting to be picked up and dumped into a rolling trash compactor. As luck would have it, the system in use in this part of the Keys was perfect for Bryce and any like-minded trash bandit: The driver pulled alongside the bins, grasped them one at a time with a remote controlled claw, and then lost sight of the containers as a robotic arm hoisted them out of his sight before inverting them over the back of the truck and emptying the contents. Not that any driver would care if he was dumping full or empty containers, but even if this one did, he would never know.

There was also a ten-cubic-yard dumpster around the far side of the building marked with a sign reading *Oversized Items Only. DO NOT place daily trash here.* Which made sense, as the fees for emptying a dumpster were four to five times higher per cubic foot of waste than with ordinary trash service. Apparently one of Stanley's few redeeming qualities was knowing the value of a dollar. Not that it would have mattered what was in the dumpster; it was within full view of the security cameras and would have taken too much of Bryce's precious time to make a worthwhile target.

The only issue remaining to consider was *how* the employees at the marina dumped their trash. It wasn't the sort of thing most people thought about, but it made a world of difference to someone in Bryce's position. The trash would either be loose or pre-bagged, with the latter being far more preferable than the former. If it was already in bags, all he had to do was grab the bags from the bins, throw them in the rear of his truck, and drive away. If the trash was loose within the bin, he would have to lift each one and dump it over the side of his pickup bed, and it was possible they might be too heavy for him to handle by himself. He said a quick prayer to the garbage gods and moved toward the marina with a purpose.

Bryce's day got better the moment he opened the first container and saw several white plastic trash bags, each bound neatly with red cinch ties. He threw them into the back of the pickup truck and proceeded to the next bin, where another half dozen identical bags were waiting for him. The final bin contained just two of the white bags, and a heavier duty contractor-sized bag which had been closed with duct tape where a twist tie might have otherwise been used.

He was in front of the marina for just over a minute. He scanned the area as he pulled away and, seeing nothing of concern, told himself the collection part of the mission had been a success. A minute later, he prepared to turn southbound on Route 1 when a Monroe County sheriff's deputy heading northbound turned left in front of him, driving in the direction of the marina. It struck Bryce as odd, given the time of day and the lack of any human activity in the area. Following a marked unit in a deserted industrial area at four o'clock in the morning was out of the question, so he made a mental note of the unit number, which was boldly emblazoned on the front, rear, and roof of every patrol car. In this case, it was 324.

He went right to work when he got home, donning latex gloves, spreading a tarp on his garage floor and dumping the contents of the first white trash bag in the center. There were no surprises, and he made his way quickly through them all. There were lots of empty and partially empty fast-food containers and bags. There was discarded junk mail and newspapers. More than a few empty quart-sized oil containers, greasy rags, and empty parts boxes from the shop where customers' boats were maintained. Plenty of paper, most appearing to be discarded receipts and other legitimate business records, none of it interesting or incriminating.

He saved the dark green contractor bag for last, using a utility knife to slice it open. He emptied the contents onto the tarp all at once, and his heart nearly stopped.

It took a moment to process, but Bryce knew what he beheld on the ground in front of him were the remnants of a murder scene. There was a complete outfit each of men's and women's clothing, both caked in dried blood. Perhaps fifty shop rags, identical to the oil-stained ones he recovered along with the other maintenance supplies, were strewn among the clothing. They were also covered in dried blood and smelled of bleach. What first appeared to be a dead rodent turned out, upon closer inspection, to be either a wig or toupee. The only item in the bag not made of fabric or hair was an eight-inch-long filet knife, its handle wrapped in the same black duct tape that secured the plastic bag.

Bryce's breath came in slow, measured increments as he pondered the horror show before him. Calling the local authorities was out of the question, given Ashley's statement about Chase Worthing having "cops on the payroll." Ditto for the state; they were all fine investigators and honest cops, but you could never know who they might talk to in the sheriff's department. There was only one place he could go to confidently spill everything he knew about Worthing, Stanley Murtaugh, and their apparent criminal enterprise. It was time to call Jose.

He scrolled to his contacts list, found his old friend's name, and dialed the number.

"Bueno?" the voice answered in a thick Spanish accent.

"Jose, it's Bryce Chandler."

"Bryce, mi amigo! How have you been? I haven't talked to you in years!"

"It has been a long time, hasn't it?" Bryce replied. "Are you still in Miami?"

"Sure am. DEA's going to let me retire in about a year. I heard you got out?"

"I did, not on the best of terms, but the pension's still the same, right? Anyway, I need to talk to you about something that didn't start out as much, but now I think I'm in over my head."

"What do you got?" Jose asked.

"I'd rather not talk about it on the phone. I need to see you, the sooner the better. It's big."

"Come on, Bryce, don't do me like that. At least give me some idea what we're going to be talking about."

"Okay. Are you familiar with Chase Worthing?"

There was a brief silence, and Bryce could hear his friend sigh. "Damn, Bryce. Chase Worthing? What have you gotten yourself into?"

"Like I said, more than I planned. I'll fill you in on all the details when we meet face-to-face."

"Roger that, amigo. But until we do, stay well clear of anything having to do with him. When are you free?"

"Now. Tonight. As soon as possible." Bryce knew he sounded desperate and didn't care.

"Okay, let me see if my colleague is available to join us. Do you like Cuban food?" Jose asked.

"Who doesn't?"

CHAPTER 48

HABANA VERDAD SAT in the middle of Miami's Little Havana, the enclave west of downtown that served as the epicenter of Cuban culture in South Florida. Founded by exiles fleeing Castro's revolution in the late 1950s, the mom-and-pop establishment gained a following among locals and visitors alike, who flocked to the cozy café-style restaurant for authentic ropa vieja, yuca con mojo, and arroz y frijoles with fried plantains, as well as dozens of other delicacies which were still prepared as they were in Cuba sixty years ago.

Bryce found Jose seated at a booth in the back near the kitchen, and saw he had company. Jose stood to greet Bryce and introduced his guest, a tall, heavily muscled and liberally tattooed Latino with sharp features and steel-blue eyes that cast an imposing gaze. Bryce wondered if Jose had brought his informant to dinner.

"Bryce, this is Larry Paz. Larry, Bryce Chandler. Bryce and I did some business between Atlanta and Miami with the…. what was it, Crips? Bloods?"

Bryce smiled. "Crips. You have a good memory. Especially since we were dealing with small amounts. I mean, fifty kilos is a pretty big haul in Atlanta, but I know down here it's peanuts, especially for you DEA boys."

Jose laughed. "It's all about building the case, my friend. From small things, big things one day come. Anyway, Larry is the case agent on Chase Worthing, so I asked him to join us. Whatever questions you have, he can answer."

They ordered dinner, and Bryce spent the better part of an hour detailing what he knew of Stanley Murtaugh, Roger Mackenzie, Chase Worthing, the incident at Tres Gatos, and the gruesome discovery in the marina's trash bins.

"So wait," Larry asked, "That was you at the taco joint? You were driving the car they shot up?" His demeanor shifted from fraternal to adversarial.

"Me, and my friend Harley, who is as we speak lying in a hospital room here in Miami recovering from the beating he got when they found him. They must have gotten the plate number on his car and tracked it down to his house. They almost killed him. How did you even know about all of that?"

Larry replied, "We have a few CIs into the organization. Your little dustup caused quite the commotion. From what I understand, those guys were just working security, watching the yacht until it was scheduled to pull out of port the next morning. Then your friend and his friends started chatting about videotaping the cars getting loaded onto the boat, and Worthing's guys didn't take kindly to the intrusion on their business. The one you hit with the car is a paraplegic now."

Bryce shrugged as if he couldn't care less what happened to someone who had tried to kill him. He asked, "And am I correct in assuming those cars were packed with drug money?"

Larry stared across the table. "Well, look at you, mister retired FBI agent. Sounds like you've been doing more than just a little snooping. Good job. Yes, you are correct."

"So if you knew this was going on, why didn't you interdict the cash?" Bryce asked.

"We did interdict some. And we let some walk. Same with the dope. We have Chase Worthing's ass ready to indict any time we want. I can put thousands of kilos on him easily, enough to put him away for thirty years. But up until now, he's still been useful to us."

"How so?"

"Chase Worthing is our highest level US target. But the ultimate prizes are the trans-national kingpins and the enterprises they run. I don't want to just disrupt a cartel's operation, I want to dismantle them from the top down. That takes years of work. It takes international wiretaps. It takes cooperation between governments. And sometimes it means we let a relative pissant like Chase Worthing keep slinging his powder so we can build the case against the boys at the top of the pyramid. In other words, the cartel bosses in Mexico. Cut off the head of the snake, if you will."

"So how much longer does Chase Worthing get to remain a free man?" Bryce asked, his irritation becoming clear. "I get where you're coming from and where you want to end up, but all this 'end justifies the means' stuff is starting to take its toll. My friend was almost killed. Ashley Oliver could be in danger for what she knows. Stanley Murtaugh has gone missing, and my guess is I've got the last set of clothes he ever wore in the back seat of my truck—"

Jose cut him off. "Jesus Christ, you brought that stuff with you? In your personal vehicle? Did you stop to think about what would have happened if you got pulled over and some cop found it?"

Bryce dismissed Jose's concern with a wave of his hand. "Well that didn't happen, and when we're done in here it's all yours. Let's not talk about me getting locked up. Let's talk about Chase Worthing getting locked up. It seems to me he's overdue."

Larry responded, "Slow your roll. Up until now, we've been waiting to see how things shake out down south. We've got most of the cartel dirtied up on phone calls, bank records, and recorded meets with CIs, but the Mexican government is slow to commit on indictments and arrests, mainly because their prosecutors don't want to wake up dead. Our AUSA is a tough old broad and she's ready to go, but it would be nice if we could up the sentencing guidelines on Worthing and Mackenzie to life. I mean, thirty to forty years is where we're at now, and that's all good, but 'life sentence' just has a ring to it, you know? Death penalty would be even better, but that would mean tying them directly to a murder, and so far we don't have anything like that, although it sucks we lost the marina. That would have been a monster seizure."

Bryce stared at Larry quizzically. "What do you mean, lost the marina?"

"You ought to know, you're the one who fucked it all up," Larry snapped. "No offense, you were just doing your job, but we had it all set. Stanley Murtaugh was going to sell the marina to Chase Worthing, and when we took it all down the marina was going in the booty bag. I've seized airplanes, boats, houses, cars, all kinds of stuff, but I've never seized a whole goddamned marina. It would have been epic."

"Wait a minute," Bryce said. "Are you telling me the DEA was orchestrating the sale of the marina for the sole purpose of seizing it from Worthing? If Stanley was using it to launder drug money, why couldn't you just seize it from him? Why all the extra moving parts?"

Larry shot Jose a glance, then answered, "Let's just say it would have been a stretch to take the marina from Stanley. It needed to pass hands to Chase Worthing before it would meet the requirements for a criminal seizure."

"I still don't get it. If they're both part of the same conspiracy, it makes total sense, unless—" Bryce stopped in mid-sentence. Jose and Larry were both giving him that "Got it now, dummy?" look.

"Oh, shit. Stanley Murtaugh was your CI?"

"One of them," Larry said. "And he dropped off our radar about the same time your attorney friend says he stopped showing up at her office. We've been by his house, his office, and the marina. No sign of him. His phone goes straight to voicemail and there's been no incoming or outgoing calls on it since he went missing. He's either cut and run, or Chase decided he was more trouble than he was worth and took care of the problem. His wife April has also disappeared. Didn't you say there were bloody women's clothes in the bag as well?"

"Yep," Bryce replied. "I mean, it could all be an elaborate ruse. Stanley definitely had the money to run and make a new life somewhere else. But I doubt he would have taken April with him. Those two hate each other."

"Yeah, the consensus around the office is Stanley Murtaugh is no more," Larry said. "To tell you the truth, we had just about gotten everything out of him we could. Chase kept him away from the operations end of the business, so he hardly ever saw any dope. We could have used him to testify on the money laundering, but we can still prove that without an eyewitness. It sucks, but I'm not going to lie and tell you I'll lose any sleep over him."

Larry continued, "Still, this is going to speed things along. It was all well and good when we were just running money and dope between Miami and Mexico, but now I've got a missing, probably dead CI on my hands. I have a meeting with my AUSA this week, and if I can't account for Stanley Murtaugh, she's going to get nervous. If Worthing can get rid of one CI, he can get rid of all of them, and the whole case goes to shit. I imagine she'll want to take it to the grand jury, roll everybody up, and call it a day. The Mexican angle will have to wait. No matter really, as soon as Worthing is out of the mix they'll find themselves another dealer and we can pick right up where we left off."

"And the beat goes on," Bryce said.

"That's about the size of it," Larry said. "I'd like to lay more charges than just the trafficking and money laundering, but we never developed a CI with an optic that deep inside the organization. If we could prove Worthing had anything to do with killing Stanley, I could indict him for murder under RICO and his ass would go to death row. Again, though, I would need some credible evidence that Worthing gave the order. Barring that, we've got what we got and he'll spend thirty years in jail like any other dope dealer."

Jose sensed the meeting had run its course, and he cut in. "What about you? Can you promise us you're done poking around Chase Worthing's business? You need to let us take it from here."

Bryce had no intention of making such a promise, and he wouldn't insult his friend by lying to him. "I'm on retainer to Ashley Oliver, and I told her I would let her know if she was in danger. As of right now, my better sense tells me she is. You want me to stay away from Chase Worthing? Put his ass in jail."

CHAPTER 49

LUKE LOWELL was born with fire-red hair and congenitally defective eyes that would need glasses by the time he was five. His MIT-educated mother and father named him after the *Star Wars* icon, and to top it all off, their last name matched that of a prominent character in the *Revenge of the Nerds* film franchise. It seemed the die was cast for the skinny young man who couldn't choose his parents or DNA. But rather than wallow in self-pity, Luke embraced his inner nerd and ran with it. In his teen years he eschewed sports and girls in favor of academic clubs, video gaming, and spirited rounds of Dungeons and Dragons with his like-minded friends. He was smart, but to his parents' disappointment, not MIT-smart. After high school, he settled for a course of study at an online technical vocational college, and three years later found himself armed with a bachelor's degree in data science and no serious job prospects. Enter the FBI.

Lowell saw an ad for the Bureau on a professional networking site and was intrigued. As a young college graduate with zero work experience, he wasn't qualified for the Special Agent position, at least not to start. But there was a list of support positions for which he felt he might be competitive, chief among which was something called "Electronics Technician." According to the ad, ETs, as they were known, installed and maintained data networks, radio systems, and other non-specific "mission-related technical equipment." It sounded interesting, paid better than slinging all-you-can-eat appetizers at Ruby Tuesday's, and at the least was a place to park himself while he figured out what to do with his life. Six months after applying, he started work in the Columbia division.

Two years after that, he was miserable. Most days found him contorted into the passenger compartment or trunk of a newly purchased Bureau vehicle, installing police radio systems, lights, and sirens. "Data network installation" turned out to be Bureau-speak for running telephone wire and fiber-optic cables through suspended ceilings in the squad workspaces, then dropping them through plastic conduit to landline phones and computers when desks were relocated after an interoffice reorganization. The cool stuff he envisioned doing when he applied for the job was hacking into phones, imaging and analyzing criminals' computers, and breaking into houses and businesses to install listening devices. Unfortunately for Lowell, these sensitive jobs were the purview of agents, and specifically Technically Trained Agents, or TTAs. Fortunately, though, the TTAs were often understaffed, and every so often Lowell would be tagged to assist with some of their more mundane tasks—tasks that he found fascinating and which allowed him to play with the Tech Agents' vast array of sexy toys.

In the end, it was one of those toys that got him fired. Generally, the Bureau gave its employees the benefit of the doubt when it came to lost or damaged equipment; damaging or even destroying a piece of a high-dollar kit in the line of duty was often written off as an acceptable consequence of the job. But that leeway did not extend to the careless loss of FBI-issued gear, and not to sensitive equipment such as the Forensic Retrieval Device, or "FRED" as it was nicknamed on the tech squad.

FRED looked like a cross between a computer tablet and the ruggedized briefcase used to carry the president's nuclear launch codes, the so-called "football." It was invented and marketed by an Israeli firm and sold around the world to governmental and police organizations under the condition that it never find its way into the public domain, lest it be used for criminal purposes. And that caveat came with good reason: FRED made child's play of breaking into cellular phones. With the right connecting cords and the stroke of a few keys, it could unlock virtually any phone, from an antiquated Motorola flip-phone to the latest iPhone or Android. Once inside, FRED could download gigabytes of emails, photographs, call histories, contact lists, and text messages to a thumb drive in minutes.

There were seven versions of FRED, each new model more technologically capable than the last, and with those increased capabilities came a hefty price tag. The latest model, FRED v.7, nicknamed ORCA, cost the FBI $65,000 apiece.

When Luke reported the loss of ORCA, it set off a panic in the office. The Israelis would not be happy with their tech marvel falling into the wrong hands, where it could be reverse engineered and used against their own security interests. Recently they had instituted inventory control measures, including requiring the return of a previous model within thirty days of the receipt of an updated one. When FRED v.8 came out and the FBI's Columbia division wanted one, they would have to return ORCA or explain why they couldn't.

Compounding the issue was the sheer stupidity of the circumstances under which Luke lost the unit. He told investigators he was working on a project for the tech agents, and when he was done, he mistakenly put ORCA in his backpack along with his own books and tools. He left the backpack in his car, which was broken into that night at his apartment complex, and everything, including the backpack and ORCA, was stolen.

The story defied credence. There was a police report, and there were pictures of the shattered rear window of Luke's car, but skepticism ran rampant among Luke's peers and supervisors. Everyone knew ORCA wasn't allowed to leave the building unless it was in an official FBI vehicle with an alarm system. The idea that he could have "mistakenly" tossed it in his backpack was also dismissed with an eye roll by everyone who was asked to believe it. The assumption quickly grew that Luke had sold ORCA on the black market, and though there wasn't enough proof to charge him criminally, there was more than sufficient evidence to terminate his employment with the FBI.

The skeptics were mostly right. The story was fabricated, but Luke didn't sell ORCA. He had been planning his exit strategy for the last six months of his truncated career in federal law enforcement, and had decided to put his newfound telecommunications exploitation skills up for sale on the open market, somewhere far from Columbia. And so a few days after being escorted out of the Columbia FBI office, Luke and ORCA made the 650-mile drive to Miami, where a new world of opportunities awaited.

Manuel Del Negro wasn't a patient man. He had been watching the computer geek fiddle with Harley's phone for nearly an hour, and he was losing confidence.

"What's taking so long?" he asked.

"You want this done fast, or done right?" Luke replied. He was taking his time, examining the device and combing through chats on hacking websites, looking for any less intrusive ways to get into the phone before hooking it up to ORCA. Even the most sophisticated gadgets had weak spots, and ORCA's was a rare but catastrophic habit of erasing data from the phone as it was transferring to the external storage device, in this case a 64-gigabyte thumb drive. If for any reason the data transfer failed, all the information on the phone was gone forever. Luke had only seen it happen once or twice, but there was something about the menacing thug standing over his shoulder that told him it couldn't happen today.

"Here we go." Luke inserted one end of the connecting cable into ORCA, and the other into the phone's charging port. The phone blinked to life, looked for Harley's face for a moment, then issued the passcode prompt. ORCA defeated the security layer in thirty seconds, and the phone's home screen displayed, the entirety of its contents now available for Luke to open, browse, and download to the thumb drive.

"Tell me again what you're looking for," he said over his shoulder.

"I need to know who he was talking and texting with on August seventeenth," Manuel replied.

Manuel started with calls, then moved to text messages, scribbling notes on a piece of paper as he scrolled through the phone.

"Well, he was texting quite a bit that day. Almost sixty in all, to about a dozen different people. Some of them are just goofy, joking around with friends. A few look like the kind of messages dopers send their dealers when they're trying to score. Let me guess. . . he's a dope dealer? That's how those guys communicate, you know. They think it keeps the cops from listening to their calls."

"Yeah, thanks for that," Manuel answered. "What time were most of the texts?"

"From one in the afternoon to about nine at night. Then there are a couple just after midnight, so the morning of the eighteenth, from the same number. Those looked a little more serious."

"What do you mean, 'serious'?" Manuel asked.

"Whoever he was texting was pissed off. Have a look." Luke scrolled through the texts while Manuel read them.

Where you at?

Ten min

Nope now

Get your ass out here NOW

"Did he have any calls to or from the same person?"

"Let me check," Luke replied. "Yep. Here." He pointed to the call log. "The same number called him at ten p.m. and they talked for three minutes."

"I need a name."

"Way ahead of you," Luke answered as he scrolled to the contacts section of the phone. "It just says 'B.C.' You want me to do some open-source internet checking and see if I can match a name with the number?"

"No," Manuel said. "I need to be sure of who this guy is before I take the next step. Google stalking isn't going to cut it.

Write the number down for me on a piece of paper."

Luke did as he was asked and handed the paper to Manuel.

"Here you go. If you can find out who his cell provider is, I might have a contact there who can hook us up for a few hundred bucks."

Manuel pulled five hundred-dollar bills from a money clip and handed them to Luke. "We've got our own people for that. Your job is done."

He turned to leave, and Luke asked, "Do you want to take the phone with you?"

"No."

"Welcome back, Mr. Petty. I'll just need your driver's license and method of payment, please."

Vincent slid his identification and credit card across the counter to the agent.

"I've got you in a Chevy Equinox, if that's okay. Unlimited mileage, bring the car back with a full tank and you won't owe us anything for fuel. Did you want the collision damage waiver?"

"No thanks."

"All right then, just initial by all the X's and sign here on the bottom. I show you returning the car in two days, is that correct?"

Vincent paused and thought. "You know what? Let me have it for a week."

"You got it, Mr. Petty. If you change your mind, you can always return it early. Shuttle bus is out the first door to your left. Just show your contract to the driver and he'll drop you at your car. Enjoy your stay."

A half hour later, Vincent drove out of the rental lot and headed south, running through the missteps of the last trip in his mind. The traffic stop in Key Largo. The unexplained absence of Bryce Chandler when he arrived at his house in the early morning hours. He would be more careful this time and would give himself the time necessary to do the job right. If his target wasn't home, he would wait. If it took longer than a week, he would extend his hotel and rental car until the job was done. But come hell or high water, Bryce Chandler was a dead man, and Vincent would have his payday.

As he drove through Homestead, his cell phone chirped, and the incoming text message banner appeared. It was from a blocked number, and read simply: *7777. Acknowledge.* The abort signal. He deleted the message and stowed the phone in the center console.

CHAPTER 50

AS PROMISED, Bryce called Ashley two days later and told her there was news. They met at 9:00 a.m. at the 7 Mile Diner, a local haunt close to the bridge of the same name in Marathon. The breakfast crowd had come and gone, and he requested a table across the room from the only other customers in the restaurant. He ordered coffee for both of them, and the waitress came back a minute later with two cups.

"What can I get you to eat, darling?" the waitress asked.

"Just the coffee for now. We'll let you know when we're ready to order," Bryce answered. A phone rang near the cash register, and the waitress excused herself to answer it. Ashley arrived a minute later.

"Good morning," she said, sitting down across from him. She was dressed for court in a conservative gray suit, her hair pulled back into a bun. Bryce couldn't help but think how much he preferred off-duty Ashley to her starched alter ego.

"Hold that thought," he replied. "I did some digging around yesterday, and you're not going to like what I found. I'll tell you as much or as little as you want to know."

"I'm a big girl. Give me the whole story."

And he did. From the results of the trash pull to his conversation with Jose and Larry, Bryce outlined everything he had learned over the past seventy-two hours, sparing none of the details save for the fact that Stanley was a DEA snitch. When he finished, Ashley looked as if she had been kicked in the gut.

"So you think the clothes you found were Stanley's?" she asked.

"His and April's. I'm ninety-five percent sure they're both dead, but there's a possibility they could have taken off together. Or she could be dead, and Stanley faked his own death. Didn't you say Chase once offered to get rid of her?"

"Yes, but that was when the marina was for sale and Chase thought April would screw things up. Which she did, of course. Anyway, I don't think that offer was still in effect after everything fell through. But if you want to know if Stanley's dead or faking it, I have an idea."

"What's that?" Bryce asked.

"Stanley had a storage unit here in Marathon. April didn't know anything about it. I don't know everything he kept in there, but I do know he had a cash reserve he called his slush fund. If you believe him, there was over a million dollars in it. I can't imagine he would have made himself disappear and left the money behind."

"Do you know the name of the storage place?"

"It's the Lock and Go just past the airport, on the gulf side," Ashley answered.

"Okay. I'll have to figure out which unit is his, and then come up with a plan for getting in. Some of those places use locks that are really tough to pick."

"You won't need to do any of that. Stanley gave me a key, and I'm pretty sure the unit number is on the key ring."

"Why did he do that?"

Ashley smiled. "I told you, he thought I was his attorney for all occasions, his 'notify in case of emergency' contact. He told me everything, and he wanted me to have a key for safekeeping. It's kind of sad, but I think I was the only person he trusted. I told him I didn't want the key, but he insisted, so I put it in my desk and forgot about it. Until now."

"All right. I'll pick up the key later today. Do you want to order breakfast?"

"No," she replied.

"Me neither." Bryce pulled a five-dollar bill from his pocket and left it on the table. They said their goodbyes in the parking lot and agreed to meet at her office at the end of the day.

———

The waitress watched them drive away, then hurried to the ladies room, where she locked the door behind her, pulled her cell phone from her apron pocket, and called the number she had written down on a napkin twenty minutes earlier.

"Hello?" the voice on the other end answered.

"I got what I could. I had another party in the diner, so I couldn't just stand over them," she said, her voice a near whisper.

"What did you hear?"

"They were talking about someone named Stanley. Like whether he was dead or alive. They weren't sure."

"Anything else?"

"Yes. This Stanley guy has a storage unit, and there's a lot of money in it."

"Did they say which storage unit?"

"All I heard was it was near the airport on the gulf side. I couldn't make out a name."

"What else?" the stranger asked.

"That's it. Then they left. He drove off in a truck and she was in a Mercedes SUV."

"Okay, thanks. My guy will come by later with the money like I promised. Thanks for your help."

"Anytime, sweetie."

———————

Bryce used a satellite photo from a mapping app on his phone to familiarize himself with the layout of the Lock & Go. There were eight long rows of buildings, and it was impossible to tell from the aerial view which ones might have internal versus external entry doors. The keychain Ashley gave him was marked "G-208," and he surmised the buildings were lettered in sequence from A to H, which would put Stanley's unit second from the end, either on the east or west side of the complex.

He drove by the business during daylight hours and plotted his entry strategy. An eight-foot chain-link fence surrounded the property, and thankfully it was not topped by barbed wire. Scaling it wouldn't be difficult, but the optics were not good. Being spotted by a random passerby would be difficult to explain, and he wanted to find another way in. The property fronted Overseas Highway and extended a block to the north, where the back side of the fence ran along a darker, quieter neighborhood street. Bryce was able to see the letters on the buildings as he drove past, and he confirmed that building G was second from the end on the east side of the complex.

There were two vehicle entry gates. The one at the front was the automatic type that slid open when customers entered a code into a keypad in the entrance lane. A pedestrian gate was situated to the right of the vehicle entry point, and it also required a code. Stanley had only given Ashley a key, not an entry code. At the rear of the property, a larger double gate was secured by a chain and a padlock. When unlocked, the two gates would swing inward to allow oversized vehicles in and out. The alternate access point was a security afterthought, cloaked in shadows, and if the rusted padlock was any indication, it was rarely used. He chose it as his point of ingress.

Bryce waited until just after 10:00 p.m., parked two blocks away, and used a red lens flashlight to check the contents of the small backpack he would need for the job. The bag held a full lockpick set, a small crowbar, a headlamp, various standard and Phillips-head screwdrivers, a pair of vise grip pliers, a slim jim access tool, a slide hammer, a door puller, fifty feet of nylon rope, and a pair of bolt cutters. Finally, there was a pair of twenty-volt power tools, a drill, and a cordless grinder affixed with a metal cutting wheel that would slice through the hinges of most safes with ease. The grinder was loud enough to wake the dead, and Bryce would only use it as a last resort. He donned a thin pair of synthetic leather work gloves, cinched the straps on the backpack, locked his truck, and walked toward the storage business.

The neighborhood was asleep. When he reached the gates, he pulled the bolt cutters from the backpack and made quick work of the chain holding them together. True to his estimate, the entry point hadn't been used in years, and a six-inch layer of sand had formed at its bottom, making a chore of pulling the drop pin and pushing the gate open. He was able to create just enough space between the gates to squeeze himself inside.

Bryce half-walked, half-ran to the end of building G, where he took a knee, returned the bolt cutters to the backpack, and put the key Ashley gave him on top of the equipment pile inside. He donned the headlamp and plotted his approach one last time, rehearsing the details of what he was about to do in his mind before turning the corner and proceeding down the line of individual storage units. Once he committed, he would be in a direct line of sight for anyone walking or driving along the Overseas Highway. He said a quick prayer to nobody in particular and turned the corner, scanning for individual unit numbers as he walked. It was darker than it should have been in a place where people stored their life's possessions, and it took a minute for him to regain his night vision.

He saw them a split second before they saw him. The storage unit was open, and they were bathed in a dim light emanating from inside. There were two of them, one wearing a sheriff's department uniform and the other in civilian clothes. There was also a pair of vehicles, a white SUV backed up to the unit with its liftgate up, and a police cruiser with the distinctive markings of the Monroe County sheriff's office, including the number 324 in reflective decals on the rear license plate. He froze about a hundred feet away from them, hoping they hadn't seen him and at the same time knowing they had.

The uniformed one spoke up. "Hey there, buddy," he called out. "Why don't you show me your hands and walk slowly this way?"

Bryce raised his hands to shoulder height and stood still.

"That's good. Now walk slowly toward me and keep those hands up."

Bryce dropped his hands, turned, and bolted in the opposite direction, back toward the gate and what he knew was his only hope of seeing another day. He could hear the deputy behind him, screaming at him to stop, and it only made him run faster. As he rounded the corner at the end of the building, he heard two shots and felt a searing pain in his back, just below his left shoulder blade. Rather than slowing him down, the pain sent an adrenaline surge through his body, and he moved faster still. When he got to the gate, he pulled hard on it, making the opening just a bit larger than it was before, enough to pass through without contorting his body or snagging the backpack on the chain link. He glanced back as he ran and saw nobody following him. As he drew to within a block of his truck, he slowed to a jog and concentrated on controlling his breathing so as not to pass out in the middle of the street.

There was still nobody on his trail when he reached the truck, but he moved as if there was. He threw the backpack into the passenger seat, started up the engine, and left his lights off. He drove west, away from the Overseas Highway, then turned north along a backstreet and followed it for half a mile until his only choice was a right turn back toward the major thoroughfare. There was still nobody in his rearview when he reached US-1, turned on his lights, and turned northbound.

He went about five miles before feeling it was safe to pull over. A Tom Thumb gas station looked empty enough, and he parked alongside a pump, turned the engine off, and went inside.

"Can I get the key to the bathroom?" he asked the pimply faced teenager behind the counter.

"Restroom's for customers only," the kid replied.

Bryce rolled his eyes and fished a five-dollar bill from his pocket, slapping it down next to the cash register. "Pump one," he said.

The clerk pulled a two-foot long piece of a wooden broom handle off a hook behind him and handed it to Bryce, the restroom key dangling from the end. The restroom was outside and was thankfully a one-at-a-time single toilet affair. Once inside, Bryce unbuttoned and removed his shirt, then turned around to assess the damage in the mirror.

It wasn't life threatening, but it wasn't just a scratch, either. The bullet had grazed him, probably at the instant he turned the corner and put his body at a ninety-degree angle to the shooter. A moment sooner, and it could have killed him; a moment later, it would have missed altogether.

The gash was about four inches long, and at least that meant there wasn't a bullet lodged in his body. The damage was more than skin deep, and blood oozed slowly from it, forming a thin red stream down his back. The biggest problem was that he couldn't reach it, at least not well enough to clean and dress the wound. Harley would have been a reliable resource if he wasn't lying in a hospital bed eighty miles away. A visit to an urgent care clinic or hospital emergency room was out of the question. The medical professionals at either location were bound by law to report even a suspected gunshot wound to the police. His list of options was down to one.

Ashley picked up on the first ring. He explained the situation to her, and her response was immediate.

"I'm sending you a pin drop to my apartment. How soon can you be here?"

It was only a few minutes away. "Let me stop at a drugstore and get some supplies. Maybe twenty minutes."

"Okay," she replied. Her voice was calm and reassuring. "Be careful."

CHAPTER 51

HE STOPPED at an all-night pharmacy near Ashley's apartment and picked up a bottle of hydrogen peroxide and several boxes of butterfly closures, gauze pads, and first aid tape. He ignored the suspicious gaze of the checkout clerk, who saw the blood seeping through Bryce's shirt but knew better than to inquire.

Ashley was waiting at the door when he arrived. She ushered him toward the couch, which she had covered in towels in anticipation of the task that lay ahead.

"Take your shirt off and lay down," she ordered.

Bryce did as he was told, and Ashley went to work. He felt the coldness of the hydrogen peroxide as she poured it on the wound, then the sting as it did its work.

"It's a little dirty," she said. "I'm going to have to scrub it with a gauze pad. Sorry in advance."

The pain was intense. Bryce suffered silently as Ashley cleaned his wound and closed it as best she could with a half dozen of the butterflies. She applied a liberal dose of antibiotic ointment over her work, and covered it all up with a large waterproof dressing. When it was done, he sat up on the couch while she disposed of his bloodied shirt and the dirtied first aid supplies and threw the towels into the washer. She went to the bedroom and returned with a Mötley Crüe T-shirt.

"It's all I have," she said, offering it to him. "Leftover from an ex. Way too big for me, but I was using it as a sleep shirt."

"Thanks," he said as he stood to don the shirt. It fit perfectly.

"Are you hungry?" she asked, checking the refrigerator for what she had on hand. "I can offer you two-day-old Chinese food," she said, holding up a pair of white cardboard boxes. She opened the pantry next to the fridge and looked inside. "Or soup."

Bryce laughed. "Does Chinese takeout ever really get old? That sounds great, thanks."

There was enough for two, and she fixed them each a plate, placing them on the coffee table as she joined him on the couch. Bryce alternated between bites of kung pao chicken and bringing Ashley up to speed on the details of his night at the Lock & Go.

"So are you sure they were in Stanley's unit?" she inquired.

"I didn't see the number," he replied. "But it was on the right row, and in about the right place, judging from the numbers on the units I did see. And then there's the sheriff's department patrol car, which was the same one I saw at the marina when I did the trash pull. There's no way that's a coincidence."

"So someone else knew about the storage unit and got there before you did. Any ideas?" Ashley asked.

"None. Do you think Stanley told anyone else about it?"

She picked up the empty plates and took them to the kitchen, answering his question as she rinsed them in the sink. "It was part of his doomsday plan. So I can't see him telling Chase. And April didn't know anything about it. Bryce, I came to you because I was concerned. Well, concern became worry, and now I'm just terrified. Between what you found at the marina and tonight . . . we're in real danger, aren't we?"

Bryce didn't want to be an alarmist, but he didn't want to give her a false sense of security either. He managed a silent nod in response to her query, and she came back to the couch and sat down, closer to him this time. Her eyes were red, her hands trembling, and he could tell she was doing her best to hold it together. *Big girls don't cry.*

"I'm scared," she said as she inched away, then laid down on her side, pulling her knees to her chest and placing her head in his lap. He rested one hand on her shoulder while the other stroked her hair, trying his best to comfort her. It felt good. It felt right. It was the first time he had been affectionate with a woman since his divorce, and he had for too long neglected the part of him that needed human contact. Ashley pushed herself up with her hands and drew her face close to his, their eyes meeting and sending the same message. Bryce pulled her in and pressed his lips to hers, and they stayed there, locked in each other's embrace, for what seemed like an eternity. She pulled her face away, and he could see that she was crying. He wasn't sure how to react, but it was a vulnerable moment, and his inner gentleman told him to dial back on the building sexual tension between them. He leaned forward and planted a single, gentle kiss on her forehead. She looked up and whispered a one-word response to his gesture.

"Stay."

Bryce sighed. "I want to. I really do. I'm not sure it's a good idea."

"Why?"

"For one, you're my employer," he said.

"You're going to have to do better than that," Ashley replied.

She was right. Theirs was not exactly a traditional worker/boss relationship.

"We're both in an emotional place. Neither of us are thinking straight. The last three days—"

She stopped him in mid-sentence, resuming their kiss, more firmly and passionately this time. Their hands wandered over each other's bodies, his head spinning as he simultaneously wrestled with Ashley and his conscience. He summoned what was left of his willpower, broke the embrace, and stood up.

"I really think I should go."

CHAPTER 52

VINCENT STOOD PATIENTLY near a patch of mangroves abutting the waters that made up the canal system behind Bryce's house. He swatted away a mosquito, another in an endless swarm of micro-sized pests the locals dubbed "no see-ums." True to their name, they were invisible, while the damage they left behind was anything but. Every inch of his exposed skin seemed to have been feasted on by the legendary bugs, made even worse by the temperature and humidity that turned the outdoors into a steam bath before the sun lightened the sky. He could not wait to return to the cool, dry climate of the high Arizona desert he called home, and hoped today would be that day. It was nearly 5:00 a.m., and he had been waiting for Bryce to show himself for nearly an hour. When a light came on in the living room, he knew his moment had finally arrived.

He double-checked the silenced Kimber, stowed it in his waistband, and moved toward Bryce's house, some hundred yards away. There were two sets of stairs leading to the second-story porch that wrapped around the house, and he chose the rearmost one, hoping to finish the job from the shadows of the back porch as his target ate breakfast or watched television.

He crept up the stairs and worked his way toward a large window that gave him a clear view of the living room and kitchen.

A single light shone over the kitchen island, but from the darkness where he stood it practically illuminated the entire interior of the house.

Chandler was seated in a chair facing the television, facing away from the window so Vincent could see the top of his head and nothing more. He raised the Kimber, placed the red dot of his laser sight on the back of the chair at what he predicted to be chest height, and fired three quick rounds, the first one shattering the windowpane but making only a little noise. The head disappeared as Chandler slumped in the chair. Vincent reached through the hole where the glass had been, unlocked the door, and went inside to make sure the job was done.

He heard the labored breathing and the familiar gurgling sounds of air escaping the lungs of a man who was taking his last breaths. He walked slowly around the chair to face the target he had stalked for nearly two months, and to give him the courtesy of looking into the eyes of the man who killed him. The dim light softened the details in the room, but the moment he cast his eyes on his prey, who now had mere seconds to live, he was certain of one thing.

It wasn't Bryce Chandler.

For one thing, whoever he just shot was at least twenty years younger than the man whose photo he had studied since beginning the prep work for this job. The face staring back at him was dark-skinned, probably Hispanic, and had a long white scar running the length of its right side. Vincent paused, incredulous, a thousand thoughts crowding his head as he tried to make sense of the scene before him. He stared at the dying man, almost wishing he had merely injured him so he could at least ask who he was and why he was sitting in Bryce Chandler's house at five o'clock in the morning.

He got his wish, but only partially. Wheezing and bleeding from his nose and mouth, the man looked up at Vincent and managed to feebly whisper, "Who are you?"

"That's funny," Vincent replied. "I was just about to ask you the same question."

"You'll see. You'll see." He took two long, labored breaths, then several more in short staccato bursts, before his chest stopped moving.

And then Vincent heard the toilet flush.

————————

Bryce raised his head and checked the bedside clock. Five o'clock. He had been sleeping soundly since they finally drifted off in each other's arms hours earlier. She was still spooned up against him, both of them naked under the comforter, which wouldn't have been necessary in his house, but was a welcome accessory in the beachfront condominium she kept cooled to 70 degrees at night. He was thirsty, but didn't want to risk waking her by walking to the kitchen for a glass of water, so he laid quietly and recounted the events of the last several hours.

Earlier, he had made it as far as the door, where he stopped, looked back at her, and reconsidered his line of reasoning. They were attracted to one another. Neither of them were married, and to the best of his knowledge, Ashley wasn't involved in a relationship. She was a strong, beautiful woman, and so what if it was an emotional chain of events that led them to one another? He stood long enough in the entry for her to rise from the couch, take his hand, and lead him into the bedroom without another word being spoken.

And he had acquitted himself quite nicely, as far as he could tell. The first time was a bit clumsy, partially owing to the unfamiliar surroundings and that moment of uncertainty when two people first lay eyes on one another sans clothing. After a brief rest, they resumed in earnest, and their second session was more relaxed, comfortable and familiar. The dressing on his back held its ground, and the pain from the wound was less of an impediment than he thought it would be.

Still, he had not been with another woman since Janet, and between what he had forgotten about relationships and what had no doubt changed over the last twenty-five years, he knew he wasn't current on the do's and don'ts of the dating game. If that was even what it was. They went to dinner, and now they'd slept with each other . . . was that dating? What expectations were there once the sun came up and they got dressed and went their separate ways? Should he call her again? Was it presumptuous to sleep over? The more he thought, the more he realized he had more questions than answers. Still, all in all it was a good problem to have.

She stirred, half-asleep and half-awake, and rolled over to face him. "Hey there," she whispered. "What time is it?"

"A little after five. You feeling okay?"

Ashley smiled. "I am. Can you do me a favor?"

"Sure."

"Run to the kitchen and get me a bottle of water from the fridge."

"You got it." He rose from the bed and started toward the bedroom door. "Anything else?"

"No, just the water. And you. It's way too early for us to be awake."

Well, that answered one question.

———————

Vincent froze at the sound of the flushing toilet, then turned his head slowly in the direction of the hallway bathroom behind him. He heard the sound of running water, as if someone was . . . washing their hands? Could this day get any weirder?

The door cracked open and light streamed out into the darkened hallway. A short, stocky man, perhaps in his early thirties, stepped out of the bathroom and turned toward the living room, oblivious to Vincent's presence.

"Hey, Manny, he's got a desk in the bedroom. I'll go through it and see if—" He stopped in mid-sentence as he saw Vincent standing over his dead accomplice. "Who the fuck are—"

"You" never left his mouth. Vincent raised the Kimber, planted the laser sight on his new target's chest, but instead of squeezing the trigger as he had trained, the surprise of the interloper caused him to jerk the weapon to the right, sending the round into the man's left shoulder instead of his heart. The target fell backward, landing flat on his back but with sufficient momentum to propel himself with his feet through a bedroom door at the end of the hall, where he disappeared from Vincent's sight.

A former special operator, Vincent knew full well the concept of the fatal funnel represented by that hallway, and he considered turning and leaving, abandoning the job altogether and living to fight another day.

But he saw me. He can identify me. This job isn't finished.

He made his way down the hall, inching closer and closer to the open bedroom door. When he got within three feet of the doorway, he began slicing the pie—maintaining cover behind the door frame while slowly rounding the corner and exposing more of the room to his field of view, in hopes that he could catch a small glimpse of his adversary and engage him. Of course, the maneuver, which he learned during close quarters combat training in Special Forces, had the reciprocal effect of exposing him to the target, but he was alone, time was of the essence, and ultimately it was his best option.

They saw each other at the same moment. Vincent was able to squeeze off two rounds, one of which struck Manny's partner in the neck, the other in the center of his chest as he had originally attempted. In return, he took three shots in his direction, two of which sailed harmlessly beyond their mark, puncturing the drywall in the hallway.

The third shot grazed the door casing Vincent had been using for cover and buried itself in the left side of his abdomen. The pain was searing, and Vincent knew in that instant he was hurt badly. Still, he could walk, and as he had no interest in attempting to question his newfound enemy, he took two steps in his direction and fired a final shot into the man's forehead, on the slim chance he might have survived the neck and chest wounds.

The mission was a failure, and there was no point in trying to salvage it. Even if Bryce Chandler came home at this moment, the element of surprise was gone. While his gun was silenced, the one used to inflict his painful belly wound was not, and no doubt some neighbor would be calling the police about shots fired at the Chandler residence. His best hope was to get to the nearest hospital, concoct a story about careless firearms handling and a resulting self-inflicted injury, and hope doctors would treat him without getting too deeply into his business. Failing that, he knew the inevitable results of a bullet wound to the abdomen, and it was not pretty. Stomach acid and intestinal contents would fill the wound channel and all the empty space in his belly, and he would die a horrible, painful, slow death. He had thirty minutes, forty-five at best, to find qualified medical assistance.

The first five minutes were spent half-walking, half-stumbling his way back to the rental car he had parked three blocks away. By the time he collapsed into the driver's seat, he was sweating profusely, the left side of his torso was tingling and numb all at once, and his entire body felt cold. He fumbled with the keys, got the engine started, and spun the wheels as he sped away from Bryce Chandler's neighborhood and toward the Overseas Highway that connected Big Pine Key with the nearest hospital in Marathon, at least twenty minutes away.

The bleeding was relentless, and Vincent could feel the life pumping out of him, pooling in the driver's seat and running onto the floorboards as he accelerated past Bahia Honda State Park at nearly a hundred miles per hour. When he made it as far as the Seven Mile Bridge, he allowed himself a small measure of hope; he upped his speed to 110 and passed no less than a half dozen cars over the length of the Keys landmark, ignoring the flashing high beams and extended middle fingers of his fellow early morning drivers as he rocketed toward his only possible salvation.

He slowed entering Marathon, not due to a lack of urgency, but because he didn't know exactly where the hospital was. He had included it in his pre-operation planning during his first trip months earlier, making note of its location but never pinning the location in his GPS. Not that it would have mattered at this point. His fine motor skills were all but gone, and manipulating a smart phone with his numb, trembling fingers was impossible. It was all he could do to manage the gas pedal and steering wheel.

He was freezing now, shivering uncontrollably, his skin ghostly pale and clammy with sweat. The pain at the wound site was gone, replaced by a dull, whole-body ache and a feeling of nausea like he had never known. His vision began to tunnel, gradually blocking out the periphery until all he could see was the road directly in front of him.

And there it was, its sign a bright, red-and-white electric glow, a quarter mile ahead on the right side of the road. Mariners Hospital, home to the only level I trauma center for a hundred miles, and the only chance Vincent Kamara stood of seeing another sunrise. He beheld the sign as a man dying of thirst eyes a desert oasis, and he drove straight toward it.

But life is cruel, and seconds after the sign appeared to him, it disappeared as Vincent's vision failed. He had slowed to fifty miles per hour when he lost consciousness, no more than a block from his destination. The car lurched left into oncoming traffic, then hard right as Vincent fell toward the passenger seat, taking the steering wheel with him.

Mamacita's Cuban Coffee was a Marathon institution, and it boasted a hardcore constituency of local sea captains and construction workers who queued up for their daily fix of the high-octane brew just before the tiny shack opened its window at 6:00 a.m. Their cars and work vans lined the side of US-1, forming a barrier between the coffee shop and traffic speeding by in both directions on the four-lane thoroughfare.

And luckily for Ada Nunez, Mamacita's owner, that line of cars and trucks did their job. Vincent's rental struck the side of the rearmost vehicle in the line of coffee patrons at nearly forty miles per hour. The force of the impact drove the electrician's van to within three feet of the service window, where a few early birds had gathered to be first in line. Two of them were knocked to the ground, but nobody was seriously injured.

Vincent's car careened off the van and down the line of patrons' vehicles, striking at least four more before coming to rest half on the shoulder, half in the roadway, pointed in the opposite direction of traffic. A crowd rushed toward his car, led by a fishing charter captain and his son, not certain what they would find when they reached the crumpled hulk of the compact sport utility vehicle.

The father was first to the driver's side window, and he peered inside at Vincent's motionless body, unsure if he should try and pull him from the wreckage or wait for the authorities. He turned to his son, who was standing directly behind him.

"Should we get him out?" he asked.

"I don't think so. They always say leave them alone unless the car's on fire. Besides, he looks dead to me."

"Did anyone call 911?"

"Dad, I think everyone called 911. There's a sheriff's station right down the road. They should be here any minute. Let them take care of it. Like I said, look at him. He's dead."

"Yeah, you're right, son. Let's go see how bad the truck is. I've got paying customers meeting us at the boat in an hour, and I don't need to lose money over this asshole."

CHAPTER 53

IT WAS A PERFECT DAY to be on the water, and Bryce loaded up the boat and made his way to the back country waters of the Gulf of Mexico. He reeled in fish after fish, every one of them undersized yet fully cooked, as if ordered in a restaurant. He threw them back as quickly as he caught them. As he tossed the last one back into the water, dark thunderclouds moved in from the east, blocking his route home, and thick, black smoke began pouring from under the boat's console. He reached for the fire extinguisher to put it out, felt Donnie Morris's hand on his shoulder, and heard the voice of his friend saying, "Let it burn. You can't stop it." Bryce struggled to reach the extinguisher, but his feet were glued to the deck, and he couldn't move. The motor began to make a loud, vibrating noise, but as with the fire below deck, he was powerless to do anything about it. It hummed on and off, rattling the entire boat, then went silent. On and off, on and off, endlessly.

"Your phone's blowing up," Ashley whispered as she nudged his shoulder.

They had drifted back to sleep, and this time when he rolled over to check the clock, it read 7:30, and the day's light was beginning to fill the room as it filtered through the window blinds.

"Sorry about that," he said. "I usually put it on do not disturb mode before bed. I guess I forgot last night," he quipped through a sheepish smile.

Ashley rolled toward him and kissed his cheek. "You're forgiven. I'll be right back." She rose from bed and walked toward the bathroom, pulling the door shut behind her. He retrieved his phone from the nightstand and checked for missed calls. There were four, all from the same number, all within the last hour.

Jordan Fleetwood was one of the first sheriff's deputies Bryce met when he moved to the Keys, and they had maintained a loose professional and personal relationship for the last several years. Jordan had access to information such as criminal history reports, vehicle registration information, and driver's license photos, all of which were invaluable in the private investigator business. In return, Bryce provided the Monroe County Sheriff's Office (through Deputy Fleetwood, of course) with street-level intelligence from his sources, including his star informant, Harley Christian. All of this was done on a strict off the record basis, and both parties benefitted from the exchange of mutually valuable information neither could have garnered on his own.

Bryce hadn't spoken to Jordan in nearly two months, and so the calls, and particularly the number and frequency of them, got his attention. There had to be a good reason for Jordan to be trying so hard to get ahold of Bryce this early in the morning.

"I need to take this in the other room," he called to her through the bathroom door as he donned his boxers and pants. He had no idea what it might have been about, but chances were it wasn't something he needed to be discussing in front of the defense attorney he had just slept with for the first time. He closed the bedroom door behind him, sat down on Ashley's couch, and dialed Jordan's number.

"Bryce, where are you?" were the first words out of his mouth.

"And good morning to you too, Jordan. Why the sudden interest in my whereabouts?"

"Because there are about four patrol units, crime scene, and the shift lieutenant over at your house right now, and they're all wondering where you are. I'm getting all this through radio traffic, but it sounds like there are two dead guys in the house, both with gunshot wounds, and the fact that you are nowhere to be found does not make it look good for you."

Bryce didn't alarm easily, but the news from Jordan sucked the air from his lungs and made it hard to think. His head spun and his breath came in quick, shallow bursts as he tried to process what he had just heard.

"Bryce? You still there? Talk to me, man."

He took a deep breath and gathered his thoughts. "I spent the night at a friend's house in Marathon. I haven't been home since yesterday, late afternoon. What time did all this happen?"

"I don't know. It was called in by your neighbor this morning shortly after five o'clock. He was letting his dog out to pee and heard gunshots coming from your house. Who's the friend you were staying with?"

Bryce snapped, "What does that matter? I wasn't at home, and I can prove it."

"Sorry, Bryce, but the investigators are going to ask."

"So let them ask. I've got nothing to hide. Tell them I'll be back to the house within an hour."

"Bryce, they may not let you in. It's a crime scene, you know."

"Yeah, Jordan, I know how crime scenes work. But I still want to go back to the house, and if the investigators are still there, they can talk to me then. Or I can come by the sub-station if they want. But let them know you've spoken with me, and that I'm on my way. I'm not trying to hide from them, and I'm not lawyering up."

"Will do, buddy." Jordan hung up, and Bryce stared at his phone. Was he dreaming? None of it made sense. He knew there were multiple parties with interests in finding him, and at least one of those parties was more interested in killing him than engaging in conversation. What *would* have made sense was, "Bryce, we found some guy prowling around your house last night," or something similar. But two dead bodies inside his home? It defied explanation.

Bryce hung up the phone and walked back to the bedroom, where Ashley was pulling on a pair of blue jeans.

"Everything okay?" she asked.

"Apparently not. I need to go."

"Okay. Want to share?"

"Right now I'm not sure what I know and what I don't. But something happened at my house a few hours ago, and I need to get there right away." He gave her the rundown of Jordan's phone call, and watched as she sat down at the end of the bed, her face blanched and her eyes affixed in a thousand-yard stare.

"When is this going to end?" she asked.

"I'm starting to wonder that myself."

CHAPTER 54

THE BODIES were still in the house when he arrived. Two crime scene technicians in white Tyvek suits made their way back and forth between their van and the rear of the home, carrying in a variety of empty plastic bags and returning with the bags filled, sealed, and ready for the laboratory. The coroner's van stood at the ready to make its haul once the scene was declared clear.

Bryce found the on-scene commander, who according to his nametag was of the clan Mullins, and introduced himself. Lieutenant Mullins looked to be in his mid-forties, supremely fit, with a large, square jaw, crew cut, and a pair of mirrored sunglasses he opted not to remove. Anything Bryce might have expected in the way of professional courtesy evaporated the moment he extended his hand and the lieutenant ignored the gesture.

The questioning began without any formalities. "Where were you last night?"

Okay, so this is how it's going to be, Bryce said to himself. *Relax, don't give this guy any reason to be a bigger ass than he's being right now.*

He pulled his hand back. "I was with a friend in Marathon."

"Male friend or female friend?"

He bristled at the intrusion. "What difference does that make?" he asked.

"Deputy Fleetwood said you were going to cooperate. Did you change your mind? Because we can do this an entirely different way," the lieutenant snapped.

You gotta be kidding me. Is this guy for real? Bryce knew better than anyone that he had nothing to do with whatever happened in his house, but he also knew the lieutenant could make his life very difficult, including dirtying the waters with regard to his private investigator's license. He decided to let patience rule the day.

"Of course I'm going to cooperate. I'm a private person, but I know you're just doing your job. I was with Ashley Oliver in Marathon, and she can confirm it."

"Ashley Oliver, the attorney?" the lieutenant asked. His expression betrayed his thoughts.

"We're just friends. Anyway, we started watching some Netflix show and I fell asleep at her place. My truck was parked there all night. I'm sure there are security cameras you can check that will verify it."

The lieutenant was irritated by Bryce's suggestion of how to go about his investigation. "Yeah, we'll look into that," he said. "Do you know either of these guys?" He scrolled to pictures on his cell phone that were taken inside Bryce's home. They were closeups of the faces of the two dead men.

Bryce studied the photos for a few seconds before tendering his answer. "No, sir. Never seen either of them before." He felt certain Harley would recognize at least one of them, but this was neither the time nor the place for that conversation.

"Mr. Chandler, when my techs are done inside, they're going to need to swab your hands for gunpowder residue. Is that going to be a problem?" With his tone and delivery, the lieutenant was practically daring him to challenge his authority.

It was unfamiliar ground for Bryce, being treated like a suspect. Still, he knew it was a reasonable request, and he also knew he hadn't fired a weapon since his last annual qualification some six months ago. He shook his head. "No problem."

"Good. One more thing. I need to collect any weapons you have on your person, in your home, or in your vehicle before we leave."

Bryce finally found the end of his patience. "Based on what?" he asked.

"Florida's red flag laws allow me to confiscate the weapons of anyone suspected of an act of domestic violence," the lieutenant replied. "You don't like it, write your state representative."

Bryce's voice raised. "Wait. . . you're calling me a suspect? With an alibi that puts me thirty miles away at the time of the crime? What the hell school of criminal investigation did you go to?"

Lieutenant Mullins stepped forward, bringing his nose within inches of Bryce's face. He lowered his voice so only Bryce could hear him, even though nobody else was paying attention to their conversation.

"Son, that mouth of yours has got you about ten seconds away from a pair of handcuffs. I know who you are, I know what you used to do for a living, and I don't care. You've been in our lockup before, and I'll take you back today if you piss me off. You're not the law down here. I'm the law. You're just some drunk-ass former fed who thinks the sheriff's office is going to cut him a break because he used to have a badge. Now be a good boy and show me where your guns are."

It was a moment Bryce would look back on in regret, but only slightly. He knew what would happen before he opened his mouth, but the words came out anyway, enunciated slowly, so as to impart maximum impact.

"Fuck. You. Asshole."

He could have fought back, but that would have only made matters worse. Lieutenant Mullins grabbed his wrist, spun him around, and pushed his chest down against the hood of his cruiser. He handcuffed Bryce and gave him a quick pat-down, feeling the bulge under his left shoulder. When he lifted Bryce's shirt, he saw the blood-stained dressing.

"What happened to your back?" he asked Bryce.

"I cut myself shaving."

"You shave your back?" the lieutenant asked.

"You don't?"

"What time did you get to your girlfriend's place last night, smartass?"

"I told you," Bryce answered. "She's not my girlfriend. And I was there from seven p.m. until Jordan called me this morning."

"Lieutenant, everything okay?" one of the deputies asked as he walked toward his boss.

"Everything's fine. Take him to the lockup and start the paperwork for me. I'll be in when we clear the scene here."

"You got it, sir. What's the charge?"

"For now, let's go with failure to surrender weapons under the red flag law, and assaulting an officer."

"He hit you, sir?"

"He was going to. I didn't let it get that far. Just transport him and spare me the questions, okay?"

"Yes, sir." The deputy put Bryce in his car and backed out of the spot he had created for himself on the front lawn. Bryce turned sideways in the seat to ease the pain and discomfort of the handcuffs, and saw Lieutenant Mullins getting into his patrol car. As the vehicle Bryce was riding in pulled away, it passed directly behind Mullins's, and Bryce chastised himself for not paying attention earlier. He was face down on the hood of that car and didn't see it. He was eye-to-eye with Lieutenant Mullins and didn't see it. The number on the back, front, and top of every deputy's patrol car was the same as their badge number.

And the number on the back of Lieutenant Mullins's car was 324.

————————————

Once back in his car, Lieutenant Mullins rolled up the windows and pulled out his personal phone. He scrolled through the address list, selected a contact, and pressed *Call.*

"Roger Mackenzie," the voice on the other end answered.

"Roger, it's John Mullins down here in Monroe County. I'm on Big Pine at our boy's house. Manny and Chico are inside. Both dead."

"Jesus. Did Chandler kill them?"

"I don't think so."

"Can we make it look like he did?"

"I doubt it. He's got a solid alibi that puts him out of town for the time frame we're looking at. We'll swab his hands when we process him into the jail, but I'd bet a paycheck it comes back negative. He didn't do this."

"You locked him up?" Roger asked. "I thought you said he's not a suspect."

"It's a long story, and I don't have time to go into it now. What do you want me to do with him? It's a bullshit charge and he'll be out on OR by morning."

"Damn it. They were just supposed to put the fear of God into him. How could it go this wrong?"

"I don't know. What should I do with Chandler? I can keep him in jail for up to forty-eight hours or let him go right away, whatever you want."

"And you're sure it's Manny and Chico? You saw them?"

"With my own two eyes. They're deader than Elvis. I'll text you photos when we hang up."

"All right. Don't do anything with Chandler until you hear from me. Just leave him where he is. I need to talk to the boss on this one."

"Roger, there's more."

"Great. I can hardly wait."

"Manny and I went to Stanley's storage unit last night. It checked out. There's a safe inside. We were about to go to work on it when somebody came walking toward us. I told him to put up his hands and he ran. Then Manny, dumbass that he was, fired two shots at him as he was running away."

"Did he hit him?"

"I don't know. We were in the light and he was in the dark, so I couldn't make him out, but he probably saw us."

"Okay," Roger said. "It sounds like you scared him off. What's the problem?"

"When I searched Chandler, he had a first aid dressing on his back. It had fresh blood on it."

"So do you think it was him?"

"I don't know. He lied when I asked him how he got hurt."

"I don't know. This sounds like one hell of a coincidence. Just handle your business and wait for me to get back to you."

"You got it."

Mullins had barely hung up the phone when his friend and counterpart to the north, Lieutenant Shane Crowley, called.

"Shane, what's up?" he asked.

"Good morning, John. Are you working a signal seven down on Big Pine?"

"A double. Why do you ask?"

"Well, do you have anyone you like for it?"

"Not yet. What's going on?"

"Maybe a coincidence, maybe not. Some dude just crashed his car on the side of Route One next to Mamacita's and took out a half dozen vehicles. When we got there, he was unconscious and barely breathing, bleeding heavy from a gunshot wound to the stomach. And there was a Kimber custom .45 laying on the floorboard. With a suppressor attached."

"What else can you tell me about him?" Mullins asked.

"His driver's license says he's Robert Charles Petty, aged forty-six, with a Kansas City address. The car is a Chevy Equinox rented from Hertz out of Miami airport two days ago."

"And where is Mr. Petty now?"

"EMS drove off with him. They were working on him like he had a chance, but I don't know. There was a lot of blood in that car."

"Did they take him to Mariners?"

"I assume so. It's two hundred yards from the crash scene."

"All right, Shane, thanks for the call. Talk to you soon."

This had gotten big, way bigger than he ever bargained for when he agreed to do a little side work for Chase Worthing. A beat-down of a junkie snitch was one thing, but a double murder in the home of a retired FBI agent meant a whole new level of scrutiny that he was not prepared to withstand. And now there was another wrinkle—an out-of-town mystery man who, in all likelihood, was carrying the gun that was used to murder Chase's two most trusted enforcers. Was it a professional hit? And if it was, how did the hit man know where to find Manny and Chico?

Oh, and the other thing. The one that, if his name was ever attached to it, would land him in prison for the rest of his life. Or if he played his cards right, could be his salvation.

Mullins had been in the business long enough to see trouble coming, and he knew he needed to get in front of it. He also knew there was only one way out.

CHAPTER 55

"CHANDLER! WAKE UP!"

Bryce opened his eyes slowly, confused as to his surroundings, but sure of one thing: His back hurt like hell. As the fog cleared, he took in the unfamiliar sights and smells of his jail cell and remembered the chain of events that landed him there the previous day. He rose from the paper-thin mattress, swung his feet onto the floor, and stared at the sergeant standing in the now-open doorway to the six-by-ten-foot room he had prepared to call home for the foreseeable future.

"Where are we going?" he asked the jailer.

"*We* aren't going anywhere," he replied. "*You*, on the other hand, are going anywhere but my jail. The charges were dropped about an hour ago. Come get your stuff."

Bryce had countless questions whirring around his brain, none of which were going to be answered by the guy whose job it was to open and close jail doors and hand out meals in Styrofoam boxes. He followed him down the corridor and into a small room where another deputy returned his clothes and personal belongings. He got dressed, signed his release papers, and walked out of the jail into the glaring sunlight. It had been just under twenty-four hours since he was dragged away from his house in handcuffs.

He checked his phone, and there was a single text from Ashley, which read simply, *Everything okay?*

Bryce was starting to like her. He knew women who would have left an endless combination of text and voice messages, each more desperate than the last, wanting to know every detail of his whereabouts and activities, and particularly so the day after sleeping with a guy for the first time. Ashley played it cool. Just a simple check-in. *No drama. I could use a little more of that in my life*, he thought.

He texted her back: *Interesting day and night. Will spare you the details for now, but let's talk soon. Thanks for reaching out.*

He called a taxi to take him home, which was just as he left it except for the absence of all the police vehicles and coroner's van. As he put his key in the lock, he assumed they had finished their business and he was free to enter the house again, and shame on them if they hadn't.

The house was by no means destroyed, but it was still clear to even the casual observer that something very, very bad had happened there. Besides the broken glass on the rear door, the most obvious sign of the horror that had been visited on his home was the blood.

And there was so much of it. Two large pools, one by his recliner and another on the floor in the master bedroom, had dried to a dark reddish brown, almost black. A heavy trail led from just outside the bedroom door through the living room, onto the back porch, and down the stairs to the ground, where it disappeared into a nearby tree line. There were spatter marks on the walls in both the bedroom and the living room. This had been a massacre. Black fingerprint powder coated a portion of almost every surface throughout the house.

The job of the crime scene technicians was to collect evidence, nothing more. Cleaning up the mess they left behind fell to the homeowner. Bryce went to the garage where he retrieved a bucket, a gallon of bleach, a fistful of rags, and a mop, and spent the next four hours scrubbing every surface that would give up its coating of dried blood. The floors were laminate and cleaned up nicely. The bedroom rug, bedding, and recliner all went into the back of his truck, and he would dump them at the local landfill when it opened. The walls would need to be repainted, but that was a project for another day. The fingerprint powder turned out to be more stubborn than the dried blood, but eventually it too gave way to the Clorox and elbow grease. He taped plastic across the broken window and made an appointment to have the door repaired.

With the house now habitable, he turned his attention back to the business at hand, that of trying to piece together the surreal puzzle his life had become. He was all but sure the two men who died in his home were Chase Worthing's goons, the same ones who landed Harley Christian in the ICU. He was doubly certain they were in his house to do the same to him, maybe worse.

But who killed them? And why?

CHAPTER 56

JOSE AND LARRY met him halfway this time, at the Square Grouper in Islamorada. They sat outside, near the water and as far as they could from the other restaurant patrons. Bryce wasted no time telling them about his trip to the storage facility and the chaotic scene at his house the next morning.

"The deputy showed me pictures of the dead guys. At least one of them probably put Harley in the hospital," he told the DEA agents. "Then they showed up at my house, I guess to do the same to me."

Larry's eyes filled with anger as he glared at Bryce. "I thought you were going to leave this alone and let us do our job. What the hell were you thinking, breaking into a business in the middle of the night? You know if you get busted there's nothing we can do for you."

Bryce was indignant. "Of course I know that, and I'm not asking you to do anything more than your job. Put Chase Worthing in jail before someone else gets hurt or killed."

"We're working on it," Larry replied. "More than you know. We have a Monroe County deputy embedded with our task force. He told us about the incident at your house, and he's been running a few leads for me. Speaking of which, excuse me while I make a call." Larry walked away from the table, leaving Bryce and Jose to themselves.

"See what I was talking about?" Jose asked. "This Worthing guy isn't the clean-cut, all-American dream he makes himself out to be. He's a monster, and he surrounds himself with the worst of the worst. You want to stay as far away from him as you can."

"Oh, I'm a believer," Bryce replied. "You think he'll keep coming after me?"

"Probably not. This thing at your house is going to draw a lot of attention to him and his people, and he'll want to lay low. But you need to stop poking the bear."

Bryce nodded. "Yeah, message delivered. Loud and clear."

They chatted about their decade-old case for a few minutes before Larry returned to the table.

"Okay, our task force officer just sent me some photos I need you to see."

"Sure. Photos of what?" Bryce asked.

"You said the deputy showed you some pics before you were arrested. Was it these two?" Larry brought up the photos on his phone, swiping left and right between the two while showing them to Bryce.

"Yep, that's them."

"The one with the scar is Manuel Del Negro. Manny to his friends. He's a badass OG, former Mexican Mafia enforcer they sent to work for Chase after they started doing business up here. The other guy is some low-level arm breaker they called Chico. Take a look at one more for me, and tell me if you've ever seen this person."

It was a full face shot, and the blue background gave it away as a driver's license photo. The subject appeared to be in his mid-forties, with short blond hair, blue eyes, and glasses. Bryce stared at the photo for a half minute.

"Nope. Never seen him before. Who is he?"

"His name is Robert Charles Petty, from Kansas City. About a half hour after the shooting was called in at your place, he wrecked his car in Marathon. When the cops got there, he was bleeding out from a gunshot wound to the abdomen. They found a silenced .45 in the car with a magazine that was seven rounds light, which matches the number of holes they found in Manny and Chico at your place. Both of them were shot with a .45. They haven't had time to make an exact ballistics match, but at this point it's safe to say they've identified the shooter."

"And where is he now?"

"They stabilized him at the hospital in Marathon, then life-flighted him up here to Miami. He's in an ICU somewhere, no word on a prognosis."

Bryce asked, "So is there anything linking him to your case? Any reason he would show up out of nowhere to kill two of Chase Worthing's trigger men?"

"That's the question of the day," Larry said. "He's a complete unknown to us. Doesn't fit into the picture in any conceivable way. Let me ask you this: Is there any chance he came looking for you, and found Manny and Chico instead?"

Bryce rubbed his temples and stared down at the table. It had been in the back of his mind, and he didn't want to admit it to himself, but now it was the only possible answer. "I can't be sure, but yeah, probably."

"And what makes you say that?"

He rolled his head back and sighed deeply. "It's been one hell of a month, gentlemen. Let me tell you all about it."

Thirty minutes later, Jose and Larry were privy to everything Bryce knew about the Network.

"Holy crap," Jose said. "And here I thought *we* were dealing with some bad dudes."

Larry asked, "So you really think this Petty guy had a contract on you, and it just so happened he ran into Chase Worthing's men instead?"

"It's the only thing that makes sense," Bryce replied. "Unless you have another theory, something that would explain how they all ended up in my house yesterday morning. The lawyer in Atlanta told me I was on the list, but I thought they would have called it off after the Network was compromised. Then the shooting, then this guy wrecks his car with the murder weapon inside. Unless he's the one they sent for me, I'm out of ideas."

"You should buy a lottery ticket, my friend," Larry said.

Bryce smiled. "The thought has crossed my mind. What's next for you guys?"

"Like I said, the Stanley situation is going to speed things along for our prosecutor. She doesn't like collateral damage. And now a double murder? She'll want to unseal the indictments this week. The only thing she'll hold out for is a murder charge, and I don't have anyone deep enough into Worthing's organization to report on that."

"I may have someone you can lean on," Bryce said.

"Who's that?" Larry asked.

Bryce laid out the chronology of his three contacts with Deputy Sheriff Mullins, badge number 324 of the Monroe County Sheriff's Office.

"Interesting," Larry mused. "Do you think he's the one who took a shot at you?"

"No idea. But he was there. And you should have seen his face when he felt that bandage on my back. It was like a light went on."

"All right." Larry looked toward Jose. "What do you say we find out what we can about this Mullins character and pay him a visit?"

"I like it," Jose said. "Sounds like a dirty cop with lots to lose. Let's see if he'll play ball."

They paid the check and continued talking as they walked to their cars. "Look, Bryce," Larry said as they reached his truck, "I really need you to lay off all things Chase Worthing, starting now. I assure you, the case has our complete attention. If you or Ms. Oliver think you need protection, I can arrange it."

"We're okay," Bryce said. "I'll take you at your word and let you do your job. Stay in touch." He extended his hand and Larry shook it.

Driving home, Bryce made a silent promise to himself. No more running down rabbit holes. He was lucky to be alive, and even though it might still not be over, the only thing his continued prodding could do was make things worse. It was time to be the gray man, disappear into the drudgery of everyday life, and let matters take their course.

He wondered if Ashley had plans for dinner.

CHAPTER 57

"**WHAT DO YOU MEAN,** he's changing his mind?" Greg Peoples screamed into the phone.

"He doesn't think we can protect him. He says he's willing to take the time for whatever crimes we charge him with."

"And does he know that list of crimes includes conspiracy to commit murder for hire, and that he's going to spend the rest of his life in prison?" the red-faced ASAC replied.

"We told him. And his response was at least he would have a life."

"Unacceptable. I want to talk to him."

"The Marshals won't let you do that."

"They will if you tell them to, Bob. You're the United States Attorney, for Christ's sake. This is the only optic we have into how the Network operates and who these so-called 'partners' are. We have to find a way. This is the kind of case that turns prosecutors into judges, you know what I mean?"

"Slow your roll, Greg. We're not all shameless careerists."

Peoples bristled at the dressing down.

The US Attorney continued. "I'll tell you what. If you can convince the Marshals to let you see him, I'll support it. And if you can convince Mr. Todd to play ball, I'll support that as well. You know I want to put these killers away. But I'm not in the business of strong-arming defendants, and neither are my assistants. If it ever got out that we coerced his testimony in any way, he wouldn't last five minutes on cross examination. You want to get him back on board, it's on you to find a way, and whatever you do had best pass every legal, moral, and ethical sniff test."

"I have an idea," Peoples continued. "Let's pull his protection detail. Throw his ass in general population down at pre-trial and see how long he lasts before he comes begging for us to take him back."

"Jesus, Greg," the top prosecutor fumed. "Do you have even a shred of decency? We agreed to protect him."

"That agreement was contingent on him playing ball," Peoples countered.

"True, but I'm not sending a man to his death because of your wounded ego. If it's that important to you, go talk to him in person. But I'm warning you, if I so much as hear about a single underhanded tactic, we are done with this witness. He's already indicted; all we need to do is unseal and take him before a magistrate to get the process started. Once that happens, he won't be in a position to cooperate any longer. And it sounds like that's what he wants anyway. Oh, and we're still going to protect him, for as long as I'm the chief law enforcement official in this district. He's already given us a trove of useful information, and we're not going to set a precedent of hanging our informants out to dry after we're done with them."

"Good point, sir," Peoples said. "Thanks for the call." He hung up and dialed his secretary on the intercom.

"Molly, get Butch Langham on the phone."

As the chief deputy for the Marshals Service in Atlanta, Albert "Butch" Langham was the highest ranking non-political appointee in the Service's 150-man office. Most of his staff was dedicated to courtroom security and managing the prisoner flow through those courtrooms. A smaller, more experienced cadre of deputy marshals were responsible for tracking down fugitives and protecting high-risk witnesses under the auspices of the Witness Security Program, or WITSEC, which was often misidentified in the media and entertainment industry as the Witness Protection Program. As was the case with most of the senior law enforcement officials in Georgia's Northern Judicial District, he was no fan of the FBI's Gregory Peoples, who he regarded as overly ambitious, under-experienced, and warrantlessly arrogant. Still, he couldn't refuse to do business with a fellow law enforcement officer based on personal animus, so he took the call when his secretary told him who was on the line.

"Morning, Greg," Butch said as flatly and coldly as he could.

Peoples got right to the point. "Good morning, Butch. I need to talk to you about James Todd."

"Mm-hmm. From what I heard, he doesn't want anything to do with the FBI. He thinks you boys are gonna get him killed."

"Great, then you already have the broad strokes. Butch, we need this guy. He can bring down a worldwide criminal syndicate, and he just needs to be reassured a little. Give me an hour with him, and I can get him back on track."

Langham was unimpressed. "Greg, just FYI, but I don't give one hot damn about an FBI case. My job is to keep this guy alive, and right now I'm doing that with four deputies split across rotating twelve-hour shifts. To be perfectly honest, James Todd being removed from my to-do list would be the best news I've heard all week. And you know we don't allow contact with outside agencies once we have them in the program."

Peoples saw his opening. "Give me an hour with him, and if he still doesn't want to work with us, I'll go to Bob Tolliver personally and end the whole thing. We'll take him off your hands, put him in pre-trial confinement where he belongs, let him run through the system, and ship him off to whatever FCI he's going to end up in for the rest of his life. I've already discussed this with Bob, and he's on board."

There was silence on the line while Langham considered the offer. "There would be conditions. We take you to and from the safe house. You won't know where it is until you get there. And no phones."

Peoples cut him off. "No phones? What's the sense in that? You think I'm going to call for a pizza while I'm there? Jesus, Butch, give me a break."

Langham continued as if Peoples hadn't said a word. "No audio or video recording equipment. You can have a pad and pen to take notes. And you dress in normal street clothes. Not a suit."

Peoples waited until he was sure the list of requirements had been exhausted. "Anything else?" he asked, the sarcasm evident through the phone.

"If you agree to the terms, I'll have the supervisor of the detail call you. When do you want to get this done?"

"The sooner the better. Today, if you can."

"We'll be in touch."

For no reason other than to irritate Greg Peoples, Butch Langham waited until the next morning to contact the detail supervisor. The Marshals Service picked Peoples up in a nondescript pickup truck and drove him to the safe house, which was an apartment in a high-rise near the Atlanta Braves' new stadium in Cobb County. As directed, he left his phone at the office and dressed in the best "I'm not a cop" ensemble he could put together: Levi's 501s, Converse Chuck Taylor sneakers, Ray-Bans, and a Ralph Lauren polo shirt, untucked of course. He noticed the driver snickering at him when he got into the truck, but didn't give him the satisfaction of an acknowledgment.

The driver parked the truck and walked Peoples through the lobby and onto the elevator, where he sent a text from his telephone and awaited the reply. "They're ready for you," he advised as the elevator reached its destination. "Apartment 2205, to the right, end of the hallway. Knock once. I'll see you downstairs when you're done." The doors closed and Peoples was alone.

The apartment door opened at the same time he knocked, and he was ushered inside. There were two deputy marshals in the apartment, and they looked every bit the part. Both were over six feet tall, clean cut, and obviously in peak physical condition. They were clad in 5.11 cargo pants and large, loose-fitting flannel shirts that concealed their duty weapons. Neither of them smiled. They motioned Peoples to the kitchen table where James Todd was seated.

Todd was the first to speak. "What's this about?" he asked.

Peoples pulled out a chair and sat down opposite Todd. "They didn't tell you the FBI was coming to talk to you?"

"No, I understand you're with the FBI. I mean, why you? Where are Morris and Chandler?"

"Mr. Todd, I am Greg Peoples, and I'm an Assistant Special Agent in Charge in the Atlanta field office. Donnie Morris works for me."

Todd laughed. "I know who you are. You're famous. The man in charge. Who looks more like a college kid on his way to a frat party than a G-man, by the way."

Peoples maintained his composure. "Let's dispense with the insults, shall we? I've come here to help you make an important decision. One that will affect the rest of your life."

"Yeah, right. I already told the lawyers I'm not testifying against anyone from the Network. You don't know these people like I do. It's a death sentence."

"That's what the Witness Security Program is for, James. Look at where you are now. Don't you think they would want you dead before you had a chance to talk about them in court? And yet here you are, safe and sound. That has to count for something."

"You're not hearing me. I don't care where you move me. I don't care what identity you give me. You can rename me Sidney Goldstein and make me an insurance salesman in Poughkeepsie, and they'll find me. It's what they do. The only chance I have is for them to know I'm not going to rat them out."

Peoples said, "But they already think that, James. They thought it when they came to your office to kill you. By the way, your instincts that day were spot on."

"Thanks. You know what my instincts are telling me right now? They're telling me you're full of shit, and that you couldn't care less what happens to me. My instincts are telling me you

just want to get me on board so you can make what will probably be the biggest case of your career and take that next step
up the ladder. They're telling me there was a reason those two
agents didn't want you involved in their investigation, probably
because they thought you'd fuck it up. And most importantly,
my instincts are telling me I'm better off keeping my mouth
shut and hoping the Network doesn't want to risk the exposure of trying to take me out. So, Mister ASAC, you can go
back to your boss and tell him 'no deal.' And see if you can do
that without announcing it to the whole goddamned world in
a press conference."

Peoples's jaw went slack as he searched for a retort. The best
he could manage was, "What's that supposed to mean?"

"I have a television in here, you know? I saw your little clown
show on the evening news. If I had any notion that the FBI cared
about my safety, that erased it. If I end up in prison, it won't be
because I ratted out the Network. But if I walk away a free man,
they'll know why, they'll find me, and they'll kill me."

The pair went back and forth for the next twenty minutes.
When Peoples realized he wasn't making headway, he ended the
meeting, asked the deputies to call for his ride, and met the driver
in front of the building.

As the truck pulled away from the apartment complex, the small
white coupe parked directly across the street stayed put. There
was no need to follow Peoples any more, at least not today. He
had been part of a three-man detail assigned to monitor the FBI

agent's comings and goings, and it appeared his diligence had finally paid off. He picked up his phone and dialed.

"McNair Industries."

"Let me talk to Mr. Jackson," he said.

"Who is calling?"

"Atlanta."

"Hold, please."

Mr. Jackson was on the line in seconds. "What do you have for me?" he asked.

"I think I may have found the lawyer. I followed the FBI guy from his house this morning. He didn't go to the office. Instead, he parked his car in a Starbucks parking lot and got into a pickup truck with dark-tinted windows. They drove to an apartment complex up near the baseball stadium, and he went inside for about half an hour. Oh, and he was dressed in some weird getup, like he was trying not to look like a fed. He came back downstairs a few minutes ago and rode away in the same pickup."

"Okay, and what are your thoughts?"

"It's out of his normal routine. There are no government offices anywhere near here, and he doesn't strike me as the kind of guy who keeps a girlfriend in a shag pad. Have the other guys pick him up again tomorrow, and let me have some time to check this place out. There are maybe three hundred units in the building he went into, so it's going to take a few days to figure out who's who. Once I have it narrowed down, I'll do some close-in work. If he's in there, we'll know."

"Sounds good. Once you confirm, our asset is ready to launch. And the big man himself is monitoring this one. Make us happy."

CHAPTER 58

THREE SHORT DAYS had done Harley a world of good. Most of the swelling in his head had subsided, and the drainage tube had been removed. His left eye was on the mend, now only partially closed but forecast to regain full sight according to his doctors. The bruises covering his face had begun to take on the yellowish edges that indicated the healing process was underway. Most importantly, he had been moved from the ICU to a semi-private room, which for the moment was a private room as the second bed was empty. A hospital food tray near the bed contained a half-eaten bowl of applesauce, Jell-O cubes, and a milkshake in a Styrofoam cup. While Harley picked at the soft food diet he would be relegated to for the next few weeks, Bryce brought him up to speed on the latest developments.

"Courtesy of our friends at the Drug Enforcement Administration," he said, as he showed Harley the postmortem pictures of Manny and Chico. "Are these the guys who beat you up?"

Harley stared at the phone for a few seconds before speaking. When the words came they were slow and indistinct, but clear enough that Bryce could understand him and appreciate the progress he had made since they last spoke. "The dude with the scar, definitely. He was the one asking the questions. The other one, I couldn't say. He was behind me the whole time. I have to tell you, Bryce, **and** I feel bad saying this, but I'm glad they're dead."

"You and me both. Look, while I'm here, I want to tell you something. I'm proud of **you**."

The remark caught **Harley** off guard. "What do you mean?" he asked.

"Just the way you've **handled** yourself. Most people I know wouldn't have stood up to a couple thugs like that. It took guts. You're one tough son of a **bitch**, you know that?"

Harley managed a **small** laugh, though his cracked ribs still made it painful to breathe. "I don't know about tough. My mother always said I was pig-headed, and all my teachers said I was dumb as a stump. Maybe that's **what** it is. Stubborn and stupid."

"Don't sell yourself **short**. You're a good man. You've got principles and you don't **violate** them. I respect that."

Harley was unused **to praise**. His eyes began to moisten, and he quickly wiped them **dry with** the sleeve of his gown before full-blown tears had a chance to **form**.

"Can I ask you a question? It's gonna sound dumb."

"Ask away."

"Are we friends?"

"Harley, nothing about that question is dumb. And yes, we are most certainly friends." He placed his hand on Harley's shoulder to reinforce his words.

Harley smiled and closed his eyes. "Thanks, buddy. Can you stay awhile, or do you need to get on the road?"

"I've got nowhere to be. I can hang out with you for a while."

"Good. I'm sleepy, though. I might be in and out."

Bryce pulled the chair from across the room, placed it next

to Harley's bed, and sat down. "You sleep. I'll be here when you wake up."

———————

Not twenty minutes from Miami Methodist Hospital, Larry Paz was drinking his morning coffee and preparing for the next day's meeting with his prosecutor. He wasn't sure how he was going to broach the subject of the random hit man who murdered two of Chase Worthing's potential co-conspirators, but he was certain the escalation of violence in the case was going to force her hand, and his two-year-long investigation was going to yield little more than drug and money laundering charges. Significant violations, to be sure, but at the end of the day, routine and uninspiring.

He and Jose were driving to the Keys that afternoon to confront Lieutenant Mullins. Their task force officer said Mullins was working overnight shifts, so the plan was to knock on his door around 4:00 p.m., after he'd had a chance to sleep. Neither of them were optimistic about flipping him, and if he told them to pound sand they'd have to do just that. They had nothing on him, and even if they did, how close was he to Chase Worthing and what could he deliver? Larry's lukewarm prediction for his case's end game was coming true.

And then his desk phone rang.

"Paz."

"Hi Larry, it's Monica in reception. You have a walk-in."

"Fuck that. I'm not on complaint duty this week."

"Watch your mouth, mister. And it's not a random walk-in. He asked for you. Or at least, he asked for the Worthing case agent."

"What's his name?"

"He didn't want to tell me anything. He's just sitting in a chair outside my window, staring off into space."

"Is he a nutjob?" Larry asked.

"Doesn't seem to be. He's pretty well-spoken, clean cut, not your usual crazy. And he's dressed in civvies, but—"

"But what?"

"Well, I could be wrong, but I think he's a cop."

CHAPTER 59

IT WAS a Chamber of Commerce day, and appropriately, the president of the South Miami Chamber of Commerce was in attendance, along with a bevy of other community heavy hitters, all of whom wanted their piece of the publicity pie when the ribbon cutting video made the local news.

The complex sprawled over twenty acres, and while the archway over its grand entrance read *Worthing Park*, there were actually four individual baseball fields arranged like pieces of a pie in a huge circle, their home plates at the center, and the outfield walls forming one giant outer perimeter. A massive set of bleachers encircled it all, providing seating for up to 1,000 fans per field, each of which boasted a state-of-the-art electronic scoreboard complete with animation effects. The outfield walls were festooned with billboards of sponsors numbering nearly a hundred, all of whom combined spent a fraction of the money spent by the park's namesake. The grass was thick, lush, and bright green. The basepaths were premium-level sand/clay/silt mix, the same as that used in major league baseball parks. But for the size, it could have passed for a Double- or Triple-A ballpark.

The stage was set up behind second base on field number one, and no less than twenty dignitaries were seated on either side of the podium. Folding chairs provided seating for three hundred parents and other attendees unworthy of a spot on the dais. A dozen teams of eight- to twelve-year-olds stood in their crisp white uniforms in front of the dugouts and along the foul fences. It was a great day for baseball, and particularly Mini League baseball in South Florida.

The crowd rose, removed their hats, and placed their hands over their hearts as the public address system played "The Star-Spangled Banner." The league president opened the ceremony, his remarks centering on the new opportunities the park would present for underprivileged young boys and girls, many of whom had never played baseball on anything other than an inner-city street or a vacant lot.

He ceded the microphone to the local representative from the city council, who blathered on about public works projects which had absolutely nothing to do with America's pastime. When he was sure he had said enough to merit at least ten seconds of audio on the evening news, he introduced the mayor, who strode to the podium to a smattering of half-hearted applause.

"Thank you, Jim. Members of the council, Mini League board members, moms and dads, and most of all, the players and coaches who will grace these magnificent fields . . . welcome to the finest youth league baseball complex in all of South Florida. Welcome to Chase Worthing Park!"

He paused for a polite round of applause, then continued.

"I am honored to share the stage with the man who made this all possible. He grew up here in South Florida, and those of you old enough to remember him during his NASCAR days knew him as one of the most competitive, daring drivers on the circuit. When he retired, he could have moved to the announcer's booth and lived anywhere he wanted. But he stayed here. He opened a business here. And for the past thirty years, he has reinvested the profits from that business back into our communities, our schools, and our children. Ladies and gentlemen, boys and girls, please join me in welcoming a hometown hero who has made us all proud. A son of South Florida who believes charity begins at home. A pillar of our community, and the name behind this glorious new sports complex . . . Mr. Chase Worthing!"

The applause was no longer polite. It was loud, boisterous, and sincere. The audience stood and chanted his name as he rose from his seat, walked to the podium, and greeted the mayor with a handshake-turned-embrace. Chase looked every bit the part of the local hero, and fifty-eight years had done little to rob him of his God-given good looks. He was tanned and fit, with a full head of perfectly coiffed, slightly graying hair, teeth that had been whitened perhaps a shade too far, and the same classically chiseled features that earned him the nickname "Chase the Face" from his fellow drivers and fans back in the day. He was dressed in "South Florida formal" for the occasion—crisp white chinos, an untucked silk flower-print short-sleeve shirt, and a pair of expensive Italian loafers, sans socks.

"Thank you, Mr. Mayor, for that most gracious introduction. I am so proud to be here with you today, and to share the field with so many future big league ball players. When I opened Worthing Motors nearly thirty years ago, I knew I wanted to use my good fortune to make a difference here in the greater Miami area. These young boys and girls you see standing behind you are our future, and they will be better prepared to meet that future by participating in youth sports. Studies have shown that boys and girls who play organized sports are better students. They are more likely to go to college and to have successful careers later in life."

"And," he continued, pausing slightly for emphasis, "they are less likely to become involved in drugs. Playing organized sports takes time. It takes effort. It takes energy. That's time, effort, and energy they won't be using to ingest the poison that has become all too easy to obtain in today's society. I hope everyone here, and especially the boys and girls who will use these fields, will join me in a pledge to stay drug free, today and every day!"

The audience rose to their feet again in a round of applause, and Chase responded with a thumbs-up gesture to acknowledge their enthusiasm. As they applauded, a pair of volunteers pulled a yellow ribbon across the stage, and a third appeared with a clownishly oversized pair of scissors which he handed to Chase, who joined the mayor at the center of the stretched-out ribbon.

"As mayor, I hereby declare that Chase Worthing Park is officially open!" he said as he cut the ribbon. "Play ball!" Chase and the mayor shook hands with each other as the cameras clicked away.

After a few minutes, the crowd began to disperse, and Chase remained on the field long enough to snap selfies with anyone who asked, which was a considerable number of Mini Leaguers and their parents.

As he said his goodbyes and walked toward his car, the phone in his pocket buzzed. It was the phone he never used in public. The one only a select few people knew existed.

It was a text message from Roger Mackenzie. *We need to talk. I'm parked next to you.*

They drove to a nearby shopping mall, where Roger climbed into Chase's Mercedes G63 and gave him the news.

"Are you sure it was them?"

"Positive," Roger replied. "I've got pictures if you want to see."

Chase dismissed the offer with a wave of his hand. "No. What the hell went wrong? Weren't they just going there to put a scare into him?"

"That was the plan. But somehow it all went south. Here's the thing, though. We don't think it was Chandler that killed them. My source says he has an airtight alibi."

"And who's the source?"

"John Mullins," Roger replied.

"Which one is he?"

"The lieutenant with the sheriff's office. He's been on the payroll for a couple years."

"Okay, if not Chandler, who killed them?"

"It looks like some mystery shooter who got shot himself, then crashed his car about twenty-five miles away in Marathon. All we have is a name. Robert Petty. I've had our people run it through their databases but nothing comes back on him. I have a driver's license picture of him, so we'll start showing that around and see what shakes out. But for now it's a dead end."

"You said he got shot and crashed his car. Where is he now? Is he alive or dead?" Chase asked.

Roger replied, "Also a mystery. He was treated at Mariners Hospital in Marathon, then airlifted to Miami, and from that point in time nobody knows anything."

"Well, tell your source to find him, find out why he killed two of my men, and most importantly, find out if someone out there has a larger grievance with our organization."

"That's going to be a chore," Roger replied. "If he's still alive, I can only assume the cops are going to have him locked down 24/7, and we're not going to get close to him."

"I don't want you assuming anything. We've got a shipment coming in a week, and the last thing I need is some replacement ninja waiting on the dock to put a bullet in my skull when the boat docks. Do you think this has anything to do with our fishing trip out to the East Hump?"

Roger shook his head. "I don't. And I don't think you need to be at the marina for a simple delivery. We have people who can handle that."

Chase scowled. "They're never simple."

"You're the boss. But mark my words, micromanagement is going to be the end of you one day. You didn't need to go out to East Hump, and you don't need to be supervising offloads of product."

"You're right. I am the boss. Now do what I told you to do."

CHAPTER 60

"I DON'T LIKE IT."

John Mullins was seated across the table from Larry Paz and Janice Swift, the Assistant United States Attorney for the Southern District of Florida, who was lead prosecutor on the Chase Worthing case. Less than three hours had elapsed since Mullins had entered the DEA's office and refused to leave until he spoke to the case agent. In that time he had teased Paz with enough information to warrant an impromptu meeting at the United States Attorney's office, where a written agreement of cooperation now sat on the table before him.

"And what don't you like about it, Mr. Mullins?" Janice Swift asked.

"There's no guarantee that I get my pension," he replied. "I've worked over twenty years in the sheriff's office, and I'm eligible to retire as soon as I'm fifty. I'm not signing anything unless it guarantees my pension."

Janice replied, "Mr. Mullins, that is entirely out of our control. If the sheriff fires you, he fires you. And to be perfectly blunt, he probably will. I know I would if I were the sheriff and found out one of my deputies was working for a drug kingpin. But I think it's more important you focus on what is guaranteed here, namely the fact that you will avoid prosecution if you are completely honest with us about your work for the Worthing drug trafficking organization. And that includes the caveat that any crimes of violence you admit to, or that we subsequently discover, are outside the boundaries of this agreement and will subject you to the full brunt of the law."

"And while we're at it," she continued, "Let's discuss the nature of the crimes you could be facing. Agent Paz tells me you have been moonlighting for Chase Worthing for quite some time now, and I would expect you've been abusing your position of trust as a law enforcement officer in order to do so. Judges and juries take a very dim view of that, sir. As to the charges themselves, you should know that we are investigating Mr. Worthing and his associates as a racketeering-influenced corrupt organization, or RICO. That means all I have to do is tie you to one of their predicate offenses, and you are exposed to a lengthy prison term, starting around twenty years. Between phone records and the testimony of other defendants, it shouldn't be hard to make that connection. So to sum it all up, while I appreciate your willingness to cooperate with the government, you are in no position to negotiate anything more favorable than what you see in front of you."

Mullins paused. He knew the pension angle was a non-starter and the federal government had no say in the personnel matters of the Monroe County sheriff, but he had to take a shot nonetheless. He had resigned himself to the inevitability of his situation before walking into the DEA office.

"So when you say crimes of violence, that means actually participating in one, right? As opposed to just knowing about it? I mean, if something happened and I had nothing to do with it—"

Janice cut him off. "If all you have is knowledge after the fact, you are fine. But if you tell us about it, deny your involvement, and later we find out you were a participant, then it is outside of the agreement and you are not protected."

"So, if somebody was already dead, and I had nothing to do with their death, but let's say hypothetically I knew where the bodies were disposed of, then what?" Mullins asked.

Larry interjected. "You said 'somebody,' then you said 'bodies.' Plural. Who are we talking about?"

Mullins shook his head. "You still haven't answered my question. If I had nothing to do with the murder but could lead you to the bodies, am I in the clear?"

Janice asked, "Who's responsible for these alleged murders?"

Mullins smiled. "You know exactly who. His name is on your case file folder."

Janice said, "If what you're telling me is that you can positively tie Chase Worthing to a murder, perhaps multiple murders, and you had nothing to do with it, then yes. Yes, Mr. Mullins, you would be 'in the clear,' to use your phrasing."

"All right, then. Where do I sign?"

CHAPTER 61

THERE WERE thirty floors in the building, and ten units per floor. The amount of combing through public records databases and Google research would have been overwhelming, and the scout had promised Mr. Jackson results within a few days. It would have to be done in person.

The pickup truck returned the next morning, this time without the goofy looking FBI agent, but rather with two large, serious looking men in their thirties or forties. One of them was dressed in the dead-giveaway federal agent getup—tan cargo pants, polo shirt, hiking boots, and a photographer's multi-pocketed vest two sizes too large, to conceal the weapon on his hip. The other wore blue jeans and a sport jacket, only slightly less obvious than his urban-safari-ready partner.

They parked the truck in the rear of the building and walked around to the lobby, where he was waiting, appearing to be immersed in a phone call but waiting for them to hail the elevator. When the bell rang and the doors opened, he finished his fake call and walked the ten feet or so to the open elevator to join them. They looked annoyed as he stepped through the closing doors, forcing them to reopen.

"What floor you going to?" the sport coat-clad agent asked.

"Fifteen, please," he answered, taking his place in the rear corner of the elevator and avoiding eye contact with his targets. The two men were as disinterested in him as he seemingly was with them. When the car reached the fifteenth floor, he glanced at the row of buttons as he exited to see which ones were still illuminated. There was only one.

The twenty-second floor.

––––––––––––

It took another twenty-four hours to figure out the schedule. Shift change was at seven, evening and morning. The other vehicle was a white Ford Explorer, and the second shift was an equally serious and no less obvious pair. Out of an abundance of caution, he waited for two full shifts to pass and made his next advance at seven the next evening, not wanting to be seen twice by the day shift.

He employed the same ruse, but this time wore a polo shirt bearing the logo of a food delivery service, and carried an insulated cooler strapped over one shoulder. As they entered the elevator, he pushed number twenty-two, moved to the rear of the car, and appeared to be engrossed in his cell phone as the three of them shared the ride.

He allowed the men to exit the elevator first, turning in the opposite direction they chose. He reached the end of the hallway just in time to hear them knocking on a door behind him, and he turned around to see them entering the last door on the left side of the hallway. As it closed, he walked back toward the target apartment, ready at any moment to stop, knock on a random door, and play the part of the lost food delivery guy. It wasn't necessary. They were oblivious to his presence, and his surveillance of the twenty-second floor went off without a hitch. He made a mental note of the unit number as he did another U-turn at the end of the empty corridor, got back onto the elevator, and returned to his car.

Once inside, he dialed McNair Industries and asked for Mr. Jackson, who picked up on the first ring.

"What do you have for me?" he asked.

"Apartment 2205."

CHAPTER 62

THE DEBRIEFING had to move to a larger room. Janice Swift's boss, the chief of the Criminal Division, wanted to hear what the newest informant in the Chase Worthing case had to say, as did Larry Paz's ASAC. A stenographer and videographer were brought in to capture everything on camera and in writing in case John Mullins decided to change his story before they had a chance to lock it down in front of the grand jury.

Janice handled most of the questioning. "Mr. Mullins, how would you describe the nature of your relationship with Chase Worthing?" she asked.

John Mullins had been offered the opportunity to retain an attorney but didn't want to spend the money. He also knew that a "Get out of jail free" card was what the government was offering, and it wouldn't get any better than that, attorney or no attorney. He had conducted enough interrogations to know how to handle himself.

"Well, to start, I've only met Chase himself a couple of times. Most of my dealings were with his attorney, Roger Mackenzie."

"Okay," she continued. "Then tell us about your relationship with Mr. Mackenzie."

"I met him about three years ago when I arrested his son for DUI in Marathon. Apparently he was some hotshot law student up at Florida State who was going to follow his dad into the family business, and Roger showed up at the jail while we were booking him in. He pulled me aside and asked if there was anything he could do to help the situation. At first I told him I couldn't."

"And what made you change your mind?" she asked.

"The roll of cash he pulled out of his pocket."

"How much?"

"It turned out to be ten thousand, but what got my attention wasn't the amount, but that it was literally a roll of cash. Held together with a rubber band."

"Doper style?" Larry Paz asked.

"Exactly. I was going through a divorce at the time, getting raped for alimony and child support. I figured there was plenty more where this came from, and if this Mackenzie guy was running the kind of weight that allowed him to throw around that level of cash, he was someone worth knowing. And worth helping."

"So where did it go from there?" Janice asked.

"About three months later, Roger called me and asked if I could keep law enforcement away from the Upper Keys Marina on Tavernier for about four hours."

"And you were able to do that?"

"I'm the shift lieutenant. Patrols go where I tell them," he replied.

Janice continued. "And how many times have you kept the coast clear for Mr. Mackenzie?"

"About once every other month, so however many times that works out to be," he answered. "And there was an incident I cleaned up for them. A nasty one."

"Tell me what you mean by 'cleaning up an incident,'" Janice said.

"A few of Chase's men were pulling a security detail, keeping their eye on a yacht that had a cash shipment onboard until it left the marina the next morning. Some stoner came around asking questions about it. Way too many questions, from what I was told. So Chase's guys followed him around the back of a restaurant, and out of nowhere somebody in a car runs them down. Paralyzed one of them, in fact. Anyway, Roger had me go the restaurant at two in the morning, make like I was taking reports from all the witnesses, then shit-can the paperwork. It was as if nothing ever happened. One of the guys who wasn't hurt too badly got the license plate of the car, so I ran it and gave the information to Roger. If you're investigating Chase Worthing, you should have heard about this. It was a big deal."

Janice glanced at Larry, who nodded without comment.

For the next several hours, they delved into the entirety of John Mullins's association with Chase Worthing, Roger Mackenzie, and the vast criminal enterprise they oversaw. Most of it was pedestrian, from working as a lookout and managing crime scenes in favor of his bosses to obtaining police reports and running license plates on the sly. The prosecutor and the drug agent covered every detail, and by the time they ordered sandwiches and broke for a fifteen-minute dinner, they had all they needed to make John Mullins a worthwhile witness, albeit a less than credible one. Everything they had would be his word versus that of the defendants, and a seasoned defense attorney would destroy the crooked cop on cross examination.

Janice saved the best for last.

"All right," she said, "Let's talk about this murder. And I remind you, Mr. Mullins, if you played any part whatsoever in it, our deal is off the table."

"Not a problem," he replied. "Actually, it was one of the few times I saw Chase Worthing up close. I always heard he meets the inbound drug shipments in person, but I was never allowed near the marina when those were coming in. My job was just to keep the cops away."

"All right, then," she said. "Tell us about it."

"It was almost three weeks ago. Roger called me and asked if I had access to a sheriff's department boat, which I do. So he had me meet him at a marina off Long Key. When I got there, he was tied up to the dock in a thirty-footer with Chase Worthing and two other guys I think Agent Paz probably knows. They went by Manny and Chico."

Larry interjected. "So we're clear, you're talking about the Manny and Chico who turned up dead in Bryce Chandler's house a few days ago?"

"That's them. Anyway, they wanted me to escort them out to a commercial fishing area called the East Hump. They didn't say why, but it was obvious to me that with a marked sheriff's boat nearby, everyone else would keep their distance. There's a lot of illegal fishing that goes on around here, and when people see the law, they tend to go the other way."

Janice asked, "How long did it take you to get to the East Hump?"

"Half an hour. They stopped in a spot where there weren't any other boats in sight. I don't know if they dropped anchor, but I do know what I saw next."

"And what was that?" Janice asked.

"They threw two bodies overboard."

Janice tried to control her gasp, but came up short. "Describe the bodies for me."

Mullins raised his hands. "Okay, let me back up. They threw what appeared to be two bodies overboard. Whatever they were, they were human-sized, and looked to be wrapped in black plastic. And it took two of them to lift each body, and another to throw something else in right afterward. I'm assuming it was some kind of weight, like a cinder block or something."

"East Hump is a big area," Larry said. "Fifty square miles if I recall. I was a deck hand on a tuna boat during high school, and we fished there. The waters are between six hundred and a thousand feet deep. It'll be like looking for a needle in a haystack."

Mullins smiled. "Maybe. Except I dropped a pin on my GPS when I saw the first body go overboard. And they were a hundred yards due east of my position."

"Why did you mark the location?" Larry asked.

Mullins smiled. "Because when you've been in the business as long as I have, you know the value of other people's secrets. And you never know when a piece of information is going to come in handy, so you gather all you can, keep it close to you, and wait for the opportunity to use it. Like today."

"Fair enough. And what happened after both bodies went in the water?" Larry asked.

"Nothing, really. They turned back toward Long Key, and I followed them. When they pulled into the marina, I turned west toward Marathon and put the boat back into our slip there. A week later I saw Roger and he gave me five thousand dollars for helping them out. I asked him what it was about, and he didn't answer directly. All he said was, 'You don't want to get on Chase's bad side, and you damn sure don't want him to think you're a snitch.' I'm pretty sure it was a warning."

They took another break. Mullins used the bathroom while Larry and Janice went over their notes, strategized, and decided to wrap it all up.

"Last bit of questioning, Mr. Mullins," Janice said. "You've made it clear your job is to keep law enforcement away from the Upper Keys Marina when Chase Worthing gets his shipments in. So they must tell you in advance when a boat is arriving, am I correct?"

"I get three to four hours' notice. Roger Mackenzie usually calls me on my cell."

"Good," Larry said. "I'm sure it goes without saying that you and I are going to be in constant communication with each other until further notice."

"I assumed so," Mullins replied.

"Oh, and one more thing," Larry said. "We're going to need those GPS coordinates."

Two days after the Mullins interview, illegal fishing in the East Hump dropped to nearly zero, as the word of the two-hundred-foot Coast Guard cutter anchored in the commercial fishery deep water spread throughout the fleets and was broadcast over marine radio. A security zone was established around the massive ship for a half mile in all directions, and any vessel coming to close was warned off by one of a half dozen pursuit boats guarding the perimeter.

The GPS coordinates were dead-on accurate, and the Coast Guard's elite deep water dive team found their targets in a matter of hours. Both bodies, as John Mullins had observed, were wrapped in thick black plastic sheeting and bound with duct tape. Each was additionally encircled with twenty feet of half-inch-thick galvanized chain, with three feet left dangling at the heads and feet. The ends of the chain were tied around fifty-pound cinder blocks.

The bodies were delivered as recovered, chains and all, to the Florida Department of Law Enforcement regional crime laboratory in Fort Myers. The forensic exploitation and autopsies took three days to complete, and the medical examiner determined the cause of death for each as a combination of exsanguination, or a fatal loss of blood, and traumatic brain injury. Both victims had a single gunshot wound to the back of their head. Both had their carotid arteries cut by a thin-bladed instrument. The medical examiner opined in his report that the killer took the additional measure of bleeding the victims in order to speed their descent to the ocean floor. Three weeks in the water had taken its toll and rendered the bodies unrecognizable, but in the end, dental records eliminated all doubt as to the whereabouts of Stanley and April Murtaugh.

CHAPTER 63

AFTER CONSIDERING all the options, Randall decided on the underground parking garage. He needed to create enough of a commotion to empty out the building, but not so much as to bring it all down around him while he went about his task. The garage was constructed almost entirely of concrete, so the only fuel would be the cars themselves, and the gas in their tanks. There were stairwells in each corner of the structure, in the event the elevators shut down at the triggering of the first smoke alarm. He winced at the idea of having to climb twenty-two floors, but knew he could do it if he had to, and it would only be in the event the device somehow prematurely ignited.

Working in his hotel room, he soldered a pair of wires to the speaker output nodes inside an ancient Nokia cellphone, and tested his circuit with a low-voltage LED lightbulb, which flashed brightly when the phone's countdown timer reached zero. Satisfied that the phone was providing enough power to trigger his charge, he removed the LED, replaced it with an electric match, and buried the match inside a gallon-sized zippered plastic bag filled with two pounds of smokeless gunpowder. He wrapped the bag in duct tape to form a neat, airtight package and, in turn, taped the cellphone to the outside of it all. Once the timer was set, he had a "toss and forget" incendiary device that would burn hot enough to turn any vehicle into an inferno, and the chain reaction among the adjacent cars would do the rest.

He chose 3:00 a.m. as zero hour. Most of the building's occupants would be asleep, giving him the best chance of moving around the parking garage and up to the twenty-second floor undetected, at least by other human beings. The complex had a security camera system, but it was not monitored in real time, and a simple disguise of a wig, hat, and dark glasses would prevent him from being identified when the authorities finally got around to examining the video evidence. Additionally, the early morning hours were when most people were at their least observant, especially when roused from their slumber, and he surmised that, in the confusion and chaos, nobody would remember him.

Randall walked the six blocks from his hotel to the apartment in solitude and darkness. When he arrived at the building, he walked around the block to the entry ramp that led from the street into the garage, ducked under the mechanical arm, which was designed to block cars but not people, and began his assessment.

About 80 percent of the vehicle spots were occupied. Any of them would do, but he wanted one with cars on each side to ensure the fire was large and fast-moving enough to require an evacuation of the building. He couldn't risk the possibility that a hero with a fire extinguisher would save the day and, in turn, ruin his. A small white crew cab pickup with a camper shell over the bed caught his eye, and he moved toward it for a closer look.

The magnetic sign on the doors read *EZ Painting*. He shined his light into the bed, which was packed full of paint cans, brushes, rollers, and tarps. Then, what he was looking for, nearest the passenger compartment: three five-gallon buckets, two labeled *Methyl*

Ethyl Ketone, and the third marked *Mineral Spirits*. He checked the door handles to see if the truck's owner was going to make it easy on him, but they were locked. A quick look around the cab's interior failed to turn up any of the telltale signs of an alarm system such as a blinking LED, and he decided it was safe to go to Plan B.

He pulled a spark plug insulator from his backpack, stood back about three feet, and threw it with moderate force against the rear passenger side window, which immediately spiderwebbed into thousands of pieces but remained in place in the window frame. With a gloved hand, he made a hole in the shattered window large enough to reach through and open the rear door. Once inside, he retrieved the package, set the timer to ten minutes, placed it under the rear seat, and closed the door.

With the countdown underway, Randall checked his watch and headed for the elevator.

———

"Sam, wake up."

It was a two-bedroom apartment, and the protectee slept in one of them. The pair of deputy marshals split the shift between watch duty in the kitchen or sleeping in the remaining bedroom. They usually swapped out at 2:00 a.m., and Sam DiGenova, senior between the two, had been sleeping for about an hour when his partner, Ron Derry, roused him.

"What is it?" he asked, sitting up in bed and squinting toward the light pouring in the door from the kitchen.

"The building fire alarm is going off," Ron replied. "Should we wait and see if it's anything serious?"

"Look out the peephole and let me know if you see smoke," Sam advised.

"Nothing," the partner said, his face pressed to the door.

"All right, let's wait and see if the fire department shows up. It could be a false alarm." He walked to the balcony sliding door to open the curtains and check for red lights, and knew in an instant it was no false alarm.

"Ron, we got a problem," Sam said. The thick, black smoke was billowing upward from the parking garage, and when he opened the balcony door to look down at the origin, it burned his lungs and eyes. He retreated back into the apartment and closed the balcony door.

"Can you see where it's coming from?" Ron asked.

"Not exactly, but it's in the building, and it's below us," Sam answered. "We need to move him. Get the car, I'll grab the go bags and we'll meet you downstairs in five minutes. Keep in mind the elevators may be out." He donned his clothes and shoes and began gathering the necessary bug out items that needed to go with them in the event of an emergency evacuation. He didn't need to answer a slew of questions from the protectee right now, and since James Todd slept like a rock, he would leave him alone until the very last minute.

"The building's on fire! Everybody out!" Randall moved from door to door, up and down the hallway, knocking loudly on each while watching his target location, waiting for his moment.

He began his move as soon as he saw the door to apartment 2205 open, then stopped when he saw only one man step out and the door close behind him. It wasn't the target. Maybe he was conducting an advance escape route reconnaissance. Maybe he was checking to see if the fire was real. In any event, the other marshal and the target were still inside the apartment. He stayed on the other end of the corridor, knocking and warning, as the fortunate marshal walked past the elevator and into the stairwell, beginning his long descent toward the parking garage, which was now fully engulfed in flames.

"Get up, James."

He had to shake his arm to break the spell of sleep, and even then James Todd seemed confused, as if he didn't know where he was. He sat up in bed slowly and stared at Sam with a puzzled look.

"What's going on?" he mumbled.

"There's a fire in the building. You need to be dressed and ready to go in one minute," Sam ordered. "You can take whatever fits in your pockets. Leave everything else. We'll be going down the stairs."

"Twenty-two floors?" James gasped, reaching for his jeans. "Why can't we take the elevator?"

Sam heard the sirens in the distance. "Elevators don't work during a fire, and that, by the way, was your last question. Thirty seconds." He pulled his phone from his pocket and texted Ron: *Headed down. Meet in front of building.*

He donned an oversized backpack, checked to see that a round was chambered in his service pistol, and holstered it underneath his jacket. "Let's go," he said to James, who was fully dressed and standing behind him.

Randall knew the next time the door opened, it would be time, and he positioned himself beside the jamb just out of view of the peephole. The other residents had scurried down the stairwells to safety, and he was the only one left in the hallway. The instant the door cracked open, he pivoted in front and kicked it open with all his strength. The door caught Sam flush in the face and knocked him backward into the living room, where he fell, stunned. He had just enough time to reach for his weapon before the first round struck him in the center of the chest, and the second in his left eye. As Sam DiGenova lay dying, James Todd turned and ran back into his bedroom, slamming and locking the door behind him.

Randall delivered a much smaller kick to the hollow core interior door, which gave way with ease. James Todd was backed into a corner, seated on the floor with his knees pulled to his chest, tears beginning to form in his terror-filled eyes as he looked up at the last human being he would ever see.

"I waited for you," Randall said.

James stared, wanting to say something but too paralyzed with fear to form words.

"I waited for you," he repeated, his voice soft and cold. "In your office. With your dead secretary behind me, stinking up the room. Did you know that? When we die, we shit ourselves. It's undignified, but what are you going to do, right? I'm sure she didn't care."

James finally managed a word. "Why?"

Randall smiled. "Oh, come on. You know why. You've known from day one what would happen if you turned on us."

He usually didn't spend this much time with his targets. The colloquy with Lashelle Washington had been an anomaly, but it was necessary in order to finish the job out of sight of the general public. This one should have been over and done already, but for some reason he was enjoying the moment, a cat toying with a mouse before its meal. The target wasn't just some random soul who pissed off the wrong person. He was a snitch. A snitch who could have brought down the entire operation, Randall included.

James shook his head as he slowly regained the ability to speak. "I didn't tell anyone. They wanted me to, but I didn't. There's no reason to kill me."

"There's every reason to kill you, James, the first of which is that you're lying to me. The marshals don't protect people who have nothing to say. Hell, the FBI was on television talking about their star witness, the one who was going to give them everything they needed to shut us down and put us all in jail."

"I changed my mind."

"Too late. Are you ready?" Randall asked, raising the gun and pointing it toward James's face. *You sick bastard,* he thought. *You're enjoying this, aren't you? You want him to know the very moment he's going to die. Finish it and get out of here.*

"Don't, please." James mumbled his final words as he brought his hands up in front of his face. Randall fired three times, then replaced the gun in its holster, pulled the dental forceps from his back pocket, and finished the job.

The sirens had stopped, but the red strobes looked as if they were right outside the building. Randall left the shell casings where they were; the gun was clean to begin with and within hours it would be relegated to scrap in an industrial crusher. He closed the apartment door behind him and made his way down the stairwell, where firemen were waiting at the first-floor landing to keep anyone from getting to the parking garage. Once outside, he made his way anonymously through the crowd of displaced renters and away from the building, gathered his things back at the hotel, and hailed a taxi to the airport.

———————

The phone rang at 4:00 a.m. mountain standard time, and it woke the old man up.

"This better be good," he said.

"It is, Sonny," the voice on the other end replied. "You said to call when there was news."

"And?"

"It's done."

"Good. I'm going back to bed."

"When can we get back to business?"

"I'll let you know."

CHAPTER 64

TRUE TO HIS WORD, Bryce kept a low profile after his dinner with Jose and Larry, dividing his attention between fishing, erasing the remnants of the crime scene from his house, and spending time with Ashley. What he thought might have been a one-night stand was slowly becoming a relationship, and he found himself enjoying her company more than he could have ever predicted when they first met as adversaries in Myron Troxley's courtroom. Most of their dates ended with him spending the night at her place in Marathon. After a late dinner in Key West, he suggested they stay at his house, a shorter drive by twenty-five miles than hers, but she flatly refused, insisting there would be zero likelihood of getting any sleep inside the scene of a double murder. Bryce couldn't blame her; he had more than his share of sleepless nights, and more than once considered selling.

He told her what he could and safeguarded the rest. She knew that a pair of Chase Worthing's henchmen came to his house, and she knew why. She knew they were murdered by someone from his past, but he stopped short of telling her about the Network or how it operated. And she knew that Stanley and April Murtaugh were murdered as she suspected, but not that Stanley had been working as an informant for the DEA during the time he was her client.

They were at her apartment when Donnie called. As usual, he had news, and as usual, the news was not good. Bryce listened as Donnie detailed what he knew of the fire and the murders of James Todd and Deputy United States Marshal Sam DiGenova. He was saddened, but not stunned by the carnage which had been brought about by Greg Peoples's ill-advised decision.

"And let me guess," he said, his voice brimming with anger. "That little turd is still running the Atlanta division, while you're sitting at home, waiting for your termination letter from headquarters. Am I right?"

"Afraid so," Donnie replied. "My sources tell me the only blowback is that he's been muzzled by the US attorney. There are to be no more statements, no more press conferences, no more investigation period until he says so. It sounds like they're in full-blown damage control mode now that their star witness is dead."

"Well," Bryce said, "he really was all we ever had. We knew that when we went to his office, didn't we?"

"We sure did. Anyway, there's a story about it in today's *Tribune*. I'll send you the link."

"Thanks. How are things going with you and Crystal? You guys holding up okay?"

"As well as can be expected," Donnie said. "Since the charges against me aren't criminal, they have to pay me even though I'm on suspension. But my lawyer says my chances don't look good for keeping my job, and I may want to consider resigning before they can fire me."

"Sounds like you need a new lawyer."

"I appreciate your confidence, Bryce, but like I said before,

I'm a big boy and I knew what I was getting myself into. And I'd do it again. Julie didn't deserve to die, and now it looks like there will be no justice for her killers. Sure, Travis Conway and James Todd are dead, but the trigger man and the organization behind him got off scot-free. It isn't right."

"No, partner, it isn't. But do me a favor, will you? Don't quit. Sometimes these things have a way of working themselves out. You can't just throw away seventeen years like that."

"I'll hang on as long as I can. But if I get notice that the termination is imminent, I'm pulling the plug. If I resign, at least I'm employable moving forward. I might even try and get my old job back, although I'm getting a little long in the tooth for that kind of work." Donnie, like Bryce, had been a police officer before joining the Bureau, and Bryce knew the thought of uprooting his family and returning to the streets of St. Louis at the age of nearly fifty was not a pleasant one.

"I understand," Bryce said. "Give Crystal my regards, and I'll see you at your reinstatement party."

Donnie laughed. "From your lips to God's ears, my friend."

A few minutes after he hung up, Bryce's phone buzzed with an email message from Donnie, who, as promised, was passing along the link to the article in the *Atlanta Tribune.*

With Murder of Star Witness, FBI Case Grows Cold

By Kevin Forrester and Rhonda Majette
Atlanta Tribune

Atlanta – The FBI's case against a mysterious murder-for-hire organization known simply as "the Network" among insiders has suffered a devastating blow, sources close to the investigation said.

Atlanta attorney James Todd was one of two people found dead in the aftermath of a mysterious apartment fire in Cobb County this week, which authorities now say appeared to have been set in order to facilitate the murders. According to sources who declined to be identified, Mr. Todd was under the protection of the United States Marshals Service as the government's star witness in the matter. During a press conference last month, FBI Agent Gregory Peoples stated there was an "...associate of the criminal enterprise" in protective custody, and sources have confirmed Mr. Todd was indeed that associate. Those sources went on to describe Mr. Todd as "...not just the government's star witness, but its only one."

United States Attorney for the Northern District of Georgia Robert Tolliver and FBI Special Agent in Charge Jonathan Turling both declined to comment, citing departmental policy regarding ongoing criminal investigations. Calls to FBI Agent Gregory Peoples, who conducted the aforementioned press conference, were not returned.

Bryce wondered who the unnamed sources might be, and dismissed the idea that Greg Peoples was continuing to try and manipulate the media to his own personal advantage. In the end, it didn't matter. It could have been anyone from the SAC down to an entry-level clerk who overheard the details of the investigation while pushing a mail cart. The word was out. The investigation had hit a brick wall. James Todd had been a stroke of sheer luck, lightning in a bottle, and their good fortune would not repeat itself. If the Network wasn't already back in business, it would be shortly.

Maybe he could do a little damage control himself.

———————

"Good morning, Judge."

"Good morning, Agent Chandler," Wendell Branch replied. "I would inquire as to why you're calling, but I'm sure it has something to do with the article in the *Tribune*. Your little side job with Agent Morris has stirred up quite the hornet's nest, hasn't it?"

"That's putting it mildly, Your Honor. It looks like the Network didn't take kindly to being found out, and they didn't care how much earth they had to scorch to stay in the shadows. And it worked. They won."

"Well, in all my years on the bench, one of the hardest things I had to swallow was watching a defendant walk out of my court a free man when I knew damned well he was guilty. But that's the system for you. It's an imperfect world we live in, I'm afraid."

"It is, Judge. Did I tell you last time we talked that Donnie is on suspension, pending termination?"

"No, you left that out. Can I assume your former boss, the one who made a fool of himself on live television, had something to do with it?"

"He had everything to do with it. He's had an axe to grind with Donnie and me since he was a brand-new agent, and now that he's an ASAC, he finally got an opportunity for payback."

"That doesn't seem right. I don't know Agent Morris personally, but from what I do know, he's a dedicated public servant with his mind and his heart in the right place. I could see him getting his wrist slapped for that stunt you two pulled, but in the end, without him there wouldn't be an investigation into the Network at all. And you say they're trying to fire him?"

"They are, Judge. He's running out of options."

"I wish there was something I could do to help."

"Maybe there is," Bryce said.

"Okay. What did you have in mind?"

"Well, Your Honor, you spent quite a long time on the federal bench. Over twenty years. That's a lot of law clerks. Did any of those clerks go on to bigger and better things?"

Judge Branch laughed. "You cheeky bastard. Somebody's been doing their homework."

"It's my job, Judge. And besides, it's not like it isn't public knowledge. Most people just forgot that he used to work for you. I remembered hearing about it once, and I double-checked his biography on Wikipedia."

"So," Judge Branch replied, "are you asking what I think you're asking?"

"I am, Judge."

"It's a big ask. And at that level, you know there are no guarantees."

"I know."

The silence was painful and long, but Bryce knew only Judge Branch could break it. Finally, he did.

"Agent Chandler, there are three irrevocable benefits for a man in my position, first and foremost among which is the pension that allows me to live out my days in one of the most beautiful places on God's green earth. Second is the fact that wherever

I go, people still call me 'Judge.' It's a title for life, and I'm not ashamed to admit I enjoy being tied to my life's work, if only by way of tradition and courtesy."

He continued. "Finally, being a retired judge frees me from the constraints I suffered while I was on the bench those many years . . . who I could talk to and who I couldn't, when I might need to recuse myself and when I could feel free to speak my mind, all in the name of blind justice. I remember times when Beatrice and I would walk out of a restaurant for fear of the appearance of impropriety because an attorney who was arguing a case in front of me was already there with his wife. But I'm old and retired now, and less is expected of me in terms of deference to societal and institutional protocols. So, what the hell? Let me see what I can do."

CHAPTER 65

"**WE'RE LIVE IN FIVE, EVERYONE!**" the news director shouted. "The usual open with Tina and Tom, twenty seconds on weather, another twenty on traffic, then straight to the live shots. Who do we have at the marina?"

"Sage is live at the marina, and Brock is in front of the car dealership," his assistant offered. "We have B-roll from the park dedication a couple weeks ago."

"No perp walks or mug shots?" the director asked.

"Sorry, boss, but no," the photography director answered. "The tip came in too late to get to the marina in time, and the feds don't do arrest photos."

"All right, then. We're going to fill the whole three and a half minutes until first commercial. Make sure Sage and Brock know I need at least a minute from each of them. Thirty seconds of Brock's piece will be voiceover for the B-roll."

For the next three minutes, the anchors read their scripts to themselves while makeup artists hovered around them, applying their final touches. The behind-the-scenes crew went about their normal business, double-checking cameras and lights, making sure the right video clips were cued in the correct order and the satellite feeds from the live shot locations were up and running.

"Cue the lead-in," the director ordered.

The screen lit up with the station's news logo as a background of dramatic music announced the beginning of the five o'clock morning news. The voiceover hadn't changed in years.

"Live. Local. Late breaking. This is Channel Six, Miami's most trusted news, with Tina Thrash and Tom Bellows."

The screen switched to a daytime shot of Chase Worthing's dealership, complete with a giant American flag waving in the breeze. Another voiceover, this one courtesy of Tina Thrash herself, teased the day's top story.

"Shocking news for South Florida, as federal agents arrest a Miami icon on drug and money laundering charges. We'll tell you who it is, right after traffic and weather."

Because the giant "Worthing Motors" sign wasn't enough of a clue, apparently.

"Tom and Tina, live in three, two—" The director held up one finger, then a closed fist as the red light on the camera in front of the anchor desk lit up.

"Good morning, Miami, I'm Tina Thrash."

"And I'm Tom Bellows. Breaking overnight, a Miami institution swarmed by federal agents, and its owner waking up in jail this morning. But first, your pinpoint weather and eye in the sky traffic, brought to you by Pollo Magnifico, voted Miami's favorite fast-food chicken five years in a row!"

It would be warm and sunny, and morning traffic through downtown was starting to build toward its usual state of gridlock. The camera returned to Tina Thrash, and the screen behind her showed the same shot of Worthing Motors, this time with the face of Chase Worthing himself superimposed over it.

"While you slept, agents from the Drug Enforcement

Agency and Florida Department of Law Enforcement were hard at work executing arrest and search warrants here in Miami and in Tavernier, just south of Key Largo. At the center of the raid is Miami's own Chase Worthing, the NASCAR sensation and luxury auto dealer who feds now say was leading a second life as a drug kingpin, importing thousands of kilograms of cocaine into the Sunshine State over the past two years alone."

Tom took over the commentary as the screen behind him switched to the live shot at the marina, and the waiting reporter.

"Our own Sage Myers is live at the Upper Keys Yacht Club and Marina in Tavernier. Sage, what can you tell us?"

It was still dark at the marina, and the camera light illuminated not only the reporter, but the massive boat she was using as the backdrop for her live shot. As she spoke, an army of agents dressed in windbreakers and body armor emblazoned with *DEA* and *FDLE* carried boxes marked *Evidence* off the boat's gangplank and into a waiting cargo van.

"Tom, all the action was over by the time we got here, but as you can see behind me, drug enforcement agents have no small task gathering and accounting for what I am told is an extremely large shipment of cocaine that was destined for Miami, where it was expected to be repackaged and sold nationwide. My sources told me the man behind the purchase was former NASCAR sensation Chase Worthing, and that he was arrested here at the marina shortly after midnight along with his longtime friend and business partner, Roger Mackenzie."

"Can you describe the scene for us, Sage?" Tom asked.

"In a word, Tom, organized. These agents clearly knew what they were after, and they came prepared. Besides the agents on the boat, there are at least a dozen more in the marina's business office, and they have been carrying white banker's boxes out of the building and into a nearby panel van for the better part of an hour. It looks as if, in addition to the drugs on the boat, they are seizing the business records for the marina as well."

The camera panned left as Sage spoke, then back toward her as she finished the piece.

"There was no sign of Chase Worthing or anyone else who was arrested here, and I'm told they are all being held in Miami, where they will have an initial appearance before a federal magistrate later today. Live in Tavernier, I'm Sage Myers."

"Thank you, Sage," Tina Thrash said from the anchor desk. "Now let's take you out to Chase Worthing Motors in South Beach, where Brock Salazar is standing by. Brock, what can you tell us?"

"Hi, Tina, a similar scene here in South Beach, but instead of drugs, these agents are seizing cars. Dozens of them, in fact, and I'm told by the end of the day there won't be a car left on South Florida's most exclusive luxury lot. Right now there is a line of car carriers around the block, each waiting to be loaded with at least eight of the high-end vehicles you see behind me. I'm told that means agents found a connection between the dealership and the drug dealing organization Chase Worthing is believed to lead. If that's the case, all the assets of the legitimate business are fair game for seizure, and in this case that includes the vehicles, the building, and even the land it sits on. And just as Sage reported from Tavernier, there seems to be a separate cadre of agents who are focusing specifically on the business offices inside the dealership, loading those familiar cardboard white banker's boxes with what we would presume is documentation of the crimes the government will attempt to prove in court."

As he spoke, the screen alternated video of his live shot with B-roll from the opening of Worthing Park, providing contrast between the Chase Worthing the public thought they knew and the man whose criminal exploits would soon be laid bare for the world to see. As he finished his live segment, the cameras returned to Tom Bellows at the anchor desk inside the studio.

"Thanks, Brock and Sage. We will have reporters live at the federal courthouse later this morning to keep our viewers abreast of all the developments in this case, so keep it tuned to Channel Six throughout your day for breaking updates. We'll be right back after this commercial break."

Bryce caught the replay of events on the six o'clock airing, and messaged Ashley with the news. He felt bad about texting Larry Paz, knowing that as the case agent he would be busy, so he kept it short and to the point.

Nice job.

He was surprised when his phone rang five minutes later.

"Good morning, Larry, and congratulations. It looks like you hit the mother lode."

"Morning, Bryce, thanks for reaching out. Yeah, we did pretty good. Worthing and Mackenzie were both there, just like our source said they would be. Counting them, their worker bees, and the crew of the boat, we locked up eleven folks last night."

"How big of a score on the boat?"

"We're still counting, but it looks like an even two thousand kilos."

"Holy cow! Two tons of coke? I've never even seen that much dope," Bryce exclaimed.

"It's a good haul, no doubt. But I've seen more. The seizures are going to be off the chart, once you add up the boat, the dealership, all the cars, and every dollar worth of Chase Worthing's personal property that we can tie to his drug money. And then there's the fact that if we can definitely tie the big man to the Murtaugh murders, the US Attorney says he will consider going for the death penalty. So all in all, a pretty significant case. I'm happy."

"Do you have a plan for tying Worthing to the Murtaughs?" Bryce asked.

"Well, the rounds they pulled out of Stanley and April were ballistically matched to Manny's gun, which they found on him at your house," Larry said. "Then we've got John Mullins's statement about watching the bodies going overboard in East Hump. So all that's left is to somehow prove Chase gave the order."

"How are you going to do that?"

"The AUSA wants to offer Roger Mackenzie a deal. Something in the twenty-year range, as opposed to the rest of his life in prison. The guys who took him to lockup last night said he was crying like a little girl all the way to Miami, so we'll see if he wants to play ball. And with that said, I gotta go. We have initial appearances starting in four hours. We'll stay in touch, and thanks for all your help."

"Sure thing, Larry. And again, congratulations on a great job."

He would share the news with Harley in person. For the first time in months, neither of them would have to worry about Chase Worthing or his goons. Still, one thought persisted in his head, and there was no denying it was the gospel truth: *If it wasn't for Chase Worthing and Stanley Murtaugh, you might be dead.*

Which in turn meant if Harley hadn't gone off the reservation and chatted up his friends at Tres Gatos, there would have been no altercation that night in Tavernier. Manny and Chico would never have known who Harley and Bryce were, and they would have had no reason to track them down.

Which means it would have been you sitting in the living room when the Network came calling.

His entire life was a series of random twists and turns, so much of it beyond his control. A pair of meth heads murder an innocent baby, and he crawls into the bottle in response. A psychopath he hasn't seen in ten years takes out a contract on his life for doing his job. A seemingly routine private investigator gig turns into a brush with the Miami arm of an international drug cartel and puts his life in jeopardy again. In a moment when he should have felt triumphant and vindicated, he was instead overcome with feelings of powerlessness, frailty, and uncertainty. The old familiar urge was on his back like a six-hundred-pound gorilla, worse than he'd felt it in years. He pulled out his phone and dialed.

"Good morning, Bryce."

"Good morning, Dan. I need a drink."

"We all need a drink, Bryce. We just can't have one. That's what makes us alcoholics. Tell me what's going on."

Bryce spilled it all. If there was a person on Earth with whom he felt secure sharing his innermost thoughts and feelings, it was his Alcoholics Anonymous sponsor.

As usual, Dan was unfazed by what he heard, or at least if he was, he didn't let on. "That's a lot to deal with. Tell me how you think alcohol will help. Tell me how taking a drink is going to make any of your problems go away, instead of just adding another problem on top of it all."

"I know it won't," Bryce conceded.

"That's right, it won't. And I'll tell you something else. You can feel sorry for yourself because you feel like you've lost control of your life, or you can take a step back and realize that so much of what happens in all our lives is beyond our control anyway. This isn't a *you* thing, it's an *everyone* thing. Why do you think we open our meetings with the Serenity Prayer? There are things in every one of our lives that we can't change. What we can change is how we deal with it. And when we're taking stock of all our curses, that's the time to be counting our blessings. Have you done that?"

"No."

"Well, there's no time like the present. Tell me about three blessings in your life."

Bryce thought for a moment. "Well, there's my health."

"Good start. Two more."

"I live in one of the most beautiful places in the world."

"Damn right. And finally?"

"I'm seeing someone. Sort of."

"That's new. Want to tell me about it?"

"She's a lawyer. Believe it or not, we met when she cross-examined me on the stand during a divorce trial. If you had asked me that day if we would ever end up dating, I would have bet the house against it. But like you said, sometimes things happen that we don't plan for, and this was one of those unplanned events that went my way."

"Is it serious?"

"I wouldn't go so far as to say 'serious.' And she's a good deal younger than me. But we've been spending more and more time together, and so far we seem like a good fit. We'll see how it goes."

"Well, I'm happy for you. Relationships are important in the recovery process. Does she know you're an alcoholic?"

Bryce laughed. "Oh, she knew that very early on. And she's good with it. Supportive, you know?"

"I do know. I couldn't have made it as long as I have without Lisa."

"Thanks for taking the time, Dan. I needed this."

"That's what sponsors are for. But I'll tell you what else you need, and that's to get to a meeting. There's one tonight. Am I going to see you there?"

"Count on it."

"Good. Remember, Bryce, control is an illusion we've created to make ourselves feel powerful. Our only true sphere of influence lies within ourselves, and how we deal with what life hands us. The secret is learning to deal with the curses with the same grace and dignity with which we welcome the blessings. I'll see you tonight."

Bryce pondered the words of his sponsor long after they ended the call. Blessings and curses. It was so easy to focus on the latter and forget the former. That's what self-pity was, wasn't it? Miring yourself in misery and failing to take stock of all that was positive in your life? He took a yellow sticky note from a pad in a drawer, wrote the words on it in large block letters, and posted it on his refrigerator as a reminder to himself:

BLESSINGS AND CURSES

CHAPTER 66

AT FORTY-TWO, Connor Bentley was the nation's youngest attorney general since Robert Kennedy, and it earned him the nickname "Boy Wonder," although nobody dared use it in his presence. Top of his class and president of the Law Review at Harvard, he shocked his professors and peers when he chose to return home to Atlanta for his clerkship rather than competing for a spot on the Supreme Court, which he likely would have landed. "If I'm good enough," he told his friends, "it won't matter where I cut my teeth."

And it didn't matter. In two short years, under the watchful eye of United States District Court Judge Wendell Branch, Connor developed a reputation for razor-sharp legal briefs and a work ethic which was unmatched among his peers. United States attorneys from across the country were always on the hunt for the next great legal talent, and the word soon spread about the accomplished young Harvard grad in Atlanta. At the end of his clerkship he had his pick of assistant US attorney positions and landed in the criminal division for the Southern District of California in San Diego.

His stock rose from there, as he garnered the highest conviction rate in the district, then in the western United States, then in the entire Department of Justice. After five years, the thirty-two-year-old was nominated to the Federal Bench as a District

Court Judge in Los Angeles, where he earned a reputation as one of the truly brilliant legal minds in the Federal Judiciary, not once having a decision overturned by a higher court. At thirty-eight, he was nominated to the infamously liberal Ninth Circuit Court of Appeals, where he served for three years as a moderating conservative voice. After only a short time in what most judges would consider the acme of their legal career, fate stepped in once again when a Republican president assumed office and wanted a young, charismatic, law-and-order man to lead his Department of Justice. Connor was on everybody's short list and sailed through the confirmation process in the Senate. With less than two years on the job, his name was already being whispered in conversations about future Supreme Court justices and even presidents.

For all his legal and political accomplishments, those who knew him best would say his finest quality was that he never forgot where he came from, and that he expected a similar level of humility from everyone who worked for him. So when his personal assistant got word to him that his former mentor wanted to chat, he blocked out an hour of his schedule, told his staff to hold all business, and called Judge Branch himself.

When the 202 area code appeared on his phone, Wendell assumed it would be a secretary telling him to stand by for the attorney general. Instead, he heard the voice of his former clerk.

"Good morning, Judge. How are things in Georgia?"

"My goodness," Wendell said. "They've got the Attorney General of the United States making his own calls?"

Connor laughed. "It depends on who I'm calling. But for the record, I can dial a phone and make my own coffee, and it drives my secretary crazy."

"I'm not surprised. You were hands down the hardest working law clerk who ever passed through my office, and I have followed your career with an enormous sense of pride."

"Thank you, Judge. What's this I hear you ended some poor soul who broke into your home?"

"It's a long story, but one you probably know about. It's all tied to the murder of the deputy marshal and the informant he was protecting in Atlanta last week."

"I've been receiving daily briefings on that case. From what I'm told, we may have hit a wall, as the informant was the only inroad we had into this so-called 'Murder.com' organization."

Wendell snorted. "Well, it didn't need to come to that. There are a couple of issues you're probably not going to hear about from the FBI, at least not from the Atlanta office. I was hoping to bend your ear for a minute about it all."

"Bend away, Judge."

"Thank you. For starters, there's an agent down here named Morris, I believe he goes by Donnie. He and a retired agent came to see me at my home a few months ago, and they are the ones who identified and developed the informant who was murdered alongside the deputy marshal. Without them, there is no case. Without them, we never would have known who or what is behind the murders of an AUSA, a federal prison guard, and almost a federal judge."

"I haven't heard his name or seen it in any of the reports," Connor said.

"And you won't. He was working the case off the books, which explains the presence of his former partner, the retired agent I mentioned. And he was doing it all because the murdered AUSA was a friend of his, and politics between the Bureau and the local police had the investigation at a standstill. So when his ASAC found out, he suspended him, and now they're trying to fire him altogether."

"Fire him? That seems a bit harsh," Connor mused. "It sounds like a procedural violation, but nothing criminal. I worked with FBI agents who screwed up worse than that and still had their jobs."

"Well, that brings me to the second issue. The ASAC, Greg Peoples. From what I've heard and seen, he's living proof that if you think there's good in everyone, you just haven't met everyone yet." Connor laughed, and Wendell shared with his former protégé the details of Peoples stealing the case from Donnie, placing him on suspension, and conducting the ill-fated press conference that cost the DOJ a major case and the life of a deputy United States marshal.

"Good Lord. He sounds like a train wreck," the attorney general said. "I wonder why his SAC hasn't reeled him in?"

"From what I hear, the SAC is retired-in-place and won't do anything to rock the boat while he's kissing ass in search of his post-FBI job," Wendell said. "And that's not just from my Bureau contacts. A couple of prosecutors and a judge I stay in touch with confirmed the fact that ASAC Peoples is practically running the office."

Connor was scribbling notes as he listened. "I have lunch with the FBI director tomorrow. Obviously I have to let him do his job, but he's going to know how concerned I am about this."

"Thank you so much," Wendell said. "Agent Morris is a good guy with his head in the right place, and he deserves better than all this."

"Agreed," the attorney general replied. "Let me see what I can do."

Three days later, all hell broke loose at the FBI.

353

CHAPTER 67

FBI Cleans House in Wake of Botched Investigation

By Edward Stein

Capitol Times

Washington – At least four senior executives in the FBI's headquarters offices and field divisions have been relieved of their duties, and several more mid-level managers have been similarly reassigned or forced into retirement, sources say. The shakeup appears connected to a closely held investigation into a shadowy murder-for-hire organization, which led to the deaths last week of a Deputy United States Marshal and a cooperating witness in Atlanta.

Citing failure to exercise proper investigative oversight and violation of the Bureau's long-standing policies with regard to media releases, Director Marcus Angiulino summoned each of the senior executives to his office at the J. Edgar Hoover building Thursday morning and informed them of his decision to remove them from their positions. The four disciplined agents are believed to be the Assistant Director of the Bureau's Criminal Investigations Division and his deputy, as well as the Special Agents in Charge of the Atlanta and Indianapolis field offices. Sources close to the investigation said both of the Special Agents in Charge informed the Director of their respective retirements, effective immediately.

Additionally, several lower-ranking managers were also disciplined, but details on their fate were unclear.

According to an unnamed law enforcement source close to the matter, "The Director lost confidence in the judgment and leadership abilities of these executives, and feels the investigation was mismanaged from its inception. A lack of coordination and cooperation between FBI field offices and other law enforcement agencies allowed a murder-for-hire ring to operate with impunity for far too long. Even when the investigation was initiated, it was not pursued with the level of rigor the Director expects, and accordingly he has sent a message to senior leaders throughout the FBI: This cannot and will not happen again."

TWO WEEKS LATER

Wings of War sat three miles from the FBI's Atlanta Office, and the combination of its convenient location and rustic charm had made it a favorite watering hole among the office's agents. Set alongside the runway of a regional airport, the World-War-II-themed restaurant and bar was the scene of countless FBI retirements, promotion parties, and celebrations whenever an agent closed a big case. It was also the location of Donnie Morris's reinstatement party, and the place was packed. Most of the office's 250 agents were in attendance, all there to support their brother while at the same time extending an invisible middle finger to those who tried to end his career.

True to his word, Bryce was also there, and he was almost as well-received as the guest of honor himself. There was a lingering resentment among the rank and file over the way in which he was forced to retire, and though it had been five years, FBI agents had long memories. Bryce felt as if he was back home again as he and Donnie played host to the bevy of colleagues who came by their table to wish them well.

As the night drew to a close, one of the last agents to join them was Atlanta's Chief Security Officer, Mike Brickhouse. Like FBI headquarters, field offices were highly secured, and anyone who didn't work there on a daily basis had to be cleared for entry and escorted throughout the building. The restriction even applied to supervisors from Washington who were in town to relieve an ASAC of his duties. And so it was that Agent Brickhouse was in the know on all the details of Greg Peoples's comeuppance from start to finish. He provided the play-by-play as Bryce and Donnie stared in amazement.

"No shit!?" Bryce exclaimed. "They had you take his gun?"

Mike nodded. "They didn't know how it was going to play out, or what his state of mind was going to be when he heard the news. So they wanted to proceed with caution. I'd be lying if I said I didn't feel a certain sense of satisfaction."

"So did they just come out and tell him?" Donnie asked.

"Pretty much. The word had already come down that the SAC had been relieved earlier in the day, so it wasn't too much of a surprise. But true to Greg's character, he tried to deny responsibility for everything. Like they were there to bargain. Like the director himself hadn't sent them to Atlanta with specific instructions to take out the trash. When it all finally set in, the poor son of a bitch looked like he didn't have a friend in the world, which is about right."

"So where does he go now?" Bryce asked. "I heard they didn't fire him outright, but there's no way he can stay in Atlanta."

Mike laughed. "Yeah, he'd probably catch a bullet, with all the people he's screwed over. Anyway, this is where it gets interesting. The director ordered him stripped of his supervisory agent status, and he's being reassigned. If he refuses the assignment, he will be forced to resign or face the mother of all OPR investigations."

OPR, or the Office of Professional Responsibility, was the Bureau's internal investigative arm, and its agents conducted inquiries into alleged misconduct and criminal behavior among FBI employees. Bryce knew them well.

"Where are they sending him?" Donnie inquired.

"Minot."

"Where's that?"

"It's a two-man office in North Dakota," Mike answered. "Northern North Dakota, in fact. Forty miles from the Canadian border. There's an Air Force base up there, some farms, and not much else. Most of the work is crimes on Indian reservations, murders, child sexual abuse, stuff like that. The average low temperature in January is minus ten degrees Fahrenheit. I couldn't have picked a better assignment for him myself."

They raised two beers and a club soda in a mock toast to the departed ASAC. Mike bid them farewell, and the crowd dwindled, leaving just Bryce and Donnie alone in the bar.

"So what's next for you?" Bryce asked his old partner.

"I was waiting until we were alone to bring you up to speed. I had a meeting with the acting SAC this morning, and the

Network investigation is **going** to be a major case, managed out of headquarters but run **locally** by a special squad in every field office that has a dog in the fight. Right now that's just Atlanta and Indianapolis, but the expectation is that as the case gets rolling, we're going to find tentacles all across the country. It could be our biggest investigation since 9/11."

"Well," Bryce responded, "at least the Bureau is taking it seriously now. Are you going to be assigned to the squad?"

"Better. The SAC asked me to supervise it."

Bryce's smile spread from ear to ear. "That's fantastic. They couldn't have picked a more qualified man for the job."

"Well," Donnie replied, "Maybe one guy. But he's already retired. And speaking of retirement, how is everything down in paradise? When do I get to meet this new lady in your life?"

"We'll see. We're not to the point of weekend getaways, and besides, she had a full calendar this week."

"You know when you two get married I'm going to tell her the story of how I predicted it all before your very first date."

Bryce laughed. "Easy does it, partner. She's a great girl, but we'll see how it goes. Neither of us is in a hurry."

"I heard that. Speaking of hurries, do you have anywhere to be?"

"Nope."

"Good. Let's close this place down."

And they did just that, reminiscing into the early morning hours, two friends bound by a shared past, and unbeknownst to them at the time, a shared future.

CHAPTER 68

"PHOENIX?"

"Here."

"Seattle?"

"Here."

"St. Louis?"

"Here."

The roll call continued until all fifteen were accounted for. The meetings used to be in person (at Sonny's insistence), but as the number of partners grew and technology made possible a secure and reliable means of communicating over the dark web, he softened his face-to-face policy in favor of a video chat platform his tech people assured him was impenetrable to law enforcement.

In theory, they were all equal partners. In reality, Sonny, as the sole surviving founding member, wielded a level of influence that gave him a de facto veto authority, though he had been reluctant to exercise it in the past for fear of being deemed heavy-handed. It was, after all, a society of murder merchants with access to the world's most accomplished hit men, and his reputation notwithstanding, Sonny had no desire to find himself on the receiving end of a rogue contract.

The James Todd fiasco had reset his focus. The Network needed to exercise more discretion, and that would start with the bidding and approval processes. There was enough work at home and abroad to keep the cash flowing and the partners happy without taking on the level of risk they assumed when they granted Travis Conway's dying wish. Targeting multiple members of the law enforcement community was a foolish mistake they would not make again.

And never again would a non-partner be given a level of access to the Network's operations that James Todd enjoyed. The lawyers would be relegated to the role of simple messengers, whose sole purpose was to facilitate communication between operators and the Network by leveraging the access afforded by their attorney/client privilege.

The work stoppage had lasted nearly a month, and as Sonny expected, it was the hot topic among the partners, most of whom seemed more concerned about their income streams than the events that led to the stand down order.

"Jobs are stacking up," Indianapolis complained. "Some of them are time sensitive. If we don't get back to work soon, there won't be any work to get back to."

"The time-out was in everyone's best interest," Sonny countered. "Some of you still don't appreciate how close we came to losing everything. That lawyer could have brought us all down, and it was a miracle we were able to get to him before he could do any real damage. Even so, they know we exist now, so we're going to take additional precautions moving forward." He explained his decision to keep the attorneys at the fringes of the Network's operation, silent and well-paid couriers who did as they were told and didn't ask questions.

The meeting continued for another half hour, as the partners debated the Network's fee schedule, their own percentages of the profit-sharing structure, and vouching procedures for new operators. As had become custom, Sonny provided the meeting's closing remarks in the form of a to-do list.

"All right, then, that's a wrap. Let's reopen the portal for customers, give it a week to populate, then notify our operators so they can submit their bids. San Francisco and Miami, you both have operators behind bars who need attorney visits. Make it happen, and remember the new guidelines. If there are no further questions, we'll call it a day and see everyone again next month."

There were no questions, and as the partners logged off around the country, they shared a collective sigh of relief. They had dodged a bullet, to be sure, but they were all risk-takers, all former operators themselves, and they knew full well the dangers and rewards of their profession. At the end of the day, what mattered most to them was that the crisis, for now, had been averted.

The Network was back in business.

CHAPTER 69

THE MIAMI PRE-TRIAL DETENTION CENTER
occupied a full city block of real estate northwest of the downtown area, and as cold and uninviting as it was on the outside,
inside it was even worse. Seafoam-green cinder block walls were
dotted with the tiniest of windows, which allowed some light in,
but due to their height did not allow inmates to see out. The
noise was unrelenting, whether from the clanging of cell doors or
the howls and wails of the two thousand mistakenly incarcerated
inmates packed within its walls, all waiting for their day in court
and the chance to convince a jury to set them free. If human
desperation had a smell, it would be the one permeating every
hallway of the massive concrete purgatory.

Some said he was lucky to be alive, but he would argue
that point if he was in a talkative mood. He was still wheelchair
bound; his prison scrubs two sizes too large in order to accom-
modate the colostomy apparatus he would carry with him for
life after doctors removed two thirds of his lower gastrointesti-
nal tract. He spent nearly a month recovering in the hospital,
guarded round the clock by sheriff's deputies, until doctors determined he could live in a prison setting, albeit with conditions.
First and foremost of those conditions was that he be kept in
solitary confinement. His fragile medical condition rendered him

defenseless, and would have made him easy prey in a community of predators.

The private cell suited him just fine. Other than the prison medical staff, there was nobody he needed to talk to anyway, and for the first weeks of his confinement he stared blankly at the detectives who came to question him almost daily. Still, they kept on, detailing the case against him in words and pictures, witness statements and ballistics reports, expecting him to break at any moment. On the occasion of their last visit, he finally broke his silence, but only to tell them he had nothing to say and they were wasting their time.

He was allowed access to the detention center library and was finishing a book on kayaking in the Florida Keys when they came for him again. Same guards. Same opening line.

"Petty. You have a visitor."

The guards strapped his hands to the wheelchair and rolled him down the same corridor, to the same room they used for the previous visits. They positioned his chair so it was facing the plexiglass partition, turned on the room's speaker and microphone, and locked the door behind them as they left. He waited for his detective friends, wondering what strategies they could possibly have left in their bag of tricks. When the door to the opposing room opened, only one visitor entered, one he had never seen before. And definitely not a detective.

Well, this is interesting, he thought, all the while casting a dead-eyed stare that made it clear he wasn't going to be the conversation starter.

After a few moments, the visitor broke the ice.

"Good morning, Vincent. I'm your attorney, Ashley Oliver. Call me Ash."

ACKNOWLEDGMENTS

WRITING, I have discovered, is a team sport. From the day I first considered testing my chops in the literary arena, I leaned on a cadre of friends, family, and professionals as I watched my dream take shape. Without them, *Call Me Sonny* would be little more than another document on a laptop, ninety thousand or so words of unrealized potential.

Foremost among those to whom I am indebted is my wife, Susan Shipman, whose reaction upon hearing my plan to write a book was an immediate and enthusiastic, "I think it would be amazing!" Since then, you have been my biggest cheerleader and my most honest critic. Your support has been unconditional and unfailing, and I cannot thank you enough.

To my beta readers, Dan Mitchell, Bob Shipman, Kim Barkhausen, Carol Keller, Mark Shipman, Brad Spacy, Philip Pearl, and Marcia Lazarus (who also happens to be my mother, an English teacher at heart, and my first de facto proofreader): Thank you all for taking the time to read my manuscript and provide honest, valuable feedback. There is something from each of you woven into this novel.

To the incredible team at Boyle & Dalton, and especially CEO Emily Hitchcock, project manager Clair Fink, and editor Ian Moeckel: Thank you for seeing something in *Call Me Sonny*, for taking a chance on a first-time, unknown author, and for turning my story into an actual book. What a pleasure it has been to work with all of you, and I look forward to many future successes together.

To Janet Jaimes at Gainovo Digital: I hired you to build my website, and got a business coach and social media guru in the deal. Your book marketing skills are simply amazing. Thank you for helping me to establish and build my author brand.

To my friends and colleagues at the Southeastern Writers Association: Thank you for helping me to hone my craft, and for sponsoring the writing contest that won *Call Me Sonny* what will hopefully be the first of many awards. You truly are what your motto says: Writers helping writers.

Finally, to everyone who is reading this: You bought my book, and that humbles me beyond words. Thank you so very much.

Steve Lazarus

ABOUT THE AUTHOR

STEVE LAZARUS is an author, retired FBI Special Agent, and United States Air Force veteran. He served twenty-two years in the FBI, spending the first half of his career investigating drug trafficking organizations and violent street gangs. Later, he became a full-time bomb technician, an assignment that led him to Iraq, Kuwait, and Afghanistan as part of the Global War on Terror. After retiring from the Bureau, he spent several years as a national security instructor in Abu Dhabi, United Arab Emirates. Steve lives outside Hilton Head Island, South Carolina, with his wife, Susan, and their amazing wonder dog, Aspen.

Learn more about Steve and keep up with his writing at stevelazarusbooks.com.

Made in United States
Troutdale, OR
12/27/2023

16482859R00228